HANLEY CASTLE

WALKING AMONG LIONS BOOK 2

BRIAN WAINWRIGHT

Copyright © 2022 Brian Wainwright

All rights reserved.

DEDICATION

To all who helped and encouraged me through difficult times.
You know who you are!

ACKNOWLEDGEMENTS

Once again, I should like to thank Kathryn Warner for her writings and for allowing me to ask questions and bounce ideas off her.

Also, all my beta readers and other friends, not least those on Facebook, who have helped me in one way or another. Special thanks are due to Mercedes Rochelle for her brilliant, improved cover design for the paperback version of the first novel in the series and for the cover for this. Also to Pam Benstead for a thorough and patient proof reading.

I should also like to give particular thanks to M.S.F. Johnston, whose excellent new translation of Froissart was particularly useful in writing this book and the one I hope will shortly follow on its heels, the third part of Constance's story.

PRINCIPAL CHARACTERS

King Richard II (Cousin Richard)

Anne of Bohemia, his wife, Queen of England.

Isabella of Valois, later Queen of England, daughter of King Charles VI of France.

House of Lancaster

John of Gaunt, the King's eldest surviving uncle, Duke of Lancaster. Lately calling himself King of Castile (or Spain.)

Constanza (Constance) of Castile, his wife.

Henry (Harry) of Bolingbroke, Earl of Derby, Gaunt's son by his previous wife, Blanche. A former Appellant.

Mary de Bohun, Harry's wife.

Elizabeth (Cousin Beth), Gaunt's daughter by Blanche. Married to John Holland, Earl of Huntingdon.

Dame Katherine Swynford, Gaunt's mistress, later his wife.

House of York

Edmund of Langley, the King's uncle, Duke of York.

Isabelle of Castile, his wife. Sister to Constanza.

Edward of York (Ned), Earl of Rutland. York's elder son.

Constance of York, Lady Despenser (Narrator). Married to Thomas Despenser almost all her life. York's daughter.

Richard of Conisbrough. (Dickon). York's son, very much junior to his siblings.

House of Gloucester

Thomas of Woodstock, Duke of Gloucester. The King's youngest uncle, by some way. Former Appellant.

Eleanor de Bohun (Mary's sister) his wife.

Anne of Gloucester, their daughter.

The Mortimers (Grandchildren of the King's eldest Uncle, Clarence, who is long gone)

Roger Mortimer, Earl of March. Considered by some to be heir to Richard II.

Edmund Mortimer, his brother, who was brought up in York's household.

Philippa, their sister. Countess of Pembroke, later Countess of Arundel.

The Hollands

Thomas Holland, Earl of Kent. Half-brother of the King. (They had the same mother.)

Alice, Countess of Kent, his wife, sister of the Earl of Arundel.

Alianore Holland, Countess of March. Kent's eldest daughter, married to Roger Mortimer.

Thomas Holland, Kent's eldest son.

Joanne (or Joan) Holland Kent's second daughter.

Edmund (Mun) Holland, Kent's youngest son.

John Holland, Earl of Huntingdon. Kent's younger brother, and another half-brother of the King. Married to Elizabeth of Lancaster (Beth)

The Despensers

Thomas, Lord Despenser of Glamorgan and Morgannwg. Wealthy heir to great lands, married to Constance of York while very young.

Elisabeth Burghersh, Lady Despenser the Elder, his mother. The Burghersh heiress.

Elizabeth Despenser, Lady Zouche, his sister.

Margaret Despenser, Lady Ferrers of Chartley, his sister.

The Mohuns

Joan Burghersh, Lady Mohun. An *extremely* wealthy widow. Elisabeth Despenser's aunt. At one time Constance's mentor and guardian at court.

Philippa Mohun, Lady Fitzwalter. Her daughter, widow of Lord Fitzwalter. Married to Sir John Golafre but maintaining her earlier, higher title, as was the custom. Elisabeth Despenser's cousin.

Other Nobles

Richard Arundel (or Fitzalan) Earl of Arundel. (Former Appellant)

Thomas Arundel, Archbishop of York (Later translated to Canterbury.) Richard's brother.

Thomas Beauchamp, Earl of Warwick. (Former Appellant.)

Margaret Ferrers, Countess of Warwick, his wife.

Richard Beauchamp ('The hawk-faced brat') their son.

Thomas Berkeley, Lord Berkeley, a cousin of the Despensers.

Elizabeth Berkeley, his daughter.

Sir James Berkeley, his brother and heir male.

Robert Ferrers, Lord Ferrers of Chartley. Thomas Despenser's brother-in-law.

John Hastings, Earl of Pembroke. Young ward of the King. Married to Philippa Mortimer.

John Montagu, Lord Montagu, later Earl of Salisbury. Lollard and poet.

Maud Francis, his wife.

Thomas Mowbray, Earl of Nottingham and Earl Marshal. (Former Appellant, but since defected to Richard II's faction.) Married to Arundel's daughter.

Henry Percy, Earl of Northumberland.

Others

Sir John Bussy – Speaker of the Commons and member of King Richard's Council.

Hugh Bygge – The Despensers' cook.

Thomas Clanvowe – King's esquire, married to Perinne Whitney.

Sir John Golafre – One of the King's knights, and high in favour.

Robert Poyntz, of Iron Acton, Gloucestershire, Despenser retainer.

Sir John Russell – Master of Horse to Richard II. Retained by the King and Thomas Despenser.

Perinne Whitney – One of Queen Anne's waiting-women.

TABLE OF CHAPTERS

Chapter	Dates	Page
1	November 1389 — October 1390	2
2	October — December 1390	22
3	January — March 1391	33
4	April — May 1391	41
5	May — June 1391	55
6	June 1391 — January 1393	66
7	February — September 1393	78
8	October 1393 — February 1394	95
9	March, 1394	109
10	April — August 1394	123
11	August 1394 — November 1395	138
12	December 1395 — January 1396	165
13	February — April 1396	193
14	Summer, 1396	226
15	November 1396 — June 1397	265
16	June — August 1397	284
17	August, 1397	305
18	August — October 1397	313

The king, inflamed with indignation,
That to such bondage he should be brought,
Suppressing the ire of his inward thought
Studied nought else but how he might
Be highly revenged of his high despite.

A Mirror for Magistrates
A Modernized and Annotated Edition
(2019) ed. Scott. C.Lucas.

Chapter 1

November 1389 – September 1390

The English chroniclers, writing or revising when a touchy usurping Lancastrian was only too ready to take offence, magnified any incident which could add to the discredit of the deposed, and were unable to appreciate that the years 1389-1396 were in some ways the most brilliant years of medieval England;

The Hollow Crown, Harold F. Hutchinson, p.129.

*

I have told how King Richard was brought low by his enemies, how he came very close to deposition, and how he gradually regained much of his power. I have told also of how so many of his friends and supporters were either executed or banished by the so-called Appellant lords, led by my Uncle Gloucester, a clutch of traitors as far as I was concerned. Now I must tell how Richard took his revenge, and became, for a time, the most powerful king England has known. You will have to be patient, for it was a slow business and I was often occupied by other matters, as you shall learn.

In the weeks leading up to the Christmas of the same year that King Richard was restored to rule we had another wedding, the return of my Uncle Lancaster, and then a tragedy.

First, on the Thursday before Advent, at Sheen, Philippa Fitzwalter was at long last married to Sir John Golafre.

Golafre had not been in France all this time — he had been back in England for the best part of the year, but had kept his head very, very, low for fear that the Appellants should lop it off. Now he judged it safe to emerge from hiding and return to court, and so it was. Indeed Richard made much of him, for he was one of very few of us left from the old days and therefore all the more valued. (Whether he *deserved* to be valued was another matter — there were many better men dead and apparently forgotten.)

Philippa Fitzwalter had spent most of the intervening time in my mother's household, and much of the rest of it attending me. (God knows why, but my mother had a high opinion of her, trusted her, and seemed to think she was a good guiding influence.) During those months she had rarely spoken of Golafre. She had certainly not wept over him, or spent hours on her knees praying for his safety. Now he was restored to favour and fortune again, she decided that she would accept their previous arrangement, and become his wife.

Her mother, my old friend Lady Mohun, also approved of the arrangement. She came back to court (from which she was nominally banished for life) for the wedding, and told me she thought it well that Philippa was settled, given that Philippa was the sort of fool who needed a man to guide her, and was better married than a source of scandal. If Golafre was a fool too, well, they were well matched, she said.

It was not so splendid a wedding as that of Alianore and Roger Mortimer, naturally. Golafre and Philippa were of lesser rank, and their coupling was of no significance to anyone except themselves. Nevertheless, King Richard made a celebration of it, gave them a feast to mark his favour for Golafre, and paid most of the cost of the business. Given that Philippa was a cousin of sorts, it was my duty to attend her and wish her well, and I did. I was, in truth, rather pleased that Golafre intended to take her off to Wallingford, where he was Constable of the King's castle. It meant she would not be sending her reports on me to my mother in the future.

At the beginning of December, my uncle of Lancaster — John of Gaunt as the common people still called him — at last came home and was welcomed to the court at Reading. The King and the rest of us rode some miles out of the town to meet him, which I need scarcely tell you was a very great honour in itself. My uncle no longer styled himself 'King of Spain', but was as grand as ever and seemed to regard the welcome as no more than his due. He was still a fine-looking man, though very close to fifty. He walked erect, without any hint of stoop, looking about him with the air and the glare of a particularly confident eagle. Although he had been forced to give up his claim to Castile, there was little to mark his demotion. He dressed just as richly as Richard himself, and with more jewels, and expected everyone (except Richard and Anne) to show him the utmost deference. I was quite below his notice; I believe he was scarcely aware that I even existed.

I cannot begin to describe the celebrations that followed, except to say that King Arthur's court could scarcely have offered more. It was now Uncle Lancaster with whom the King walked about arm-in-arm, and they even went so far as to exchange livery collars with one another as a token of their unity. Some whispered this was excessive, but they only whispered it. Before long, the King's retainers were wearing the Lancastrian 'SS' device as well as the White Hart and the angry whispers grew.

Almost at once my uncle fell into a quarrel with my father. The Duke of York had been under the impression that in return for his previous renunciation of his and my mother's rights in Spain, he was now entitled to a share of the spoils. My uncle had come home with whole barrels of gold coins paid to him in compensation, to say nothing of a huge pension which was to be paid to him for life. However, he refused to part with a penny, though my father had much more need of money than he had himself. After this dispute they were not on speaking terms for many months.

What made it worse was that my uncle publicly condemned the actions of his son, Harry Bolingbroke, who had, of course, been one of the Appellants. He pretended great anger with him, going so far as to say before us all that he would kill Harry if the King so wished. It was obvious to me that this was a mere gesture, a figure of speech, and that Richard could not possibly order such a thing, even if he was inclined to do so. Indeed, I very much doubt my uncle disagreed with much that Harry had done. He himself had been no friend to Robert de Vere. My father took him at his word, however, and as he was fond of Harry — God knows why, but he always was — it was a further reason for distance between him and his elder brother.

As for my aunt, she summoned me into her presence within a day or two. She was, as I have mentioned before, my aunt twice over, as well as my godmother, and she had some interest in me. She was not at all like my mother, being much taller and very much more serious in her manner. She was pious too, although not quite the saint some have made her out to be. She enjoyed rich clothes and fine food just as much as the rest of us, and was not averse to a dance, either, so long as it was a stately one.

She told me that I was the very image of her daughter, Catalina, or Catherine as we say in English, who had been left in Spain as part of the settlement, married to the son of the usurper. She did not expect to see her again and the sight of me, she said, was a sort of compensation. She did not exactly catechise me, but she asked me any number of questions, some of which I found inconvenient. So I answered, 'yes madam,' and 'no, madam' and 'if it so pleases you, madam' until she grew weary. She did however, give me a fine brooch, with an emerald in it, which I still have. It was our only booty from Spain, unless you count the fact that my brother Edward had been named residual heir if Catalina and her husband should have no children. This had been included in the treaty, just as my cousin, Lady Huntingdon, had told me, and my father was supposed to be satisfied with this provision and nothing more.

The tragedy followed just before Christmas. John Hastings, the Earl of Pembroke, was practising jousting with an older knight, Sir John St. John, when, by sheer misfortune, a lance which St. John had dropped (in obedience to the instruction of the fellow who was supervising the practice) somehow pierced Hastings through the groin. Physicians were rushed to him from every corner of the court, but the loss of blood was too great, beyond staunching, and John died, to the sorrow of us all.

The Queen wept for days, for John had grown up in her household, and she loved him like a younger brother. He was but seventeen. The rest of us mourned him too, for he had been amiable and gentle, and popular with all from the King to the least of the grooms. That sorrow began to turn to anger, and Sir John St. John saw fit to flee the court, accident though it had been. (He was one of my husband's feudal tenants in his marcher lordship of Glamorgan, and went to ground there in his little castle at Fonmon, where no English writ could touch him and where he could surround himself with a guard of fine Welsh archers. He was as safe there as it was possible for a man to be.)

My cousin, Lady Pembroke, made a great show of being prostrated by grief, but she had never given a rap for John while he was alive and the greater part of us were well aware of that. She was soon consulting with attorneys though, with a view to collecting her extensive dower rights — John Hastings had been very rich, though of course he had still been in wardship and their marriage had never been consummated.

Philippa Pembroke was within her rights, I cannot deny it. It was her pretence of sorrow that sickened me, and I itched to tell her exactly what I thought of her, to remind her of the many occasions when she had treated John with complete contempt before the rest of us, as though he was some knave quite unfit to look on her. I did not dare, because I knew it would not end in words, that I was likely to find myself rolling in the dust with her. I also knew that in the particular circumstances of the hour I was certain to be the loser in such a conflict. The calamity of John's death had won her the Queen's sympathy, and Anne fussed over her as though she were a dying puppy.

Instead, I wrote to my mother. I told her I had grown

unhappy at court (which was true for one reason or another) and asked to be recalled. I spoke to Anne as well, naturally, and soon, between the two of them, it was all arranged, and I found myself back at Fotheringhay.

*

It was interesting how people now spoke of King Richard. Some said that he was ruling wisely. Others that he had learned his lesson, and was now being guided by the counsel of his uncles, especially my Uncle Lancaster. There were even those who said that in truth it was Lancaster who reigned, that Richard was little more than his puppet.

I was, for most of the next two years or so, far from court, and for much of it in Elisabeth Despenser's household, learning, as my mother put it, the ways of my new family. (She told me it would be *good experience*, a term she sometimes used when cajoling me into performing some unwanted task.)

Elisabeth I found no easier to live with than I had during my earlier time at Caversham. We scarcely moved from her great house at Tewkesbury, set in its park close to the abbey and the small town under its shadow. She worshipped, ruled her household, managed her estates, and received visitors — though she did not encourage any unless they were her close friends or blood kin. (Lesser folk were commended to the hospitality of the abbey. As she was a great patron of the monks I suppose she saw this as a way of regaining some of her bounty.) It was from these few visitors that I received most of my news, and that only by listening to conversation at table.

Elisabeth did not encourage me to ask questions, or still less to put forward my opinions — though I can say without exaggeration that I knew more of King Richard and his family than any of these people. It was her view that I should sit silently, my hands folded in my lap when I was not working or eating, and speak only when addressed. She considered this proper behaviour for one of my age, and I had little choice but to endure it.

The most frequent visitor was 'dear cousin Berkeley' as Elisabeth referred to him. You would have thought, by the way he was received and welcomed, that he was her brother, and I suppose it may be that he was a proxy for the one she lacked. I could not deny that he was courteous, and the serious, urbane way he had of speaking gave the impression he was wise. I could not like, though, the way he spoke of the King.

'I hear,' Lord Berkeley said as we sat over one of Elisabeth's plain suppers, 'that the King has sent clerks and friars and a pack of other fools to Gloucester Abbey. Their task, madam, if you can credit it, is to compile a book of miracles performed by the second King Edward. Well, that should be the thinnest book ever written. Some say our King has lately grown in wisdom, but here is certain proof he has not shed all his follies. You will scarcely credit it, my lady, but he intends the book to be sent to the Holy Father in Rome, asking that King Edward be made a saint!'

He threw back his head and laughed, as though nothing could be more of a joke. Elisabeth smiled, which she did not do very often, but at least she had the grace not to comment, and to wipe her mouth with her hand-towel to conceal the extent of her amusement. I frowned, but controlled myself by taking a long sip of the wine that stood before me. It was heavily watered — Elisabeth always saw to it that it was — and barely fit for a petty squire's table. (If such wine had been served in my father's household, my mother would have poured it over the boteler's head.)

'King Edward was my great-grandfather,' I said, as meekly as I knew how, which I suppose was not so *very* meek. 'I have heard many strange tales of how he came by his death, my lord. Are they true?'

That went home. I saw the angry flash in his eyes, just for an instant before he assumed his usual smooth expression. King Edward, it was said, had been horribly murdered in Berkeley Castle. Some claimed that this fellow's grandfather had been responsible, at least in part. He had certainly been one of those responsible for the King's custody.

'My lady,' he answered, 'you should not listen to lies, put about by the rabble. I believe the late King Edward came to his death quite naturally. You should also bear in mind that he was as wretched a king as we have ever had, the very opposite of your grandfather of blessed memory, whom God pardon. The second Edward, whatever else he may have been, was certainly *no saint!*'

I said no more. There was no need. I knew I had caught him on a sore spot, and for the time being that was victory enough.

*

Another source of information was my brother, Edward, who wrote to me from time to time, when he had nothing more interesting to occupy him. He was Earl and Sheriff of Rutland now — though of course he delegated all the sheriff's duties and in return kept most of the profits of the office. He was, as he told me, not so much pleased with the promotion as by the fact that he no longer had to extract every penny he spent from my lord father's purse.

It was from one of his letters that I learned the astonishing news that my cousin and enemy, Philippa Mortimer, Countess of Pembroke, had secretly married — of all men! — Richard Fitzalan, Earl of Arundel, that bitter, ugly little man who was about thirty years her elder. Of course, they were both of them very rich and I knew my cousin well enough to know that she would be delighted with her new status, and not be troubled by the treasons her new husband had committed. For treasons they were, as far as I was concerned. The secrecy meant that they had to pay a fine to the King, but for the likes of them it was no more a punishment than if I had had to forfeit a farthing.

The thought of that insolent girl — she was barely older than me — parading around the court in her furs and fine jewels, while I was secluded in country obscurity with my Lady Elisabeth, living more or less as her waiting-gentlewoman, made me furious. The only consolation I could find was that I did not have to go to bed with Lord Arundel.

On the other hand, I was not allowed to go to bed with Thomas either. I had broken the matter to my mother, thinking myself old enough in every way that mattered, and that was the main reason she had packed me off to Tewkesbury. She had absolutely refused to listen to my arguments, simply stating that I was too young and that was an end to it. (She was quite right, of course, but at that age I did not agree, and thought myself very ill-used.)

My mother also wrote to me from time to time, but never told me anything interesting beyond family news. She was far more likely to admonish me for some imagined fault — I suspect, and I am all but sure I am right, she had regular reports of me from Elisabeth, and those reports were not as glowing as the Queen's had once been.

Thomas sent me occasional letters, but it seemed my father kept him busy. When he was not on some errand of business or another he was with Edward at court, or more infrequently, with his uncle, the Bishop of Norwich, or visiting the households of one or the other of his three sisters. I had not thought the Despensers a close family, but I now realised that they were, and that they all doted on Thomas, who was the youngest of them all by some way. The sisters came to Tewkesbury sometimes to see their mother — I liked best of them Margaret, Lady Ferrers, the nearest one to him in age

— but it seemed to me there was something of a conspiracy to keep Thomas himself away. It did not help my moods, which at this time were swinging about like a broken gate in the wind, much to Elisabeth's dismay. I have never been much given to crying, but there were days when I cried from pure frustration. Always in privacy, though. I would never allow Elisabeth to see my weakness.

Another visitor we had was Lady Fitzwalter — she still styled herself as such as it was a higher title than plain Dame Golafre — and it said something about my low spirits that I was pleased to see her, even though she brought her husband with her. They had much to tell us about the King's great tournament at Smithfield. Golafre had taken part (with his wife leading him to the lists at the end of a chain, as was the fashion at that time, all the way from the Tower) and according to Philippa's account only the wilful partiality of the jury (the Queen and her ladies) had deprived him of one of the major prizes.

Sir John said far less than usual — I had an idea that he was wary of Elisabeth's tongue — and seemed quite content to allow Philippa to boast of his prowess, while he sat back and smiled an indulgent smile. He had, I suppose, some reason for complacency. Though he had been born a bastard, he had risen high in the King's service, and was now more in favour than ever, one of the very few who had survived the late upheavals and remained in prosperity. He was in truth a great fellow in the lists and it was not only his wife who admired his skill. He had made a marriage that linked him to many of the greatest families in England, including mine. Small wonder that he had the look of a cat in cream.

It was he who announced the reason for their visit. King Richard was on pilgrimage to Gloucester, to the tomb of King Edward II. He was gathering there various bishops and canon lawyers to discuss the case and formulate the necessary evidence to submit to the Pope. It was only a matter of time, Sir John said, before King Edward was canonised by the Holy Father. The King was determined that it should be so, and neither petitions nor offerings would be lacking to bring it about. That King Edward had been evilly used by his nobles could not be denied, he said, and nor could it be denied that he had been most horribly murdered. King Richard had drawn his own lessons from that history and he was determined to prove that King Edward had been in the right all along, his enemies not only traitors but the murderers of a saint.

I saw the parallel at once, and I believe Elisabeth was no less acute. She frowned.

'I think it folly to open such ancient wounds,' she said. 'There are still those around who remember that time, and they say that King Edward was a long way short of sainthood. I don't say that he deserved to be murdered — no one does, least of all an anointed king — but I well remember my grandfather saying that he was the greatest fool ever to wear a crown, and that his son was twenty times the man. I cannot believe the Pope will ever be persuaded to make a saint of one who brought himself to ruin by his crazy dealings.'

Golafre snorted into his wine. 'My lady, you should remember that the Holy Father in Rome needs our King's support. Not least because there is another Holy Father in Avignon. In a world with two Popes, there is some competition for business, and prices cannot be set too high.'

Elisabeth hissed — I know not how else to describe it. I believe she thought it irreverent even to mention the second Pope, or anti-Pope as that fellow is rightly described. The division in Christendom was a scandal then, and so it remains, though all the kings and princes of Europe have sought to cure it. Golafre was right though. King Richard was one of the chief supporters of the true Pope, and his wishes were scarcely to be ignored, even in so sacred a matter.

'We are here because the King wishes his cousin,' he pointed at me as if to remove any doubt, 'to attend him at Gloucester and make an offering at the tomb.'

'For what possible reason?' asked Elisabeth. 'My daughter Despenser is neither a bishop nor a doctor of canon law. What purpose will her presence serve?'

'It is the King's command, madam,' Golafre said bluntly.

'By no means to be questioned,' Philippa added, looking at me.

'The King will have his reasons,' I said. 'He cannot be disobeyed.'

I had an inclination for any adventure, no matter how mild it might be, after so many weeks mewed up at Tewkesbury, scarcely allowed beyond the gardens. I was also motivated by a desire to disoblige Elisabeth, given what she had said. I was surprised when she did not make further objection, but she did not. Perhaps she did not think the argument worth it. Instead she gave me some minor commissions, orders for her favoured mercer in Gloucester, which I was to obtain on her behalf, or at least cause to be put in hand.

Next morning therefore, after we had broken our fast, we set forth on our journey. We had all the time in the world, for the distance is no more than can be walked in three hours, and we did not urge our horses beyond an easy pace. We were a fair company, for Golafre had brought half a dozen servants with him, with Philippa's woman and then there were my own people, besides a couple of Elisabeth's fellows tacked onto the party as guides. (We had no need of guidance on so straightforward a journey, but she insisted, perhaps fearing that without them to watch over me I might decide to run away to Fotheringhay.)

Golafre began to talk of my cousin, Harry Bolingbroke, presumably assuming that I was interested in his doings. Harry, he said, had taken himself off to Prussia to fight the heathens, being in bad odour with both his father and the King. There was some hope that a Lithuanian spear would be the end of him.

'Mind you,' Golafre went on, 'there are those who say that Lancaster is not as displeased with his son as he would like us all to believe. That would not surprise me. He's a crafty rogue, that one. More faces than there are heads on London Bridge.'

'You speak of my uncle, sir,' I said, for I thought he needed to be reminded of it.

He laughed. 'I know, my lady. A fine uncle too. Far too grand for any of us. Why, we are scarcely fit to lick his boots.'

That made Philippa laugh too.

'You need not fear,' Golafre went on. 'I know how great a prince my lord of Lancaster is, for he never tires of making it clear to all of us at court. He's the King's right hand, and his left, and I fancy his head as well. You there — dog!' He turned his attention from me to address a fellow who was leading a creaking, empty wain along the road in front of us at something less than walking pace. 'Do you not see us coming? Get out of our way, you scum.'

The carter bowed, knuckled his forehead, and dragged his old, skeletal horse onto the verge out of our way. As we passed though I intercepted the stare he gave Golafre, which was one of purest hatred. I could not blame him, for there had been no need for such discourtesy. We were in no haste; it was just that Sir John could not stomach being baulked by a humble carter. Philippa tittered into her hand; she evidently found the business amusing.

'Sir John does not tolerate insolence from inferiors,' she said, and sounded proud of the fact.

I looked at Golafre's florid, angry face, and it struck me that if dressed in russets he would be indistinguishable from the lowest bumpkin. A bumpkin with his hair and beard elaborately barbered, admittedly. He was loyal to the King, and I gave him credit for that, but he had the manners of a churl.

Suddenly, he let out a great belch. 'God's truth, my stomach aches for dinner,' he declared. 'Wife, it seems to me that your cousin keeps a scanty table. Nothing to break our fast on but bread and ale, and a supper last night that was fit to be a monk's penance. I hope there is better fare in Gloucester, when at last we get there.'

'Elisabeth keeps no state, but she is a good woman,' I said, for I felt compelled to make a defence.

'Indeed, I hear she is right godly,' Golafre answered. He exchanged a glance with Philippa and I sensed that they were enjoying a private joke together. 'Like all such, she would be better placed in a cloister. Better so for you, my lady, for she would be out of your way. You should recommend it to your lord husband when next you see him.'

I glared at him, but saw no point in prolonging the conversation. We rode on in silence.

When at last we came to Gloucester, Golafre led us into the courtyard of one of the large inns near the Northgate and at once began to bawl for stabling, a private room where we could take dinner — for he had no intention, he said, of eating in the common hall and being gawped at by yokels and apprentices — and the finest food and wine that such a place could supply. All of which was delivered more swiftly than he deserved, for it was a good inn and its people served us well.

Even Golafre was silent for a time as he filled his belly, and we were there for some time before this was fully accomplished. By questioning the host he established that the King was not yet in the city, but a day or two off. He paid the reckoning without a quibble, threw coins at various servitors, and then we were off again, to the Abbey, so short a distance away that it hardly seemed worth remounting our horses. We did so, nevertheless.

We were not the only pilgrims that day; indeed I was surprised to see a great crowd ahead of us, so that we, with our people, could barely enter the building. John Golafre was much displeased, and crooked a finger at the nearest monk.

'I am Sir John Golafre of the King's household,' he said, 'and this,' gesturing in my direction, 'is my Lady Despenser, the King's cousin. We are here to worship at the shrine of King Edward Second, and my lady does not stand waiting behind crowds of rustics. Clear a way for us, fellow!'

The monk did better than that. He led us through the building to the abbot's lodging, where we were welcomed with wine and little saffron cakes and an abbot who fawned so much that even Golafre was placated. The abbot spoke passionately of the holiness of King Edward, the cruelty of his martyrdom — which he dwelled on for longer and with more detail than I thought necessary — and the wickedness of his enemies, drawing some very proper parallels with King Richard's opponents. He was certain that when the King arrived he and his bishops would accept the truth of the miracles, and authorise a petition to the Pope to confirm King Edward's sainthood. For himself, he had no doubt of it.

Sir John grunted and nodded his approval, and the abbot conducted us to King Edward's tomb so that we might pray before it. The people were held back by the monks to give us space, but the place was still crowded, and as I knelt I was very conscious that two score or more pairs of eyes were watching our bearing. It was hard to focus on our veneration of the saint – for that King Edward had been a saint I chose not to doubt. If my cousin wished him to be regarded as such, that was quite sufficient for me.

After we had made our offerings we stood back, and were just about to return to the abbot's lodging when Philippa let out a gasp.

'That fellow there,' she cried, 'it's the rogue from Caversham. The one who claimed Our Lady had cured his lameness. Look, he has his crutches again. He will be here to pretend another miracle, to win alms for himself. Sir John, you must have him taken for the fraud he is!'

I followed her pointing finger, and saw at once she was correct. It was the same old man looking, if anything, more frail, dirty and helpless than he had at Caversham. It astonished me that a rogue could be so bold in his villainy. He was not at the front of the crowd, but patiently making his way forward now movement was permitted.

'Hush, wife!' said Golafre, suddenly quite fierce. 'The King's Highness would have King Edward made a saint. The more miracles the better for his purpose, whether feigned or not. Hold your tongue. If he finds a cure here, we shall marvel at it with the rest. Do you understand me?'

We stood in silence for a time, while the abbot babbled of miracles already brought about by the intercession of King Edward, of which there was no short supply, from a baby rescued from choking to a cow in a parlous state whose life had been saved to the delight of its very poor owner. I had my eyes on the old man, and was not in the least surprised when he let out a loud cry, fell on his knees with an expression of ecstasy on his wrinkled face, and cast his crutches aside. He had the strength of his legs again, he said, in a voice loud enough to fill that great church. *Deo gratias!* Praise be to King Edward the saint!

He rose to his feet, astonished, or so he wished us all to believe. The people crowded around him, as though anxious to touch so blessed a man, and there was something of a race between the good abbot and John Golafre to be the first to give him alms. Then, at the abbot's direction, we all knelt to offer prayers of thanksgiving, with the abbey bells ringing their acclaim in the background. I believe we were on our knees for a full half hour, for the abbot was filled with joy, and proceeded from prayers to a lengthy sermon on the greatness of God's mercy.

I itched to denounce the rogue, and it was much against my conscience that I did not; yet there was truth in what John Golafre had said. The King's purpose was more important than any trickery. I looked at the faces around me. Philippa's expression was pinched, and I knew that she was seething, but almost everyone else was lost in wonder and delight. Sir John was the other exception, but he had a look of deep satisfaction, that of a man who could scarcely believe his good fortune. I knew he would report the day's events to the King, and that Richard would glory in it too. No one would thank me if I told the tale of Caversham. Silence was the only course.

*

I spent that night in the abbey guest house with Philippa and our women, for of course Sir John could not lie with his wife within the holy precincts.

Philippa told me that there was to be another great tournament once the King returned from Gloucester, and that her husband would surely take part. All men, she said, admitted he was a great hand with the lance, and he was a good man, she claimed, much trusted by the King and likely to have great advancement in the years to come.

'Even so,' she said, very quietly, 'I begin to wish I had not allowed my mother to persuade me to marry him.'

I stared at her, for I was well aware that this was a distortion of the truth. Lady Mohun had said that she needed some husband, and that Golafre might serve, but she had scarcely pressed him upon her.

She sighed. 'You do not know my mother. She doesn't issue commands in plain words, but she knows how to make her wishes plain. She wanted me to marry a rising man, and Sir John is certainly that. He is — not kind. When I say he has a short way with inferiors, he does. He includes me among them.'

Silence lay between us, because I had no idea what to say. It was scarcely a surprise to me that Golafre was not an amiable husband, but Philippa had chosen him. Her mother was certainly not to blame.

'Perhaps,' she said, 'when you have your own household, and all is established, and when Sir John has no need of me — as you know, he is much at court — I will be able to stay with you. After all, Thomas is my cousin. We are close kin.'

I answered nothing, for I had no intention of being caught in a promise.

*

Next morning, just before dinner-time, King Richard arrived, bringing with him the Archbishop of Canterbury, a psalter of other bishops, and a whole host of holy clerks, canon lawyers and their like, together with his usual company of knights and great lords, though there were fewer of the latter than usual and my brother was not among them.

As you will understand, I had no proper place in such company, and was very much in the background, scarcely, as I thought, to be noticed. I did not understand the reason for my summons because, as Elisabeth had so kindly pointed out, my counsel on such a matter was of no weight whatever.

Nevertheless, we had no sooner eaten our dinner than Richard sent for me. He gave me a warm greeting, and told me that Anne sent her best wishes. She was a little unwell, so had stayed behind at Easthampstead.

'Golafre tells me that yesterday you witnessed a miracle with your own eyes, dear cousin,' he said eagerly.

'Yes,' I said hesitantly, 'that is so, your Grace, if it pleases you.'

'It pleases me very much! A miracle witnessed by my own cousin? I could ask no better. You shall set down the truth of what you saw in writing. It will be included with all the other evidence we shall send to the Pope. For evidence there is of our great-grandsire's holiness, do not doubt it. Some of my bishops are naturally reticent about the matter. They do not accept miracles too easily, lest there be fraud. Yet here is no fraud! Here is truth. I shall persuade them so, and at length the Holy Father with them.'

I was dismayed by his words, but what could I say? I promised that I would dictate the tale to a clerk, and I was well aware that my report would lack some salient facts. I might confess my doubts one day, but I knew that if I did it would be to a priest, not to Richard.

'I sent for you precisely because you are here in Gloucestershire,' he said. 'I would have you seek to foster the cult of King Edward in every way you can. You must talk to the ladies of the county, and to their husbands. Speak of this miracle, and the other miracles. Tell them that it is my particular wish that they reverence King Edward, and bring offerings to Gloucester. That they will do it as they hope for my good will. Do you understand?'

'Yes,' I said, 'but Highness, Cousin Richard, you must know that I have little influence here. I am in the household of my lord's mother, and she lives quietly, without keeping any great company. I will do all that I can, I need not say.'

'Time will amend that lack of influence,' he said, nodding at me. 'How old is Despenser now?'

'Seventeen, or close to it.'

He nodded again, sharply, then paused for consideration. 'That is old enough,' he said, 'for me to do something for him. To give him some authority and you, perhaps, a trifle more standing in the shire. I shall look to it, I promise you. You will do as I ask?'

'Of course,' I promised. 'To the limits of my power.'

***

Chapter 2

October—December 1390

As on a May morning on Malvern Hills
Me befell a ferly, of Fairy me thought.
I was weary of wandering and went me to rest
Under a broad bank by a bourne side.
And as I lay and leaned and looked on the waters,
I slumbered into a sleeping, it sweyed so merry.
Then gan I to mete a marvellous swevene:
As I beheld into the East and high to sun,
I saw a Tower...

William Langland, Piers Plowman

It was only a short time after my pilgrimage when news reached us of the death of my friend, Sir Guy de Bryan, the kind old knight who had treated me with such courtesy on my journey from Windsor to Caversham, and who had tried to raise my spirits with his generous gift of goldfinches. Elisabeth had been fond of him too — not least because she was old enough to remember him in his prime as a great jouster and warrior, a dear friend of her husband — and for once we were united in mourning, kneeling together to say many prayers for the benefit of his soul.

His beautiful tomb (almost as fine as that of King Edward at Gloucester, and built to a similar pattern) in the abbey remained empty, however. He had died at home in Devon and his people had buried him down there, not wishing to be troubled with the cost of carrying his corpse to Tewkesbury. It seemed a great scandal to me that they had not observed his wishes, but at least the unused tomb provided a focus for our prayers. The effigy on it pictured him as a much younger man — Elisabeth pronounced it a good likeness — and showed him in the act of drawing his sword, quite fitting for the great warrior he had been.

Elisabeth's husband also lay in the abbey, of course, as did many of his ancestors. He was beneath a plain slab, but it was her intent to build a tiny chapel over his resting place, just large enough to hold a small altar and a priest to say masses for his soul. The sight of Sir Guy's tomb seemed to renew this ambition, and she sent for some fellow from Gloucester, who presented her with sketches she did not consider fine enough. So he was sent off to reconsider, and returned with even more sketches. This time she was content, and before Christmas a contract was signed, so that at last her mind and her conversation turned to other matters.

It was a dull time, with even fewer visitors than were usual. The Abbot of Tewkesbury shared our table from time to time, but he rarely brought news of any interest, but only more talk of tombs and chapels and donations — Elisabeth was generous to his house, but he always had some new project in mind for which more coin was required. (If a roof was not leaking, there would be an altar in need of better furniture or a bell that needed to be recast or a statue that needed fresh gilding.)

Then, at last, Thomas came home; not only that, he brought with him a grant from the King, newly enrolled in the Chancery. He was henceforward to have a share in his own wardship — to be associated with his mother in the governing of all his Welsh lands and many of his English ones. It was not freedom — they had still to pay a great sum to the King each year — but it gave him a degree of independence and meant that he was no longer reliant on his mother for every last coin.

We feasted our eyes on one another after our long parting, for we had both changed very significantly, were close to being man and woman together. After so many months of tedium, after a time when I had even welcomed Philippa Fitzwalter's company for the week or two she had been with us, I was beyond excitement. That Christmas was upon us only added to the occasion.

Thomas had brought my father's troupe of musicians with him, and several young men besides whom he had taken into his own service. Suddenly, Tewkesbury was a place of laughter, of merry tales and songs, and above all of dancing. We danced and carolled endlessly, joyously, and Elisabeth's dull household was quite transformed. I believe I had all but forgotten how to laugh — Elisabeth had all but trained me out of it — and as for dancing, why, for many months there had been no one to dance with except my damsels, and even that had not been encouraged.

We had quite a gathering for the festivities. There was Thomas's sister, Margaret, and her husband, Robert, Lord Ferrers, who was somewhat older than she, beyond forty and with flecks of grey in his brown beard, but with all the energy of a youth and very agreeable company. Thomas Berkeley, 'good cousin Berkeley', was with us, and with him his lady, a quiet, unassuming woman on whom he clearly doted, rather to my surprise. There was Judge Cassy and his wife from Deerhurst, near neighbours of Elisabeth. The judge was a solemn fellow, and more than plump, but he was amiable enough. Then there was Sir John Russell and his wife, from Strensham. Besides a score of lesser people, who could recognise the rising sun in the sky when they saw it and thought it wise to make themselves known to Thomas, and to me.

Berkeley and Judge Cassy spent hours talking at each other. Berkeley expounded at length about how difficult it would be to achieve peace with France while retaining England's honour, giving all manner of complicated reasons why this was so. The judge wanted to grumble about the many disorders in the county, largely caused, he implied, by men under Berkeley's patronage. He wanted to know what was going to be done about it. Neither man seemed to make the slightest impression on the other. It was almost as if each was speaking in some incomprehensible foreign tongue. Neither lost his temper though, which was quite impressive. It may be that they had had enough of Elisabeth's wine to make them mellow.

As for John Russell, he had much to tell us about the jousts he had attended earlier in the year, near Calais, after three French knights had issued a challenge to all-comers. He made little of his own deeds (although from what I heard from others, he did as well as any), but praised my cousin's husband, Huntingdon, whom he called the best of the English knights. Both Harry Bolingbroke and Thomas Mowbray had been there too, as well as John Golafre — which surprised me, as Golafre had not spoken of it during his visit. There had been many other English knights and squires engaged, but Russell said the greatest honour belonged to the French, for they had each met multiple opponents and had held their own. He said that it was in part that they were better horsed. He had brought home a French destrier, purchased for some ridiculous sum, and said that he intended to breed from him, to improve his own stock.

Lord Berkeley hooted at this, saying that our English war horses were as good as any in God's world, and that Russell had wasted his coin. The French, he said, would never have sold an animal that would give any advantage to our knights. An argument ensued, but fortunately it remained a friendly one.

Thomas's eyes had taken on a distant look at all this talk of jousting, and I knew that he wished he had been part of it. He had not had the funds to equip himself according to his rank for one thing, and another factor was that my father had kept him busy with other business. Now, however, he had the means to be his own man, at least to some extent. How it came about I am not sure, but he began to talk of going on crusade to Prussia. Before very long I realised that this was no dream, no mere talk. He meant to go, the following summer. It was obvious from his talk that his plans were already settled.

I remembered that evening at Fotheringhay when Harry Bolingbroke had spoken of his damned crusade and Thomas, along with most of the rest of the young men and boys had grown enraptured by his talk. I had never expected it to come to anything, but now, it seemed, it had.

I rose silently, and withdrew from the company. When my damsels sought to follow me, I sent them back, because I wanted to enjoy that rarest of luxuries, solitude. I went to my bedchamber, and considered kneeling before my image of the Blessed Virgin, but I had not the stomach for prayer, so simply sat on the bed in idleness, my thoughts wandering. What hurt most was that in all his words to me since he had arrived Thomas had made no mention of Prussia. Not only had he not thought to consult me, he had not even had the grace to tell me of his decision, yet now was happy to speak of it before all, as if it were the common knowledge of the shire. Perhaps it was! Known to all but me.

After a time, there was a brief knock on the door and Margaret Ferrers entered.

'Are you ill?' she asked.

I shook my head. 'No. Why should you think me ill?'

She sat next to me. 'My dear sister,' she began, before hesitating. 'May I call you that?'

I was puzzled. 'Of course you may.'

'I was unsure. You may not know it, but you are — *intimidating*, Constance. We are all a little in awe of you. Even my lady mother, who would face down a basilisk.'

I was astonished by her words. Margaret was not only my elder by some years, but the mother of several children. I could not believe that she was intimidated by my mere presence, and the idea that Elisabeth was seemed too ridiculous for words.

'I cannot think why,' I said.

'Thomas is going on this adventure to Prussia for you — or at least, to prove himself worthy of you. Don't be angry with him on that account.'

'He has no need to prove himself, to me or others,' I snapped. 'I bring him no lands, no dowry, nothing but my clothes and jewels, such as they are.'

I held out the hand with the Queen's ring on it, shrugging as I did so.

'You bring him much more than that,' she replied, taking my hand in hers. 'I don't just mean your quarterings either, splendid though they are. A man might be pleased to win you if you were but a mere gentlewoman. Thomas is so *proud* of you. I know not how else to explain it. He doesn't think himself *worthy*. So he seeks to earn your favour. Do you really not see it? It's as clear as can be.'

'It's folly!' I said sharply.

She shrugged, smiling at me. 'Perhaps, but it's a man's folly. You cannot hope to keep him forever quiet at home. At least, not until he is very old, and has aches in his bones and silver hair. Now that we have peace with France — well, a truce at least — there is no glory to be found there, so he must and will find it elsewhere. You had better learn to make the best of it, and be as proud of him as he is of you.'

'Do you think I am not?'

'Then why not let him know it? Sulking will not serve. nor harsh words. Let him have his way in this small thing, and show that you approve it. You know, he must make *some* decisions for himself, you cannot command him in everything. My mother has accepted that, and you should do the same.'

I sighed. It was annoying to admit she was right, but of course she was. We returned to the company, our arms linked together in amity. By this time Thomas was talking to John Russell about practising combat together, a suggestion that had Russell nodding with pleasure. My absence did not seem to have been noticed, and that was just as well, for I knew that I had been childish and ill-mannered. If Elisabeth had been in the room she might have reproved me for it, but there was no need, as I reproved myself far more severely than she would have dreamed of doing.

*

Thomas suggested that some of us — those who wished to do so — should go for a long ride on St. Stephen's Day, if the weather proved fair. Dawn revealed a crisp, cold morning with every promise of winter sunshine and so, after hearing the morning Mass and breaking our fast on wine and sops, we set out, with Lord and Lady Ferrers, Russell and his wife and a suitable escort of our people.

We rode through the little town and across the long, stone bridge over the Avon. Thomas was reticent about our exact destination and at first I thought we might be on our way to Strensham, to visit John Russell's manor. However, I was mistaken, as we continued down the Worcester road.

We were a merry company. Some of my father's minstrels were with us, and one of them played bagpipes as we rode along, familiar tunes to which, for much of the time, we could sing the words. I had no idea where we were going, or even if Thomas had a destination in mind, but I decided it did not matter. I had exercise and good company, and was scarcely bothered by the chill wind that was blowing directly into my face. I was quite determined to enjoy the day, and take pleasure in whatever came of our small adventure.

After some time, Thomas led us down a by-road to the left. This was new territory for me. I had travelled with Elisabeth on pilgrimage to Our Lady of Worcester, but what there was away from the main road I did not know.

Hanley Castle

'They say the bridge is down at Upton, but the ferry should be working,' he said, as though I was familiar with the area. I had *heard* of Upton — it was a small town or large village belonging to Elisabeth — but I had not visited it and had no idea what to expect when we arrived there.

It was not so far to the river, the Severn, and it was dark and sluggish in the winter light. As Thomas had said, there was a bridge, a wooden structure, but it was in sad disrepair with a great gap in the middle where the flooding waters had broken it down. There was little sign of life about the ferry either, which was moored on the far bank, the side, as I could see, where the village lay, a cluster of small houses around a church. One of our musicians sounded a clarion, and in a very short while the ferryman emerged from hiding and began to pull his vessel across.

The ferry was not nearly large enough to take us all — not by the half. Thomas and I were among the first to go across, with our horses, but it took some time to complete the passage. Thomas went straight into the nearest inn, where, as was fitting at this time of year, he bought all those present a fresh drink. Long before the last of our people had joined us I had my nose deep in a cup of mulled ale, very warming and very welcome.

I thought this might be our destination for the day, though I marvelled that we should take so much trouble to reach the inn when there were any number on the other side of the water. Of course, I was mistaken. When everyone was refreshed for the road — a process which took some time because the ale was very good and a second cup was irresistible — we set off again.

After a mile or so, a small castle came into sight to our left, its dull, whitewashed walls visible through the bare branches of the trees.

'Hanley Castle,' said Thomas, pointing. It seemed to me that he was struggling not to grin at me, though I saw no obvious joke.

'Is it ours?' I asked.

'My mother holds it in dower.'

'Oh!' I said, feeling unaccountably disappointed.

I realised this was our destination, nonetheless. The path to it was not direct. We carried on a little way before turning to the left along a road which took us into another small village, past a church and then through what was quite obviously part of the castle park, though it was much overgrown and without any sign of deer.

It was clear that we were expected, because the drawbridge had been lowered and the caretakers, few in number though they were, stood waiting for us in the courtyard in what must have been their best liveries, well-brushed. They bowed low and bade us welcome.

The castle was, indeed, quite small. Not at all on the scale of Fotheringhay. What was more it was evident, now we were close, that the rendered walls had not seen fresh whitewash in many a long year. The windows were shuttered, and many of those shutters lacked paint, while a few hung limply on their hinges as though the supporting ironwork was rusted to the point of death. Grass grew abundantly in the court yard, and ivy was making its way up many of the walls. There were more loose roofing tiles than you could count. Even so, there was something pleasing about the place — I had this strange sense of having come home.

As Thomas helped me down from my jennet I was surprised by the sudden clanging of a bell, and when I looked around I saw there was a great clock built into the gatehouse and saw that two little figures in the shape of knights were engaged in striking the hour. This was one luxury we did not have at Fotheringhay, nor at any of my father's castles.

Thomas smiled. 'My father had that put in,' he explained. 'He gained so much from the French wars that he could bear the expense. There's one at Cardiff too, but not as grand as this. At Cardiff, it just strikes the hour — this one has a hand.'

As I looked, I understood his meaning. Time here at Hanley was so precise that you could judge it to the quarter hour. Even the King's great clock at Westminster was no better.

'We have to employ a man to keep it in order,' he went on, 'but it's worth it, don't you think? Even Warwick has nothing so fine, and Berkeley cannot dream of it.'

We went inside. Of course, the walls were bare, except where there were murals, and there was scarcely any furniture. Nor were the caretakers very particular, for all their fine liveries. Dust lay thick on every surface, and I judged that the floor rushes had not been changed in years. Still, we went from room to room, climbing the staircases of every tower, peering into every corner. At last we came to what, from its size and grand vaulted ceiling, I knew must be the lord's solar. Dilapidated and dirty though it was, it was still a very fine room, with fine red and white floor tiles decorated with Despenser griffins and the peculiar Burghersh lions with their double tails.

'If you like it, it is yours,' Thomas said.

I span to look at him, puzzled.

'My mother has no use for the place. She has agreed we may have it, once we come to live together.' He smiled. 'I fancy she has no mind to have us under her feet at Tewkesbury, disturbing her peace and quiet. Once I come of age, she will give us a proper lease, but there will be no rent worth mentioning. It's her New Year gift to us. What do you say?'

We were standing rather closer together than I had realised, so close that it was easier to kiss him than answer. It was no ordinary kiss, either, but something quite new to me, that set lightning flashing through my veins. Before I knew it we had our arms about each other and we were repeating the experiment. It was perhaps as well that we were interrupted.

'Here are the lovebirds!' It was Robert Ferrers, his kindly face appearing in the doorway. We sprang apart, as Margaret followed him into the room.

'Do you like Thomas's surprise?' she asked me. She was grinning like her husband, but I knew they were not mocking us, that they wished us well.

'It's as good a surprise as I have ever had,' I said.

'It should keep you occupied while Thomas is in Prussia,' she went on. 'There's much to make good, but nothing that can't be mended.'

I could not stop myself. I hugged her. I hugged Thomas. I even hugged Ferrers. It was the finest gift I had received in the whole of my life, and I lacked the words to express my gratitude.

***

Chapter 3

January-March 1391

It was Elisabeth who decided that my lord husband should go to Glamorgan, to see that his interests there were not being mismanaged by the officers she had set in place. She herself had not set foot in Wales for over a decade, although she suspected the revenues were not what they should be. Since he was now her equal colleague in managing the Welsh lordships, he should, she said, show himself there. It would, at the least, be good experience.

When I offered to go with him, she told me not to be absurd.

So, quickly and effectively, Thomas and I were parted again. I was still too young to live with him as his wife, Elisabeth said. It was not her opinion, she added, as I began to protest, it was the expressed will of the Duke and Duchess of York, to whom we had to defer. There was a twitch of her lips as she said this, the nearest she came to a smile.

I wrote to my mother. It was difficult to find the right arguments while remaining suitably deferential, but I did my best. I told her that Thomas was for Prussia before the end of summer, and that he might well die there, even if he was not drowned on the voyage. I mentioned he had no brother and his only surviving uncle was a bishop. (The Duchess was well aware of these facts, but in my folly I thought it proper to refresh her memory.) His line might die, I pointed out. Unless —.

I calculated how long it would take Elisabeth's messenger to reach Fotheringhay, and how long to return. I allowed time for my mother to write her reply, and allowed a day longer for security. It seemed to me that the entire transaction could not take longer than eight days. Ten at most. I might even have an answer in a week.

A week went by. Then ten days. There was no answer. I persuaded myself that the Duchess might be at Conisbrough, or Sandal, or Vasterne. She might even be at court, wherever that might be. Then I decided that Elisabeth's man was an idler who dawdled on the road, sitting for hours in every alehouse, instead of covering the forty miles in a day that I expected such a fellow to complete. I cursed him, and developed the impatient habit of opening a casement from time to time, despite the freezing weather, and looking out to see if the man was approaching. Each time I looked I found that he was not.

I all but gave up on receiving any answer. Then, late one afternoon, with the winter sun so low in the sky that darkness was scarcely a dozen Paternosters away, a tremendous clatter of hooves and wheels on the courtyard paving reached my ears. Berkeley and his entire meinie might have made so much noise, but he was not expected. I could not think of any other likely visitor who would bring such numbers with him.

I opened the casement — to the displeasure of my companions, who were cold enough already without an icy blast from outside — and looked out. What was below was my mother's great carriage, with its five horses and two postilions, accompanied by a sizeable escort of our people. They filled the courtyard almost completely, to the point where you could barely see the cobblestones. I shut the casement hurriedly, astonished. I was in my workaday garb, my hair under a plain linen cover-chief, my nose red as a burning coal and streaming, for I was in the grip of a miserable cold. I was scarcely in a state to receive the Duchess, but there was certainly no time to tidy myself, let alone to change into a more suitable gown and headdress.

However, it was not the Duchess who had arrived. She had

sent three of her women (headed by the chief of them, Marie de St. Hilaire) and with them a letter. Elisabeth scanned it, and passed it to me without a word. My mother required my return to her, at Fotheringhay. She had sent her carriage to convey me. She neither asked nor suggested, but commanded as only a Spanish princess knows how to do. It was a courteous letter, after a fashion, but it brooked no evasion, let alone refusal.

It was too late to set out that night, but there was time enough for a hurried packing of my belongings between supper and bed. In the morning, I heard Mass, swallowed a hasty meal of bread and small ale, offered a respectful farewell to Elisabeth (which was coldly received) and set out on my way.

That journey seemed endless. It was bitterly cold, even though we were all wrapped in blankets on top of our clothes. Thomas, I knew, would be in Cardiff by this time, and every mile was another mile away from him, to my discontent.

On one occasion, the road was blocked by flooding, and there was no choice but to turn the carriage in an adjoining field. No sooner was it off the road than it sank into mud up to its axles, and we had to alight and stand on the verge, shivering in the wind, while the men of our escort struggled to extricate it. Even when the road was firm and empty before us, the carriage made no great speed, and we did well if we managed fifteen miles in a long day.

My mother's women showed me every proper deference, but I was in little doubt that they blamed me for their involvement in such an unpleasant and uncomfortable expedition. There was the occasional tart remark, and the more than occasional long silence. My own damsels, I sensed, were scarcely more content to be taken away from their customary comforts.

I was grateful indeed to reach Fotheringhay at last, although I was uncertain as to the reception I should have, given the peremptory tone of my mother's letter. I went at once to her apartments.

She was sitting in her great gilded chair by the fire, and I saw at once that if she had been angry the storm had passed. She looked weary, and, I thought, rather thinner than when I had last seen her.

I knelt for her blessing, and her hand gave my cheek a gentle caress. She was smiling, very definitely not displeased with me. I stood, and waited for her to speak.

She pointed to the stool next to her. 'Sit, child. My neck will ache if I have to keep looking up at you. I hadn't realised just how much you've grown.'

There was silence for a few moments, setting aside the occasional sharp crack that came from the logs burning in the fireplace. The Duchess shivered as if, despite the fire, she was feeling the cold.

'Do you know why I sent for you?' she asked.

I shook my head. 'No, madam my Mother.'

'First, to separate fire from kindling,' she said, fixing me with her piercing eyes until I lowered my gaze. 'Next, and just as importantly, because I wished to see you again.' She stroked my cheek again, very softly. 'I have missed you, my dear, and I grow lonely. Your father and Edward are with the King — I've not seen either of them in months. There's your brother Richard, of course, but his conversation is all you expect from a five-year-old boy and no more.'

We ate supper together in the Great Chamber, my mother and I at the high table, our women and the senior household officers (such as were present) at the others. Even though we had braziers full of charcoal burning away, it was still rather chill, with the east wind battering against the shutters and fierce draughts playing with the candle flames and casting dancing shadows across the tablecloths.

The Duchess barely picked at her food, nor did she speak much during the meal. Of course, there were a few feet of space between us, as was proper given her rank, and so it was not the place for private words. It was true that my mother had never been one to empty a dish, but as I watched her I sensed that she was also very tired.

'Are you unwell, madam?' I dared to ask.

She smiled thinly. 'Not at all, my dear. All is well with me, now that you are come home. I'm just a little tired and ready for my bed. You must be weary too, after such a journey.'

I shook my head in denial. I felt awake enough to stay up half the night if necessary. My cold was all but gone, and I was much the better for its leaving me. I was, perhaps, not quite in the mood to dance, but I should have been happy enough to sit up and hear some poetry read, or listen to music. Better than either would have been a long talk with my mother, especially as she seemed so amiable.

Next morning, I rose very early, and was in good time to attend the Duchess to Mass in our chapel. Even so, I found her already dressed and about to leave her rooms. She greeted me kindly as I knelt for her blessing but said very little beyond that. In the chapel, where she often talked or sat reading her Primer except during the Elevation, she was silent and attentive to the priest's every word and gesture. Our breakfast meal was as well-supplied as ever, but she barely picked at it, taking less bread than would satisfy the appetite of a sparrow and barely sipping the wine.

I spoke to her of Hanley Castle, a circumspect approach, I thought, to the subject I wanted to broach with her.

She smiled at my description of the place.

'Elisabeth Despenser has more sense than I imagined,' she said quietly. 'I must write to her again. A kinder letter this time, as I can see that she means well by you. When I sent for you I was in an impatient mood, and I fear I was a little short with her.'

That was putting it mildly, I thought, but of course I didn't say so.

'Your father and I decided, long ago, that you should not be bedded with your husband until you are quite sixteen. This is for your good, Constance, no matter what you may think. Too many girls are ruined for life, or killed, by breeding too young. I will not have that for you, and I may add that your lord father and I do not care to have our decisions questioned in such matters.'

That was brisk, and for a moment she sounded much like her old self. My face fell. I could not help it.

She laughed, for the first time since my return. 'Oh, my dear child. You've not changed. You've *still* not learned to hide your displeasure. I thought Elisabeth might have taught you that at least, for I'm sure her will crossed yours more than once.'

I was silent, and after a little time she went on: 'This matter of Prussia is a complication, that I must admit. I really do not understand the attraction. If what I am told is correct, it isn't even a proper crusade any longer. The King of Poland, who rules these Lithuanians, is as much a Christian as we are; if some of his peasants and slaves are not, not yet at least, he will no doubt make them so in his own good time. Still, I am not a man, and don't have the inclination to fight for the sake of it. It seems your Thomas does, and he's not alone. Your Uncle Gloucester means to go at about the same time. Perhaps it is as well. Your uncle, despite what you may think of him —' (she had evidently seen my nose wrinkling) '— is a very great lord and has some experience of war. I will ask him to keep a kindly eye on Despenser.'

This, I thought, is growing worse and worse.

She sighed. 'I will speak to your father, when he returns from court. Perhaps something can be arranged to please you, although I make no promises.'

I tried to thank her, but she held up her hand to silence me.

'Until then,' she said, 'I do not wish to hear another word on the subject. If I do, I promise I will send you to the nuns at Delapré and leave you there until Despenser is landed in Prussia.'

*

I had to be satisfied with that, because I knew the Duchess was more than capable of keeping her word. I busied myself as best I could. There was still work to be done on the new bed curtains, and I attacked them with my needle until my fingers ached, working through all the hours of daylight and often by candlelight as well, for I was determined the task would be finished.

My mother also found work for me. She told me to deal with various matters brought to her by the household officers, acting as her deputy. I had wit enough to know this for a test and did my best. For example, when the Parker came to her with some tale about deer dying in the park, she told me to ride with him and see what the problem might be. This I did.

Had they been struck by murrain, I should have had the bodies hanged from the trees, to counter the risk of infection, as was the custom, and common sense besides. However, it was soon clear that this was a matter of simple starvation, a lack of fodder in these cold winter months. So I had the fellow arrange for hay to be distributed about the park, which was well enough until I learned we lacked sufficient hay, for there were horses and our herd of cattle to be considered and our stocks were a good deal lower than they ought to have been. How this had come about, I cannot say. There was much shuffling and making of excuses.

We had to buy more to make up our stocks, which was ridiculous, as the demesne and parks should have produced ample hay for our own needs even in a bad year. I suspected some wretch in our livery had been selling it off for his own private profit, but of course, I couldn't prove it. I wrote to my father though, and told him, very humbly of course, that he had fools in his service and quite probably rogues. I ended it with the new *raison* I had invented for myself: *Constant et Loyale*.

To make matters worse, our credit was at a low ebb at this time, not least because my father was elsewhere, and in the end I had to ride into Peterborough and pawn two or three of my rings to pay for the hay and other necessities. I had them back before too long, when the Lady Day rents came in, but it was still infuriating.

***

Chapter 4

April — May 1391

I waited impatiently for my father's return from court, feeling, at times, as excited as a five-year-old child who has been promised a whole jar of sweetmeats — tomorrow, when father comes home, tomorrow, if you are good, tomorrow, if you learn to say your catechism. Tomorrow, as ever in such circumstances, seemed exceedingly reluctant to dawn. Until, at last, it did.

It came in the shape of my brother, Edward, who arrived quite unexpectedly, not having had the courtesy to send a harbinger or messenger before him — I have an idea he enjoyed creating confusion and chaos by taking us by surprise. His advancement to an earldom had not made him more dignified, nor had it removed the familiar hint of mockery from his eye. He ran his eyes over me from head to foot and let out an oath.

'By God's nails, you are changed since last I saw you, my sister! You've sprouted out in all directions. Let me kiss you.'

He did at once, and without waiting for my consent. Still, it was a brotherly kiss and entirely proper.

He had Edmund Mortimer with him, still wearing my father's livery. This surprised me, as I had had the distinct impression that he had quit the Duke's service to attend upon his brother and live with him and Alianore in Kent's household. Clearly I had misunderstood, but there was no misunderstanding the look he gave me. I swear it made me blush, as though I stood before him in my shift. He kissed my hand, and hurriedly let it go, but I knew that he would have liked to kiss a great deal more. It is never exactly *unpleasant* to be admired by a good-looking young man you have a liking for, but it can be awkward and embarrassing, especially when you are under the eye of an elder brother who knows a great deal more than is good for him.

Edmund stuttered something, and I made myself say something suitable by way of polite welcome, but I had the distinct impression life had become complicated.

Edward had brought a letter from my father. The Duke wanted my mother and me to come to Windsor for the coming Garter feast. It was not exactly a command, but it was very close, especially as he was careful to state that the King and Queen were looking forward to seeing us.

My mother was reluctant. I could see her struggling to find the words to refuse. In the end though, after my brother had plagued her with persuasive words for a good hour, she gave way, with the sole condition that we would have to travel by easy stages. I believe she would very much have preferred to remain where she was, but the habit of obedience was too strong. My father's wishes, when coupled with those of the King, were as good as law to her.

It was a tedious journey. I supposed we covered, each day, about half the distance Edward and I would have thought reasonable, and sometimes less than that. The only consolation was that the weather was in our favour, with very little rain, and the roads were as good as they ever are, neither deep in mud nor coated with layers of dust.

It was very tempting to ride with Edward and Edmund, who sometimes galloped off across the fields or disappeared to explore the adjoining woodlands, taking their hawks with them and looking for what sport they could find, careless of who owned the land. I decided, however, that it would be prudent to stay with my mother in the jolting, lumbering carriage, and console myself by caressing my greyhound, Edith and scratching her ears, something which she would tolerate for as long as the day lasted.

As we, at long last, approached Windsor the roads became busier. We were not the only retinue making the journey to the castle by any means, although my mother's rank meant that everyone we met gave way and allowed us precedence, despite our snail-like pace. One of the parties had Arundel's banner flying above it, and there indeed was the fellow himself.

He climbed from his horse and walked over to the carriage to pay his respects to my mother, kneeling courteously to kiss her extended hand. He glanced at me, and nodded by way of acknowledgement as I averted my gaze. I was pleased to note that his young countess did not seem to be in his company. She, of course, had not been given her Garter, and I am glad to say that she was fated never to receive the honour, much to my satisfaction. It must have torn at her heart. Philippa Mortimer, Countess of Arundel, could have all the coronets, all the furs, all the jewels, all the fine gowns that she desired, but not *that*. *Honi soit qui mal y pense*.

It was perhaps another hour before the great castle came into sight, set on its hill, the little town spread out below at its foot. I was delighted to see it – here at last was the prospect of rest in a comfortable bed, with no more travelling for perhaps a fortnight, perhaps even longer, depending on what the King and my lord father had in mind. My mother was anticipating a brief visit to court, purely to attend the Garter feast, but there was really no telling what would transpire. It was not in her hands to decide, still less mine.

We were received by some of the King's household officers with all due ceremony, and perhaps a little more, and conducted, with many bows and flourishes, to the apartments allocated to my father, which were not as extensive as I had hoped. It took me about a Paternoster-while to realise that I should have to bed down with my mother's women, as in the old days when I was but a child. (Of course, now that Uncle Lancaster was home, we were pushed down a step, so to speak.)

Still, there are worse places than Windsor, especially when you are given one of the better lodgings. The rooms are large and airy, and lit by huge windows that let in a great deal of light. Some of my father's hangings covered the walls, familiar hunting scenes and tales of King Arthur and the like. In our principal room a substantial fire burned in the grate. My father was not present, but several of his men were there to wait on us, and we were soon seated on chairs, stools and cushions with large glasses of wine in our hands.

Edward muttered something about essential business to which he had to attend and departed. We were just finishing our wine and having the first thoughts about preparing my mother so she could present herself to the Queen when the doors were thrown open without announcement and Anne herself came into the room.

This was, of course, a very great honour. We all rose to our feet in confusion, and made our reverences, while my mother began to stutter apologies, thinking, I suppose, that she had lingered too long and that Anne had grown impatient. However, Anne merely smiled, embraced her, and welcomed her to Windsor. Then she did as much for me.

The Queen and her women stayed with us for some time, exchanging what family news there was. Anne had miscarried yet again, I gathered. Richard had suffered with pains in his face in the weeks after Christmas, but had taken physic and was well again. Bolingbroke's wife had had another child in his absence — that was no great surprise. My Uncle Lancaster was closer to the King than ever – his advice was greatly to Richard's liking, and Anne hoped there would soon be a lasting peace with France, not merely another truce. My uncle and the King were in full agreement on this point, although Uncle Gloucester had some reservations. He was back on the Council now, I learned. So was Arundel. Richard had wished that

Robert de Vere should be allowed back to England before long; his Council was against it, though — no wonder, I thought, if the likes of Gloucester and Arundel were giving their advice — and Richard, well, he did not think it wise to overrule his counsellors. I agree, said Anne, smiling at us. We have peace now; it is worth keeping Robert in exile to preserve it. Much as we still love him.

Robert's annulment of his marriage had been reversed by the Pope. So my cousin his wife was Duchess of Ireland again —there were many, including my mother, who had never thought of her as anything else — and drawing revenues from such part of his lands as she had been allowed. She was not at court though, not even for the Garter ceremony. She preferred to live retired in the country. Anne said that she had suffered from smallpox, that her face was —well, not what it had been. My mother sighed, and said it was a great pity.

I was just beginning to grow tired of the talk when Anne leaned to speak some private words in my mother's ear. The Duchess, glancing at me, nodded, giving a brief smile.

Anne rose to her feet. 'Come, cousin,' she said, extending a hand towards me. 'I have a fine surprise for you.'

What could I do but follow her from the room? I had no idea what she intended. Perhaps, I thought, Cousin Richard wishes to see me. Or Aunt Lancaster. Or perhaps it is a gift, though I can't think I've done anything to earn one.

We walked for some way, Anne just a foot or two ahead of me, although she kept turning to look at me, as if unsure that I was following, and I had the distinct feeling that she longed to link arms with me, or lead me by the hand. (It would not, of course, have been proper to do such a thing, certainly not when at times we were passing through public rooms, with all manner of great men bowing low before her as she passed.)

At last we reached a closed door, guarded by a man wearing,

of all things, Despenser livery. He threw the door open so the Queen could pass and knelt before her. In the room beyond, dressed in Garter robes, was Thomas! I was so astonished my knees buckled, although in truth the presence of that man in livery should have prepared me. Thomas went down on one knee and kissed the Queen's hand. Then, almost before I could make sense of what was happening, Anne was gone, the door was closed behind her, and we were alone.

I ran to him. We were only a few feet apart, and he was still on one knee as he had been to salute the Queen, so in my haste and clumsiness I all but knocked him over. He kissed my hand, as he had kissed the Queen's, then stood and took me in his arms. It was strange but I was at the same moment aware of his strength *and* his gentleness.

'Garter robes?' I asked, after some time.

He looked very pleased with himself. Very pleased indeed. 'The King has ordered my election as a Knight,' he said. 'I don't know why – there must be a dozen more senior and more worthy — but he sent a man all the way to Glamorgan to summon me. So here I am. I thought I might earn this one day, but I never dreamed —.' He paused, gave me a sharp look. 'Is it your doing, perhaps? Did you ask for this?'

I shook my head. 'I've not seen the King in months. I've not even seen him today. This is not of my doing, I promise you. Though I wish it was! It would be a fair gift, equal to Hanley Castle.'

'Better,' he said, 'far better. I am honoured far beyond my deserts and the King shall have my life service and my life blood in exchange. That I swear, by all that is precious to me.'

I don't think I imagined it; at these words a chill ran through my veins. It made me recall those others who had given their life blood for Richard — or had it taken. It was only a momentary fear.

No enemy, I was sure, would ever overcome us.

*

There were the usual services in the great chapel, the usual processions, the usual solemn conclave at which, to my pleasure, Thomas received his Garter, and the usual great feast. I felt as though I was drunk, or walking on air. None of it mattered – it was simply a kind of elaborate dream through which I was passing. Only Thomas mattered. I had eyes only for him, and was filled with an inexplicable mixture of pride and joy that set my belly trembling as though a tiny bird was fluttering within it.

We had jousting that year, after the other ceremonies were done. It was held out in the park, with the castle walls at our back as I sat with my mother in the stand to enjoy the spectacle. Spectacle there was in plenty, with a great procession of the knights taking part, the cries and proclamations of heralds as they announced each event, and a great concourse of minstrels in various liveries, including my father's, who made merry music whenever there was a pause in activity.

On the far side of the lists, behind a six-foot barrier built to contain them, was a whole mass of humble folk from the town and beyond, standing on sloping ground that gave them a good view, and making a great clamour. It was, I suppose, a local holiday, with most work stopped, save for those who carried trays of pies and the like to sell to the spectators. Here and there columns of smoke rose from their cooking fires. A great cheer rose from these people when the King and Queen made their way to their seats in the centre of the stand — whether this was any true sign of loyalty I cannot say. I suspect most of them would have cheered just as loudly if we had been hanging a thief.

It was the first time Thomas had been involved in such an event — given the circumstances he could scarcely have avoided it, although several of the older and more senior knights were sitting in the stand with the ladies, either because they had received bruises enough in their life or because they had grown too infirm for such sport. Even my brother was actively involved, although Edward was scornful of jousts, saying they were a pastime for fools. Fortunately, he was in the same team as Thomas, so there was no chance of a contest between them.

I had my eye on Thomas's pavilion, with its Despenser banner flying from it, from the very first, foolishly imagining that if I did not keep it under close scrutiny I might miss his appearance. It was ridiculous, of course, but I was absurdly excited. He was carrying my favour (a garter, appropriately) and I was all but bursting with pride. If I was troubled by unpleasant memories of the fate of John Hastings — and I was — I thrust them to the back of my mind and maintained a smiling face.

My lord did not win any prizes that day — he was too inexperienced, too raw — but nor was he disgraced. He was not, unlike Edward, knocked from his horse, and he broke several lances, which was all to the good. Above all, he was not hurt. At least, not in any way that was visible.

The ones that did win the prizes were Arundel — to my disgust — Thomas Mowbray, who had, among other things, put Edward on his back — and inevitably, the handsome John Holland, Lord Huntingdon, a man I had to make an effort to like, for all that he was the King's half-brother and my cousin Beth's husband. However, I must own it — he was one of the first to say how well Thomas had done in the lists, and that made me think a little more kindly of him.

Later, when the day's feasting was done, Thomas and I joined in the dancing, but he was weary, and before too long we found a dark corner to settle in and talk. We were just beginning our discussions when Arundel found us and interrupted.

'You did well today, Despenser,' he said briskly, nodding his head up and down.

'Thank you, my lord,' Thomas answered, climbing to his feet. I, of course, did not stir from my seat, though I could feel my spine stiffening.

'You need a better horse, my boy. That one you have is a little shy, and you have to put too much effort into keeping him on his proper line. However, you managed very well despite his failings. The training you had in my household has served you well.'

'Yes, and of late I have been much at exercise with a most skilful knight, Sir John Russell.'

'Russell, you say?' Arundel sniffed as if he had just detected the first hint of a vile smell. 'Warwick's man that was? A troublemaking fellow, and, from what I've heard, an ingrate. Knows his horses though. Does he go with you to Prussia?'

'I think not. Though my cousin, Sir Hugh, is minded to go with me. I'll be glad of his experience'

Again there was an expressive sniff. I began to think Arundel must have a cold.

'A good man, Hugh Despenser,' he allowed. 'A worthy knight. You do well to choose him. Well to leave this court, too. I myself will be off to Holt in a few days, to join my wife. She is in pup, you know. No, we are all of us well away from a court where Lancaster reigns as a second king, and no man dares to cross him. Look at him now.'

He jerked his head towards the far end of the hall, where my uncle, dressed in a most elegant violet velvet and loaded down with jewels and gold chains, was sitting as close to the King as Anne was at his other hand, but leaning to speak into Richard's ear, making some point that required him to sweep his arm in a dramatic gesture.

'He's already talked the King into making the palatine of Lancaster a hereditary honour, whereas before the palatine powers were but for his life. Then even that was not enough; he had Richard make him Duke of Guienne as well, as if one duchy is not sufficient. Before we know it, he will be making himself heir to the throne, thrusting my brother March aside. Mark my words, he has the ambition for it. He's always wanted to be a king, and if the Spanish will not have him, he'll gladly take their gold and then turn his ambitions to England itself. We shall do very well to stop him.'

With that, he gave a brief tilt of the head, and departed, leaving us to stare at one another.

'What do you make of that?' Thomas asked.

I sniffed. 'Arundel seeks to make trouble, and hopes he can involve you in it. He knows you to be March's friend.'

He laughed. 'So I am. Yet this talk of your Uncle Lancaster is, I think, but jealousy. Arundel would give an arm to be the man the King heeds first. He's opposed to this peace, too, and blames Lancaster for pursuing it. So I judge it. Even so, in one respect he may be right. A man might be safer in Prussia, chasing infidels, than meddling in his quarrels with the King and your uncle.'

'I wish you were not involved in either,' I said, and I meant it.

'My time in Prussia will not be long,' he promised, clasping my hand. 'A few months. Once it is done, we shall be at Hanley together — Arundel may do as he pleases, but I have no mind to break my teeth on the Duke of Lancaster.'

*

My mother was very soon wearied of life at court.

'All the men talk about is this peace with France,' she complained, 'and how difficult it will be to negotiate it. I really don't see the difficulty. Make peace, end it, say there will be no more fighting by land or sea. But no, that is too simple for them. They draw out ancient chronicles and take words from them and say: "We once had that. We cannot yield on that. We must keep the lilies in the King's arms." All shadow, no substance. It's not just the men, either. Your aunt of Gloucester is just as bad; though I doubt she does more than repeat what your uncle says, like a trained starling.'

It was unusual for the Duchess to say so much at once, and of late it had become even more unusual. She sighed far more often than she spoke.

'I am for Fotheringhay,' she went on. 'You, my dear, are going with me. I have need of you. As for the other matter, your lord father and I have given it a great deal of consideration. Thomas is to go to Tewkesbury for a little time, to complete his arrangements for Prussia and array his men — he will take fifty or sixty with him in all, including clerks and priests and such like, so that will occupy him for a time. After that, though, it shall be as you wish. You shall have at least a couple of weeks with him before he goes, perhaps three, and he may share your bed.'

I struggled to find the words to thank her; they all seemed insufficient. Indeed, I yearned to hug her, but that would have been unsuitable, with her women and various other inferior persons watching us. It was difficult enough to keep my feet still, to refrain from dancing for joy at having carried my point.

She held up her hand. 'Do not give me too much gratitude, Constance. When you find yourself in childbed, you may yet wish that you were with the nuns at Delapré. I will pray that all goes well with you.'

So I was parted from Thomas again, but this time with hope in my heart. There was still much to be done in preparation, of course, and only a very limited time in which to do it. When I was not busy with my own needle I was fussed over by the Duchess's tailors, or choosing jewels and peltry. If I was not doing either I was discussing with my mother who should be bidden to the feast and what viands should be served to the guests.

We decided it should not be so great a celebration. It was not a wedding — you cannot repeat the sacrament of marriage, and Thomas and I had been formally married for years — simply a confirmation of what had long been in place. That the occasion should be marked was proper, but there was no need to have half of England there. However, keeping numbers to a minimum also had its problems, because such winnowing can give great offence. My lord father and Elisabeth Despenser had to be consulted, of course, and both of them added people to the list that I should have preferred elsewhere. Still, at last it was done, and messengers sent off in all directions to summon our guests.

We had scarcely sent the last of them on his way when we had an unexpected visitor. My cousin, Harry of Bolingbroke, Earl of Derby and various other titles that he claimed for himself. He sent his herald ahead of him to announce his coming — although he was making no great journey from his house near Peterborough, scarcely an hour's ride, or perhaps two if you were going slowly and praying at every church on the way.

He arrived only a short time after the herald, bringing with him half a dozen minstrels, who piped and drummed their music into our very courtyard, as if they intended to wake us up. At his side was his wife, Mary, looking thin and grey-faced, and behind them rode a good dozen assorted knights and esquires and a host of lesser men, all in his livery, and a litter bearing Mary's women. It was not so much a visit as an invasion.

Harry himself was dressed in red and white, the King's colours, with a bright red hood, a doublet richly trimmed with ermine and with dagged sleeves so long that they all but touched the floor. I swear there was not a finger that lacked a ring, and when he bowed to my mother — very low — he straightened up with a huge smile on his face. Poor Mary looked like a ghost next to him, although she smiled too, very thinly. Well, she had a husband who only came home to make her pregnant, and then set off on one pointless venture after another, so she had no great cause to be content.

He was in a very fulsome mood. Perhaps because my Uncle Lancaster was no longer suggesting he should be killed, and was instead pouring gold into his purse.

I soon gathered from his talk — for Harry could talk a great deal when he was so inclined, as he was that day — that he was already planning to spend the summer and autumn travelling from one tournament to another, wherever such events might be found. Moreover, he was already toying with the idea of another venture to Prussia. He had greatly enjoyed his time there, it appeared. I cannot say that he boasted, but he let my mother and I know something of the great battles he had fought in and the many hardships he had endured. I dare say there would have been a great deal more detail given if my father or Edward had been at home, but, fortunately for them, they were not.

He had no sooner come home than he had set off on pilgrimage to St John of Bridlington, barely pausing to kiss his wife, even if he bothered to do that. He had only just retraced his steps to Peterborough. He was a strange fellow, to say the least.

We had not invited Harry to our feast, because my mother had thought him still in Prussia, nor yet Mary, because we had imagined her to be in Brecon, or Monmouth, or some such place, occupied with her brood of children. (She already had four sons.) Of course, there was now no choice but to include them, and to my dismay they promised to be there. I had no objection to Mary, she was amiable enough, but I could have lived quite happily without the company of Harry Bolingbroke on such an occasion. Still, there was nothing to be done about it. I was astonished he could spare the time from his programme of jousting and visiting shrines, and wondered whether I was to think myself honoured.

***

Chapter 5

May — June 1391

My lord father came home from court only a few days later, bearing gifts for me that included a fine new saddle. Edward was not in such haste, but he arrived in due course, bringing with him a retinue of young fellows, mostly penniless but for the wages he gave them, but richly dressed in bright liveries. They were respectful enough, but restless and full of energy. They occupied themselves by horse racing in the park, indulging in mock fights and troubling the local women in every village between the castle and Stamford.

As the day approached, the first of our guests began to arrive. The first were the Earl and Countess of Kent —my parents' particular friends — and it was only to be expected that they brought with them Roger Mortimer and Alianore, who were still living in their household.

Alianore confided to me that she was with child again.

'A son, this time, I hope,' she said, very quietly, her hands in the posture of prayer. 'A son; and once he has a brother, I shall be free to do as I please.'

She grinned at me, to remind me of our previous conversation on the subject.

'You do not mean it,' I said.

'Oh, yes I do! What's more, Roger and I are in accord. He will not make any difficulty. I suspect he no more wants to share my bed than I wish to share his.'

'That's one thing,' I said, quite shocked, 'but for any man to agree to be a cuckold, a wittol, let alone a great lord — are you *sure* he is in accord? Besides, you must think of the sin. You will be forever doing penance.'

She laughed. 'Oh, my sweet, I wish you could see your face! Did I ask to marry Roger? Did he ask to marry me? Of course not! Neither of us was given the least choice. Besides, I shall always be discreet. As for adultery and sin, ask your Uncle Lancaster about that! *How* many bastards does he have? And no discretion there — he flaunts them. Half the court lies in a different bed each night, as you well know. We are not all as fortunate as you, to love where the marriage ring binds.'

I sighed. Alianore was no more interested in my advice now than she had been in the past. It was fruitless to argue.

'You must do as you think best,' I said levelly.

She smiled at me. 'We Hollands have always gone our own way in matters of love. I should not be here if my grandfather had not seduced my grandmother when she was twelve years old and already as good as promised to another man. If he had not come back to claim her, years later, from her supposed husband. If he had not taken the whole matter to the Holy Father himself. Do you suppose *anything* I might do in my life will even *touch* the scandal they created between them? Holland born or Holland married, we have a way of choosing our own path, whether it pleases the priests or not.'

I did not answer. The warm breeze of a summer evening was drifting in through the window and bringing the odd fly in with it to enjoy our hospitality. When will Thomas arrive, I thought? I itched to lean out of the window and look for him, ridiculous though it was. He would certainly not be here today, no matter how my belly tweaked at the thought.

'You remember my grandmother, of course?' Alianore asked.

I nodded. Certainly I remembered her. She had only been dead six years. The King's mother, a very great lady, fat and amiable with a huge jar of sugared figs and an ample lap. She always spoke in French, though she was as English as could be. I had sat on that lap when I was young, and later, when I was older, I'd been promoted to sit at her side sometimes, to be petted and fed sweetmeats, pieces of gingerbread, honey cakes and the like. She had been kind to all children, and very generous.

'God knows how many ells of cloth it took to make her a gown at the end,' Alianore chuckled, 'but once she was young, like we are now, and men worshipped her, wrote her poems, swore they would kill themselves if she didn't at least smile at them. They all wanted her in their bed, even the King's father. (Though of course *he* got her in the end, even if he did have to wait for my grandfather to die.) When we are grandmothers, you and I shall perhaps be so fat we can barely move, and have to sit in our rooms all day long, just like she did. At least she had her memories of being loved, and so will I. I certainly want to remember something better than March mauling me, farting and belching wine in my face.'

*

Thomas arrived at last, bringing most of his following with him — the remainder being pledged to meet him at Lynn at the end of June, ready to take ship. I saw little enough of him, though, for my mother kept me busy. For one thing, we had a good dozen noble ladies to keep entertained, some of whom, like Elisabeth Despenser and my aunt of Lancaster, were not easy to amuse, and seemed to think that I needed to sit down with them and listen to long litanies of advice, much of which, I am ashamed to admit, I completely ignored. My head nodded up and down in seeming agreement and submission, but my ears were closed.

My Uncle Lancaster, of course, did not appear, he being too

much occupied with weighty matters to pay any attention to me. His son, my cousin Harry, on the other hand was very much present and anxious to tell everyone — not least Thomas — about the fascinating towns and castles of Prussia, and the names and natures of all the principal men who ruled that benighted wilderness. When that paled he spoke of the enemies Thomas might encounter, and what cruel and uncivilised beasts they were — quite unlike Harry, of course, that peerless knight who had never performed an evil deed. I swear that he sickened me to the point where — God forgive me! — I prayed that he would break his neck in his next joust. (Had I been able to foresee the future, I would have wished him a good deal worse; as it was this evil thought gave me something to confess to my father's chaplain on the evening before our ceremony.)

By this time the castle was so crowded that our every room was now packed with folk after the fashion of herring in a barrel, and that many were spending their nights in pavilions erected in the Lesser Park. I kept reminding myself that my mother and I had intended only a small gathering, but it had somehow grown, to the point where my father was now musing on whether he should have more lodgings built. (It was only a dream. He lacked the money to make such an improvement; even the work to expand our chapel had stalled, the scaffolding standing around it as a mute comment on ambition outstretching income.)

It was as well, perhaps, that the King and Queen had not been able to join us, or Thomas and I might have had to be accommodated in one of the tents. However, Richard and Anne sent us kind letters, wishing us well, to say nothing of a very generous purse of gold. That these things were brought to us by Sir John Golafre and his wife was perhaps a little less pleasing, but then again Philippa Fitzwalter was Thomas's cousin, so I suppose she had some right to be there. You could even say the same about Lord and Lady Berkeley, two of the guests added to appease Elisabeth Despenser, but her other nominees, the Earl and Countess of Warwick, who arrived on the very eve of the feast, were about as welcome as Beelzebub as far as I was concerned. Still, there was no choice but to be gracious and pretend otherwise.

I barely slept that night, but it seemed that no sooner were my eyes closed than a great company of ladies, headed by my mother and my Aunt Lancaster, arrived to hale me out of bed. There were so many in the room there was scarcely space to breathe, and the noise of their chatter, their advice, their congratulations, their good wishes, all but deafened me. I cannot recall who said what, or who dressed me, because I was scarcely given a moment to think.

My mother had decided that I should wear my hair loose, which seemed very odd to me, and made me feel nervous about appearing in public, as though I was to be half naked. It was the tradition for brides, she said, and that, in effect, was what I was. (Though of course I had been married for almost all my life and so was not really a bride in the true sense.) On my head I wore, not the chaplet of flowers such as cotters and the like have on these occasions, but a borrowed circlet with silver gilt flowers and leaves. I recognised it as something Alianore had worn at her wedding to March, though I believe it truly belonged to her mother, Lady Kent.

As for my clothes, they were quite new, the kirtle crimson samite, the side-less surcote cream velvet with ermine trimming. This set off a debate among the women crowding the room as to whether these colours suited me. There were those, Elisabeth Despenser among them, who thought a pale blue, or a shade of green might have been better. I did not care a damn for their talk. Like Harry Bolingbroke, I was wearing something that brought King Richard's colours to mind, the difference being that I was sincere in my allegiance, whereas he was as false as Judas, but doing his best to pretend otherwise.

I met Thomas in our chapel, which was so overcrowded that there was scarcely space left to pass through. His uncle, the Bishop of Norwich, in the full splendour of his pontificals, demanded to know of us whether we objected to the promises we had made while below the proper age for marriage. We both confirmed our consent, staring at each other as we did so, fighting hard to restrain the laughter that inexplicably rose in our throats. Then we prostrated ourselves before the altar as the assembled clergy censed and aspersed us. The Bishop spoke some words of blessing, we knelt together to receive the sacred Host, and that was all the ceremony we received.

From the chapel we went straight to the Great Hall for the feast. Thomas and I sat at the centre of the dais, sharing a mess, his task being to serve me, picking out the choicest morsels from the various dishes. Though, in truth, I ate very little. In part it was because I was too excited, too overwhelmed by the occasion, but I also knew that these proceedings would last all day, and that if I did not eat and drink with care I should end up gorged with food and befuddled by wine, and spend the night voiding the contents of my stomach down the shaft of the garderobe. I was still young, but I was not quite a fool.

My father's musicians played all through the meal and after it, with scarcely a break to rest. I wondered at their stamina, although of course, with this being a special occasion they would be rewarded far beyond their usual wages. Bolingbroke's fellows reinforced their numbers, and there were a few random minstrels brought along in various retinues, so their gallery was crowded and the music loud enough to soar above all the various conversations that were in progress.

Later, of course, we had other entertainments. A troupe of tumblers had arrived from somewhere, quite uninvited, as though they scented free food and a distribution of largesse. Our own minstrels descended to the body of the hall, and sang quite beautifully of love to great applause and much throwing of coins. Then there was dancing.

My mother had warned me of the usual traditions on such occasions. (I think there are many traditions better buried and forgotten, but I knew there was no point in my disputing the matter with her.) I must dance with anyone who asked, whether I cared to do or not. I should not be surprised if they kissed me; it was part of the custom. Even if they proceeded to other liberties I ought not to make too much of a fuss about it, as it was all part of the sport of the day. A degree of licence was permitted, and no cause should be given for quarrels. She would, she promised, keep a careful eye on me and be sure to intervene if anyone went too far.

So I found myself dancing with Harry Bolingbroke, though I must admit he danced well, and treated me with perfect courtesy, just as he might have done at court, so I could find nothing to complain about, which was annoying. You could not fault his manners any more than you could his steps. In truth, like his sister, Beth, he was a more accomplished dancer in those days than I shall ever be. I dare say he could have earned the occasional sixpence by giving lessons had he been so inclined.

Next was Edmund Mortimer, who said nothing to me, nothing at all, but just stared at me with his relentless eyes, like a puppy in hope of petting. It was only when the dance ended that he spoke, forcing the words.

'I love you,' he said, struggling to form the words, 'and I always shall. To the death.'

I was irritated by his folly, however flattered.

'Edmund,' I answered, 'you have ever been my friend, and I love you as a brother, but I am not for you. I never was. You know it well enough.' I lightened my tone, trying to make him laugh as he had often made me laugh when we were children together. 'Besides, you need an heiress, not a set of fine quarterings on a lozenge and nothing else. You should seek one out.'

'If the world was different — ' he began.

'If I had wings, I should not need a horse. If I were Queen of Spain, I should be living in Burgos. Do not waste time with "ifs". Find your heiress.'

He kissed me, lingered over it just a little longer than was proper, and was gone. I did not see him again for hours.

Before I could give another thought to Edmund, John Holland seized me. His grip was near strong enough to break my wrist, and I could no more have wriggled free of it than flown up into the rafters.

My turn now,' he said boldly, imposing a kiss on me, forcing his tongue into my mouth.

'Delicious,' he pronounced, escaping before I could bite it off. 'Shall we dance?'

So we did, as the music rose again. 'A fine present for young Despenser to unwrap,' he said, as we drew close. He lifted an indolent hand, toyed with my hair. 'I envy him the task. Though if he proves an inadequate tutor, you may always apply to me for additional lessons.'

'You are insulting, sir!' I snapped.

He grinned. 'On the contrary, I am offering you a compliment. I'm very particular about those I admit to my bed. It's not an invitation I give to every woman I meet, not even the highborn. Besides, we should not quarrel, my lady. Do we not both love and serve my brother, the King?'

'I find it hard to credit that you *are* his brother.'

The dance parted us for a moment. Near to us, Harry Bolingbroke was in conversation with Warwick.

'Of course I support the peace,' I heard him say, 'the King wishes it, and so does my father. Why should I disagree?'

'The terms — ' Warwick began, but the rest was lost to me as John Holland took my hand again and the dance led us away from them.

'I am not a changeling, lady, whatever else I may be. Of course, the King and I are but half-brothers. They say I take after my father, rather than my lady mother. So perhaps that explains the difference. I shall still live and die with him. That, and give him counsel not to be so soft.'

'You dare to say the King is *soft*?'

'Do you deny it, with so many of his enemies still above ground?' He sniffed expressively. 'Softness is not a trait I admire. It is particularly unsuitable when training a spirited young filly.'

He laughed, so loudly that people stared at us, and gave me a sharp slap on the behind. I let out a gasp at the shock of it, and was sorely tempted to give him the good kick which was the least he deserved. However, I decided not to be provoked — it would only add to his mockery. So I set my lips and said nothing. It only served to make him laugh the more.

Later, when I told my cousin, Beth, about her husband's treatment of me she laughed as well.

'John is just an overgrown boy playing the man,' she said, shaking her head. 'He means no harm, it's but teasing and talk. In truth, they are most of them but overgrown boys. Look at my brother, Harry. My father has given him *thousands* of pounds. What does he mean to do with that money? He will spend the summer riding from tournament to tournament, showing off, throwing coins to the crowds to make himself popular. What folly!'

The day passed swiftly, because I was scarcely allowed a moment to myself. When I was not dancing or eating there was someone with me, wishing me well, giving me advice, telling me some anecdote or reminding me of something ridiculous or embarrassing I did or said when I was but a child.

At last, with the light beginning to fade, someone decided it was time for Thomas and me to be bedded. I was carried off by a whole pack of women, most of them half-drunk, nearly all of them full of bawdy remarks and suggestions. That they meant well I do not doubt. Perhaps they imagined I was nervous and in need of cheering. In truth, I was not nervous at all. A little light-headed, perhaps, because despite my moderation I had taken on a fair quality of wine.

They all but carried me to my bedchamber, and had me stripped to my shift and slid between the sheets almost before I knew what was happening. Then the men arrived, in another noisy crowd, and almost as bawdy in their talk, John Holland and Edward taking the leading part, Thomas between them, held like a prisoner ready for the rope, left with nothing to cover him but his shirt.

Thomas's uncle appeared from somewhere, dressed now in his ordinary clothes and looking more like a nobleman than the bishop he was. For a few moments there was silence as he solemnly aspersed the bed and blessed us, but then the clamour rose louder than ever as the company treated us to all the usual jests and coarse suggestions. I wanted to curse them, to order them to the devil, but of course it was not for me to do that. I had Thomas to do it for me, and at last, when they grew weary of the sport, they heeded his words.

It was not yet full dark, so we had a good view of one another. Neither of us spoke. We kissed for a little time, and then it seemed quite reasonable that we should remove our remaining garments and lie naked in each other's arms. It was strange, but I did not feel in the least awkward or uncomfortable. It was as if I had been sharing my bed with Thomas all my life, as if it was the most natural place for me to be.

My new life had begun, and it was far better than I had envisaged.

***

Chapter 6

June 1391-January 1393

We had two weeks together before Thomas had to leave for his campaign in Prussia. I urged him to delay for at least a day or two; he granted me one, saying he would make up time on the road. I was up at first light to watch him ride away, clung to him for as long as I dared. Then he was gone, and I ached for his loss. I knew now why minstrels sang of love, why almost every poem had it as its theme.

When the dark of the moon came at the end of the month my blood came with it, and I knew I was not with child. I was bitterly disappointed, for I had wanted Thomas to come home to find me staggering around, big-bellied and ready to give him his son. It was not God's will, and I had to accept it. My mother was first to tell me that I must do so. All is in God's hands, she said. We may pray, we may weep, but we must not complain.

What was I to do? Again, my mother answered. I must do as I thought fit. She and my father would always offer their advice, if asked, but I was now answerable only to my husband, not to any other.

I decided to go to Tewkesbury, and to begin my work making Hanley Castle fit to be lived in.

Elisabeth welcomed me kindly enough, and when I explained my purpose she said she would help me all she could. In particular, she would assist and advise me on the hiring of servants. Thomas had set a certain amount of money aside, and I could draw from that as I pleased. If it was not enough, she would lend me more, within reason. My father had granted me the eighty marks a year he had from the King for my maintenance, and said that it would now be mine until Thomas reached his majority, so I also had some money of my own. In addition, I should have the rents of the manor itself, as they came in.

So the work began. I hired labourers to scrub out the little castle from cellars to attics, banishing spiders and their webs, clearing away layers of dirt and grime. I had broken windows replaced and fitted with new glass, bringing skilled craftsmen in from Gloucester to insert our quarterings and cognizances, until you could scarcely find a room without a Despenser griffin and a York falcon-and-fetterlock. I had broken and missing tiles replaced on our roofs, and down spouts and gutters unblocked. I had the exterior walls improved with new rendering to replace that which had cracked or fallen off, and had the whole brightened with fresh whitewash.

The gardens were a wilderness of neglected chaos. I had them dug over, and new paths laid. I saw to it there were arbours fashioned by carpenters from the local oaks, and roses planted, as well as all the useful herbs every household needs. Some of these last I established in the ground with my own hands. You would have laughed to see me kneeling there, in an ancient gown and a straw hat, looking like a cottager and scandalising my damsels, but I was content.

I had some furnishings from Elisabeth, including a number of threadbare hangings that were barely fit for a steward's room, but which had to serve for the time being. There were even a few items from Fotheringhay, brought out from the depths of my mother's store rooms, but most of it had to be bought new from the craftsmen of Worcester and Gloucester.

This depleted my store of money severely, and eventually I had to take up the option of borrowing from Elisabeth. It was irritating that she asked for an explanation of almost every shilling spent, but I had little choice. You cannot manage even a small household on pennies, least of all when you are establishing it from nothing.

At last the day came when I no longer had to go back to Tewkesbury to sleep each evening, but could stay at Hanley, attended entirely by our own people, fed from our own kitchens. It was a small household, such as a minor knight's widow might have — I doubt whether there were thirty of us all told, including my women — but it functioned.

One of my better recruits was a cook by the name of Hugh Bygge. (He was a tiny man who barely came up to my shoulder.) He had been dismissed by the Earl of Warwick for stealing, and since cooks have all manner of natural perquisites I think his dishonesty must have been exceptional. He promised me he would not steal from me, and I assured him he would not steal from me twice. It was a gamble, but one that paid off, for Hugh was to stand by me through triumph and downfall. He also proved to be an excellent cook who knew well how to manage a kitchen, and I soon had as fine a table as could be found in three counties. (I often had to go out and take game with hawks and hounds to provide adequately for it, but that gave me sport and kept me from idleness. It is better for the soul to be up early and go hunting than to lie in bed until dinner.)

Our fish ponds proved to be well-stocked, better than I had hoped, especially with carp. From time to time I paid local men sixpence or eight pence a day to fish the ponds for me, and it was a rare occasion that I did not make a handsome profit on the transaction.

At the end of September I had a letter from Alianore, asking me to come to her at Brockenhurst if I could, for she hoped to see me at her lying-in and asked me to be godmother to her child, principal godmother if it proved to be a girl. This was an honour, quite apart from the claims of friendship, so I made the long journey, even if I had to borrow three or four of Elisabeth's fellows so that I could have a fitting escort without leaving my castle entirely deserted.

The child, when it came, proved to be a son, Alianore's first, whom she named Edmund after his late grandfather. She was quite delighted.

'I am half way to my freedom now,' she said.

Lord and Lady Kent (for it was their household) gave a feast as splendid as any you might have seen at the court itself. March was a generous fellow – he gave all the ladies in attendance gifts, including a ruby clasp for me, and celebrated the birth of his heir by getting gloriously drunk with his cronies.

It was a pleasant enough gathering, for Brockenhurst is a fair manor, set in the New Forest and the weather was kind to us, making our ventures out of doors very agreeable. The only real inconvenience was that March's sister, Philippa, Lady Arundel as she now called herself, was one of the company. You might have thought her the Queen from the way she bore herself, with a different fine gown every day, the plague of jewelled rings she wore on her fingers, and the sparkling coronet she insisted on wearing at all times – she claimed it was only her second-best, that she had a superior one under repair at the goldsmith's. How she enjoyed looking down her nose at me, brushing her sleeves to emphasise their newness, gesturing with her hands to show off the glory of her rings, smiling at me as she capped my remarks.

Still, it was I that carried the child to the font and made the responses on his behalf. A few weeks later, it was I who made the godmother's offering at Alianore's churching and sat next to her at the feast that followed. What was more, it was I who had the young husband, high in the King's favour and likely to advance. That was all the compensation I required for any victory over me she imagined she had.

That Christmas, I was able to offer a modest feast of my own at Hanley Castle. Elisabeth was my guest and I took great care to ensure she was offered the finest food and wine in great quantity, and to house her in the best of the guest chambers with a roaring fire to keep her warm and thick rugs to keep her feet from the cold touch of the floor tiles. She seemed pleased by my hospitality, and as we both longed for Thomas to come home and talked of little else, we made good cheer together and had not a single cross word.

Then, as the leaves began to sprout on the trees and the days grow longer, Thomas returned to me.

I ran down the castle steps to greet him, quite forgetting my dignity.

'Careful!' he cried. 'I've cut my hair short and washed it a dozen times this week, but I'm not sure I'm clean of my cattle yet. I'd better have a bath.'

I hugged him anyway. Be damned to the lice, I thought.

Poor Thomas had faced storms at sea on his return voyage, and some of his baggage had been lost. Some of his clothes were fit only to be burnt, and his men and their horses all looked as if they could do with a mountain of food and drink followed by a long sleep, so I arranged for these things in short order.

(Despite his troubles, he had done much better than my Uncle Gloucester, who had set out later in the year than was wise. No doubt he had thought he could command the waves and the winds. He was blown back to Scotland, and many of his men were drowned. Had it not been for the truce those that survived would have been taken prisoner by the Scots.)

Soon, after Thomas's bath, I found myself sitting on the window-seat in our solar, running a fine-tooth comb through what was left of his hair (which looked as if it had been cropped with sheep-shears) trying to catch what were left of his 'cattle', crushing the few creatures I found with my fingernails until I was quite sure all were gone. Then I washed his hair with rosewater just to be certain.

Meanwhile, he told me of his adventures, reaching out from time to time to the food and drink I had had placed within his reach. It was simple fare, manchet bread and sliced beef, with a cup of our finest Rhenish, but I knew it would serve for his present need.

'We were about as welcome as the pestilence,' he said. 'The Teutonic Knights seem to think us as much a burden as an ally, and they weren't slow to let us know. Mind you, it's hard to blame them. The English and Germans among us spent as much time fighting the Scots and French knights as we did the Lithuanians. I don't mean knightly sports, Constance. There were no jousts or tournaments. It was more in the way of brawling and rioting, with no one with the authority to keep order. Harry Bolingbroke's tales made me imagine there might be glory to be won. Yet I think I might have been better to stay at home.'

I restrained myself from saying that I could have told him so. Sometimes it is wise not to say too much.

Thomas got me with child almost at once, which added to my complacency. Even Elisabeth was pleased with me, although her way of showing it was to draw me aside and give me a great deal of quiet advice. I should not lie with Thomas, she said, it was sinful. I should not ride, either, and I was best staying indoors. If I had to travel, it had better be by litter. She advised me not to take baths, not to dance, not to do much of anything except pray or sew. As for the lying-in, she would make all necessary arrangements. She would secure the best midwife in this county or the next, and arrange, when it was the proper time, for a suitably virtuous woman to act as wet-nurse. In the interim, she would tell her beads for my welfare every single day.

I ignored her advice, naturally.

When I look back — and it is like looking through a glass that has been scorched with smoke and flame — I realise that I have rarely been as happy, and certainly I have never been happier — than I was during that time at Hanley Castle. I had a husband I loved dearly, a child on the way and a castle over which I was undisputed mistress, set in as fine a piece of country as you will find in all England. What young woman of noble blood could possibly desire more? I could chatter and dance and sing with my damsels, for they were a lively and merry crew and good company. I could ride out on my fine jennet, with my lord beside me, and enjoy the park, or ride further into Malvern Chase. We hawked together in season, and coursed our greyhounds, and loosed arrows at our deer.

The summer was fading when a letter reached us from my mother, carried by a messenger in York livery who by the look of him had come with much haste and little rest. Unusually, it was addressed to Thomas rather than to me, and he opened it at once, read it briefly and handed it across.

The Duchess had written in her own hand, which was perhaps why the letter was so brief. She asked Thomas if he would give me leave to visit her. She had need of me, and hoped I might be allowed to stay at Fotheringhay with her for some weeks.

'May I go?' I asked.

'Of course you may,' he said, as if it was a foolish question. 'What's more, I intend to ride with you. That is a strange letter. Something is wrong. I can tell from what your lady mother does *not* say. We set off tomorrow. Have your baggage packed.'

It took us the best part of a week to reach Fotheringhay. Thomas insisted on a slow pace, for my sake, and I rode pillion behind him for most of the way, on the oldest, gentlest palfrey our stables could supply. (We could in any event make no greater speed than that made by the litters bearing my women and the sumpter carts carrying our goods, but it was frustrating to make so long a journey at no speed greater than a walk.)

We found the Duchess ill in bed, and, although she sought to hide it, in great pain. Her women had been dosing her with poppy juice for weeks, but the household physician could do no more than wring his hands and whine about the impossibility of bringing her humours into the proper balance. The aspects of the planets were entirely adverse, he explained, babbling something about Venus being in Capricorn, or some such gibberish, I know not what.

My mother stared at me with what seemed to be huge eyes, and took a tight hold of my hand. There was no flesh left on her, and her skin had a sickly, yellow tinge. She spoke, but I could scarcely make sense of her words, except that she was glad to see us.

My father and Edward were with the King. I wrote to them as soon as my mother slept again, urging them home. If my letter to the Duke was suitably respectful, I wrote plain words to my brother: 'Get you here as swift as a horse will carry you if you would see your mother alive.' It was already growing dark when the messenger set off, but I gave him gold and told him to make as many miles as he could before night, and be away next morning as soon as there was light enough to mark the road.

I then returned to my mother, to see that she was as comfortable as was possible, but found her already asleep. Her women had done well by her, and that was good, for the rest of the household had descended into chaos. It was late before Thomas and I were able to eat supper, for no fool had thought to take order for our needs or those of our people.

Although I was exhausted from the journey, I had but a fitful night of sleep before beginning again. As soon as I had broken my fast, I wrote a letter to my Aunt Lancaster (whom I believed to be at Hertford) as she was entitled to know that her sister was so ill. I wrote another to Lady Kent, who was at Maxey, and in plain terms asked her for help. If she could not come to Fotheringhay herself, could she please send Alianore?

Thomas and I then began to set the household to rights, with many harsh words and rebukes. I must admit that Thomas did most of this work, not least because he kept insisting that I rest, saying that I looked tired and unwell. In truth, it took little effort to weary me, and I was reluctant to stray too far from the Duchess's bedchamber. She was, I thought, a little brighter, and she talked for a while, but as we kept dosing her with wine and poppy juice against the pain it was no great wonder that she was asleep for much of the time.

How my Aunt Lancaster arrived as quickly as she did I do not know – it seemed a miracle to me. If my messenger managed fifty miles in a day, she cannot have ridden much more slowly. She embraced me, asked a few breathless questions and took charge at once. I had never been so glad to yield up responsibility to an elder as I was at that hour.

I remember little detail of the days that followed, except that on at least one occasion Thomas carried me to bed, literally carried me, because through lack of sleep and worry about my mother I was left too weak to stand on my feet. Lady Kent and Alianore arrived the day after my aunt, having made a more leisurely journey than she, and between us we maintained a constant vigil over my mother, at least one of us being with her for every hour of the day and night. I admit that I did less of this than was my fair share, but then again, there was little to do but weep and pray and seek to comfort one another. I think my aunt barely slept at all.

My father and Edward arrived at last. Edmund Mortimer came with them, in attendance on the Duke. The court had been at Langley, Edward told me, and they had ridden hard all the way, or as fast as my father could bear, for his joints ached and gave him much pain if he was too long on a horse.

'Is it really so bad?' he asked.

'As bad as can be,' I told him, leaning on Thomas, for my legs felt like they were made of lead, as did my belly. I did not so much walk as waddle like a duck. Strictly, according to etiquette, I should have retired to my chamber by this time, surrounded by fussing women, not showing myself before the men of the household. The circumstances, of course were extreme.

Edward turned pale as milk when he set eyes on the Duchess, and for once in his life could not find words for the occasion. He merely stood there, head bowed, mouthing silent prayers as he tugged at his beard. Nor did he mock when Edmund Mortimer wept openly, like a little child. Edmund had barely known his own mother, who had died when he was no more than five years old, and mine had fostered him. I had not realised how much he loved her, until then.

At first my lord father could not bring himself to believe that my mother was in an evil case. He tried to persuade her to get out of her bed and dress, saying that it was but a fortnight to Christmas, and she must take her proper place for the festivities. Then reality seemed to dawn on him. There would be no Christmas celebration for us, not this year. My mother would not see it.

She passed from us two days before Christmas, and the only consolation was that we were all gathered around her at the end, which came in the middle of the night, candles lighting her as we stood around, half-undressed. Even my little brother Dickon was present, though at his age it might have been kinder to spare him. My father and my aunt were holding her hands as she left us, the rest of us kneeling in prayer while one of the chaplains intoned *De Profundis*.

*

The plain truth was that I could not attend my mother's funeral. The King, no doubt intending to honour her, had ordered that she should lie in the church of the Order of Friar Preachers at Langley. (At that time it was his intention to be buried there himself, although, as you will learn, he was later to change his mind.) It was quite impossible for me to make such a journey, even by riding in the Duchess's carriage, for my time was too close. So I had to be content to stand on the castle steps and watch as the great procession set off on its long, slow journey, all clad in black, the wind howling from the east and bringing a few flakes of snow with it. I swear I was frozen to the marrow, but I stayed where I was until the last of the riders vanished beneath the gatehouse, weeping because I could not be with them to play my proper part.

Then I could only do what I ought rightly to have done weeks earlier; to retire to my chamber to await the birth, and after confessing to the one chaplain left with us, saying farewell to the company of men until the deed was done. Lady Kent stayed with me out of duty (my aunt and Alianore were gone to Langley with the rest). Although she fussed and clucked over me like an old hen I was more than grateful to have her.

When the child came — and Lady Kent told me that I suffered less than was usual for a first babe, though I thought the pain adequate and prolonged enough — it was a son, but so weak that the midwife (one of our people from the village) insisted on baptising him at once. When I protested that it would not take more than minutes to fetch the chaplain and take the child to the chapel, she cried that she dared not answer for such a delay. So baptised he was, there and then, Edward, after my lord's father, my own brother, or St Edward of Caernarfon, as best pleases you. He lived long enough to suckle the wet-nurse's milk, but only to cast it up again. Then he died, and all my work and effort was in vain.

At least he could be buried in the church, not forlorn in unconsecrated ground, and for that I had to thank the wise midwife and the grace of God. It was the only consolation that remained to me. I blamed myself for his death. If I had remained at Hanley Castle. If I had done this thing, or not done that. It was fruitless, of course, to repine in this way. Lady Kent told me it was God's will, and that I had to submit to it. Thomas, when he returned from my mother's funeral to find me desolated, said much the same, although more kindly. The child should have a little tomb, he promised, and Masses said over him. An innocent child would not linger in Purgatory very long. Besides, there would be others. Not to replace him, but to compensate for the loss. All that mattered was that I was safe. So he said.

***

Chapter 7

February — September 1393

I was churched as soon as I could be, but saw little cause for the usual feasting and celebration, so there was little ceremony about it, though of course I made the proper offerings, and there was a small gathering with a few guests, notably the Countess of Kent and her elder daughters, Alianore and Joanne. Next morning, Thomas and I went home to Hanley Castle.

There we resumed our easy way of living, and slowly the pain began to ease. After a while there were days when I no longer thought of either my mother or the lost child. We kept an open door for guests, and soon had a fair portion of the gentry of the three counties of Gloucestershire, Worcestershire and Warwickshire paying court to us, particularly the younger and less established elements. Indeed, it *was* a court of sorts, a small one, where I was queen. As the King had ordered me, I did all that I could to encourage the cult of King Edward among them. Sometimes Thomas and I led pilgrimages to Gloucester, which, if it served no other purpose, was an agreeable journey which helped us know these people better.

Sir John Russell was one of our more frequent visitors. He had in his time been one of Warwick's retainers, but when he had taken the King's livery Warwick had promptly dismissed him from his service and begun to persecute him by setting his lackeys to harass him in one way or another. The worst of these lackeys was Nicholas Lilling, a knight to his shame, who among other matters caused Russell's bailiff in Pershore to be murdered by his hirelings, or so Russell told us.

Thomas had given Sir John a collar of our livery, the Griffin, and appointed him to his council, but until now we had lacked the power to defend him properly from the depredations of Warwick's minions, who were determined to make his life difficult. However,

Warwick himself had now gone on pilgrimage to the Holy Land, and that gave us an opportunity. Thomas and I said a word here and a word there, our letters travelling even to the King, and Russell took a petition to Parliament. It did not solve his problems at once, but his enemies drew back and became more cautious.

Sir John was useful to us, and we to him. By Thomas's patronage, he had found a place as one of the King's household knights, and had pleased Richard so much he was soon made Master of Horse as well. So we had a friend close to the King, which cannot but be profitable. He was as much with us as he was at home in Strensham. He exercised with Thomas and the gentlemen of the household in the small tilt yard we had devised, and proved himself a right worthy man with the lance. Not only did he know horses, but he bought and sold them, and we used him as our agent in these matters, if not to our great profit then certainly to our convenience.

I found that some of the local people, the women in particular, were apt to come to the castle to ask my advice, to seek my assistance, or even to arbitrate their small disputes. They came with hesitation and reluctance at first, very humbly, but then with greater confidence when they found I was willing to give them my time. It was very odd — I felt it even then — that these women, who were often old enough to be my mother, or even my grandmother, and who had far more experience of the world than I, should petition me rather as I myself would petition the King. Yet I tried to do my best by them, to listen carefully and make such suggestions as I could. Sometimes they needed but a kind word. Sometimes they needed my intervention with whomever was at the root of their problem — perhaps the parish priest or the manor bailiff, perhaps a brother or a husband. Occasionally they just needed a coin or two to feed a child — or bury one in a seemly fashion. I was their lady and, although barely a woman myself, they trusted me. I discovered — by indirect means — that they were rather proud of me. To have the King's cousin in their castle, and to be able to talk to her — however ignorant she was of their lives — was something they boasted about to other wives when they attended the local markets. I was unsure whether to be amused, humbled or pleased.

I saw nothing at all of Alianore, Lady March, but letters arrived from her quite frequently. She was often at Usk, or Ludlow, or one of her lord's other castles, not so far away that a messenger could not travel between us with ease. The impression I had from her writing was that she was more at ease, if not quite contented. She was expecting another child, and kept me aware of its progress. In the week before Ascension tide I had a letter from her that was full of joy and triumph. On St. George's Day she had borne another son.

'I am free at last,' she wrote, and I was glad for her, and wrote back at once to tell her so.

I should have been wise if I had been content to ask for nothing better than this life. If I had stayed at Hanley with Thomas, and watched our cattle grow, if we had lived like a simple esquire and his wife, attending the quarter-sessions, perhaps bringing a child into the world every two years, enjoying the company of our friends and the simple pleasures of our estate. Looking back, it would have been as near to heaven as we are allowed in the sinful world. But that is to speak with the infallible benefit of hindsight.

You cannot keep a gyrfalcon in a tiny cage, where it may not spread its wings, let alone fly, and expect it to be happy. Perhaps it will tolerate such treatment for a while. Fed, and petted, it may not complain too much. But sooner or later, you must take it out into the open air, and allow it to soar as high as it pleases. Only then will it know contentment.

I wanted advancement for Thomas — and thus for myself. I wanted to dance at court, and sit with my cousin the King, perhaps reading to him from one of his jewelled books, perhaps riding at his side, stirrup to stirrup, in the hunt, perhaps listening to him talk of his plans for England and offering my own humble suggestions. I wanted news of the world that was not a month old. I wanted power.

Ah, I hear you say, so it was you, Constance, who brought the disaster about. Your folly, your foolish ambition, your influence over your lord. But no, Thomas's ambition was every bit as great as my own. Perhaps greater. When all was said and done, *I* had nothing to prove. I was the daughter of York, granddaughter of two kings, cousin to a third. *His* great-grandfather, Hugh Despenser the Younger, had been hanged from a gallows fifty feet high and the family had been disgraced and stripped of all its wealth.

It was true that his father and his great-uncle had repaired much of the damage. The Despensers had served my grandfather the third King Edward well, and were rich again, although they had never recovered all the estates, and still less the portable property that had been lost. Edward Despenser had been honoured as one of the greatest knights of his day, one of the most revered of those in my grandfather's circle, which is to say a great deal. Yet still a little of the stigma lingered. There were in those days still men alive who had seen Hugh Despenser hanged, and even more who remembered when the family was eclipsed and of no account. On top of that, you must remember that during my lord's long minority, his mother may have managed his estates well — I do not grudge her that, because she did, however harshly — but almost all the family's influence was lost. Lord Berkeley was the great man in Gloucestershire, the Earl of Warwick in Worcestershire, and they commanded everything. Our influence was scarcely greater than if Thomas had indeed been a squire of low degree. In effect, it did not exist.

We used to talk about it in bed, when we had nothing better to do.

'One day,' said Thomas, 'I shall be a greater lord than Berkeley, greater even than Warwick, and they shall both sue to me for favours. Only then will I be worthy to be your husband.'

I thought this merely flattery, but when I laughed he grew quite angry.

'I shall have back every acre my family had taken from it by injustice. You know my great-grandfather never had an honest trial, that his only fault was he was too loyal to the second King Edward.'

I was more than fond of Thomas, and ever-ready to stretch a truth in his favour, but even I knew it was not so simple. I knew his family history as well as my own. Had I not been taught it as part of my training in life? His great-grandfather had been *hated*. Indeed, he had ruled the second Edward so completely that he had been known as 'the King's husband'. You could dress that as you liked, but you would struggle to make an innocent lamb of such a man.

As for winning back all the lands he had held, young, naïve and ambitious though I was, I knew it to be quite impossible. For one thing, some of those lands had been stolen in the first place. For another, many were now held by the likes of my Uncle Lancaster and the Earl of March. Such eagles as these would never disgorge their prey. Certainly not when they and their forebears had been digesting it for half a century and more.

'To gain such power,' I said, 'you will have to return to court. What is more, you will have to devote yourself to the King's service and secure his particular favour. If it is what you want, you know that I will be at your side, and do all that I can to aid you. The King and Queen have always been good to me, and I have some influence. It will not be enough though, unless you climb very high; and since there is no war, nor like to be, you cannot serve as your father did. You will have to help the King overthrow his enemies here in England, help make him as supreme and absolute in power as a king should be, so that he in his turn may reward you.'

I am not quite sure, even now, whether I intended to encourage or dissuade him; certainly I wanted him to understand the enormity of the task he was setting himself. For a time, he was very quiet. I wondered whether he had gone to sleep.

'Fine figures we should cut at court,' he said at last, 'with our empty purses. Beggars at the feast. I will not have you shamed before the other ladies; you must have the finest — clothes, jewels and horses. Nor will I appear there looking like some petty knight from the depths of Wales. I must have my own adornments, and new armour for the jousts in which I shall carry your favour — if you deign to grant it. We must be very splendid, *treschere*, and taken together it will cost a great deal of money. I shall speak to my lady mother — ask her to open her purse again. God knows it is full enough, and it's time someone other than the monks of Tewkesbury saw the benefit of it. Besides, it will only be a loan, until I come into my own. When that day dawns we shall be prosperous enough to pay for all. Croesus will be jealous of us.'

I hesitated. I doubted whether his mother would be happy to put in funds, given that much of it would be spent on my adornment, and given that she had already advanced a great sum towards our life at Hanley Castle. She was not overly fond of me, and I was certainly not the bride she would have chosen for her son. That woman would have been an heiress; she would never have said a word to Elisabeth except 'Yes, madam my Mother', 'No, madam my Mother' and 'How right you are, madam my Mother.' She would have produced a child each year, and made no demands on my lord except those absolutely necessary for the getting of those children. She would not have advised him on any matter beyond the walls of the castle, and she would *certainly* not have tried to steer him in any particular direction. She would have been as meek and humble as a mouse, with no opinions of her own at all. Indeed, she would have been almost my direct opposite.

That I was interested in the doings of the court, and of the King in particular; that I was personally acquainted with all the great men of the realm, and had my opinions of the character of most of them, including her 'dear cousin Berkeley' and her 'good friend and kinsman Arundel' was anathema to her. That I should tell her what I thought of them — even in the privacy of our household, for example when we were at table — shocked her no less than if I had spat the sacred Host from my mouth in church and crushed it under my heel.

I do not wish you to think that I had no respect for my lord's mother. For one thing, she was exactly that, and for another she was my elder. I gave her all the reverence that was her due. Yet, when all was said and done, she was but the daughter of a knight. An estimable knight, no doubt, a banneret and a right worthy man, but still a knight. The simple fact was that I was born at least two steps above her, for she had no kings in her quarterings. I was *entitled* to make my offering in church before her; to take precedence over her in processions; to sit above her at table. If I did not always do so, it was by my condescension and grace — not her right.

Of course, she had been little at court, where such things become second nature; you soon learn to whom you must defer and from whom you are due deference. It is simple courtesy, and the mark of good breeding and a proper education. It is also a matter of importance. I have seen two knights fight over the right to go first through a door. Indeed, had I not quarrelled with Philippa Mortimer over just such a matter?

No, the issue was not my lack of respect for Elisabeth, but her lack of respect for me. You would have thought, from her attitude, that Thomas had chosen me from among her launderers, or out of a Southwark stew. She even made veiled comments about my mother from time to time which gave me great offence. For, whatever my lady mother's faults may have been, I would not tolerate hearing her abused by an inferior. The King, the Queen and my father alone had the right to say such things, and they had more courtesy than to do so. From anyone else it was insufferable insolence.

So I suggested that the matter was not urgent. That it could wait until he was allowed livery of estates, which would not be so very far into the future. Then he would not have to ask favours from anyone. He said he would think on the matter, and this time did fall asleep. I found he slept very easily in my bed, but then we were comfortable together, as though we had never been otherwise. A blessed state to enjoy, and one which is rare and worthy of cherishing when it is your fortune to enjoy it.

Then a serpent entered our Eden, and its name was my brother, Rutland.

*

Edward gave us no notice of his arrival until his man arrived just a few hours ahead of him. He came from the King, and where he was going next was not disclosed to us, although I had my suspicions. He brought with him his usual tail of youngish followers, handsome men who smiled and spoke loudly, and wanted to dance and sing and show us how proficient they were in courtly ways. I doubt any man of them had more than five pounds of inheritance before him, or anything else much beyond what my brother doled out to them by way of wages, but they dressed like great knights, if not earls, and swaggered around as if they were nothing less. I kept my damsels on the tightest of reins, for I was responsible to their parents and kindred for their good reputation, and these fellows were just the sort who, if they were given half a chance, would think nothing of spoiling a maidenhead and laughing about it in the morning.

The girls, for the most part, were by no means reluctant. They led a dull life at Hanley Castle in the normal way of things, and had a fancy to be adored and mooned over, to say nothing of a natural eye for potential husbands. It was as good as a holiday season, as far as they were concerned. I was not so very much their elder, but I had my experience. I had lived at court and knew what went on there in dark corners, and, of course, I had a loving husband and understood how easily young blood could be stirred and what followed from that stirring, unless you were made of stone.

I told my brother to keep his randy dogs on leashes too, but he laughed at me.

'You have grown pope-holy, fair sister,' he said, leaning back on his cushions. 'Young men and maidens must have their sport; it is the way of the world. It was so long before we were born and will be long after we are all dust. They will come to no harm. As for you, I see you blooming. You all but glow. Despenser must know his business, or you would not have such a look on your face.'

He was doing his best to make me blush. It was his way. Edward never simply talked to you. He always wanted to stir you to one emotion or another. I sometimes wondered if he kept a score: so many made to laugh; so many reduced to tears; so many left raging — and so on.

'Father has decided to marry again,' he told me, and smiled amiably.

I was not altogether surprised. Those of my mother's women who had not found other places were still at Fotheringhay, living at the Duke's charges. He had told them they could wait on his new Duchess, when he chose one. I had not expected him to move quite so quickly, however. It was little more than six months since my mother's funeral.

'Who is it?' I asked, when it became clear he was not going to volunteer a name.

'Joanne Holland.'

'Joanne Holland?'

Did he *really* mean Joanne Holland, Alianore's younger sister? Or was there perhaps some other Joanne Holland I had not considered? I could not think of one, but I knew they had any number of obscure cousins up in Lancashire.

'Kent's girl,' he confirmed, with an abrupt nod. 'She grows tall and quite pretty. More to the point, there's a very useful dowry. Kent is an extremely generous man.'

'She's younger than I am!'

'Even so. I suppose he'll give her back to her mother for a year or two. Nevertheless, they'll be married before Advent. I take it you and Despenser will be there to see it?'

I frowned. 'Thomas might be. I shall be too far along by then.'

'Far along? Oh, I see. I hadn't realised. Well, I am pleased for you both. And it's a most useful excuse.'

'It's not an excuse. This time I mean to take no risks. No risks at all. I'll not ride that far, or anything like it.'

'By St. Jude!' he cried. 'Are you serious? I wouldn't have known you were carrying if you hadn't told me. You should be able to ride for months yet as long as you don't fall off. It isn't your way to be so cautious.'

'Well, it is now.'

He shook his head. 'You should come back to court,' he said. 'The Queen is always asking about you, and Richard would welcome you both back, as he welcomes every friendly face. You know he has enough sour ones around him! You can imagine it, can't you?'

I could well imagine it. My Uncle Lancaster with his inevitable look of hauteur. Uncle Gloucester, sour-faced, finding fault with every new policy. Arundel, grim as ever. His brother, the

Archbishop, looking as though the troubles of the world were on his shoulders. Perhaps Thomas Mowbray, airing his latest grievance.

'We're waiting for Thomas to come into his own,' I said. 'As matters stand, we are little better than beggars, and I should be disgraced in my gowns that are three years old at best and let in and let out until they are not fit to be seen in such company. Besides, as I told you, there is the child.'

'You *are* a little more rounded than you were,' he said, surveying me with an appraising eye, 'but only in the right places. *Borrow* the money. There are creatures in London— I can give their names to Despenser if you please — who would lend you a thousand pounds tomorrow. Two thousand. These men have a proper understanding of such matters, and know the value of every last manor and lordship that will come to him. They'll expect to be paid back of course, and with a consideration, but it'll be worth it. We can persuade the King to allow Thomas to come into his inheritance before the proper time. It is a thing easily done for those in favour, and you and I between us could gain it in an hour — perhaps in five minutes, for our cousin loves and values us. (We may thank our *other* cousins for that! We owe some of our kinsmen a great deal, for making themselves so obnoxious.) The money is nothing. You can have all that you desire, and still have gold nobles spare to throw around as you please.'

To Thomas he said (a little later, when the wine had gone around and they were alone.): 'The King has it in mind to take an army to Ireland. He wants it better ruled, and it won't be until he goes there himself. He will need warriors — *loyal* warriors. You could lead a great company, my dear brother, for it would be an insult for me to suggest that you should go as part of any other man's retinue, even if it were mine. (Did I not tell you? I shall be one of his commanders.) For that you shall have war wages, for yourself and your men, and although you will need some cash in hand to set things in train, why, can you not borrow it? My lady your mother is rich; she will be proud to see you so engaged, for was your father not a very great knight in the wars with France?

'In return, I shall speak to Cousin Richard on your behalf — for I have much influence nowadays. I shall say that you need and deserve possession of your lands before you come of age. That will solve your problems, will it not? You need only come to court. Bring my sister if it pleases you, for you know she is great with the Queen and much loved. It'll do her no harm to travel, no matter what she says. Then the ladies will also make their suit to the King for you. You know, he listens to the Queen even more than he listens to me. Even my Uncle Lancaster— who rules all these days, I fear — has not the influence that Anne has.'

All of which Thomas reported to me in due course, for he asked my counsel. I suggested he should think on it, but not be too anxious to let Edward imagine he had persuaded him, since my brother never in his life served anyone without some thought to his own advantage. It was not, I said, to *our* advantage for Edward to think that we were at his call and willing to jump to his bidding. For I had no wish that he should think us his servants.

Nevertheless, the thought of a campaign next summer — even in Ireland — with the command of soldiers pleased Thomas, and it played on his mind, just as the thought of returning to court, dressed in silks and ermine, played on mine. We could each, in our own way, see the path to advancement ahead, and it would be a lie to deny it. We hid our feelings from my brother behind wooden faces, saying only that Thomas would decide on the matter in time, and that we were quite content with our present way of life; but Edward had a way of raising his eyebrows when he doubted you, and those eyebrows were raised a few times before he left us with his noisy and disruptive train of followers.

Thomas, because of his involvement in the management of the family estates, had regular meetings with his mother and her council, usually at Tewkesbury. He told me that at the next of these he would open the matter with his mother, and seek to borrow from her. Eventually the day dawned and he rode off, while I remained at Hanley Castle, trying hard to keep my mind occupied by working on his shirts (which it was my wifely duty to fashion and maintain) and listening to my damsels singing. (They were in a deflated mood after the departure of so many good-looking and admiring men, and most of the songs were doleful, but at least they were all still virgin, to the best of my knowledge and belief.)

When my lord returned he looked as downcast as my damsels, though he was not in the mood to sing. On the other hand, nor was he spectacularly angry. It was still only mid-afternoon, and we walked out together through the gardens, hand-in-hand, because it was the most sure place to have a conversation without half the castle's population overhearing you and passing the news on to the other half.

At first, he was inclined to say very little, and we inspected the growth of the plants in the new arbours. I pointed out this and that flower, the scents rising from the herbs, and so on, and with smiles and touches tried to cheer him. At last the tale came out. He had been refused, absolutely. Not a clipped penny would be advanced beyond what had already been delivered or promised.

'My mother is within her rights,' he said. 'She has already been generous, as she sees it. She must pay great fees owed to the King for farming my estates, she must find the annuity for my lord your father, and the eighty marks each year that goes to him for your maintenance. We already have a fair sum each year from the estates, or we should not be able to keep our household, small though it may be. We have this place without rent, and you must remember, it is hers by right, part of her dower. She has spent great sums at Caversham and Cardiff for our future benefit, to keep them in good order. If my lands had been in any other hands during my minority, we should not have fared so well.'

These were obviously Elisabeth's points made in answer to the request, and they were fair enough as far as they went. On the other hand she had a third of the Despenser lands in her own hands by right of dower, to say nothing of the manors of her own Burghersh inheritance, which were considerable in themselves. Her daughters were long since dowered and married off and her household was modest. She rarely left Tewkesbury these days. She could certainly not be short of money. It was not even as if we were asking for a gift. She was certain to be repaid, and quite quickly.

I was tempted to be angry, but I knew that with Thomas in his present mood it would not serve. So I kept my thoughts to myself, and sought to cheer him. I did not even mention the London merchants Edward had told me about, as I thought they should be a last resort. I pretended that I was perfectly happy as we were — which I should have been, had I been half as wise as I thought myself.

Next day I wrote Elisabeth a very humble letter, though it galled me. It took me a long time to write, as there were several drafts and I made use of my own pen, since I wanted to keep the contents between us. I addressed her as my 'right worshipful mother', entreated her daily blessings and hope that I might hear news of her good estate. All of which was proper and formal, and written in as submissive a style as I would have used to the Queen herself, if not more so. There was nothing there of which she could complain.

Then I *thanked* her for refusing the loan. I told her as I was with child again, Thomas would probably have left me behind at Hanley Castle in the event of his returning to court. We were very well as we were, I said, and the last thing I wanted was to be parted from him for a day, especially in the circumstances. The court had temptations for men, even the best of them, and I preferred to keep him under my eye.

As for Ireland, I said that I was in horror at the thought of his going on another campaign, no matter what glory might arise from it. We were better living quietly in the country. I knew that other men might say that he was avoiding the danger, and failing in his duty to the King, but that we two, who knew him well, would always honour him and it mattered not what the world thought. Moreover, I had heard that my uncle of Gloucester was to have a great command under the King, and that the last thing I wanted was for Thomas to fall under his influence, which was pernicious to say the least.

I asked her to keep this secret, especially from my lord, who might be angered by it, and I signed myself her most humble daughter and beadswoman.

This I sent off, wondering whether I had baited the hook too generously. Elisabeth was not my particular friend, but I respected her. She was a capable woman who had guided her own affairs for almost twenty years and anything but a fool. There was a perfectly good chance that she would see through me and my trickery.

For several days there was silence; then she chose to visit us, bringing a small company with her. This was an unexpected visit, but I made her good cheer for it was no part of my plan that she should feel unwelcome or that she should think me sullen and disappointed by her refusal on the loan. I told her that we hoped that she would honour us by staying for several days, as we would both be glad of her company and counsel.

I bore myself very lowly towards her. After I had shown her to the finest of our guest chambers and settled her in comfort I asked her advice on several small matters, which seemed to please her. I listened to her answers and suggestions as attentively as if they were holy writ, nodding and smiling at all she said and promising to be guided by her. I pretended to feel faint from time to time, and barely picked at my food, though the truth was that I could have walked to Worcester at need and had an appetite that a horse would have thought excessive. Thomas fussed over me as a result, asking if I ailed, and this was all for the better.

Next morning, Elisabeth asked me to show her the gardens, and I did so more than willingly, pointing out the improvements I had made. The arbours were well-established now, and kept neatly trimmed by our gardeners, while the herber was positively flourishing, providing almost all our needs. The pleasaunce was bright with flowers, although the roses were already past their best, with the hips forming and beginning to show bright red. It was a fair morning and we walked together quite amiably, our women trailing behind us chattering about this and that, admiring the flowers, discussing what could be done with herbs and the care needed if they were not to die before they became useful.

Suddenly, she became serious. 'I have many books at home, Constance. Written in French and English. I have no difficulty reading and understanding any one of them. You I can read more easily than a child's ABC poem.'

I said nothing, although I knew I had made a foolish misstep. One should never underestimate an adversary; least of all a clever one.

'You long to be at court again, I know. You've never been happy to be away from it. From the King. Our life here in the country must be infinitely tedious to one of your kind. Then your brother comes here, telling his tales, no doubt making great promises. As for Thomas, I'm sure he's easy enough to tempt. You have him all but jumping to command.'

There were untruths and half-truths in her words, almost too many to count. I could feel myself bristling, but could scarcely decide where to begin.

'If you imagine, madam my Mother, that I can make Thomas do anything he doesn't wish to do, you are sorely mistaken,' I said, carefully keeping my voice level.

'You encourage him to folly, nonetheless. That you may do, but I shall not pay to enable it.'

I shrugged. 'As you please. I told you no lie when I said that I was content here at Hanley. So I am. It's Thomas who loses by not being able to advance himself. If that's what you wish for him, well, so be it. He can wait, and owe you nothing.'

I was already thinking of those men in London, the ones my brother had said would gladly lend Thomas money. I hoped Edward had left us a note of their names.

***

Chapter 8

October 1393 — February 1394

We decided that I should not lie-in at Hanley. The reasons were purely practical. We had occupied it for many months, and, even though the days were growing cooler, it was beginning to stink and was in much need of a lengthy visit from the gong-farmers.

'Cardiff,' Thomas said, 'is the place to be. It's the *caput* of my lordship of Glamorgan, and it would be fitting for the heir to be born there. Besides, it's time you saw it.'

'Where were you born?' I asked.

'Llanblethian. But that's a poky little place, only half-finished, and hasn't been lived in since. Cardiff is much grander. You'll like Cardiff, I promise.'

'What if I don't?'

He laughed amiably. 'You will. But you can choose Caerphilly instead, or Llanblethian. Or Llantrisant or even Kenfig. We don't just have the one castle in Glamorgan, but Cardiff is by far the best of them. No one with any sense would prefer one of the others, so I *know* you won't.'

We travelled by barge from our quay at Hanley, making our first stop at Tewkesbury, where Elisabeth welcomed us kindly enough. She had a new member of her household, Berkeley's young daughter, Elizabeth, whose mother had died the previous year. This unfortunate child was only seven or so, very quiet, and quite unobjectionable.

'Cousin Berkeley is quite devastated,' Elisabeth told us, once the girl was despatched to her bed and we settled to our supper. 'He has sworn he will never marry again.'

'But he has no son!' Thomas objected.

'Quite so. Little Elizabeth will be his heiress. Although some of his lands, as I gather, are entailed, and must pass to his brother, Sir James.'

'That will cause trouble. Such partitions always do. James is a good man, though.'

Elisabeth sniffed. 'Perhaps. But his brother has been a good friend to me – to us – and it's hard to see him as broken as he is. It unsettles the whole county.'

'Mother, Berkeley has been unsettling this shire for years. He's behind half the rogues that disturb its peace, as Judge Cassy will tell you. No one can touch him, or his lackeys, and so the people have no justice. The fact that he's your friend does not change that. It will be amended, before long. I shall see to it myself.'

Elisabeth sucked her teeth. 'Berkeley is a powerful man,' she said, 'with great influence in these parts. I advise you not to be swift to make quarrels with him.'

'Oh, I shall take my time, madam my Mother. For one thing, I still intend to go to Ireland with the King next summer. Even if, for lack of sufficient funds to do more, I must enlist as one of my brother Rutland's knights.'

'That's senseless. Ireland is a poor, benighted country. There'll be no booty worth having, no great ransoms, and even if the King grants you lands there — which I suppose he might, if his flatterers speak for you — they will not be worth the having.' She flicked a brief glance in my direction. 'Next September you come of age, and will have all your lands in England and Wales to put in order. You'd be better employed if you set your mind to that, instead of wasting time in more profitless adventures like your folly in Prussia.'

He shrugged. 'As to my lands here,' he said, 'Constance is more than capable of managing all that needs to be done, given the counsellors I shall leave to advise her. A man wins no renown, madam, by serving as his own land steward. Besides, I have my duty to the King. If he makes war, then I must serve under him, no matter where the war may be. Would my father have chosen differently?'

It was an astute point to make, and it silenced Elisabeth. I watched her as she struggled to come up with a suitable rebuttal, her face contorting with the effort. To do her justice, she did not lie, did not pretend that Lord Edward would have chosen another path.

'You have no cause to smile, daughter,' she said instead, turning on me.

I was not aware that I had been smiling, and apologised out of courtesy. I was, I must admit, rather pleased with the turn the conversation had taken. Thomas was asserting himself in a way I thought very proper.

From Tewkesbury we sailed, next morning, as far as Gloucester, where of course we made a point of visiting King Edward's shrine with our people and making an offering. Then next day we boarded a larger vessel, and made our way down the river and out into the Severn Sea. The voyage seemed interminable, but at least the waters were smooth, there was a cabin into which we could withdraw, and even a bed of sorts to lie on.

Cardiff, I discovered, was little more than an overgrown village. We had to ride (on hired horses) through it from the quay to the castle and I saw that most of the houses were little better than miserable hovels, their timber frames, as I learned, filled with a mixture of earth, straw and animal dung, which the Welsh call *clom* and roofed with thatch. However, some of the richer merchants had stone houses; there was at least one large church and two friaries. The whole settlement was protected by a defensive wall, although Thomas assured me that the Welsh of these parts were as just peaceable as our own people in England.

'You're as safe here as you are in Gloucestershire,' he said, 'although if you venture into the hills you'll find people who have no

English, though the better sort always have French as well as Welsh. They're good folk, or at least, as good as most folk are, but you might struggle to find one who doesn't think himself your equal. They don't grovel, but you shouldn't take offence. It's just their way.'

The castle was splendid, as fine, in its own fashion, as Fotheringhay. However, it had not been lived in for years except by a skeleton staff of caretakers, and the distinctive smell of damp and mould hit my nostrils as soon as I entered the door. Of course, I knew it would look and feel better when our furnishings arrived, but much of the stuff was travelling by road and would not be with us for days, along with our horses. We had only brought the bare essentials by water.

However, it was not long before Hugh Bygge and his fellows had contrived a passable supper for us all, and I was able to retire to a warm and comfortable bed, even if the walls of the room in which I lay were bare and their ancient paint flaking away.

*

It is vain to complain of the pain and discomfort of childbirth; it is the common fate of all women, high and low, part of our punishment for the sins of our distant grandmother, Eve. To do so is close to heresy, and in these days, with Archbishop Arundel sniffing around for heretics to burn — and no doubt wringing his hands in frustration at their perversity — I am careful to say nothing that might offend the Church. (In Richard's day we would often freely discuss such matters at court, but then, as you know, King Richard was a *tyrant*.)

It is, however, permissible to question such traditions as the one that says a woman of noble birth must be confined in her chamber for weeks on end, served only by women and seeing no man at all once her confessor has heard and absolved her sins and taken his way out of her sanctuary. It makes it a tedious business, one that seems to last far longer than in truth it does.

There was, of course, no question in any case of my seeing Thomas. He had gone to attend my father's wedding to Joanne Holland and could scarcely be expected back before the child was born. The wedding also meant that Alianore could not come to me as I had hoped – she had a higher duty to her sister, as I understood.

Instead of Alianore, Elisabeth arrived, and at once took charge of everything, as though I were a child of five, or an idiot. It was annoying in a way, and yet at the same time I was glad to have her, for my own women were all young and inexperienced, while Elisabeth knew the business well, and saw that everything was arranged properly. She even found a suitable wet nurse, a Welshwoman I was allowed to inspect for myself. She was clean and obviously respectable, so I had no cause to demur.

Elisabeth said that Edith should be cast out and put in the kennels. On this point I did demur, and fiercely. I said in plain words that if Edith was to go to the kennels I should move there myself. If Our Blessed Lady could give birth in a stable, I could most certainly do it in a kennel. Elisabeth accused me of being irreverent, but gave way. So, however slowly the hours went by, I at least had Edith's head to fondle, and when, as occasionally happened, she ran about the rooms chasing shadows, I was set laughing. There was certainly nothing else to amuse me.

Elisabeth had brought Philippa Fitzwalter with her. From what I could gather, with her husband away at court, she had gained permission from Sir John to attend me at Hanley. (She had had no invitation, but presumed her welcome.) Finding us gone she had hurried to her cousin, Elisabeth, just in time to join her journey to Cardiff.

Philippa talked to me a good deal more than I talked to her. She was full of complaints about John Golafre; told me that these days he was always angry about something or other, and forever finding fault. She was grateful he was with the King, and hoped he might stay there. She hoped to stay with me for several months, and had the idea that Golafre was most unlikely to recall her. I resigned myself to her company.

I had written to my cousin Beth, Lady Huntingdon, hoping that she would come to me and act as godmother to the child but not expecting that she would do so. (I thought, at best, she might be godmother by proxy.) To my surprise she made the journey, travelling from her home in Devon by crossing the Severn Sea, which was, of course, the quickest way. I was delighted to see her and the days suddenly seemed much shorter as we talked, for Beth had much news of the court and of the world in general, and was happy to share it all with me. She had much to say of her brother, Harry.

'He went again to Prussia, of course.' She laughed, and gripped my wrist as if it hurt her. 'He found he was unwanted. He, the noble Harry, the famous warrior with his great retinue, was turned away from the door, so to speak, like an old woman selling stale fish from a tray. They have a truce there, I imagine, or something of the sort. So what do you suppose he did? Well, of course, he didn't come home, that wouldn't have done at all. No, instead he set off for Jerusalem.'

'*Jerusalem?*' I repeated. 'Is it not in the hands of infidels?'

My head was swimming, or I would not have asked such an obvious question, but Beth did not mind.

'Oh yes, but pilgrims are allowed. And Harry, being Harry, did it very properly, walking through the desert, or the wilderness, or I know not what, for miles and miles. He saw all the Holy Places, and talks of little else now he is home. For he is home, though not much at court. My lord father has advised him that he is best out of our Cousin Richard's eye. Good counsel, I think. Out of sight, out of mind as they say. Though Richard, of course, has forgiven all offences. So he says.'

I picked up the note in her voice, though it was very subtle. 'You don't think he has?'

Hanley Castle

She grinned at me. 'Do you?'

I shrugged. 'I'm not sure,' I admitted. 'Being so long away from the court, I know only what people tell me, and most say that Richard is ruling well, and that the troubles are forgotten.'

She leaned closer. 'My John is much about the King, and he says that Richard has neither forgotten nor forgiven, and that it will be a long time before he does. Of course, Arundel refreshes his mind from time to time. That fellow is always making trouble. You have heard of the risings in Cheshire?'

I shrugged. I had heard something of the trouble there, but Cheshire is a long way from Hanley Castle, and neither Edward nor any other reliable informant had written to me on the matter.

'The men of Cheshire,' Beth went on, 'are ever ready for a fight, and many of them fight for their living. So they think this peace with France a great threat to their future, and many of them rose in revolt against it, blaming my father, Uncle Gloucester, and even Harry for it, since all three had been ambassadors to France to make the peace. They particularly wanted my father's head, and there were some other fools, in other parts of the North, who rose in sympathy.

'It was not all that serious, I think. At least, my father went up there with a force of men and put an end to it all very quickly, with little bloodshed. He took many of the fellows into his service. (He needs soldiers for Guienne, you see, and they are as good as any.) So, all was settled. But here's the rub. Arundel was up at Holt Castle, which, as you likely know, is right at the gate of Cheshire. He had a great number of retainers with him, all armed to the teeth. But not a finger did he stir! Not to repress the rebels, at any rate. Some say he encouraged the rising. I know my father believes it so. He is furious with Arundel and, as you can imagine, that pleases our cousin the King more than a little.'

I had no difficulty in imagining at all. If Arundel had been fool enough to make an enemy of my Uncle Lancaster it was all to the good, for there was no doubt which of them must prevail. Richard would scarcely need to lift a finger to have his revenge. Though, of course, it would only be on the one of them, Arundel. There were another four to bring to account and I saw no hope of progress there. So much had been forgiven for the sake of peace — or so I thought.

*

My daughter Elizabeth came easily enough, or at least as easily as a child ever does. Her baptism was not hurried, for she was in good health, but my cousin Beth served as her principal godmother, with Philippa Fitzwalter, for want of anyone better, as the second. The Bishop of Llandaff, who by some oversight happened to be residing in his see at the time, did duty as godfather.

When all the ceremony was done there was a feast in the Great Hall, a very splendid and expensive celebration, from which I, naturally, was excluded. Custom — that dread tyrant — required me to keep to my rooms, though I was up on my feet, pacing about, and suffering from nothing worse than a trifling soreness and an insatiable appetite for food and drink.

My women served me my meals, of course, but on Elisabeth's orders they were plain and simple fare, with none of the splendours our guests were enjoying, not so much as a dish of *viande royale*. Indeed, if Elisabeth had had her way, I should still have been lying in bed, leaning on my pillows and allowing myself to be fed on sops, but there were limits to my patience and I made that clear to her. Perhaps, I must admit, without the proper deference due to an elder.

At last, Thomas returned, to my joy and relief. It quite made up for my weeks of isolation and my exclusion from the baptismal feast and the Christmas celebrations. It even made up for the cold – the weather had frozen the moat and scribed icy patterns on the window glass and even all my blankets and furs and the great blaze Elisabeth had ordered built in the fireplace could not exclude it. My feet felt as if they had turned to ice and I was plagued with chilblains.

It is only natural for a man to want a son to carry on his name, but if Thomas was disappointed to have a daughter instead he gave no sign of it.

'She is beautiful,' he said, 'and it will be my business to make her a great marriage, which I shall, I swear to you.'

I laughed, for it seemed madness to talk of marriage for a child just born. 'There are years to think of that,' I said.

He made light of it, and yet I sensed he already had someone in mind. I pressed him on that point, but he denied he had any such thoughts. I could not very well call him a liar, but I knew that at the least he had some design at the back of his head. Contrary to what Elisabeth would have told you, he was more than capable of developing ambitions of his own, without any suggestion from me.

It was not long after this that I found Philippa reproving the wet-nurse for speaking to my daughter in Welsh. She had already reduced the young woman to tears, and I had to take her aside and give her plain words. I was grateful for her company at this time, I said – courtesy makes hypocrites of us all! - but she must not meddle in the ordering of my household. She was not pleased with that, as I could tell from her face, but she apologised, saying that she had meant well but would remember what I had said.

As for the wet-nurse, I told her she might speak to my daughter in what language she pleased, whether it be Welsh, French or the tongue of the wild Irish, as long as she took good care of her. Then, to dry her tears and make her content, I gave her several coins by way of a bonus, and told her she had but one mistress to please, and that mistress was me, not my lord's cousin.

Thomas, I should say, had not come home to me empty-handed. As well as various gifts from the family, he brought me as much rich cloth as I had ever seen, some of it fine enough to make me gasp with pleasure and provoke me to run my fingers over it. Still better, he had brought a tailor from London, an addition to our household, a soft-voiced fellow who took my measurements and spoke of the new fashions seen at court.

Thomas had borrowed a great deal of money from a mercer of London, a man of good Gloucestershire family called Whittington. (This fellow has since grown in importance. He has been Lord Mayor more than once, and has more money than the King that now is. Even then he was a man of some substance, and more than ready to serve us, knowing that he could make good profits for his trouble. It is how such men make their living, and perhaps the cost of their service should not be grudged, though it seems to me they take little risk for great reward.)

I asked Thomas about my father's wedding, and, in particular, what he had made of Joanne Holland.

'Oh,' he said, 'she has grown very fair. She presided very nicely over the jousting, and gave out prizes with full courtesy – the Queen herself could not have been more gracious. She is very young though. Your father has not bedded her, but has left her with her mother for the time being.' He hesitated, just for a fraction. 'She asked after you, of course. Said she would pray for your welfare, and that she longs to see you.'

'I'm sure she does,' I said, 'and no doubt longs to hear me call her 'mother'. How strange that will be!'

He shrugged. 'Well, it is as it is, and could be worse. You can't say you don't know her. You're also in my Lady March's prayers, by the way. She made a point of speaking to me, and seems very happy. Perhaps she and Roger have grown contented after all. He goes to Ireland with the King in the summer, as do I, of course. The difference is that he'll be staying there – he's to be Lord Lieutenant. Whether Alianore goes with him, I know not.'

I suspected I knew the answer to that, but I held my peace.

*

I shall not speak of my churching and the great feast that followed, splendid though the occasion was, nor yet of the tedious journey back to England, tedious though it was. My heart was so full of joy that I could scarcely take anything in. I was free again, able to breathe the fresh air – though that air was still very cold, and there were times as we rode that sleet blew fiercely in my face. Even this did not depress my spirits, though it reddened my face horridly and made my nose feel as raw as if I was suffering from a streaming cold.

At last we came to Caversham, where we intended to rest for a few days. Much to my surprise, my brother Edward was already there, waiting for us as it seemed. I presumed Thomas had written to him with word of our intentions.

Edward greeted us very warmly, embracing us both.

'Your petition is granted,' he said to Thomas, 'and has but to pass the Great Seal. That should not cause any more delay than is usual with those fellows – you know how clerks work, and how many bribes it takes to speed their business. I have spoken to the Chancellor for you, and he made no difficulties.'

(The Chancellor at this time was Archbishop Arundel, who had regained his post. It was all part of the truce that still held, and at least he was not as noxious as his brother, and knew how to manage business.)

We were free at last; or at least Thomas was now, or soon to be, his own master, a good six months earlier than was his right by law. His revenues would be his, and he would no longer need his mother's assent every time he settled a lease or appointed a steward. Moreover, during his absence in Ireland, I should rule over all, by his authority. It was a great change for us both.

Edward made a circular gesture with his wrist. 'There are some small reservations. My father's annuity for one. You must maintain it until you are truly of age. Nothing onerous, though, nothing to tie your hands.'

He was so amiable that it made me suspicious. He even

insisted on being introduced to his new niece, and made a great fuss of her, although usually he had no time for young children, let alone babies. (Even as a boy he had treated the more obtuse of our young pages with a mixture of impatience and contempt.) I began to wonder what reward he expected in return for what I knew he would perceive as his services. No attorney born was ever swifter to render an account than my brother.

*

'March is with the court,' Edward told me. It was the next morning and we were strolling through the gardens together, alone save for Philippa and my damsels, who followed us a few paces behind. (My lord husband was busy dictating letters, including one to his mother at Tewkesbury, giving her the good news.) It was pleasant enough in the open air, and I was glad of the chance to consider what changes needed to be made, now that the place was in our control.

I did not respond at first, because my mind was woolgathering. I believe I was busy with thoughts of a new arbour, how much it might cost us, and how long it would take to build. I supposed there might be carpenters in Reading ready to take on the work, but I had no idea of their names, or where word might be sent to fetch them.

'Thomas would do well to make less of his friendship,' he went on. 'It provokes suspicion.'

'What friendship?' I repeated, shaking my head. I'd not been listening well enough to make sense of his words.

'For one thing, you should bear in mind that March's sister is married to Arundel now, and Arundel, I promise you, is a marked man. That Cousin Richard detests him is the least of it – Uncle Lancaster is his enemy too, especially since the fellow as good as accused him of treason at the last Parliament. That enmity is like to spread to Roger March, and to Roger March's friends. Must I say more? You were not apt to be dull-witted, back when we were children at court together.'

'I understand your meaning well enough,' I answered. 'You know as well as I that March is no friend of Arundel, and his sister's marriage was not made with his approval, but the very opposite. That I know from Alianore herself, and Alianore is well placed to know.'

'Oh, yes, Alianore.' His eyes turned towards the river for a moment, then flickered back. 'In some ways, Alianore is a surprisingly loyal wife. In some ways. It should be enough for you to know that Richard has suspicions about March, and has his reasons. As for Arundel, he would dearly love to have a king he could control, and Roger Mortimer is just such a one.'

'Even if all that is true, you are wrong to think that I can command Thomas,' I said. 'I mean in any matter, let alone to tell him what friends he may or may not have. He and Roger March were boys together in Arundel's household —'

'Precisely!' he cried, leaping on my words like a lawyer seizing on a point of law. 'Do you not see? *That* is what makes it worse! As for the rest, never tell me you lack influence over Despenser. He dotes on you almost as much as Arundel dotes on Philippa Mortimer — which is to say, not quite so far as to make himself ridiculous, but as far as any man should. It's your duty to guide him in this matter. Not just because it's the King's wish — though it is! — but in his own interests if he hopes for further favour and advancement. It's your business to make sure that he sees sense.'

'I've told you, I can't command him.'

'Then make suit to him!' he snapped back. 'Fall on your knees. Weep. Plead. Use the other tricks women use to win their way; I'm sure you know them better than I do. It's for his benefit, you fool, not mine.'

I was minded to call him an insolent dog and slap his face; so I should have served any lesser man who named me 'fool'. Yet there was a voice within me, sounding very like my mother, which said:

'Subtlety, Constance. Subtlety.'

So I restrained my temper, and my hand, and said: 'I make no promises; but I will speak to him.'

There was no lie in that. I certainly intended to speak to Thomas, on every day that we were together. However, I had no intention of telling him what friends he might have. I might hint, but hints bounced off my lord like a feather off plate armour. Most men are made like that, I have always found.

The truth was that my brother had power, and we, for the time being, had very little. We had need of him, and to quarrel was not in our interests. Yet nor would I be his lackey, rushing to do his bidding. Subtlety was all.

***

Chapter 9

March 1394

'I want all your news. Tell me everything,' the Queen demanded of me.

We were sitting together on one of the window-seats in *La Neyt* at Sheen, just as we had sometimes done in the old days, before all the trouble started. So much was the same — the rich hangings covering the walls, with their scenes of Camelot, the painted glass in the windows, Anne's kind, happy face — but just as much had changed. The absence of so many old friends, banished or dead for one thing. Perhaps the greatest change of all was in me. I was no longer a child, uncertain of my place in the world and fearful of speaking too boldly. I had a child of my own and Thomas to protect and care for me. I had grown fearless, sure of my opinions, sure of my standing. Too much so, if the truth is told.

I took a breath and began, for there was much to tell, and even more before all Anne's questions had been answered. We laughed so much that at times we did not so much drink the wine we had in our hands but snorted it down our noses.

'I'm glad you're so well settled,' Anne said, leaning closer so that our faces were scarcely a hand apart. 'As for me,' she went on, speaking softly so as not to be overheard, 'I have been dosing myself with potions, *and I believe they have worked!*'

I was unsure of her meaning until she gave a little, knowing nod, and then hugged me as though we were sisters.

'I pray it is so!' I cried.

She held a finger to her lips. 'I am keeping it as secret as I can, at least until I start to show. By all means pray for me, after so many disappointments the more prayers the better.'

I knew from my own time in her household that it would be no secret from her women, and if no secret from them the chances were it was no secret from half the court. Even so, I understood her wish not to make too much of her hopes.

There had been many other changes at court since I had last lived there. The most obvious was that my Uncle John of Lancaster had become so influential that nothing was done without his advice and consent. Whenever there was any form of ceremony or celebration, there he would be, standing or sitting next to Richard. At every hunt, every hawking expedition, there he was again, standing at the King's side or riding half a length behind him as if acting as a watchdog, guarding Richard from harm.

My cousin, who would once have found such close attendance infuriating, seemed completely at ease with this shadowing. On many days, he still wore the Lancastrian livery collar as well as his own as a token of their alliance. They had also retained the habit of walking about the court arm-in-arm. How my uncle enjoyed that! All the obeisances made to Richard were made to him as well, and I'm sure he thought it no more than he deserved. Had he not called himself King of Spain for years? I've no doubt he still considered himself the equal of any man on earth.

There was to be peace with France. As part of the settlement it had been agreed that my uncle would be given Guienne, and not only the lands we held then, but much of the hinterlands long lost to the French. What was more, he was to hold it as a vassal of the French King, not of Richard, whose inheritance it was. There were many who thought this madness, and muttered about it in corners, not daring to speak openly because that would offend both the King and my uncle — to say nothing of my cousin, Harry Bolingbroke, who stood to inherit all this.

Arundel was one of those who objected, and for the first time in my life I found myself in agreement with him. It irritated me to think that my uncle should be given such vast power and wealth, almost for the asking, while my poor father often had to battle with officious, low-born clerks to squeeze coin from the Exchequer. (Much of his livelihood came that way; more, in truth, than came from land.) My father had served the King loyally, through all the darkest of his troubles, but his rewards were scant. He had to think himself fortunate if he was found another manor or two. Lancaster, who already had more wealth than he could hope to spend in a dozen lifetimes, had only to hint at a desire for more, and it was given. It was unjust. Or so, at least, it seemed to me.

When I spoke of this to Edward, he laughed at me.

'You fail to see beyond the end of your nose, my dear sister,' he said. 'Our uncle will have to live in Bordeaux, not here. In his absence, we shall have plenty of room in which to bustle. Besides, it will bring peace, and that means our cousin the King will have less need for taxes, and thus very little cause to summon parliaments. He'll be able to rule without the tedious interference of petty squires from the back of beyond. That can only be to our benefit, as well as profiting the whole realm.'

'Uncle Gloucester,' I said, 'will also have more room in which to bustle.'

He laughed, and tweaked his moustaches gently with his fingers. It looked very much as if they had received attention from the curling-tongs that morning — certainly they looked too artificial to be entirely natural. I wondered if he coloured his whiskers — they had a touch more red than was present in my hair.

'Yes,' he said, 'and doesn't he know it? Why do you think he has been converted to our cause of peace? It's not solely because he's devoted to Uncle Lancaster and his interests, as a fool might suppose. What he forgets is that the world has changed. Arundel might still stand with him, but Warwick grows old, and has Mowbray on his tail, pursuing a claim to Gower. Do you know of that? Never mind, it's enough for you to know the case will keep him occupied for a long time, and cost him hundreds of pounds in lawyers' fees. Apart from that, I am no Simon Burley or Robert de Vere. Nor for that matter is Huntingdon, or Mowbray, or your Thomas. Richard can rely on all of us — and others besides. There will be no repeat of Radcot Bridge, nor of their treasonous Parliament. Oh yes, the world has changed, and very much in our favour. The day I promised you is coming — it's coming soon.'

We were standing beneath one of the windows of the Great Hall at Sheen, tucked so deeply into the oriel that the glass was almost touching our faces. We were quite alone, having sent our attendants away to entertain one another across the room, so that we could talk in privacy, something that is not always easy to achieve at court. There is always someone who wants to eavesdrop, and you cannot forever converse in whispers.

Just as the last word left my brother's mouth, Roger Mortimer and Thomas walked by us, each carrying a hawk on a gloved hand, much absorbed in conversation and followed closely by a train of servants and hangers-on, many of them in March's livery or ours. Not one of them did as much as cast a glance in our direction, not even Thomas.

At the time, I must admit, I found it infuriating to be so ignored. Since then, I have grown in wisdom. I have learned that men are like greyhounds — when their eyes are focused on one thing, be it a hawk, a woman, or an enemy, they are blind to all else. Indeed, I have long since concluded that in their vision, and in their hearing, they are much inferior to women, and see and hear very little. (As they possess much greater physical strength and are the lords of creation, I suppose it is only just of God to give *some* advantages to lesser creatures.)

Edward gave me a wry look, his head tilted to one side like that of a bewildered dog.

'I begin to see that Despenser does not heed your counsel,' he said.

'I shall give him counsel, when next I see him,' I answered, for I was angered beyond all reason. I was older in years, and yet in some ways I was still a wilful child. It does no harm, now, to confess it.

*

That evening I spent much time dancing with Edmund Mortimer, laughing at almost every other word he said. (Edmund was good company, and always had been, but in truth he was not *that* entertaining. I merely sought to punish Thomas for daring to ignore me. It gives me no pleasure to set down that I could be so absurd, but so I was.)

Edmund had long since left my father's household by this time, and now served as his brother's deputy, aide and shadow. He had been knighted by the King, and was to take part in the Irish campaign.

'The chances are I shall never return,' he said wistfully, 'or at least, not for many a long year. You know, of course, that Roger is to be Lord Lieutenant? Well, I shall serve under him, and when he comes home — which he will have to do from time to time, even if it's to attend Parliaments and take order to his estates — I shall stand in his place. Imagine me, in command of Ireland!' He laughed. 'Constance, I've not yet done so much as managed a single manor. How shall I fare, do you think?'

'Very well,' I said. 'Do not decry yourself. You were born to such a rule.'

He shook his head. 'Birth I may have, but that is not enough. You must also have the head for such work, the experience, the judgement. All these I lack. I can couch a lance, perhaps. Sing a song. Dance after a fashion.' He grinned at me, as if to deprecate his efforts. (He was not the best dancer at court by a long street, but he did well enough. He had not trodden on me once.) 'Train a dog, I suppose, or a horse or a hawk. To rule a country? I am no more fitted to that than

I am to ride a horse over a steeple.'

The dance ended, and we walked together to stand by the wall, beneath one of the King's most splendid hangings, a representation of knights jousting in some verdant woodland, while eagles and hawks soared above them.

'You should have more faith in yourself,' I said. 'You are so high-born that nothing should be beyond your ambition, or your ability. I know you do not lack courage or honour. Be bold. Men will be glad to follow you, if you but choose to lead.'

'I will remember what you have said,' he answered quietly. He was silent then for perhaps a dozen heartbeats, before he went on in quite a different tone. 'I am grateful for your friendship — and Despenser's. So many at court have turned their backs on Roger and me. You must surely have noticed? For some reason, I believe some think us to be Arundel's friends, and he's hated by the King and by Lancaster, which is more than enough for most. It's *madness*. He was one of Roger's guardians I grant you, but he never gave either of us cause to love him. He married my sister without Roger's knowledge or consent; without mine either.'

'This I know,' I said. 'Alianore told me as much.'

'They arranged it between themselves, them and our uncle, Thomas Mortimer, who is indeed in Arundel's pocket. For the love of God, it was not *political*. At least, not on our side. It would be a kindness if you would explain that to the King, and to anyone else who will listen. Anyone *at all*. My lord your father for one. The Queen. Anyone you think fit.'

He had barely finished when we were joined by his brother. March bowed low to me, and invited me to join the dance with him. I complied, out of courtesy.

I had always thought Roger Mortimer awkward and clumsy, and so he was, but he danced well enough, though with more energy and enthusiasm than precision. This was a more energetic measure, and there was little scope for conversation, but unlike his brother he did not speak of politics or of grievances but of commonplace matters. When the music halted, he led me over to his wife, for she, he said, particularly wanted to speak to me.

I had not realised that Alianore was in the room, or even at court. When we had finished greeting and hugging one another, I learned she had arrived only that afternoon — with her parents, and with Joanne.

I could see Lord and Lady Kent across the hall — they were standing close to the Queen and exchanging conversation with her. There was no sign of Joanne, though.

'I shall take you to her,' Alianore said.

She led me to Kent's lodgings, and there indeed was Joanne. It was more than a year since I had seen her, of course, but I was not prepared for how much she had changed. She was still very young, but she had grown into a beauty, the equal of Alianore, which is to say a great deal.

There was nothing for it. I made a reverence. 'Madam my Mother,' I got out, though the words seemed absurd.

She smiled at me, but did not rise from the bed on which she was seated. Instead, she patted the coverlet. 'Please sit next to me, Constance,' she said.

'I'll leave you,' Alianore said briskly. 'I've some hope of dancing with your brother, Constance, if he can be found. I think he may be in hiding.'

She was gone, and Joanne and I sat there together quietly, looking at each other by such light as was provided by her oil lamp.

Unexpectedly, she took my hand.

'I'd like us to be friends,' she said, 'just as you are my sister's friend. When we are alone or in privacy, I would have you call me "Joanne" or plain "Joan" if you prefer it. I know we must be more formal when it's necessary — it is but proper courtesy, and people will expect it. We both know better than to be unmannerly. That's all, though. I shall never be able to think of you as a daughter — that would be quite ridiculous. I am, of course, your father's wife.' She paused to blush. 'In name at least. You know he has not — not yet. Still, he is very kind. It will be much, much easier, if you do not choose to dislike me.'

'You are very — gracious,' I said. (It was as good a word as I could find.) 'Of course I don't dislike you. You've given me no cause.'

She let out a breath. 'I'm not sure I could be so forgiving of one who took my mother's place. Even so, I'm glad we are in accord. There's much I have to ask you.'

There followed many questions, some of which were inconvenient and might more properly have been asked of Lady Kent. However, I answered as well as I could, and we chattered together for a good hour. It was, I reflected later, time well spent, for we had reached an easy accord, and I had quarrels enough elsewhere. Family unity is well worth a concession or two, and, as she had said, she was now my father's wife, and I had to be on terms with her.

*

It was not the last strange interview of the day, for later still, not long before midnight, with the dancing very much still in progress and a rere-supper in contemplation for those of us high enough in favour to be bidden to it, I was approached by Sir John Golafre. To do him justice, he showed himself more courteous towards me than I had ever known, perhaps because he no longer saw me as but a child, perhaps because he knew that my lord would not tolerate any disrespect and was capable of bearing a sharp lance.

'My lady,' he said, 'I believe you have my wife in your household?'

'Yes,' I admitted, 'she is still our guest, as you must surely know, but she's not here. We left her at Caversham with our daughter and the greater part of our people.'

(Thomas and I had brought but a small number of attendants with us, just sufficient to maintain our proper dignity. Lodgings are sparse at court, and the King's officers look down their noses if you bring more than they think convenient. Each mouth, of course, is another to be fed at the King's cost.)

He laughed, but for once in his life he was not mocking me. 'You mistake me, madam. I do not seek her return. Indeed, I was about to beg a favour of you. That you keep her about you. You see, that way, I am sure she will not find her way into any mischief. Besides, I am but a mere knight in the King's service, and she has no proper place here. His Grace keeps me busy, and I am ever in one place or another in his service, either in England or across the sea. I am soon to go to Poland on a mission for his Grace and am likely to be away for many months. It is not as if she is one of the Queen's ladies. Nor do I want her alone in the country. For one thing, I'm not sure of her honesty.'

I stared at him in astonishment, wondering what on earth he meant. Did he think Philippa was playing him false, or that she was muddling his household accounts?

'Of course,' he went on, 'once I am back in England you may send her home from time to time. When I am there to watch over her. Yet, to be truthful, I'd not mind, even then, if it was not more than twice or three times a year. I find I have no great use for her company.'

'I thought —' I began.

'That she wanted to be away from me?' he laughed again, this time bitterly. 'No, my lady, you can spare me her tales. No doubt I am included in them as Satan in boots. I promise you, whatever distaste there is, it is quite mutual. Suffice it to say we are better apart, and in that regard my duties in the King's service are a great convenience. Yet if she can have an honest place — and I can think of none better than in your service, since you are a great lady and she is Despenser's cousin — it would ease my mind.'

I should, of course, have told him that I would not have her, and that if he had doubts about her honesty I did *certainly* not want her in my company. Yet, I must admit, I had grown used to Philippa, and in some ways she was of value to me. At that time, for example, was she not supervising my daughter's nurses? Indeed, was she not managing the whole of Caversham on my behalf, and thoroughly enjoying the task? Besides, as he had mentioned, she was Thomas's cousin, and I could scarcely turn her from the door. My mind was already occupied with thoughts of enjoying the King's rere-supper, and there was little space for consideration. So I told him that Philippa could remain, and might, if it pleased him, consider herself a member of my household.

*

My lord husband had assumed new arms, by the King's licence, quartering the de Clare blazoning with his own, and putting them in a position of prominence, for theirs was the greater inheritance. Their three chevrons, *gules*, on their field of *or*, were a mute challenge to all those who held part of the de Clare lands, whether it was my Uncle Lancaster or indeed Roger Mortimer, Earl of March. Thomas did not lack for ambition, and I admired him for it, though I thought him reckless. Then again, recklessness in a man is not unattractive, unless it becomes sheer folly.

My ridiculous attempt to make him jealous had failed completely. Indeed, he thanked me for showing the Mortimers kindness.

'There is a chill wind that blows about them,' he said, 'though God knows why. The King is not offended by anything they've done. If he was, he'd scarcely make Roger his lieutenant in Ireland, would he? He's said nothing to me that makes me think they are not in his favour.'

I had quite forgiven Thomas by this time. I could never remain angry with him for long, no matter how he exasperated me. I shook my head, though.

He gave me a sharp look. 'What is it?' he asked.

'Remember the Appellants,' I said. 'They had the heads off the men they hated most. (Those that had not fled abroad, anyway.) Those they hated somewhat less, they banished to Ireland. It's a barren land, far away, and not healthy for an Englishman.'

'Yes, but Roger is to *rule* there. He isn't banished, nor stripped of his livelihood. He's Earl of Ulster too, don't forget, and has great lands over there, which I dare say need to be set in order.'

Such lands, I thought, as are not already overrun by the wild Irish. This though I did not say.

Instead I said: 'Thomas, I don't presume to know more than you do. Yet allow me this — I've lived at court longer than you. The King does not always give orders in plain words. (In truth, when he does, matters have gone far along.) He *lets it be known* what his wishes are. If you hope to regain more of the de Clare lands than you already own, you must have my cousin's favour. Without it, we may just as well go back to Hanley Castle and sit on our hands.'

'I'll not abandon a friend!' he said sharply.

'I'm not suggesting that you do.' I sighed. I hesitated for a moment. 'You're steering the ship. I do but remind you of the direction of the wind, and warn that it may grow stronger. You cannot sail directly into the wind, Thomas. The ship will sink, go down with all hands.'

He let out a bitter little laugh. 'A pretty figure,' he said. 'I suppose you think that I should be guided in my steering by a lodestar, and that lodestar is your brother, Rutland.'

I shook my head. 'I will never counsel you to do *anything* that is not to your advantage. Nor will I ever be fool enough to tell you what you must do. I know you too well ever to do that! All I say is you must be careful and not lose the King's good will, because if you do you will find what enemies you have, and we shall both of us — *both of us!* — be brought low. I seek your profit because it is my own.'

He sighed. 'My claim to the de Clare lands is a slow business. It can't even *begin* until I return from Ireland, and set attorneys to assemble the evidence I shall need to take my case to law. Once March is over there, out of sight, the chances are that the King will forget all about him. He really is no threat, Constance. He has no ambition at all. Even when in drink, he never, ever speaks of having any hope of the crown. As God is my judge, I swear he intends no more harm to the King than you do yourself. No, if there's ambition in that family it lies with his brother, and Edmund does not aspire to any crown.' He smiled at me. 'The way he looks at you at times makes me think I should tilt at him with a sharp spear. It's as well that I trust you, and know that you're too proud to indulge in folly.'

'I thank you for your faith in me, my lord,' I said, tilting my head back to let him think I was offended. (The fact that I addressed him as 'my lord' when we were in complete privacy was another marker for him to chew over.) I was not really offended at all. In truth, I was flattered. I simply did not want him to be so sure of himself. A husband is none the worse for a few doubts to keep him on his toes.

*

There could be no final peace settlement with France. For one thing, the Gascons were — quite literally — up in arms against the suggestion that they should be removed from their allegiance to England. The idea that they should have a lord in Bordeaux instead of one, far away, in Westminster did not sit at all well with them, and nor did they want to be answerable to King Charles of France.

My Uncle Gloucester — who was suddenly a fierce advocate for the King's prerogative and authority — told everyone that would listen to him that the men of Guienne were rebels and traitors, and must be put down by force of arms. This was quite impracticable, of course, as well as ridiculous. Far from being rebels, these fellows were *insisting* that they remained Richard's subjects.

The result was that there had to be another temporary truce, and my father and my Uncle Lancaster (but not my other uncle on this occasion) were sent off to negotiate it. Not that any difficulty was envisaged, for the French wanted peace as much as we did, if not more. Until quite recently, their King Charles had been much the same as other men. Now he was beset by a malady of his mind. Sometimes he was entirely lucid, but when he was not he imagined himself to be made of glass, or made violent attacks on his attendants, swearing they were assassins, or on his wife, claiming that he did not know her. His brothers and uncles took over the government when he was unfit to rule, but were far too busy quarrelling among themselves to want to fight us into the bargain.

The embassy set off, although not without first a great feast in celebration of its departure and various ceremonies, including a sermon — by Archbishop Arundel of all priests! — on the virtues of peace and concord. I marvelled that the chapel roof did not fall about his ears.

They had, I suppose, been gone for a week or two when word came to the King from Leicester that my Aunt Lancaster had died suddenly, unexpectedly, and we were all obliged to put on black again.

*

We were still in Lent, of course, which is a doleful enough time without having to wear mourning. I have never cared for the sight of myself in black (an unfortunate disadvantage as matters have turned out over the years) although there have been many anxious to tell me it suits my colouring. Perhaps it does. Then again, I have never thought of myself as any great beauty, certainly not when standing next to the likes of Alianore, or even my stepmother, Joanne, her sister. My nose is that shade too long, my eyelids are too heavy — in that respect I could be King Richard's own sister — my mouth is too large to be fashionable and I am a trifle too tall for a woman. All this, swathed in black, is nothing to admire. My hair is my best point, but of course, one cannot display *that* to the world.

    I had never been close to my aunt, and I will not pretend that I wept over the loss. I was of course sorry to receive such news of her, and it is certain one must show the proper respect for the dead, and say the appropriate prayers. It is a duty, it is expected and it is right. There could be no funeral of course, not in my uncle's absence abroad, and my aunt had to stay above ground until his instructions were known. That it would be an elaborate and costly business I did not doubt. His pride would allow no less, and although he had never even pretended to love her, she had brought him his claim to Castile. To give him his due, he was too well-bred, too steeped in courtesy to forget such a service.

***

Chapter 10
April — August 1394

Thomas and I returned to Caversham for a time. Philippa Fitzwalter had written to say that our daughter was unwell, and we were both concerned enough to hurry back as quickly as horses could carry us.

As it proved, Philippa's fears were exaggerated beyond all reason, and by the time we reached Caversham the child was well again, and her nurses were anxious to assure me there had never been cause for concern. Philippa, who was red-eyed and claimed she had not slept for a week, told the very opposite tale. It made for an awkward hour, because when all was said and done she was Thomas's cousin, and the nurses but low-born Welsh girls. Yet all my instincts told me that the nurses had the right of it. I gave them all a suitable gift, the finest, several ells of rich scarlet cloth, naturally going to Philippa in honour of her rank. Any ruffled feathers were soon smoothed. I could not be angry with Philippa — she had fallen into panic and confusion, and caused us some unnecessary worry, but she had meant well.

In any event, we remained at Caversham for a time as there was no particular reason to hurry back. Thomas was still recruiting his retinue for Ireland, but he could as well sign and seal the contracts where we were as he could at court, indeed in some ways it was easier, for in our own house we could receive knights and esquires more fittingly, and there was plenty of space for our clerks to prepare the indentures that set out what lesser men, archers, spearmen and the like each must bring with him, and what pay he should receive for his trouble. Thomas was also making his personal preparations for the campaign, so that he seemed to be forever in armour or practising combat out in the park with any fellow who was available. His horses, his pavilions, his stores of everything essential from chapel furniture to horse blankets — all had to be carefully checked and the details recorded on a roll. He even needed a new banner now that he had changed his arms, and we had a skilled craftsman out from Reading to do the necessary painting at eight pence a day, plus all the cost of materials.

We had left the court at Langley, but now it was at Sheen again, as I learned from Queen Anne's occasional letters to me, each new communication hinting at our return with less subtlety than the one before. It is not sensible, or courteous, to wait upon command in such circumstances. In any event, the Garter Feast, delayed by Easter, would soon be upon us, and we had a duty to attend that, unless there was a very good reason not to do so.

We returned in some style, with Thomas's new banner flying above our company, the largest riding-household we had so far possessed, all splendid in bright new liveries, the knights and gentlemen with bejewelled collars of our livery about their necks and looking quite splendid. I myself rode in the splendour of my new carriage, which was as fine as my mother's had been, but all the better for being new-minted, with five horses, chosen according to my fancy with no two of the same colour, the equipage guided by two young and handsome postilions. If it was not as comfortable as riding a horse, still less than being conveyed by water, it more than satisfied my pride.

So we appeared at Windsor, where the feast of St. George took place with all its usual magnificence and I stood nearer to the Queen than ever and was much contented. In the jousts that followed next day, Thomas did more than well, and he wore such armour as he had never owned before, designed for this work and not for the commonplace of war. The mere sight of him made my heart leap, as did the certain knowledge that there were others watching with me who envied me in my possession. For he was mine, not just by marriage but by those strange invisible strings that grow in the heart and bind. God help any creature that dared try to take him, I thought! She would know my vengeance. Better still, she would know his contempt. My sister Margaret Ferrers had been right

Hanley Castle

when she said he was *proud* of me. I could not understand why I had been so slow to see it, nor can I tell you on what day it was that I realised it. The truth is we had both, for different reasons, thought ourselves unworthy of the other. Now we knew we were as one.

From Windsor, we travelled on to Sheen, and there the court settled, with Thomas and me at the heart of it, as high in favour as we could wish to be. Often, we found ourselves visiting *La Neyt*, which was as much a distinction as it had been in the old days, the only difference being that the company, apart from Richard and Anne themselves, was naturally rather different. Indeed, most of our former companions were dead, one way or another. Robert de Vere, for example, had been killed during a boar hunt in Flanders.

The King still spoke of him occasionally, but it was notable that he did not do so except in such privacy as *La Neyt* provided. He would not, for example, mention him in the presence of any of his uncles, not even my father. Yet he had not forgotten. I realised that now.

What was more to the point, he had not forgiven either. He'd begun to talk of vengeance. Only, as yet, in the company of those he trusted most. He would speak of it before my lord and me, but if Thomas Mowbray happened to be in the room the subject was never mentioned. Oh, yes, Mowbray was forgiven. Some nights he would be with us in *La Neyt*, playing cards with us and dancing with the Queen, but if he thought he was one of our fellowship, he was not.

All was very well with us, until the evil day came. A day forever accursed. Worse than that day in the Tower when Richard was all but deposed, worse even than the day of Burley's execution.

It came without warning, like a thunderbolt out of a cloudless sky.

It was the first week of June. The evening began like many another. Thomas and I were among those chosen to take a rere-supper with the King and Queen in *La Neyt*. My brother Edward was of the company, and so was Alianore, though her husband was not. Where March was I am not sure, nor did I much mark his absence. I presumed he was either with his cronies, drinking himself into a stupor, or making arrangements for Ireland.

Perinne Whitney was with us, for she was still one of Anne's ladies, one of very few from the old days and also her husband, Thomas Clanvowe, one the King's most trusted esquires. Like Perinne he came from the Marches. He was a little older than us, a courteous fellow with a plain honest face. I thought him very ordinary at first. Thomas was talking of his plans for recovering his ancestors' lands — speaking judiciously because he was uncertain of how far the King's favour would stretch — and Clanvowe made some sharp remark about the legal process which made me wonder if he was trained in the law.

That particular conversation did not continue long. All the men were going to Ireland, and it was inevitable they should talk of the campaign and what was to be expected. Richard told us he had no intent to be oppressive. That he sought only to placate the land. If there were just grievances, he would hear them. If some of his officers on the island were abusing their power, he would not hesitate to remove them if they could not be amended. Ireland had not been a profitable possession for years, but it was part of his inheritance and if he could set the place in order and thereby restore peace he was certain the revenues would recover.

We were not there for business, but to eat, drink and play cards, and gradually the talk turned to lighter matters, and the coins began to change hands. (There is little point in games of cards unless money is staked, and the stakes must be high enough to make the game interesting, yet low enough not to be ruinous.)

For once, the cards fell in my favour, and I began to make a serious profit. This was so unusual I could scarcely believe my fortune. At first, therefore, I was too occupied to see that Anne was in discomfort. It was Alianore who mentioned it, Alianore who urged her to take another cup of wine. The wine made no difference. I noticed that that there was sweat starting from Anne's forehead, as though she had a fever.

I laid down my cards. That Anne was ill was obvious — equally obvious was her reluctance to admit anything was wrong. We had to persuade her. Richard now also saw that she was not well. He did not exactly command her to bed, but his advice was very persuasive. She struggled to her feet, and made her slow way to her bedchamber. Alianore, Perinne and I went with her, of course, and when the door was firmly closed behind us Anne admitted that the pain was as much as she could bear, and growing worse, low down in her belly.

We undressed her, and there was blood on her shift from her secret parts, but nothing that looked serious. We persuaded her onto the bed, and tried to settle her, but she cried out with the pain. It seemed to me she was miscarrying, and that was a sorry business, but one she had endured before. For a time she seemed a little eased, and I noticed that her belly was scarcely rounded. She cannot be as far on as she imagined, I thought.

What was to be done? I wished we had Lady Mohun to lead us, but she was far away on one of her own manors. The other two looked at me as if they expected me to instruct them, which was strange given that I was the youngest person in the room. Alianore looked as if she was going to be sick and Perinne was in tears, clutching Anne's hand as she sought to comfort her.

'We had best send for a midwife,' I said. 'Perhaps a physician. Better to be safe.'

I went back to the men and told Richard what was needed. Clanvowe needed no instruction. He was through the door, hurrying to the ferry before the King opened his mouth. Richard stood up.

'I will see her,' he said.

There was no gainsaying that, so I followed him into the

bedchamber. Anne held out her hand to him and he hurried to her.

'It is nothing,' she said. 'Just a little pain.'

I knew she was hiding the truth from him, seeking to reassure. That was Anne's way. She was, I think, more concerned for him than for herself. The pain was none so small though. I could see that from her face, from her gritted teeth. We gave her more wine and she drank it down right willingly.

After a long time — perhaps a full hour — the midwife arrived and I thanked all the saints for their mercy. Where Clanvowe had found her I know not. Perhaps from the village. She was a small woman, with brown, wrinkled skin, probably older than the ages of Alianore, Perinne and I put together. Her first act was to shoo the King of England out of the room as though he was a troublesome child.

'Men!' she spat out. 'Always under the foot. Now, let me look at you, lady.'

She examined Anne very thoroughly, asked questions, and made a strange humming noise. I think this was for reassurance.

She drew me aside. Again, why she chose me above Alianore I do not know.

'This is no miscarrying,' she said, bluntly. 'If we cut her open, I doubt very much we should find a child in her belly. Not even one barely formed, like a blob of jelly. This is something other. It reminds me of something I saw when I was young, learning this trade. If I am right, there is nothing to be done but send for a priest to confess her and then give her poppy juice. Lots of poppy juice. This is bad.'

My blood ran cold.

'Are you sure?' I demanded. 'Before I tell the King?'

She shrugged. 'I am not sure. I think she should see a priest though, and that right swiftly.'

At that moment, there was a knock on the door. The physician had arrived. He was one of those belonging to the court and looked as if he had been plucked from sleep, as he probably had at that hour. He was bare-headed, except for a little coif, and his hair was an unruly tangle of pure white. Once more I thanked the saints. I hoped and prayed that he would say this was nothing. A mere gripe of the stomach. That a purge would set all well.

Instead, he talked quietly with the midwife, taking her into a corner. I could not hear a word they were saying, but at length they went to Anne together and repeated the examination, except the physician did not pry into her secret parts.

The man looked grave. He did not say a word to us, but went to report to the King. A moment later I heard my cousin's voice raised in anger and disbelief. He came bounding into the room again, and stood by the door, staring at Anne.

'Is there nothing you can do for her?' he demanded of the physician.

That man wrung his hands, as if mimicking Archbishop Arundel. 'Pray,' he said bleakly.

*

Of the rest of that nightmare, I remember very little, which is a mercy. Chaplains were fetched to her. Anne, unable to stand the pain longer, screamed for mercy. The midwife dosed her. Richard paced around, weeping, sometimes shouting. Thomas and the other men stood, staring, near the table where our discarded stakes still lay. No one knew what to say. For a time we knelt in prayer, Alianore and Perinne and I, and even the little midwife. Then, all at once, Anne died.

Hours later, I woke in my own bed. How I reached it, who undressed me, I have no idea to this day. It was full light, around noon, and Thomas was next to me, holding me. At first I thought it had all been an evil dream, but then I remembered. Anne was dead.

My cousin, my dear kind friend was gone. As I have said, I am not given to weeping, but I wept like a little child after a whipping.

'I must go to the King,' Thomas said at last. I thought he was going to say more, but he only shook his head and repeated his words. 'I must go to the King.'

It was duty calling him, so I let him go. In truth, I was not altogether sorry to be left alone with my thoughts, to be allowed time to compose myself. Nothing will ever be the same again, I told myself. Richard will run mad. He will be like King Charles of France, who conceives himself to be made of glass. Perhaps worse. God help us all.

There were many foolish rumours about Anne's death. One was that she died of plague. Nonsense! At least one of us would have died with her, if not all of us. Another was that she was poisoned — Richard himself was inclined to say this in private, as I learned some time later from my brother. How could it be? Anne did not eat or drink anything that the rest of us did not, so it would have to be a very subtle poison, as none of us was ill, not even mildly, let alone killed. No, I believe it was some problem with her woman's parts, something that gave way and killed her. Perhaps the problem lay with the mixtures she took to aid her fertility. I cannot be sure, and nor can anyone else. Perhaps it was just God's will.

*

Thomas sent me back to Caversham. He himself remained with the court, to be of what service he could be to the King. Even before I left I heard of another sorrow in the family. Harry Bolingbroke's wife, Mary, had died in her latest childbirth, just a few days before the Queen.

I suppose I ought to have travelled to Leicester, to her funeral and that of my aunt, for they were held but a day apart. I can only say I lacked the stomach for it, though of course I included them in my prayers. How could I not? I had left Caversham full of pride and hope for the future. Now there was nothing but sorrow. Anne's funeral was to follow, and I gathered from what my lord wrote to me — he did not quite write every day, but very often — it was to be a very great ceremony. Richard wanted it to exceed the precedent of that given to our grandmother, because Anne was an Emperor's daughter.

There was also to be a great and expensive tomb at Westminster, Thomas told me, depicting them both lying hand-in-hand. Richard had decided the one he had prepared for himself at Langley was not glorious enough. Of course the new tomb would take years to make, but the King wanted the best, at whatever cost.

Part of the delay was that that the entire nobility of England was to be summoned to attend. All of us, no excuses accepted. Not just the King's close family, not even just distant cousins, but every last baron, every last baron's wife. They were to travel up to Sheen even if they lived in Northumberland, or Cornwall, or some remote corner of the Marches. Even if they were elderly, or infirm. Richard's command was absolute.

I thought of those messengers, sergeants-at-arms, perhaps even knights, carrying the letters to every corner of the kingdom, of the heralds who were no doubt dusting off old rolls giving precedents from previous ceremonies, of the work of the King's household, procuring black cloth and wax torches in unprecedented quantity. How busy everyone must be! Here I was, red-eyed, moping in idleness. I had prayed, prayed until my knees ached, and I had Masses said, but even so, I felt useless.

At last the day came when I must travel to Sheen, where we had been ordered to gather. Once more I travelled in my new carriage, but this time not in pride but in sorrow, clad from head to foot in black, as were all my people. I took Philippa Fitzwalter with me, for her husband had ordered her to appear. For once, she was almost taciturn, and I was grateful for that. I could not have borne her endless prattle on such a journey, and might well have tipped her out of the carriage.

As we grew close to Sheen, the roads became more and more crowded, and I realised that mine was not the only retinue heading there, nor even the most important. At last we were brought to a halt, and for a time could not move at all. When we edged forward again it was at less than walking pace, and we had barely started before we had to draw to a stop again. Various fellows, some in the King's livery, were riding back and forth along the road, trying to establish order, but it was hopeless.

At last we reached the palace, but I was not surprised to find that even in the courtyard all was chaos. Such a crowd that it might have been one of those games of football that involve a whole town, one half against another, save that no one was trying to kick their neighbour. There was a babble of voices, many of them loud and protesting, men dismounting and throwing their reins at servants, women hectoring their waiting-women as they descended from carriages and litters or were assisted from horseback. The nobility of England, or some of them, gathered together, impatient, confused, all expecting the King's officers to receive and lodge them on the instant.

I should not have been surprised to find myself directed to a pavilion in the park, given the press of folk. As it was, one of my lord's men had been placed to watch out for me, and made his way over to the carriage as quickly as was possible given the circumstances. He guided me inside, where I found the crowds were just as thick as they were outside, and by stairs and passages until he came to a particular room with a shield of my lord's arms displayed above the door. Thomas was within, working on some letter, but he put down his pen at once and hastened to receive me.

It was a small room, or at least it was when it had to accommodate both of us and our personal attendants, but we were fortunate enough to be accommodated at all, and not lying on a pallet in the hall or outside under canvas. There were the bed curtains to give a degree of privacy, but that was all. However, I was so glad to see Thomas that I cared nothing for a cramped lodging.

Anne lay in the palace chapel, surrounded by more burning candles than I could count, so she seemed to be bathed in a light brighter than day. Once again I found myself kneeling, praying for her soul, but this time surrounded by many others, some of them with tears streaming down their faces. One of those present was my Uncle Lancaster, much to my surprise. He was, of course, on the other side of the aisle, but that made it all the easier to watch him, and it seemed to me he was in genuine distress, as though he had lost a daughter of his own. I had thought him far above any display of emotion, yet here he was, bawling like a child. It astonished me, but there he was.

*

Next morning, very early, we were somehow marshalled into a great procession. The heralds and pursuivants bustled up and down, ensuring no one was in the wrong place, quietly (and very respectfully) adjusting the order of our going where it was necessary. How they managed it I do not know, for they could not possibly have known everyone by sight and there was little to distinguish between us. No heraldry was on display, and we must have all looked much the same beneath our black, hooded cloaks. Yet somehow it was done, and with very little fuss or argument.

Then we walked, all of us, behind Anne's hearse, led by the King, line after line of us, all the way to St. Paul's in London. It was no small walk for the elders, those troubled by the infirmities of age. Yet we were all there, young and old. All but for two. The Earl and Countess of Arundel. Where they were, no one knew, but their absence was noticed and, when the ceremonies of the day were concluded, much talked about.

Nor did they appear on the morrow, when the procession formed up once more, this time to follow Anne to Westminster for the final time. The Londoners came out in force to watch us pass, for

Anne had been well-loved by the citizens. They remembered the occasion, two years earlier, when Richard had quarrelled with their leaders, and forfeited their liberties for a time. It had been Anne who had knelt before the King to plead for them to be forgiven. Of course, it had all been part of a reconciliation ceremony, with everything agreed and arranged in advance, but if the Lord Mayor and such folk knew that, the common people of the city did not.

At last we came to Westminster Abbey, for the final ceremonies. My father's wife, Joanne, took first place among the ladies, as was her right, for there was no one alive of higher rank on the distaff side of the aisle. I wondered how she would bear herself, for she was still but fourteen, and I remembered — from my complacent seniority of eighteen summers — just how awkward one felt at that age when thrust into prominence. She bore herself well, uncommonly well, with every sign of dignity and assurance. I am sure she had been well-advised, not only by her mother but by the heralds, but even so, she proved herself worthy of her place.

I stood a little behind, among my cousins. It was, of course, an occasion of great solemnity, with no scope for conversation, not even of the most hushed kind. We prayed, and made our responses, and at the appropriate time went forward to make our offerings in due order of precedence.

All at once, in the middle of these ceremonies, Arundel made his appearance, bringing with him his wife, she who had been Philippa Mortimer, the Countess of Pembroke, my cousin and adversary of old. No one said anything, of course, but there was a strange sound, made of the in-taking of many breaths all at once. It was an outrage. Across the aisle I saw that my Uncle Lancaster had drawn himself erect and was white with fury. My father was scarcely less outraged, and even Uncle Gloucester looked displeased. (He was very good at looking displeased. I had seen that expression many times.) The King scarcely seemed to notice the interruption. I believe he scarcely knew where he was, or cared.

Lady Arundel came thrusting among our ranks. She knew better than to grapple with me, but one of my young Gloucester cousins was thrust rudely aside. Of course, no one made any remark. Tacitly, we were in agreement that there should be no stir at such a time.

What was the reason for their delay I never knew, but there are times when there is no excuse for lateness, and this was certainly one of them. It was an insult in itself.

The ceremony proceeded, and, I must admit, it seemed endless. Arundel's brother, the Archbishop, spoke a sermon. It was a generous one, that related all Anne's virtues, and elaborated on them at very considerable length.

Suddenly, there was a stir across the aisle. Lord Arundel had stepped forward from his place and approached the King. What was he about? I could not guess, but having at first been ignored he began to tug at Richard's sleeve, like a child importuning its nurse for a drink or a toy.

The silence was all but complete, so I was near enough to catch some of Arundel's words. (He was, of course, not a man who spoke in whispers.) It was something to the effect that he had urgent business and begged to be excused. I could scarcely believe my ears. That anyone, let alone a great lord with many years of experience in life, could be so crass!

For a moment, Richard simply stared at him. I doubt he could believe his ears any more than I could. Then he snatched a staff from one of the vergers and struck Arundel with it, across his head. Not once, not twice, but several times, very hard, so that the fellow fell to the floor. What was worse was that his blood flowed onto the tiles, polluting one of the most holy places in all England. They were but a stride or two away from the Confessor's shrine.

It was my Uncle Lancaster who dragged the King off Arundel, and he did this very gently, while the rest of us stood around, gaping in disbelief. For a moment my eyes met those of Lady Arundel, and I saw that even she was appalled, although whether by her husband's actions or the consequences I cannot say.

'Get that man out of my sight!' Richard's voice set off echoes in the silence of the great abbey. 'Now, before I kill him.'

Some men hurried forward, knights of the household for the most part. First, they had to hoist Arundel to his feet, for he was barely conscious.

'To the Tower with him!' barked my Uncle Lancaster, taking charge with his usual ready assumption of authority. 'See him safe lodged until the King's further pleasure be known.'

No one contradicted him. Not even Richard. In truth, I was not sure he quite comprehended what was happening. All around was a stunned silence. We all looked at one another, but no one spoke. My father stepped forward, gently removed the bloodied staff from Richard's hand, as if this was all part of the ceremony. He handed it back to the verger, who was quite literally trembling with shock. The return of his symbol of office seemed to restore some part of the man's wits and he backed away, bowing almost in half.

The bishops, of whom there were many in attendance, gathered together in a huddle, whispering. There could be little doubt of the subject of their conclave. The abbey was desecrated, and would need to be reconsecrated before the service went any further. Someone though, was required to explain this to the King. This duty fell to Archbishop Arundel, who shuffled across and whispered.

'Do what must be done!' Richard said, impatiently, loudly enough to allow us to hear. The Archbishop bowed low and backed away, looking shamefaced and wringing his hands in despair. I almost felt sorry for the man. He must have felt the humiliation keenly.

It takes a surprisingly long time to reconsecrate a great church. First, they had to find some unfortunate fellow from among the abbey servants to clean up the blood. The bishops and their acolytes kept finding splashes in all manner of infeasible places, and until every last drop was scrubbed away they could not even make a start. It was well after midnight before the obsequies could be concluded. Before we reached our beds, it was beginning to grow light again.

***

Chapter 11
August 1394 -November 1395

I had imagined the Irish war might be postponed, if not cancelled, but King Richard soon made it clear that it would be conducted as planned, and so all the arrangements continued to be made.

Arundel was released after a week or so, having found sureties, and removed himself and his wife to one of his more distant castles. He had no place in the Irish campaign, even though he was one of our most experienced warriors.

Nor was my cousin, Harry Bolingbroke, among those required for the expedition. He was to remain in England, neither attending the King to Ireland nor going with his father to Guienne. For my Uncle Lancaster was to journey to Bordeaux and it was my lord father who was to be left to govern England in Richard's place.

I came upon Harry at Westminster in the aftermath of Anne's funeral. I condoled with him on his loss of Mary, and promised that I would pray for her. He thanked me, saying something to the effect that he was glad someone had remembered her when *most* had quite forgotten. He was courteous in his dealings with me, but I sensed an underlying bitterness. The very next morning, he left with all his followers. I saw him go, bent low in the saddle, looking like a banished man.

Thomas and I were not so far behind him. In our case, we moved slowly west. First back to Caversham. Then on to Hanley Castle. Then, to Cardiff, going part of the way by water. At each point more men were mustered, until we had not so much a household as an armed camp. It seemed to me that scarcely a day passed without Thomas greeting some knight or esquire who was to follow him, or long hours of practice with weapons.

At Cardiff the other contingents began to arrive, the first led by my brother, Edward. He looked extremely pleased with himself, and I must admit his men were well-arrayed and kept well in hand. In the outer court of the castle, encircled by a curtain wall, there was a good deal of space, and his fellows were able to set up their pavilions and cooking fires close to our own people, yet with sufficient room to avoid quarrels.

Edward was Admiral of England now, having replaced Arundel in that appointment almost as soon as Richard had regained his power. He knew about as much of ships as I did, or as my little daughter did for that matter, but it was an office of profit, as any dispute between seafarers was settled in the Admiral's court. Not that my brother sat in judgement, of course, he left such tasks to his underlings. It added to his status though, and his power and authority seemed to grow by the day. I remembered his boasting that he would become high in Richard's counsels. Now he was.

The King arrived last, bringing the main body with my Uncle Gloucester. (I wondered where March and Edmund were, but soon learned they were taking ship with their men from Chester, or some such place.) It was a surprisingly convivial company. Richard was not himself, of course. He said very little, and there were times when it seemed to me his thoughts were not with us, were not even on his Irish war, but were living somewhere with Anne.

He had altered the style of his arms. He had impaled the arms of the Confessor with those of England and France. Why he had done this I do not know. Perhaps to make amends to the saint for the bloodshed near his shrine. He had also ordered that all who bore the royal arms with a mark of cadence — my father and my uncles, for example — must also make the change.

I suppose it made work for painters and embroiderers, but the banners looked very strange, until you got used to the new look.

Richard drew me aside for a moment.

'When I return from Ireland, do not be surprised if I ask you to return to my court,' he said. 'I am minded to ask you to perform a service for me.'

I must have looked bewildered. He gave me a little, sad smile and hastened on: 'You need not fear. It is nothing to your dishonour. That part of me died with Anne. Promise me that you will do as I ask.'

'Of course,' I said. 'I am your Grace's servant, always.'

We sat long at table, and Hugh Bygge and his fellows presented us with a fine feast. At the conclusion there was a subtlety made of sugar, as much to look at as to eat, showing two ships. One was made to seem to be sinking below the waves and was meant to be a defeated Irish vessel.

Edward and Thomas Mowbray were in competition to say the most, and both were doing their best to flatter Richard. There were no quarrels though. Even Uncle Gloucester seemed content for once — perhaps because he knew he would soon have plenty of opportunities to kill people.

The wine flowed freely, and after a time I thought it better to leave them to it, so they might speak freely and enjoy themselves. Richard granted permission amiably enough, but there was pain in his eyes and I suspected he had had quite sufficient of the conversation. It was just that he lacked the spirit to say so, or to impose his wishes on the company. He was a man so sunk in melancholy he knew not what to do with himself.

Thomas was late in bed that night, and too well-refreshed to do more than sleep. He also had to leave my bed early, for the entire army was to set off as soon as could be contrived. I overslept, woke in an empty bed, and had to be content to say my farewells on the castle steps, in the presence of half the archers and men-at-arms in England. I knew it would be many months before I set eyes on any of them again.

Hanley Castle

*

In the interim, I withdrew to Hanley Castle, where I was most at my ease. Had I been myself I should have relished presiding over Thomas's Council and managing his estates. As it was, I found it an unpleasant and tedious duty, and left as much as I dared to the officers he had left to advise me, not all of whom I trusted as much as I should have liked. A man may be gently-born, even a knight, but still a thief by inclination and an abuser of any power put into his hands. I knew this, but could not find the energy to assert myself.

I had my daughter; I had my dogs and horses; and I had my women, including Lady Fitzwalter. That was more than enough company. I had thought to spend this time riding about the country in my carriage, making pilgrimages to Gloucester and Our Lady of Worcester, so that people could see how splendid I had become. However, I did not have the spirit for it. I rarely went even so far as our park, except to exercise my horses.

Elisabeth decided to pay me a visit. Perhaps she had grown weary of waiting for me to come to her, although we had exchanged occasional letters, on matters of business as much as anything. (Now that Thomas was of age, she had leased her Glamorgan dower lands to us — I say 'us' because Thomas had insisted it be in jointure in case any ill befell him. This meant she had an assured income for her lands there, while at the same time the management of the lands was simplified. It was an arrangement that benefited us all.)

As I said, she came.

'You are looking very wan,' she said, taking my wrists as if that would cure the difficulty. 'Are you breeding?'

I shook my head. Assuredly I was not, though I wished I were.

'I can see you are not in good sorts. You must not worry about Thomas. I'm sure he will not come to harm in Ireland. The wild Irish barely have armour themselves, and have not the means to hurt one who wears good harness. It is not like fighting the French. My cousin

Berkeley says it will be more like cutting down unarmed peasants. A slaughter, not a war.' She frowned, as if the thought troubled her. 'I do not say it is dishonourable, Constance. Never that. But it is not like fighting the French.'

'I have evil dreams,' I said. 'They keep me awake.'

It was true. Often they involved Anne. It was as if she was still alive. Then I would wake with a jerk, and remember, and find myself unable to sleep for sorrow.

At other times, I found myself back in the times when the King had been in danger. Or I would see Burley's execution again. In the dream, it would all seem as real as if I were living it.

No matter how long I prayed, no matter what offerings I made, no matter how much I fasted, these wretched nightmares would return. Sometimes I might escape them for as long as a week, and think myself free of them. The respite never lasted.

'Would you like me to stay here for a time?' she asked.

To my surprise, I found myself answering that I would. I was grateful to have her there, to take some of the weight from my shoulders. So low were my spirits that we lived together for some weeks in complete amity, and it must have seemed to her that by some sorcery or other I had been transformed into the meek, submissive daughter her heart had always craved. I don't recall a single cross word between us, so willingly did I assent to every proposal she made. If I was not sick of my body — and it may be that I was — there was certainly a sickness in my heart and in my soul.

Part of it, of course, was that I missed Thomas, in every possible way. We had been apart before, of course, even in the time I had truly been his wife. Even at the beginning, he had no sooner bedded me than he had been off to Prussia. Yet this, somehow, was not like those other times. It was far worse.

It was Elisabeth who suggested we make a pilgrimage together to Our Lady of Worcester. It is certain to lift your spirits, she said. If your conscience is troubled, it may serve to ease that burden too.

It is no great journey from Hanley Castle. I could have gone on foot — it was less of a distance than my walk behind Anne's coffin from Sheen to London — but out of respect for Elisabeth's years I decided we should go in my carriage. The horses were certainly in need of some work, and my women would make less fuss. I also decided to take only the smallest of escorts — for once, it was not my intent to make a show, but to go modestly. Or as modestly as one can in a great, brightly-painted carriage that blocks the road and scrapes the stones of every bridge it crosses.

When we arrived in Worcester I saw at once that mine was not the only carriage in town. Another was waiting just outside the cathedral, its canvas roof bright with paintings of the bear and ragged staff. Lady Warwick! It could be none other. I glanced at Elisabeth and saw her face was quite composed. It was as if she had planned this meeting. Perhaps she had. She was not on ill terms with Warwick and his lady, counted them among her friends. I had not kept track of all the messengers who had come to Hanley and left again with letters from her. It had not even occurred to me. Now I began to suspect that at least one of her missives had been sent to Warwick Castle. I could already feel my spine stiffening, my head tilting backwards. No knight entering the lists was more prepared for battle than I was at that moment.

We met Lady Warwick before we reached the shrine. It was inevitable in the circumstances. She greeted us courteously enough, and Elisabeth was so amiable in her replies that my suspicion grew that this meeting had been contrived.

Margaret Warwick was a good deal younger and less long-faced than her husband, who thankfully was not in her company, but, as she explained, back at their manor of Salwarp. I suppose she was about fifteen years my elder, and perhaps twenty years Elisabeth's junior. She had a kindly face and a gentle voice, and it was annoyingly difficult to dislike her.

She had come with her son, whom they had had the effrontery to name Richard, as though they were loyal subjects; a hawk-faced brat of about twelve or thirteen with restless feet. (I was surprised he was still at home, not away serving as someone's squire or page.) He was Elisabeth's godson, and, as emerged from the conversation, was already betrothed to Elizabeth Berkeley. It was clear that Elisabeth saw this as a good thing. She was too purblind to see that it was an alliance set up against Thomas and me, and very much against our family interests, designed to keep our power in check.

It was agreed we should dine together. At least, Elisabeth and Lady Warwick agreed it, and, as we were in a church, I did not trust myself to speak against the proposal.

After Elisabeth and I had visited the shrine and made our offerings, we met with her in the Prior's Lodging, where high-born pilgrims are always made welcome, and where the table always groans below the weight of food and drink placed upon it. They were courteous enough to insist that I sit above them both, which was proper, but more than I had expected to gain without contest. Then we set to our meat, for which I was more than ready, having fasted since the previous evening in honour of our pilgrimage.

My elders soon began to discuss young Elizabeth Berkeley, whom Elisabeth had left at Tewkesbury, in the care of a governess. They soon agreed that we should all go there together to enable the hawk-faced brat to enjoy the company of his future wife. (I'm sure the lad wanted nothing more!) We could all then go to Tewkesbury Abbey and venerate the relics there.

Lady Warwick turned to me. 'I know that your husband and mine have had disagreements, but I believe most of them are caused by other men. John Russell, for example. An ambitious man, my lady, but also a great troublemaker. The petty quarrels of men like that, their breaches of the law, ought not to be a cause of enmity between great families.'

'It is the business of ladies to be peacemakers,' Elisabeth added, 'and it lies within our proper sphere.'

'My business, madam my Mother,' I said tartly, 'is to obey my husband and support him in all his purposes.'

There was silence for a few moments.

'However,' I added, 'I do have another suggestion. That is that we extend our pilgrimage and go, all together, to King Edward at Gloucester.'

This time the silence was profound. Elisabeth's nose wrinkled.

At last Lady Warwick spoke. 'I'm very willing to go with you. However, I'm expected back at Salwarp this night, and there is not the time to travel so far and back. I shall write to you, and agree a date.'

I thought it strange, this sudden need to be back at Salwarp. It had not been a problem when it had been a matter of a visit to Tewkesbury, and I did not see how that could have been accomplished in the day. I might have won back to Hanley, but she would certainly have had to travel to Salwarp in darkness. It was surely more likely she had thought to lodge with Elisabeth.

It was obvious, when I thought about it, that she wanted to seek instruction from her husband.

*

I was not greatly surprised when no Beauchamp liveryman came hastening to Hanley Castle, letter clutched in his hand. A week passed. Then two. I knew Warwick's answer by the lack of one.

I decided to make pilgrimage to Gloucester alone. Though, of course, not quite alone. I took with me my entire household, save a handful of folk to hold the castle, and also invited many of those in the county who had showed themselves friendly to my lord and me. Not everyone responded, for some offered excuses or proved to be on their lands in another county. We still made up an impressive procession though, and I called at Tewkesbury to see whether I could persuade Elisabeth and her people to join us. I felt a demonstration of family solidarity would be no bad thing.

She gave me dinner, but said she was too unwell to travel. I knew this as an excuse, as she was not the sort of person to be ill, but I did not press her. What was the point?

I did not return to Hanley Castle until the following day, and found a letter waiting for me. Not from Lady Warwick, but from Thomas. Letters, I had found, did not pass easily from Ireland. If the wind was adverse, ships simply could not make the crossing, for it was far too hazardous. Moreover, he was not on the coast, but somewhere in the interior of the country. That was almost as remote as if he had been in the wilds of Prussia.

I was glad to have this word of him, and hoped it might contain some indication of an early return. In that at least, I was disappointed. He said the campaign was going well, but that the King expected to stay there over winter, perhaps until after Easter. He wanted to be quite sure the island was settled in peace.

He spoke of missing me, and the postscript at the end, written in his own hand, was warm enough to make me blush. It was, however, small compensation for his absence for so many months.

*

It was a long, cold, hard winter. For weeks we lay under a blanket of snow; the roads, at times, barely passable; the river so swollen that more than once it broke its banks and spilled out over parts of the manor. We had to bury wandering beggars who had frozen to death, either on the main road or, in one case, far out on the Chase. Even some of my own people went hungry, their stores all but exhausted, for it had been a thin harvest that year. Crops had been damaged first by excessive heat and then by weeks of unrelenting rain. Some came to the castle to be fed, and received a dole. Others were too proud, and simply starved to death in their cottages, unable to withstand the cold, unwilling to ask for help, either from me, their priest, or their neighbours.

My father, in his capacity as Keeper of England, commanded a parliament to gather, for the King had need of fresh funds. My Uncle Gloucester came home to sit in it and report on the campaign, but my lord remained in Ireland. My uncle brought letters with him, including one for me from Thomas and another from my brother. Eventually these reached me, borne by a man in York livery. I gathered that the fighting was over, that it was now all diplomacy and agreement. Richard had taken many of the Irish chiefs into his peace. He had even knighted several of them. Now he was trying to amend their manners by persuading them to wear English clothes and abolishing the strange custom they had whereby all men from the chief to the lowest slave in his household (for these men still had slaves!) all ate together at the same large table, without distinction of rank.

Lent went by, and Easter, and land began to grow warm and green again. Then came May Day, when my women and I rose before dawn to gather dew in the woods for our complexions and flowers with which to make garlands; there was a maypole in the village, and a feast for all who came to the castle. Everyone was drunk, whether they favoured cider, perry, ale or wine. As night fell there were bonfires, and our people danced around them, joyful to have survived the winter. I knew many babies would come into the world in nine months' time, for some did more in the woods than gather flowers.

Still there was no sign of Thomas. Then one morning, just as our great clock was striking the hour for dinner, there he was, leading his fellowship into the courtyard with no more fuss than if he had merely been away for the day to visit his mother at Tewkesbury.

I was down the stairs to the hall, out in the courtyard and at his stirrup before he could even dismount. It was disgraceful. I believe I actually broke into a run, and gave the household the sight of my shins, if not my knees, but I could not help it. What they thought of me, God knows, but at the time I didn't care.

Thomas was equally lacking in decorum. Before I knew it, he had dismounted and I was being swung in the air, like a child. Then we walked, clinging to one another, to the Great Chamber, where I had food and drink set before him, and where we ate in the company of all our principal people. I sent for our daughter, and Thomas sat her on his knee, remarked her growth, called her his jewel and fed her tasty pieces from our dish. Some of which she was prepared to accept, though I believe she scarcely knew who he was. It was all very contrary to the proper ordering of a dinner, but there was no one there to command us to more elevated behaviour.

There was also a great deal of talk, for Thomas and those fellows he had brought with him were naturally desirous to speak of their adventures in Ireland, and the strange sights they had seen, while there were those among his officers left at home who thought they had matters of business to bring before him that could not be left for another day. His chief attorney, for example, who had been pestering me for instructions on various matters for some weeks, now thought it would be profitable to pester Thomas.

My lord dealt with some of this, in between petting his daughter and sharing his anecdotes of Ireland, but when he had eaten and drunk his fill, and washed his hands in the silver basin brought to us for that purpose, he brought an abrupt end to it.

'Enough of talk for now,' he said. 'I must have a private conference with my lady before I decide anything further. Ladies and gentlemen, you will forgive me for the next few hours. After supper, when I have rested from my journey, I shall be at leisure, and ready to deal with whatever is brought before me.'

He gave me a glance that was quite frank in its meaning. We

retired to our bedchamber, pausing only to tell my women that they would not be required. Philippa, in particular, looked highly amused. It was well for him that I was in a receptive mood, for in another I might have thought myself humiliated.

Thomas closed the door behind us and bolted it, the bolt going home with a loud thud that reflected the force he had applied to the task.

'All those months in Ireland,' he said, 'I dreamed of nothing better than serving as your waiting-gentlewoman.'

'*Nothing* better?' I laughed.

'I had a very *particular* part of their duty in mind,' he said, archly.

He began his work by unpinning my headdress, and unwinding my hair from its coils. As he stood behind me and pressed close, his spare hand securing my waist, I received a very clear indication that his ambition did not end there, and that he possessed at least one faculty that my damsels lacked.

When at last both of us were sated — which took some time — we lay in companionable silence, both of us naked except for the rings on our fingers, both of us somewhat breathless but very content.

'You must tell me what you have been doing in my absence, *treschere*,' he said at last.

'I've scarcely been off the manor,' I said. 'Life has been very dull. Your mother stayed here with me for a time, and I was glad of her company, for I was low in spirits.'

'You must have been, if you were glad of my mother's companionship.' He grinned. 'You and she have rarely been in accord.'

'I don't deny she is a good woman. Or that she loves you very much. Nor can I deny that she guarded your estates through your minority, so well that no man in England could have done better. I respect her, Thomas. I would respect her even if she had done no more than bear you. I only wish I pleased her better.'

'You please *me* well enough. I may have given you evidence of that. Next time I go to war, I shall be very tempted to take you with me. I'd dress you as a boy and call you one of my squires, but I doubt anyone would be deceived.'

'I ought to play a game of love and pretend I have not missed you at all.' I believe I may have blushed. 'I cannot. It would make me a liar and I was not brought up to tell lies. The truth is I have often lain awake, thinking of you. This is no idle flattery. I've missed *this*. Having you at my side. Hearing your voice. Sleeping in the same bed. I must own myself a wicked, lustful creature. Quite shameless.'

'I may not stay here long,' he said, and laughed as my face fell. 'The King wants me back at his court. There is some talk of a Great Council I may be bidden to attend. Do not look so downcast! You are to come with me. For one thing, he has a purpose for you, as I gather you've been told. He also says he cannot bear the thought of a court without the presence of ladies, so you will not be alone.'

'He and Anne were so close he must feel he has lost a hand.'

'He speaks of little else.' He shook his head. 'No, that isn't true. I do him an injustice. When he was at leisure, perhaps. When it was late in the evening, and we had nothing to distract us but wine and dice, and when certain people were not about, *then* he talked of her.

'He was a different man in Ireland. He ordered the campaign very well — even Gloucester could not fault him, and I need not tell you that your uncle is no flatterer, nor slow to complain. We were in wild country at times, but he bore the hardships as well as any of us. When the Irish chiefs yielded, he could have humiliated them. Or hanged them from trees. Instead, he was conciliatory, even though they were entirely at his mercy. He gave them fair terms, as long as they did him homage. He even made knights of several of the more important. Not all agreed with that, but he said that although they were foes they were men of great courage, and deserved the honour.'

He fell silent for a moment, drew a breath. 'So they were, Constance. Even the chiefs were clad in indifferent mail, with not a piece of plate armour between them. As for their commons, most had no protection at all, not even leather, except perhaps for a small buckler. Our archers cut them down like driven deer. Yet, God knows, they were brave fighters and kept coming on, doing what they could. They had no chance. I was glad that the King let them down so lightly. He said all along that what he sought was peace and accord, that he would concede a great deal to achieve it. Well, achieve it he has. Though whether our Irish friends will really adopt English clothing and the English way of ordering their households, I very much doubt. They remind me of the Welsh. Proud people with their own ways. You cannot force them to be what they are not, any more than the French could force us to be French.'

*

That night, I woke from my sleep screaming, loud enough to bring the castle down around our ears.

Thomas, rudely awakened, put his arm about my shoulders, sought to comfort me, thinking I was struck by some sudden pain. He asked me what was amiss.

'A dream,' I explained, shuddering. 'An evil dream. I dreamed of Burley's death.'

(Except it was not Burley. It was *you*.)

I could scarcely believe that a man had so much blood in him.

*

We found the court at Leeds Castle in Kent, which is a very beautiful place, with the castle set in a lake and surrounded by a vast park. I found I was by no means the only woman in the King's company. The one highest in rank was Joanne, my father's Duchess, who was now living with him and, for the time being, taking first place in all ceremonies. She greeted me with warmth, and seemed happier than I expected her to be. From what I could gather from her words, she found my father gentle, understanding and generous, although somewhat easily tired. He could not dance late into the night as she could. Still, if she had complaints, she kept them from me.

Her sister, Alianore, was also at court, which pleased me very much; though not as much as it pleased Edward. That they were seeing more of one another than was proper was quite obvious, although no one spoke of it, apart from Alianore herself. She was even more contented than Joanne, not least because Roger March had remained in Ireland, as had been planned.

It was Alianore who told me that the Council was pressing the King to take another wife. She had this information from my brother, although it did not surprise me. What *did* surprise me was that my cousin had, according to Edward, accepted their advice and that the necessary search had begun. Yolande of Aragon had been chosen — but then the French had made a counter-offer. Their suggestion was that he should marry their king's daughter, Isabella.

'She is, of course, very young,' said Alianore. 'That's the difficulty. Not yet six, as I understand it. It seems folly to me, when my uncle has such need of an heir. Yolande is bad enough. A little older, about ten. Oh, there's another candidate I haven't mentioned. Your uncle has offered his daughter, Anne of Gloucester. The King will not have *her* though, says they are too close in blood. That did not please your uncle.'

I shook my head. My cousin was not above twelve. What were all these men thinking about? Richard needed a grown woman, or at the least a girl of an age fit to bear children. I could not make any sense of it.

It was as if Alianore had read my mind. 'It may be that the King is not yet ready to move on from Anne. You know what they were to one another.'

'But it's his duty!' I said.

She smiled. 'Perhaps you would like to tell him that? Let me know when you plan to do it, so I may make sure to be a mile or two away at the time.'

She knew very well that I would not dare to broach such a subject with my cousin. To be in favour is not a licence for impudence or impertinence. You may not tell a king what he must do. Unless, of course, you are my Uncle Gloucester or another of that stamp.

It was not long after this that Richard sent for me. I had no idea what to expect, but I took Philippa with me, for want of a better attendant, and followed the gentleman who had brought the summons through the outer apartments where the King's knights and squires loll about when not needed, and where sundry petitioners cool their heels as they wait to be received, beyond all these, into Richard's very bedchamber, where great lords such as my father might enter without ceremony but from which lesser mortals were barred, unless they had a specific invitation.

My cousin seemed in better spirits than he had been at Cardiff. He told me to sit on the chair opposite to him, and although he did not extend the same privilege to Philippa, he acknowledged her presence, greeting her by name. Of course, as Golafre's wife she had a certain station in his esteem, for he valued and trusted John Golafre out of all proportion.

'I have decided to have an altar piece painted for me,' he said. 'A small one, for my private oratory, that can be taken wherever I go. It will show my patron saints presenting me to the Blessed Virgin and the Christ Child. It is my wish that you shall be painted as Our Lady.'

I heard the snort that emerged from Philippa, though it was hastily repressed and I doubt it was loud enough to carry to the King's ears.

'It is too great an honour,' I protested. 'For one thing, I am a married woman.'

He shook his head. 'Consider how many statues and paintings there are of the Blessed Mother of God. They are all based upon some sinful woman or another, many, I think, far less virtuous than you are. In any event, it is my wish and your lord husband has given his consent. I consider there is nothing more to be said.'

Outside, I could hear birds squabbling. One was perhaps meddling with the nest of another. What could I say? It *was* too great an honour. Quite absurd. Yet it was clear that he would brook no refusal.

'Very well,' I said, 'if it is your Grace's command.'

'Not my command. My request.'

That was a quibble. It amounted to the same thing, as he well knew. I could no more refuse than spit in his face.

'My uncles will be painted in the character of my patrons,' he went on. 'Your father, for example, will be St. Edmund. That is very appropriate! Of course, it cannot be entirely completed until Uncle Lancaster returns from Guienne. He is to be the Confessor. Also appropriate, in that he has always longed to be a king, and to appear as a King of England will flatter his pride nicely. I must recall him soon. He is doing very little good out there, and, besides, I need his counsel on the matter of my marriage. You have heard of that business, I suppose?'

I said I had heard something of it.

'It may be a way to peace, if the right choice is made. So, I must follow my Council's advice. That is how matters stand. You know what Anne was to me — there's not a woman on earth who could take her place. I can never go back to Sheen. Still less *La Neyt*. The thought of ever entering those rooms sickens me. I have ordered the whole place razed to the ground, not one stone to stand on another.

'I can never forget Anne, but I have no choice but to marry again. Peace is a great prize, and I must grasp it.'

*

Thomas laughed when I told him what Cousin Richard wanted of me.

'Did you not know of this?' I demanded, and quite sharply.

'He swore me to secrecy, as he wanted to tell you himself. You cannot say it's not an honour, because it is. He had any number of kinswomen to choose from and he decided it should be you. Yet I have an idea you are not pleased.'

'To my mind it borders on blasphemy.'

'Scarcely. Someone must form the basis of the painting, or no such work could be contrived. Better you than some I could mention. It's not as if it's to be put in some great church, where any jack might marvel at it. It's intended for the King's private worship, and few other eyes will ever fall on it.'

'And my father and my uncles to stand as saints also! What do you say to that?'

'That it seems very fitting. In their different ways they have guided him, helped make him the man he is. The King will have taken advice from his confessor, or some other holy father in God, before proceeding in such a venture. There's no more blasphemy in it, Constance, than when some mercer or goldsmith plays the part of a saint — or even God — in a town's mystery play. No one thinks that some fat alderman is *really* St. Peter. He merely *represents* him. Where is the offence in that?'

'Your cousin found it all very amusing.'

He shrugged. 'Philippa would. In some ways, she and Golafre are well matched. I think you should perhaps let him have his wife's company for a few months.'

'I'm more than happy to allow that. Whether Golafre wants her under his feet is another matter.'

'He's on duty, here at court, so I shall ask him. I have a feeling about my cousin that I do not like — that she knows too much, and watches us too closely. I wonder at her purpose.'

I shrugged. 'I doubt she *has* a purpose. Even her mother says she's a fool, and although all women are curious by nature, she is more than usually so. I shouldn't have taken her with me to see the King; now she knows a secret I'd have preferred kept close. Yet she is my senior lady, I couldn't have taken another in preference, and I had to have *some* attendant.'

He sighed. 'I'll speak to Golafre. At least you should have a rest from her. She can devote herself to her husband for a few months, as is only proper.'

'Have you heard what is intended for Sheen?' I asked, for I scarcely believed what Richard had told me, that he would destroy a whole, great palace in Anne's remembrance. Perhaps I had misunderstood.

'In another man I should call it madness,' Thomas said, with a shrug. 'Still, he has not ordered this in haste. He must have been thinking about it all the months we were away in Ireland. If it eases his sorrow, perhaps it is well done.'

*

Some ancient French knight called Philippe de Mézières had written to my Cousin Richard. When I say ancient, I mean he was almost as old as Lady Mohun. When I say that he wrote, I do not mean that he had sent a letter. It would be more correct to call it a book. It was passed around the court after the King had read it, making some, such as my Uncle Lancaster, nod in agreement, and others, like Lord Arundel, bristle like angry dogs. Others merely laughed, as if they had read a witty poem. At last it came to me. It was very long, and more than a little tedious, and of course, given that it was written for a king, it did not lack for flattering phrases. This Sir Philippe did not merely counsel peace between England and France. He also proposed a joint crusade against the heathen, gathering together as many knights as was possible for this purpose.

He had also sent a banner, of what he called the Order of the Passion of Jesus Christ, with the idea that English knights should swear to take part in the crusade. It was an excuse to have a ceremony and to dress up — there were robes specified even for wives — and because it pleased the King the suggestion was taken up. My father took the oath — to my surprise — as did my brother and — not at all to my surprise — Thomas. (I believe my lord was one of the few who took the business seriously.) Harry Bolingbroke did not volunteer, although you might have thought he would have been one of the first to step forward. Uncle Gloucester offered only to be a supporter, not to go himself.

To be truthful, I thought we should hear no more about the matter. That was not quite right, but in the end, as you shall see, it came to nothing.

*

We were many months at court, although we kept our household at Caversham, or at one of my lord's London houses (he had two, one in Friday Street, near St. Paul's and another close to the Minories.) Sometimes we withdrew to one of these places for a few weeks to tend to our own affairs, to take pleasure in our daughter's growth and progress or simply to rest ourselves where we had more privacy and more space, and where we could talk freely to one another without much fear of being overheard.

When Golafre's turn of attendance on the King came to an end, he took Philippa with him into the country, to Wallingford, I think. However, it seemed but a week before he was back at court, busy with his duties, and Philippa, instead of staying under her own roof like a good wife and managing his household and his affairs of business, returned to plague me.

The painter proved to be a squat little man, old enough to have very wrinkled darkish skin, almost like a Moor, and more grey hair than brown, a Fleming who spoke French with a guttural accent and no English at all, so that we understood one another only with difficulty. Fortunately, little discussion was necessary. I had but to stand in one place while he sketched me with a fine piece of charcoal, and this was no hardship for me, given that I had been trained to stand still while still a child, and had practised my art through many a tedious ceremony. I gathered, from what he said, that there was further work to complete, but for the time being there was no more to it than that.

Thomas, almost as soon as he had returned from Ireland, had set his attorneys on the task of having the judgement against his ancestors reversed, with the idea of recovering as much of their forfeited property as possible, or at least forcing the present owners to compound with him.

This was a costly and tedious business, for the Despenser archives were anything but complete due to the various upheavals the family had endured. Among other things, it was necessary to find ancient men willing to give sworn testimony on our behalf. How much of it was honest I cannot say, but honest or false it cost many a bag of coin, for the attorneys and their lackeys took their full share. Slowly, patiently, a petition was prepared, that was to go before Parliament. Yet the attorneys were never satisfied. They always wanted another piece of evidence to add, and that meant more endless searching through dusty documents, more lengthy expeditions in search of witnesses. It seemed to me that the task would never be complete, not least because it served our advisers and their purses all the better if it was prolonged.

I judged that the game was not likely to be profitable enough to pay for the candle, and I said as much to Thomas. He answered that he had the King's approval for this work, and that the sentence against his ancestors touched on his honour. I knew then that there was no point in arguing, so I held my tongue on the matter.

I believe Elisabeth would have been astonished to see me so submissive; though I have no doubt at all that in her mind the petition and the trouble it would stir were all my doing, and that Thomas was but my puppet, dancing to my tune. So she had persuaded herself, again and again, and even if I had presented her with reams of evidence to the contrary, gathered by all the attorneys in England, signed, sealed and attested, she would still have believed it. Why she thought her son so feeble a creature that he would meekly jump to a woman's bidding I cannot imagine. I had influence over him, that I do not deny, but I didn't have rule of our policy. Nor did I wish to have. I supported Thomas to the hilt, right or wrong, and I told him what I thought, but never once did I command him. Nor would he have consented to be so governed.

The talk was now all of my Cousin Richard's marriage, and the peace with France that was linked with it. Little Isabella of Valois, the French King's daughter, was now considered the most likely choice. There was even a suggestion that my brother, Rutland, should marry her younger sister, Jeanne.

I ribbed Edward about this. It was pleasant to have the upper hand for once in my life, to be making a jest of him, when usually it was he who made a jest of me.

He looked rueful. 'Well,' he said, 'it would make the King my brother, and you his sister. Perhaps that is worth having. For the rest, as you well know, a man need not look solely to his wife for pleasure. There are many others more than willing to accommodate me.'

'One in particular,' I said.

He sighed. 'One I should much prefer as wife. But, as you know, her husband is most inconveniently alive. Though there is a good chance Ireland will shorten his life. It's a vile country, Constance. It makes the wildest parts of Yorkshire seem like a tranquil paradise, and those native Irish fellows, even the ones Richard knighted, are no more than bare-shanked barbarian savages. Still, Roger Mortimer probably feels quite at home among them, being the witless oaf he is!'

'If you hurt her—' I began.

He held up his hand. 'I've no intention of hurting her. Though really, fair sister, it is none of your business either way. Moreover, I'd be grateful if you didn't tattle about us. You may have gleaned our secret, one way or another, but I don't want it generally known.'

'Secret?' I repeated. 'How many years is it since you first came to court? There are no secrets here. The lowest turnspit knows when you last changed your underlinen, and how many pennies you have left in your purse after you lose at dice.'

He shook his head. 'There is a lot of gossip, that I grant you. What people *know* is another matter. The King has plans you cannot begin to imagine. Even I only know a part of his mind. The peace with France is merely a beginning, not an end.'

'This peace, is it really so difficult to achieve? I don't see why it should be, if both sides are willing. Perhaps you should send women to negotiate with the French ladies, because that way we might see some progress! All I hear are quibbles about whether Richard should pay homage to King Charles for Guienne, and if so, in what form. I have no patience to listen to it.'

'These are not trivial matters, Constance.' He let out another sigh. 'You may think they are, but they really aren't. They touch on England's honour, and thus on the King's. I believe Uncle Gloucester is now resigned to peace — God knows he has been richly bribed for his consent! — but he is very particular about the form it takes. Reluctant too, in all truth. Peace, he says, is all very well, but it must not be secured at whatever price is demanded. The French must make concessions too. There are many who agree with him, who will be angered if we concede too much. A balance has to be found, to preserve honour.'

'Honour! Another word for horseshit!' (I still recalled my mother's words: Make peace, end it, say there will be no more fighting by land or sea. But no, that is too simple for them.)

He raised his eyebrows. 'You would not say that if *your* honour was in question. It would suddenly be the most important question in the whole world. Don't even think of denying it. You flattened Lady Arundel, as she is now, merely for wanting to walk through a door before you, when you were both mere girls. Don't pretend that you think honour unimportant.'

'Shall I never hear the end of that? I was young, and I could never stand the sight of that creature. Besides, the case was altogether different.'

'Yes, because it touched on Constance! Do you suppose the rest of us hold our honour more cheaply than you do yourself? Uncle Gloucester is a king's son, and not only is he is conscious of it, he demands that the whole world acknowledges it. How is that different?'

'More to the point,' I said, 'is that this marriage you all seem to favour must leave the King without an heir for what — ten years, at the least? Perhaps more, given that God chooses when babies arrive, even when we provide the means. As I have some cause to know. I cannot think it wise, even as a price for peace.'

'But our cousin thinks it is, and it's his decision. In the interim, I believe he means to make other provision for the succession, but as you know, such matters are not for discussion. Richard himself will decide, not any parliament, and certainly not any uncle or cousin. He will announce his choice when he thinks the time is proper, and until then I would not advise any man — or woman — to press him on the matter, or even to talk of it.'

'Ned, they *will* talk about it! They've been talking about it for *years*, but at least while Anne was alive there was some prospect of a child. Now there is absolutely none, at least not if this marriage is chosen. Not for years and years. I agree that it's dangerous for people to gossip about such a matter, but nothing will stop it. It's a huge gap in the King's armour; it makes him vulnerable to any kinsman with a grievance and sufficient ambition.'

'It's almost as if you've someone in mind,' he grinned.

'The candidates declared themselves some years ago, if you recall. It isn't hard to imagine it all happening again.'

He smiled. 'The difference is that this time we are prepared. As I told you once before, we that stand around Richard now are not of the stamp of Robert de Vere.'

Robert de Vere! That handsome mountebank that in my youthful folly I had once thought the perfect knight. Witty, courteous, and as good a jouster as I have seen, and I have seen many. I had all but forgotten him. King Richard, however, had *not*.

He had long desired to allow Robert home, but his Council had objected and the King had had to give way, for fear of shattering the very peace he had achieved in England. Then de Vere had been killed, as I mentioned, and you might have thought that would have been the end of it. It was not. Richard chose this time to bring his body home, and announced that he intended to attend his funeral. The only concession he made was to allow Robert to lie in his own country, at the priory at Earl's Colne in the depths of Essex, rather than in Westminster Abbey.

There were many who said they would not attend such a ceremony. My own father was one of them. The very prospect of it created urgent business at Fotheringhay which he and Joanne needed to manage. He was far from alone in wanting to stay away.

Thomas and I were there, as was my brother Edward and the Earl and Countess of Huntingdon. However we cousins and the other nobles present, such as good Lord Lovell — lately brought to court by Richard's decree after many years of exile — were far outnumbered by bishops, abbots and lesser clergy. Even Robert's widow did not appear — I mean my cousin, Philippa, Duchess of Ireland, not Agnes Lancecrona, who had vanished into obscurity — although his mother, the Countess of Oxford, was most certainly present, her head high with pride.

Richard had the coffin opened, so that he could look on his old friend for one last time. (Robert had of course been embalmed, and was still recognisable, though I cannot say that, after the manner of saints, he had remained as he was in life.) My cousin was in tears, though they were silent. He produced a ring from somewhere, and slid it onto one of de Vere's fingers.

I looked around, and saw general bewilderment. Some were clearly shocked, others horrified, and one or two even looked amused.

I knew a pledge when I saw one, and no pledge is ever more sacred than one given to the dead. It was a pledge and a warning — though none of those warned were there to see it.

***

Chapter 12

December 1395 — January 1396

Just before Christmas, my uncle of Lancaster returned from Guienne. Richard had sent for him to come home, not really because he wanted his advice on the matter of the marriage to Isabella of Valois — that matter was now quite resolved as far as the King was concerned — but because he needed him as counterweight to my other uncle, who kept finding small objections and reasons for delay.

We were all gathered at Langley, and it was a very busy time, quite apart from the ceremonies and worship appropriate to the season. There were many secret gatherings behind closed doors, quite apart from regular meetings of the King's Council. It was clear we were moving towards peace and the French marriage, but not without much discussion and bargaining as Uncle Gloucester was persuaded to conform.

It seemed to me that although my Cousin Richard had received my elder uncle with full courtesy and all due ceremony, there was not quite the same warmth as before. They no longer walked arm-in-arm through the court, Richard maintaining a distance so that my uncle had to kneel and bow with the rest of us. It was a subtle change, but the change was there to be seen and interpreted by all.

The little painter had finished with me. My part of the altarpiece was finished. It was a small panel, fit to be carried from place to place; and there you could see me, somewhat disguised by the Virgin's discreet and flowing blue robes, surrounded by a host of angels, all of whom wore the White Hart. My Uncle Gloucester, in the shape of St. John Baptist, and my father, disguised as St Edmund, presented the kneeling King. We had all been subtly amended. Uncle Gloucester had darker hair than in life; my father a less barbered beard; I had been given a more fashionable mouth, closer to a rosebud. All that remained was for Uncle Lancaster to be added; and this was put in hand, much, I suspect, to my uncle's frustration. When it was finished, I found that the painter had given him an unruly beard, and made him look more ancient than he truly was. If you allowed for his age, he was still a fine-looking man, and in good health. It was very strange to think that the King would look at us all each day, during his private devotions.

There were all manner of rumours in circulation, even as we danced and carolled, and laughed at the follies of the Lord of Misrule. One was that Harry Bolingbroke had had a serious argument with his father. It was claimed that they had been heard shouting at each other by half the palace.

This, I doubted. Harry had many faults — I could fill a page listing them, for he added to and built upon them in later years — but he was unfailingly courteous, even when that very courtesy concealed an underlying contempt. He had always showed my uncle the greatest deference. I could no more imagine him shouting at his father than kicking Archbishop Arundel down the palace steps.

It was true that Harry looked unhappy, but then he always seemed to be ill at ease at Richard's court, and rarely lingered long, preferring, it seemed, to sleep under one of his own roofs. He had, of course, little cause to be merry, with his wife dead and his six children scattered around various households of retainers and relatives. Nor was he happy with the suggestion that had been made that he should marry yet another of King Charles's daughters, a babe scarcely out of leading-strings. In his heart, I believe he was as much opposed to the peace as Uncle Gloucester, but outwardly he conformed, because it was his father's policy as well as the King's.

It was the morning after the great Christmas feast that Joanne came bustling into my room. I was bleary-eyed and half-dressed, for it was still early, and after the celebrations of the previous day I was tired, bloated, sickly, and in an irritable mood. Joanne was little better. I had the impression she had dressed herself, for her gown was not properly laced upon her, but hung loose, and she had nothing on her head but a simple linen coif, as if she was just out of bed.

'You will not believe this!' she cried. 'I scarcely believe it myself, but I had it from your father, and he had it from Lancaster's own mouth. The King has given your uncle leave to marry. To marry his — his *woman*! I am to give way to, to walk behind, a petty knight's widow, a raddled old whore. As soon as Christmas is over, he is leaving court, riding up to some ghastly little village in Lincolnshire where she lives, and he will wed her. *Have you ever heard the like?*'

I thought she was going to start screaming.

'My father told you this?'

'Yes. Last night. I've barely slept for thinking about it. Can you imagine the shame? The disgrace! Imagine what the French will say when their princess is received by such a creature. As she must be! I have told York I have no intention of being there, and I hope you will say the same. None of us should have anything to do with it.'

She started to weep, which was awkward as Philippa and the rest of my women were listening and no doubt delighting in the gossip this would create. What could I do? I murmured soft words, and comforted Joanne against my shoulder as if she was a child. (She was, in truth, little more, in sense if not in age.)

I thought of Dame Katherine Swynford. She had been attending the Garter feast for years, as was her right, and was often about the court. She was older than us, certainly, but to call her a 'raddled old whore' as Joanne had was more than unjust, indeed slanderous. I had always found her an unassuming lady, and had no doubt she had been very handsome in her youth. As for her four children, the Beauforts as they were called, they were my cousins when all was said and done, and were also often at court. I preferred the least of them to Harry Bolingbroke. The eldest son, Sir John

Beaufort, was about the same age as Thomas and Edward, a good-looking fellow and accomplished in the jousts. He had been retained by my Cousin Richard for some years, and wore his livery as one of his knights.

In any event, as I sought to explain to Joanne, there was nothing we could do about it, so it was better to be gracious. My father had had his differences with his elder brother over the years, mostly about Castile and the rights arising from it, but he would not quarrel with him for the sake of it, and certainly not over such a matter. If the King approved, that was an end to it.

'Richard can never do *any* wrong in your eyes, can he?' Joanne protested, pulling away from me. I was surprised that she took me up on that particular point.

I shrugged. 'You must choose your battles. If the King, my father and my uncle are all in agreement on this matter, you cannot hope to prevail. No power in England would be sufficient, let alone you and your complaints, or even the protests of every woman at court. Cousin Richard needs my uncle's support — that's why he called him home from Guienne. This will be part of the agreement between them, one concession for another. Besides, my uncle must want this very much. Whatever you may think about the woman, he must love her and their children very dearly to make such a decision.'

'*Love!*' she snorted. 'What great lord marries for love? Or marries a mistress? I still say it's shameful. I think he must be in his *dotage*. For that matter, your father is little better, and I think my uncle the King must have parted from his wits to give consent to such a scandalous connection. In all my days, I've not heard of such folly.'

She bustled off, highly dissatisfied with my response.

*

It was not long after this that Thomas and I found ourselves bidden to dine at my father's house in London — that is to say the one he was renting at the time. He had had several over the years, but the only one he had been granted by the King, long ago, was too small for a duke's household and dignity. I suppose we could have let him have one of ours.

My father was most splendidly dressed in blue velvet, with a multitude of rings on his fingers and a heavy gold chain about his neck that bore his falcon device. He even wore the very pointed shoes that were fashionable among the young men at court, the tips exceeding in length even of those that Thomas was wearing, which were quite long enough.

Despite this finery, he looked drawn, as though he had not slept. That was quite possible, I thought. During his life he had had many falls from horses, as well as injuries received in battle and in jousting, and many broken bones, some of which had perhaps not healed perfectly. He had never been one to complain about his ailments, but I noticed that when he moved he did so with a certain care, as if uncertain which leg to favour to minimise his pain.

Joanne also looked heavy-eyed. Her mouth was sealed in a tight bud, and she scarcely spoke at all. She too was most splendidly clad, and wore a headdress studded with pearls that made her look a good foot taller than her true height, and a gown with a heavy, furred train that at times she seemed to struggle to manage, as if she was not used to wearing such gear. It was certainly more fit for a great feast than a quiet dinner with family, and I wondered which of us she was trying to impress with such splendour. I was scarcely in rags myself, but next to her I looked like a country gentlewoman just arrived at court.

We settled down to eat and I saw at once that one of the servitors was my brother, Dickon, who had evidently been promoted to this role. He was not yet eleven, of course, so he played a subsidiary role, mainly fetching and carrying. The chances were he had not yet been taught to carve, or that if he had, he was not yet skilled enough to allay a pheasant or unbrace a mallard. Still, he was fit to hold a bowl for us to laver our hands, even to pour wine, and although his movements were a little stiff and awkward, I could not call him clumsy. Given that this was a private meal, and not some great state occasion, he was adequate enough.

Another of the boys serving us was Mun Holland, Joanne's youngest brother, who had evidently joined my father's household for a time. Mun was about two years Dickon's elder, and it showed. He was deft with the carving-knife, and broke the venison before us with a skill that would not have been out of place at the King's own table at a reception for some great foreign guest. Like all the Hollands, he was tall and well-made, allowing for his age. (No one can be thirteen, or thereabouts, and lack a few spots and blemishes.) He was also beyond that age where boys think women are below their notice. His eyes fell on me more than once, and quite obviously saw something of interest. It really was quite amusing. I doubt he would have known what to do with me if I had made the offer, but that did not keep him from *looking*.

Such conversation as there was at table passed mainly between my father and Thomas. At first they talked of horses — John Russell had lately found a fine new destrier for Thomas, already well-trained for the joust. Then they turned to hawks — for the Duke had lately procured a fine gyrfalcon from a London merchant for some ruinous price. They discussed the hunting they envisaged and the conclusion of the peace with France. I heard much more of this than I should normally have done, as I could barely extract a word from Joanne beyond 'yea' and 'nay'. That she was sulking was beyond doubt, but I had the impression she was almost as displeased with me as she was with my father.

The meal was drawing to its conclusion when my father revealed the point of our invitation.

'My son,' he said, gesturing towards Dickon, who was

standing by the wall, awaiting orders, 'is now of an age when it would serve him to train in another household instead of idling away at home. He's shown you something of what he has learned, but he needs to be polished, and his training with weapons has scarcely begun.

'I must consider his future. He has an annuity from the King, but not a single foot of land. I'm not so wealthy that I can afford to buy up manors to provide him with a livelihood, as my brother of Lancaster has done for the Beauforts. Nor am I so well provided with heirs that I can safely make a priest or a monk of him, though that might be his proper course, since he enjoys his books, has some skills with writing and has the makings of a clerk. He would make a fair land steward, but that is too lowly an office for one of his birth.

'He may well have to earn his bread with his sword, as part of the King's retinue, or that of some great lord, because that at least would be honourable employment. So I would make a warrior of him. If you would take him, Thomas, I should be grateful. I think you are the example he needs, and I can think of no one I should prefer above you.'

There are some requests that cannot be refused, and this was one of them. My lord gave me a glance along the table, as if to secure my assent. I nodded briefly. I knew we had no choice. The chances were that it was a concession Joanne had demanded, and which my father had felt obliged to concede as a means of maintaining peace. Besides, I had no objection to having young Dickon as one of my household. It seemed to me that he would fit in well among the other boys, and Thomas would certainly make a man of him.

*

I began to long to live at Hanley Castle again. It seemed like an eternity since I had last set eyes on it, and yet, of all the places we had, it was where I had known most happiness, most security. There was talk about the court that Richard intended to visit a number of shrines in Gloucestershire and Worcestershire, so we would soon be moving in that direction. It seemed to me that this presented an opportunity.

I spoke of this to Thomas. 'I should be more content there,' I said, 'and when a woman is content she is far more likely to breed. Everyone knows that. It's high time you had a son. You know, your mother has mentioned it to me more than once. (I fancy she thinks I bar you from my bed except at Christmas and Easter, and put wool soaked in vinegar up inside me on the very rare occasions when I deign to permit you to touch me.) Well, I have a feeling. If we have a few weeks at Hanley, I shall conceive one.'

He gave me one of his wry grins. 'I thought you were enjoying life at court.'

'So I was. Yet I find that when I am at Hanley I miss the court, and when I am at court I miss Hanley.'

'Well, you do but confess yourself a woman. Fickle and changeable in your desires, as in the indictment. Not,' he added, holding up his hand before my mouth could open in protest, 'that I would have you any other way, *treschere*. This is not, I take it, anything to do with your new aunt?'

'Of course not! I am not Joanne. I know what I can hope to change and what I cannot. She has become used to being the most important lady in England, but that was always going to end when Cousin Richard married again, as he must. My uncle has merely advanced the change a little. She should be grateful at her age to stand as high as she does.'

'I see no difficulty at all. The King plans to visit our country very soon. He has not forgotten King Edward II, nor yet Our Lady of Worcester. I have already written to my mother to warn her he is likely to pass through Tewkesbury, at the very least, and that she must be ready to receive his Grace. So we may go with him, and ask leave to have a little time to ourselves at Hanley. I can't think he'll forbid it. Once you've grown weary of the place again — say in a fortnight or a month — we can soon rejoin the court. It will do no harm to spend some time at Hanley, and to arrive in the district in the King's company will be even better. Warwick and Berkeley will be reminded that the world has changed.'

*

So it transpired. The court moved westwards, by slow stages. We had a whole week at Woodstock, for example, where I was glad to huddle by the fire with Joanne while the men hunted in the keen frost. They would come in one day soaked by heavy rain, on another with their faces reddened by hail or icy winds, but they were in excellent spirits. My father seemed to shed his aches and pains if you gave him a courser to sit and a deer to chase. Edward was equally happy. Alianore was in the company, and he spent most evenings dancing with her, or sitting in some corner or other mooning over poetry. He wrote some himself, though I thought his verses were execrable. Still, it was very much the fashion, and it was better than debating heretical ideas, as some of our knights were all too apt to do.

In those days we had more than a few Lollard heretics at court, but these knights and squires were all moderates, and did not have the extreme views of some of their fellows, who objected to swearing, saying it was blasphemous, and held the quite ridiculous belief that all property should be held in common. Yet even most of those at court rejected the miracle of the Mass, saying that the holy wafer was but bread and did not become Christ's Body. This I thought *outrageous*. There would be no comfort in communion if one thought it mere bread and not that which unites all true Christians. So far I agree with Archbishop Arundel. Where I differ from him is that I cannot think it right to burn men alive for being fools.

Some of their ideas were more interesting, but I was wary of paying too much heed to their wild notions. For one thing, Cousin Richard did not approve. Every so often he would lose his temper and threaten the Lollards at court with a terrible death. At which they would draw in their horns for a time. However, the King never followed through with his threats, and I believe he was more tolerant than he admitted. Certainly, these men retained his favour as long as they did not become too outrageous. The most important of them was Sir John, Lord Montagu, old Salisbury's nephew and heir. He was an agreeable fellow, despite his absurd opinions on holy matters, and he wrote far better poetry than my brother. He was a good twenty years older than Thomas and me, but we quite often had him in our company, along with his wife, Maud, who was only a little older than Thomas and a very agreeable woman, despite the fact that her father had been but a merchant of London.

At Burford, on our way to Gloucester, we had to share a lodging with the Montagus, and think ourselves fortunate not to be lying under canvas in one of the frozen fields. (Burford was a Despenser manor, but more of a place for passing through than residing, and possessed of considerably more sheep than people. There was precious little in the way of proper accommodation.)

The four of us sat together that night, dicing by the light of the cressets for want of anything better to do, though we talked as much as we gambled.

'God listens to every petition,' John Montagu said. 'The lowest bondsman, praying while making good a hedge, or even sitting in the place of easement, is heard. We need no saints to intercede for us, so pilgrimages such as this, from one shrine to another, are but vanity, and a waste of time and money.'

'Surely,' I objected, 'just as the King is more likely to heed one of us than he is some mere digger of ditches, God is more likely to hear the petitions of the Blessed Virgin or one of the saints than he is to listen to wretched sinners such as we are.'

He laughed. He had a kindly, pleasant face, and his laugh was gentle rather than mocking. 'Madam,' he said, 'I mean no least disrespect to the King, and still less to God, when I say they are no more to be compared than a popinjay is to a war horse. The King is a mortal man, with only so many hours in the day, much work to complete, and with a body that grows as weary as ours do. He cannot *possibly* give attention to all his subjects. Imagine some girl, who labours in an alehouse. What chance has *she* of receiving any consideration from him? I suppose, if she was *very* lucky, and importunate, and if he was in the right place and in the right mood, he might give her a hearing. God though, will *always* hear her. Wherever she is, and at whatever time of day or night. As readily as he will hear you or me. God's capacity to receive petitions is unlimited by its very nature. Surely you see that?'

I saw Maud's eyes roll towards the ceiling. Clearly this was such familiar ground to her that she found it tedious.

'Pilgrimages are long established by custom,' said Thomas, 'and approved by all the holy fathers of ancient times. Besides, I do not see what harm they do. Many enjoy a season on the road, to be away from their daily lives, and the cost and effort *must* be of some benefit to their souls. Hardship in a holy cause cannot be other than a balance to our sins.'

'No harm to us, perhaps,' John Montagu conceded. He paused in his argument to cast his dice, tutted over the disappointing result. 'Our revenues still flow in whether we are here or in Rome, whether we sweat over our estate accounts or lie in bed all day. Yet to a working man every day away from his trade or occupation is a day without pay, and a loss of useful work that benefits the commonwealth. All for folly. What do people do on pilgrimage but swill drink, stuff their stomachs and fornicate? In many cases, more sin arises from the supposed act of contrition than was committed in the first instance.'

'John, John!' cried Maud, despairingly, 'You are becoming tedious!'

That made us all laugh, even Montagu himself, because although he took his beliefs too seriously for my taste, he did not lack humour, like some sour creatures who dwell too much on religion.

He also knew when he had said enough, and our talk turned to lighter matters, such as whether we could hope to get beyond Northleach next day, and whether we should find any better accommodation there than at Burford.

*

At Gloucester, the King went in procession to venerate King Edward, not only with those of us who had followed him but also with a great company gathered from the surrounding country. Even Lord Berkeley was there, to my surprise, no doubt trimming his sails to the prevailing wind. The little abbot was so delighted he scarcely had the breath to lead the prayers, let alone to preach. The offerings his house received that day must have been enormous.

In return, the King was given a great and splendid feast, after which he received many of the knights and gentlemen of those parts, hearing their petitions and receiving their professions of loyalty, some of which, I thought, were rather high-flown and exaggerated, given that not a few came from men who had supported his enemies in the various parliaments and in some cases in the field at Radcot Bridge. I was in a position to judge, because at Richard's command Thomas and I were standing at his right hand, for he wished to make it clear to all that my lord stood for him as lieutenant in that county, and that service to us was regarded as service to him. This I had not expected, but it was a great mark of his favour.

When this was over, he drew us into the lodging he had been given for his use, and sent out all his people so that we were left alone with him. He settled on a chair before the fire, and had us standing before him.

'Thomas,' he said, 'I hope one day that I shall have a parliament that will do my will, not the will of my Uncle Gloucester or any of the others who imagine they could rule this land better than I can. First, I want you to think of a man who is fit to be sheriff of this county, a man loyal to you who wears your livery. Not a fool, not a man who can be intimidated, a man who will do as we tell him. While you are at Hanley Castle, think of a name, and let me know. I will order the Chancellor to appoint him when the time comes.'

He paused, just for a moment, and went on. 'Some years ago, I asked Constance to do what could be done to promote the cult of King Edward in this county and hereabouts, and I believe you've both worked to do my will in that matter. The crowds gathered here today say something of your influence. Now you must labour the county again, both of you. I want loyal men elected for Gloucestershire in the next parliament. Preferably men who have taken Despenser fees and livery, but in any event, men who are loyal to me and will serve me. You will see to it, I trust?'

'As your Grace pleases,' my lord said. What else could he say?

As we left the King's rooms, and as soon as we were out of the hearing of his knights and esquires, Thomas turned to me, a wry look on his face.

'I doubt I have the power,' he said, shrugging.

'Then you will have to find it. The right sheriff will make a difference. Does he not manage the elections?'

'Yes, but all men of note have a voice, and my cousin Berkeley's influence is still very strong.'

It was pure chance, but as we turned the corner there *was* Berkeley, with two or three of the county gentry trailing in his wake and wearing his livery collar. An ill omen, I thought.

'Cousin,' he said, bowing low. 'My lady.' He bowed even lower.

'Cousin, we were just talking of you,' Thomas said. 'I know the King was glad to see you here, paying reverence to King Edward, as he desires.'

That was well said, I thought. Not a challenge, merely a reminder of present realities.

Berkeley nodded. 'I am the King's servant. Though, as you know, I spend most of my time here in this shire, and very little at court. You seem to be quite the opposite, cousin, unless it is in your mind to change your ways and involve yourself in the business of the county.'

'I intend to be at Hanley Castle for some little time,' Thomas said. 'Perhaps you would care to visit us there?'

'Perhaps. I believe the King is for Tewkesbury tomorrow. If so, I shall do myself the honour of following in his train at least that far. It's some time since I've visited my lady your mother. I understand young Richard Beauchamp is also there at present, so it should be quite a reunion of our families.'

'Tomorrow, then,' said Thomas.

'Tomorrow,' Lord Berkeley agreed. He had a smile on his face that I longed to wipe away.

*

Tewkesbury. The King was to be the guest of the abbot; for Richard was on a pilgrimage. There was no shrine as such to venerate; but there was a miraculous statue of the Virgin — not as famous as the one at Worcester, still less Caversham, and far below Walsingham — but still worthy of reverence. Then there was an entire collection of holy relics including Christ's own crib and the bed on which the Blessed Virgin lay to give birth to Him. Then there were the tombs and chantries of my lord's ancestors from his father, Lord Edward, through the de Clares, to his distant forbear, Robert Fitzhamon, who had founded the abbey long ago, about the time of the first King Henry, as I understand.

So there was a great deal to see, and many prayers to be said, as well as offerings to be made, and a great swell of people at least as great as the company that had gathered at Gloucester. Elisabeth was there, of course. Her husband's little chantry was finished at last, complete with his kneeling effigy above it; and she was anxious to draw attention to her work, which, it must be said, was very fine, and entirely worthy of our family.

Berkeley was present, as he had promised, and for most of the time walked at her side, flattering, admiring, no doubt telling her how wise and pious she was, and how the world had fallen away since they were both young. That hawk-nosed little runt, Richard Beauchamp, was there too, just as Berkeley had told us he would be, walking arm-in-arm with Berkeley's little daughter, who was not yet ten. They were pretending to be grown-up.

What was worse was that his parents were also present among us. I suppose I did not much object to Countess Margaret. Her husband's long face, however, was an uncomfortable reminder of evil days, when he had more or less acted as jailer to King Richard and those about him, including me. Warwick looked older — much older. He had always been tall, but now he stooped and his walk had lost some of its bold, striding confidence. I wondered if his legal dispute with Thomas Mowbray was wearing him down. That case was still dragging on — a falling out of thieves; for as you will recall, both had been Appellants — and it was no small matter for Warwick, for Gower provided a fair proportion of his revenues. I wondered if he meant to use this occasion to appeal to the King, especially as Mowbray was not with us. Good luck with that, my friend! I said inwardly, smiling to myself.

The King, and most of the court, were, as I said, lodged in and around the abbey, for the monks had ample provision for guests. Thomas and I were to sleep under his mother's roof, but we were far from alone. The company included Berkeley, the Warwicks and their children, so you may well imagine what a cheerful supper we had.

Elisabeth set me in the highest place — I had taught her one or two things about courtesy over the years — but that meant I was seated between Warwick and Elisabeth herself. They talked across me as I picked at Elisabeth's offering of pigeon pie smeared with some vile sauce and sipped at her thin wine which would have been a hard bargain at three pence a gallon.

It was the eve of St. Agnes, when unmarried girls are supposed to see their future husbands if they perform certain bizarre rituals. I could see mine well enough, sitting between Lady Warwick and Lord Berkeley and apparently finding Margaret Warwick's tattle congenial. Montagu and his wife were on my other hand, below Warwick. As for Philippa Fitzwalter —. Where was Philippa? As Elisabeth's cousin she was certainly entitled to a place at one of the boards in this room, and as my waiting-woman I expected her to be at hand. She had helped me dress for this supper, had seemed quite cheerful, at least by her standards. I had expected her to sup with us, but she had evidently slipped away. Either she was eating in the hall with the lesser members of our households — I thought that unlikely — or her husband had sent for her to eat with him at the abbey, where he was in attendance on the King. I shrugged, and gave it no more consideration. Golafre and his requirements were the probable explanation, and it was not unreasonable that she should go to him.

'I intend they should be married this year or next,' Warwick was saying, obviously referring to the hawk-nosed brat and the Berkeley child. 'At least, to perform the sacrament in church before a congregation. Clearly, it will be a few years before they can be bedded, but I want the matter secured, lest there be — *contingencies*.'

'I know what you mean,' said Elisabeth. 'If anything but good should befall, and your son is taken into wardship.' She sighed. 'A true, canonical marriage is more difficult to dissolve than a mere betrothal, and there's no saying whom he might be required to take to wife if the matter is left unresolved. I think you very wise, cousin, to make provision. The child is an example to other girls and has given me no trouble whatever. She's entirely douce. Obedient, willing, and happy to accept correction for any small fault. Better her for your son than some *unsuitable creature* who thinks herself far above him.'

Did she think me so obtuse that I did not recognise her allusion for what it was? By the bones of the living God, it was too much! It was not sufficient merely to insult me, she had to do so in a conversation with Warwick, as if her conspiracy against our interests with him and Berkeley was not betrayal enough.

Subtlety, Constance, subtlety! I heard my mother's advice in my head just as clearly as if she were sitting next to me. If I had not, I might well have thrown my glass of miserable wine in Elisabeth's face, and that would have served me badly. Instead, I gripped its stem and fought against my rising fury. It was something of a miracle that the glass did not shatter, but it did not. Slowly the anger passed and I recovered my poise.

I turned to Warwick. 'Is it true, Lord Warwick, that most of the Berkeley lands are entailed to the male heir? To Berkeley's brother, Sir James?'

'It is, my lady,' he said tersely.

'I know Sir James well,' I said — the truth was that I barely knew him from Adam — 'and I have thought him a kind and generous man. These entails to the male are so unjust, in my opinion. I'm sure that if you talk to him he'll be more than ready to be generous to young Elizabeth. He might even concede the inheritance of Berkeley Castle itself.'

There was more chance of my accession to the throne of Spain, and all three of us knew it. Warwick's long face took on a look of bewilderment. Perhaps he was wondering whether I really was *that* naïve.

'My own daughter,' I went on, 'stands to be a much more important heiress unless God grants her a brother. I know that my lord intends a *very* great marriage for her, although he has not yet said with whom. I do not press him on the matter, of course. As his wife, it is my place only to be *douce*.'

I was delighted by their expressions. I had unveiled an image for them to look upon that they did not care to venerate. Perhaps I had even shown them that their petty schemes against Thomas and me *would not work*. That we had our own allies, more powerful than could be contained within the intrigues of this petty little county. I longed to tell them that Thomas had just been asked to nominate the next sheriff, and to find two of his own men to sit in parliament. Yet I judged that premature. Let them discover our power in due course.

*

Next morning, Thomas and I were on the road before it was fully light. The King was to spend another night at Tewkesbury Abbey, but he had promised to visit us at Hanley Castle on his way to Worcester, and we had to be sure that all was ready for his reception. Our household — that is all bar those who attended us to court and formed our escort — was already established there with my daughter, having moved from Caversham.

Philippa was back in our company and positively *glowing*. It was the look of a woman who had spent a merry night with her husband — though how she had contrived *that* within an abbey precinct I could not imagine. It is sometimes better not to know every detail. Golafre, I knew, was not a man to allow decorum to stand in his way, and it would not have surprised me to learn that he had requisitioned some cottage for his purpose, or perhaps a private room in one of the inns. Such things could be contrived, if you made arrangements with the King's harbingers, who had the task of selecting accommodation on these progresses. A little coin can do a great deal.

I did not grudge her. On the contrary, if it meant her marriage was amended, then I might see less of her, since Golafre was sure to send for her as soon as his present turn of duty with the King was ended. She might even start to spend more time under his roof and less under mine.

'What is this you have been telling my mother about our daughter's marriage?' Thomas asked, as we rode across the long bridge over the Avon. I gathered she had been at his ear even before he had broken his fast.

I told him of the discussion I had with Warwick and his mother, and made him laugh.

'You take pleasure in setting hares running, don't you?' he said.

'I was provoked.'

'I dare say you were. You didn't lie, either, for I *do* have a great marriage in mind for her. In fact, I have had in mind since she was born. Now you have prompted me, it might be the proper time to discuss it with the other family. I believe we can make such an alliance as will put Warwick's nose well out of joint, and Berkeley's too. What would you say to her becoming, at some distant time I hope, the Countess of March?'

It was cold on that bridge, for a stark wind was blowing straight down the river from the direction of Evesham. Now, however, my blood felt a still greater chill.

'I think you should consider very carefully,' I replied, 'not least because any such marriage would need the King's consent. I would take advice, because I think it could cause great trouble and make you dangerous enemies. The other matter is that the boy is my godson. I believe that makes him Bess's spiritual brother. You would need a dispensation.'

'We probably need one for blood kinship anyway,' he shrugged. 'I thought you would be pleased, especially since you and his mother are such mighty gossips. In truth, I'm a little surprised that you and Alianore have not already agreed the marriage between you, in the common way of women in such dealings.'

I knew from his tone of voice that I had disappointed him, even angered him, but what else could I have said? This was no mere private matter between families. It could be presented as nothing less than an attempt to make our daughter Queen of England one day.

There had been those who had said as much when Kent had married Alianore to March. However, Kent was the King's half-brother, and everything had been done with Richard's full knowledge and consent. Besides, it had all been arranged before Parliament had named March heir, when such a possibility had had no substance beyond speculation, and before it became clear that Richard would have no sons for years, if ever.

'All I am saying,' I explained, 'is that Bess is still very young, and there is no cause for haste. In any event, you know Roger is in Ireland and likely to be there for some time. Such a matter is better discussed face-to-face, in a private room. It's too delicate to be managed by letter, and letters, in any case, can go astray and fall into unfriendly hands. I suggest this is not a fence you should rush.'

'As you will,' he said, even managing a smile. I was not sure whether I had carried my point. Thomas was not one to wear his counsel on his sleeve. 'As you say, the girl is young, and there is no cause for undue haste.'

I had expected much to amend at Hanley Castle, but our officers had managed all very well, and there was little with which I could find fault. They had even prepared the guest chambers, which was wise because although the King was not expected to stay overnight, kings can and do often change their minds, and it is well to be prepared. The rushes on those floors we had not yet equipped with new tiles had been replaced and dried herbs had been scattered everywhere, so that the very act of walking produced an agreeable scent. Those rooms that lacked fireplaces had charcoal braziers burning to drive away the chill and damp.

I was pleased, and I let it be known.

My daughter was growing well. It seemed to me that she was a good inch taller than when I had last seen her, some weeks ago, at our London house, but that was probably my imagination. Her nurses were proud of her quick wits and willing obedience, which they praised to me. I sat with the child for a while and played at ninepins with her, allowing her to win, which made her squeal with delight.

We were barely finished with that when her father appeared, to take her on his shoulder, and swing her about, and tell her that she was his sweet beloved, all of which delighted the child, even if it excited her more than was desirable. Tomorrow, he said, she would be presented to the King. He made it sound as if Richard's whole purpose in our country was to set eyes on our daughter. Still, I thought, it will do no harm. If my cousin had faults, a dislike of children was not one of them. The pity was he had none of his own, although if he had they would assuredly have grown up spoiled beyond measure.

*

Next morning we were up again betimes, and most carefully dressed, knowing that the King could arrive at almost any time. It was true, of course, that my cousin would probably break his fast at leisure, hear Mass in the abbey, and take an unhurried leave of his hosts, but you can never be sure and it is better to kick your heels in idleness for an hour or two than have to rush around in panic like a beheaded chicken.

His harbinger arrived just before our great clock struck ten. He took wine with us, and talked for a little time, for he was an amiable fellow, not like some harbingers I have known who imagine themselves as important as their principal. His Grace would be by Ripple now, he said, but he was not moving with great haste. He would bring only a small company to Hanley; the great bulk of the court would be going straight down the main road to Worcester, avoiding the ferry at Upton. Then, with wine downed, he was on his way to Worcester himself, taking the byroad on our side of the water. He and his fellows would have plenty of doors to mark with chalk in that city as they allocated the lodgings.

He was not through the village before Thomas and I were mounted up, and with a suitable escort behind us, on our way through the castle gate. Our retinue was large enough, for it included several of our retained men from the district as well as household folk, all bright in our livery. We must welcome the King as he approached, it was but courtesy, and with any luck we knew we should be at the Upton ferry before he reached it.

So we were, but with less time to spare than I should have liked. He was already setting foot on the ferry, with as many of his company as would fit onto it, and a horse or two. I knew from experience it would take some time to bring everyone across. The bridge was still standing half-built, half broken-down, something of a reproach to us given that Upton was Elisabeth's town. It had already been like that for the best part of a decade, to my knowledge.

Thomas and I dismounted and knelt in the road to greet my cousin. I cannot speak for Thomas, but I chose my piece of road with some care. At that time of year there was an ample supply of mud and icy water on its surface, to say nothing of the leavings of various animals that had passed along it. Fortunately, Richard did not keep us kneeling long.

Among those with Richard were John Holland and his lady, my cousin, Beth, and my brother, Edward. The Montagus came across with the second ferry, but it was a small company, and in many ways that was so much the better. When all were assembled and remounted, Richard led the way, of course, with Thomas at his side, and I was a little behind with my brother, who seemed quite pleased with himself and had a great deal to say, much of which, I admit, I ignored. He did say, however, that it pleased him that Thomas and I were so honoured, and that he hoped we would have greater honours still, if Thomas served the King as well as Richard expected. The rule of our district was important, he said, and we must keep a close eye on Warwick. The man might be growing old, but he still had many followers and was dangerous. It was unfortunate, he said, that Elisabeth seemed to be on such friendly terms with the fellow. It had not gone unnoticed.

I said I was sure the King had far more important matters on his mind.

He shook his head. 'Constance, you have known our cousin long enough not to underestimate him. *Nothing* is below his notice, and nothing is forgiven. You might mention that to my Lady Despenser the Elder when next you see her.'

No point in that, I thought. I might as well hunt a hare with a tabor.

'At least Warwick is not here today to remind him,' I said lightly. I did think my brother was being a little absurd.

'No, but I believe he and his lady have gone straight to Worcester, in some hope that Richard will receive them there. That little legal case about Gower will be preying on their minds, and I expect they hope he will hear a petition in their favour. He won't of course. They'll be fortunate if he deigns to grunt at them.'

Perhaps I should not have laughed, but I did. I could imagine them in their finery kneeling before the King and merely being grunted at. A small repayment for old debts.

I had thought that Richard and his company might eat their dinner with us, and Hugh Bygge and his fellows had produced all that was necessary to do the household credit. However, the King said that this could only be a briefest of visits, for he was expected in Worcester and did not wish to disappoint his hosts. He promised to come again, now that he had seen our fair castle, and said that when he did he would certainly stay a night or two.

He took wine though, and wafers, and some sugared plums we had set out, my brother Dickon acting as one of the servers and not failing us. If the King was pleased with the castle, he was no less so with the many gentlefolk gathered there to be presented to him.

I also brought forward our daughter; when I told her to kneel before the King she did so at once and quite gracefully for one of her age.

'A poppet!' cried Richard, and before I knew what had happened he had her seated on his knee and was calling for someone to fetch over the sugared plums. He seemed entranced by her. 'She is the image of you, Constance, although I see something of Thomas in her too. I believe she has his nose, rather than yours.'

'If so, she is fortunate,' I said, which made some of the company laugh.

'If you are the King,' she asked him, 'where is your crown?'

'Bess!' I hissed, but my cousin merely laughed, and fed her one of the plums, which she accepted graciously.

'I only wear it on special days,' he explained. 'Only then because it's the custom and expected of me. It's heavy and uncomfortable, you know.'

'Then how do people know you're King?'

I was appalled, but again, he merely chuckled happily.

'That is a very good question,' he said. 'I've no idea, little maid, but I find that generally they do. I suppose they must look at my banner, or perhaps my face.'

She nodded, as if that was a satisfactory explanation.

'You know,' he went on, 'I have a new Queen coming to England very soon. The daughter of the French King. She is not all that much older than you, and your cousin. She might like you as a playmate. Would that please you?'

Bess nodded vigorously.

'Then it is settled and agreed.' He turned to me. 'This child reminds me very much of someone I know when she was younger; but I cannot think who it is.'

Everyone laughed. Of course, a king does not need to be particularly witty to make people laugh, but in this case the joke was aimed at me.

'Bess,' I instructed, 'you are to say, "Thank you, your Grace."'

'Thank you, your Grace,' she repeated.

'Down you go,' said Richard, dropping her onto her feet so suddenly that the child was confused, and ran to me for comfort. I held her close, for she was suddenly shy, her eyes buried in my skirts. Still, she had done well. She had pleased the King, even if she had done it in her own particular way.

'I hope your Grace will forgive the child's sauciness,' I said.

'Forgive?' he repeated. 'There is nothing to forgive, cousin. Your daughter is a delight — I only wish I had one like her to brighten my days.' He fell silent for a moment, his eyes distant, and I suspected he was thinking of Anne and children they might have had between them. 'I was in earnest when I spoke of Isabella. She will, of course, have many ladies and damsels about her, most of them much her elder. A child though, needs other children. Isabella is of course somewhat older, but, if memory serves me correctly, little girls often enjoy having someone smaller to order about. In another year or so, perhaps.'

'Favour upon favour,' said Beth Huntingdon, as we followed Richard back down to the hall. 'Will you *really* let her go from you, so young?'

'If it is Richard's wish, I have no choice,' I said.

'Remember that she is my god-daughter. I have an interest here, and I think her too young to be taken away from what she knows. I would not allow it for a child of mine, and I shall give our cousin my counsel on the matter.'

'It could be much to her profit, if it means she grows close to the Queen of England. Beth, it is not as if she is being sent to another land beyond the sea. I shall probably see her as often as I do now, and she would live well in the Queen's household, I do not doubt it. In any event, it may all come to nothing. Richard may well forget.'

She rolled her eyes. 'You aren't speaking to a stranger, Constance. We both know perfectly well that Richard forgets *nothing*. I only wish he *would* allow some matters to fade from his memory. Many would sleep more easily in their beds, including my brother. You know, Harry is at his wits' end since Mary died. He doesn't know what to do to please my father, let alone the King. He tries; he really tries. He's even supported this peace with France, though it wrings his heart. What do you think he must do to be forgiven?'

I shook my head. I had no idea. My view was that *all* the Appellants had great cause to thank God, fasting, that they were still alive. That certainly included Harry of Lancaster, who had won Radcot Bridge for them. They had piled humiliation after humiliation on Richard, murdered his friends, driven others into exile. Arundel had even insulted Queen Anne after her death. There are some dealings in life for which no amends are possible.

*

The King rode out of our castle just as the clock was striking eleven. He will be a little late for his dinner in Worcester, I thought. He had, perhaps, lingered a little longer than he had intended, but all had gone well, despite my daughter's pertness. In part, perhaps, *because* of it, as she had evidently charmed him.

The dinner was not wasted. I had our people brought up from the village, as many as pleased to come, and in our hall was a feast in honour of King Richard, which was much enjoyed. There was food enough for all, and if some beggars and outlaws from the Chase found their way to the lower tables it would not have surprised me, nor did it matter on such a day.

Thomas and I ate in the Great Chamber, of course, with my ladies, our chief officers and the most prominent men among our retainers, with a few other gentlefolk who had remained instead of going after the King. We made merry, for all had gone well and that is always a relief after a visit from an important guest. There is always an uncertainty in the stomach until you see them leave and know that there has been no misstep or folly to mar the reputation of the household or bring one into disrepute. The world is ever ready to mock, to take pleasure in any failing. Now we could take our ease, and we did so, sitting long at table and enjoying the music of our small troupe of minstrels. When we wearied of food and drink, we began to dance, and so passed the time until it grew dark, the sconces were lit, and the gluttons among us began to have thoughts of supper.

For my own part, I took a little time to visit our chapel, to kneel before the statue of the Blessed Virgin to give thanks, and also to ask for a blessing upon my marriage. I had not forgotten my purpose in coming to Hanley Castle, nor my feeling that this would be the place where I should conceive a son. It was a matter of the greatest importance to us both, but it needed the favour of God, which is sometimes much harder to gain than that of any earthly king. One may make pilgrimages, do penances, offer charity, say endless prayers and not gain any result if God's will is to the contrary.

I had all these reservations, and yet I felt peace.

***

Chapter 13

February — April 1396

It was full dark. Outside, the clock struck, four times. I could not sleep.

'I wish we could stay here longer,' Thomas said, drowsily. The flickering night-light enabled me to see the contented grin on his face. He was, unlike me, just on the point of drifting off. A moment later, no more, and he was snoring like a pig. It was tempting to kick him, but it would not have been dutiful. Besides, it was not his fault I was wide awake, with thoughts racing about in my head like a litter of young greyhounds turned out into a field for their recreation.

Instead, I moved closer to him, tucked my legs up behind him so he was almost sitting on me, and had the satisfaction of feeling him stir, of hearing him grunt with approval. It was if he had woken for an instant, just long enough to register my closeness, and then relapsed into unconsciousness.

My clinging to him was not purely for affection — though there was affection enough in my heart — it was also for warmth. We had a good number of sheets and blankets above, a greater weight than was entirely comfortable, but I was still cold. It was scarcely surprising that the room should grow chill at that time of year, but it seemed to me that there must be a heavy frost outside. As I listened, I realised that there was a strong wind to go with it. It was beating against the shutters with a rare venom. Indeed, the draught created was enough to stir the bed curtains, to set them trembling.

As he had said, we had only a short time allowed to us at Hanley. Richard was planning to move to Nottingham, once he had completed his tour of shrines. There the whole court would gather, and remain in place for some weeks, with all our wide family expected to attend, to receive and pay homage (as it were) to the new

Duchess of Lancaster. I wondered what Joanne thought of that! No, I did not wonder, because I knew the answer. I could not but smile as I thought about it. She would be making my father's life a misery over it, but what, in all honesty, could he do but accept the King's wishes?

My uncle had already secured a dispensation from the Holy Father in Rome for his marriage, and Richard had agreed that a statute should be made by Parliament to declare the Beauforts legitimate. It was all settled and sealed, and as I had told Joanne, there was nothing to do about it but be gracious. Dame Katherine Swynford had done me no harm — I preferred to reserve my spite for those who had earned it.

*

Thomas had agreed with my father that we should meet him at Leicester, and travel with him to Nottingham. It was intended, I suppose, to make the Duke's retinue more impressive at such a time, although we should not make the journey as a family, as Edward was already with the King, indeed had not left his side since we had all been together at Hanley.

We found my father waiting for us at Leicester, lodged with the black canons at St Mary's Abbey. He had Joanne with him, of course. She was no longer sulking, but was very far from cheerful. However, that was not all. They had other company, the Earl and Countess of Arundel, who were making their way north from Sussex. This was pure, evil chance, not something that had been arranged.

Arundel, by his standards, was positively affable. He grumbled about the French peace over supper, but that was no wonder, for he was a great lover of war, and taking that away from him was rather like telling my father that he was no longer allowed to chase after deer or set his greyhounds to pursue hares. However, for once he said nothing against King Richard, except to suggest he was badly advised, and he did not even condemn those giving him that advice, perhaps out of deference to my father, given his elder brother was chief among them, and that the Duke himself was of the same mind.

Joanne, although courteous, said very little, and my cousin, Lady Arundel, somehow contrived to say even less. It was a somewhat tedious evening, and when the food was finished — which did not take long, given that this was a religious house in Lent; there were only a couple of courses and only three dishes at each — the conversation did not improve.

Next morning, Joanne asked me to ride with her in her carriage, and although it was no better than my own it was not an invitation I could easily refuse without seeming discourteous. What I did not discover, until it was too late, was that she had issued a similar invitation to Philippa Arundel. That made trouble almost inevitable unless I bit my tongue all the way to Nottingham, which was all of two days' journey away.

We had barely turned onto the highway before Lady Arundel began her complaints. It was inevitable, and for a time I listened in silence, wrapped in my thick mantle against the cold as the carriage lurched from one pothole to another, moving at what was barely above walking-pace because of the condition of the road.

Then Joanne began. 'Imagine what the French will say, when that low-born creature arrives in their land to receive the new Queen! It may be enough to set the war off, all over again. Well, this I know. I shall not be there to stand in second place to witness such shame.'

'Madam,' I said mildly, 'you will have no choice. An indulgent husband will tolerate disobedience in small matters, but this is not a small matter, but a great one, touching on the whole realm. You shall have to do your duty, because my lord father will insist that you do. He has no choice either. If you are not there to receive the Queen, it will bring great disgrace on our family, and he will not stand for that.'

'I tell you, *I shall not go!* It would be a degradation. Even having to meet the woman, to acknowledge her, is humiliation enough.'

'I blame the King,' Philippa Arundel blurted out. 'It seems to me that Richard has become nothing more than Lancaster's puppet, dancing as his strings are pulled.'

I had to answer that. 'I suggest you say that to the King, or to my Uncle Lancaster. You will have your opportunity when we reach Nottingham.'

That silenced her for the time being. We rolled on down the road, a little faster now for the surface was smoother and there were fewer jolts. Joanne turned her attention to the tiny dog that she held in the crook of her arm, fussing over it as if it was on the point of death. It was a most agreeable respite and it lasted to our first stop, when we paused at a wayside inn to water the horses, while cups of ale were brought to us to drink. It was vile stuff, barely warmed, but it quenched thirst and kept Lady Arundel from talking and provoking Joanne afresh, so it was not without some merit.

It was however, only a respite. We were scarcely set on the road again before they began to discuss their favoured topic once more. It gradually grew worse and worse, with any attempt I made to soothe them or change the subject completely ignored.

'It is shameful,' Lady Arundel declared. 'I have never before heard of ladies of high birth in any Christian land, or even in the land of the Turkish infidels, being required to give place to a common trull.'

I had had enough. 'Surely,' I said, 'it is not so shameful as some of your lord's deeds over the years. The Duchess of Lancaster has never levied war on the King's Grace. Nor has she caused his true friends to be murdered. Nor did she stand by, uncaring, while Queen Anne was grossly insulted. Nor did she arrive late for the Queen's funeral, and then ask to be excused while the ceremony was but half done. *These* things I call shameful.'

'Constance!' cried Joanne. 'This is not courteous.'

'Courteous enough, madam, after what has gone before. I have heard enough spite for one day. It sickens me.'

With that, I opened one of the flaps in the side of the carriage, just sufficiently to summon young Mun Holland, who was riding close by. I told him to have a horse saddled for me, and to have it fetched up.

He was quick about his task, which was well, since the icy silence that had fallen could easily have developed into something far worse. The carriage was halted long enough for me to descend, and with Mun's willing assistance, I mounted up. The jennet he had found was not one of mine, but belonged to the Duchess. It did not much matter, although it was a very placid beast, which could have carried some octogenarian dowager or a tiny child without risk of upset. It took some persuading before its speed exceeded a slow walk, and I doubt it could have galloped to save its life. (I had no whip about me to quicken it and had to rely on words.) Eventually though I left the carriage behind, and achieving something that was almost a canter, caught up with Thomas, who was riding with the other men at the head of the procession, their banners marking their positions, my father leading the way, as was proper.

Arundel was telling the peasants harrowing the fields about his brave deeds in France. At least, his voice was pitched loud enough for them to hear, and half the county besides; but as he was speaking in French it was probably no more than a meaningless babble in their ears.

'This is an unexpected pleasure,' my lord said as I reached his side. 'I hope you have not displeased the Duchess by deserting her.'

'I should have displeased her a good deal more if I had slapped Philippa Arundel as she deserves,' I answered. 'Come to that,

I was close to slapping Joanne herself. She has no respect whatever for my lord father.'

'That is your father's business,' he said. 'It's not for you to correct her.'

I snorted. 'I know that well enough! That's why I am here, and will ride in my own carriage tomorrow. I can only stomach so much folly, Thomas. God knows, Joanne lacks the wits of a sheep, and Lady Arundel is as vile a bitch as I have met in my life, and has spent the whole morning pouring poison into her ears. What will come of it in Nottingham, I have no idea, but if Joanne baulks at paying her respects to my aunt, there will be no end of trouble. I only know I don't want my father, or the King, to think that I played any part in influencing her.'

He shrugged. 'I'm sure they both know you better than that. I'm also sure that the Duchess won't defy your father. Talking is one thing, deeds are quite another. He may be gentle in his ways, but that doesn't mean he'll allow her to shame him before the whole court. No, I think you'll find she'll do as she is bid. Grudgingly, perhaps, but she will still do it.'

'Hmm,' I said.

'I've noticed that Lent has a way of putting you into an ill mood.'

'Not Lent. Though God knows that I grow weary of the sight of fish after the first week. I doubt I'm alone in that.'

'Montagu says it's an idle superstition.'

'Montagu's a fool as well as a heretic or he'd keep his mouth shut. I say it isn't Lent that puts me in an evil mood: it's that wretched Arundel woman, as she now is. She and I have been like cat and dog from the moment we were first set free from leading-strings.'

'At least at Nottingham we shall be able to lie together again,' he said, a certain light in his eye.

'It will still be Lent.'

'Hang Lent. I will do penance for both of us, as the sin will be on my head, not yours. As my wife, you have no choice but to obey.'

That was true enough, but I still felt myself blush. How ridiculous it was! After all, it was not as if we were new-wedded. The thought of sin did not displease me as much as it ought to have done. It very distinctly did not. In truth, the thought made the tedious journey considerably less tedious.

*

Nottingham Castle was crowded, to the point where gathering one's train under one arm was a necessity if it was not to be trampled underfoot by every second person who pushed by. Despite the season, the atmosphere was one of feasting and celebration rather than contrition. There were few significant absences — my brother Rutland and Thomas Mowbray were the most obvious, but they had a good excuse, for they were at the head of an embassy to France to conclude the agreements for the peace and the King's marriage. We expected them back in England for Easter.

The ordeal that Joanne had dreaded had come upon her. It may be that my father had words with her, or even more than words. After our arrival I heard him shouting at her from the next room. Her replies were also fierce, although I could not make out the exact words on either side, only that he used French, she English.

She submitted, in any event, made her curtsey to the new Duchess, even went so far as to call her 'sister', though I believe the words all but choked her. She certainly seemed to be close to tears.

For my part, I thought it no ordeal at all. A curtsey, a few words of respectful congratulation, and it was done. The new Duchess was no more finely dressed than when she had arrived at Garter Chapters as plain Dame Katherine Swynford. Nor was her manner much changed. She was doing her utmost to be amiable and agreeable and I had no objection to her or quarrel with her.

My uncle was evidently pleased with me. He not only smiled at me, but kissed my hand. Since he usually paid me no more attention than if I were but the wife of some obscure esquire from the back end of Cornwall, this was recognition indeed, and no doubt intended as a reward for my courtesy towards his new wife.

A little later, I found myself in conversation with Lady Mohun, whom I had not seen for some years. She was not much changed, perhaps her hands were a little more gnarled, her legs weaker so that she preferred to sit at every opportunity. It was no surprise when you considered her years. She was now nearer eighty than seventy, but she still stood straight, and her gown was as fine as any in the room, not excluding the three duchesses. It was of red cloth-of-gold, grandly edged and lined with ermine, while pearls by the score jostled for position on her headdress with an array of precious stones. She was, of course, a very rich woman, and she left no one in any doubt about it.

We exchanged our news, which took some little time.

'Is my daughter Fitzwalter still in your service?' she asked.

'Yes. At present, though, she is with her husband. I believe she and Golafre are on better terms these days. It may be she will not return to me at all, but manage his household while he is away at court.'

'Hmm,' said Lady Mohun. Then was silent for a moment. 'I've heard some tales of her on the wind. They may be false. Very likely they are no more than idle gossip. God knows, I've been slandered myself over the years, as you know. If the King was as rich in gold as his court is rich in liars and other false rogues — well, for one thing, he would never need to ask a parliament for taxation ever again. Nevertheless, if I were you, I'd keep my eye on her. Philippa was ever a strange creature, even as a child. I never understood her, and I liked her least of all my girls. Secretive, and not half the fool she seems. A glib liar too, almost from when she first walked, no matter how often she was whipped for it. So, keep an eye on her, dear girl, lest you be deceived.'

There was silence between us for a moment, and then she jerked her head in a particular direction.

'Harry Bolingbroke looks less than pleased with his new mother,' she said lightly.

I followed the direction of her gaze, and there indeed was my cousin. He was clad entirely in black, albeit black velvet of the finest quality, embroidered in silver, with a great jewel in his hat, a ruby the size of a pigeon's egg. His expression was as dark as his clothes. He was in a little group with my Uncle Gloucester and Lord Arundel, among others, and they were engaged in what seemed to be a desultory talk, with long periods of silence when none of them could find anything to say.

'I suppose,' Lady Mohun ventured, 'that when you have long been the only lawful son of your father, it must be quite a shock to find that your three bastard brothers are to be advanced to be your equals. In birth at least. Of course, as you will know, most of the Lancaster lands come from Harry's mother – the Beauforts can never have any claim to that inheritance. This change has given quite a few people I could name a bruise or two, and I believe the King is enjoying himself no end.'

There was no denying that Richard looked pleased with himself. He was seated on a high throne at the far end of the hall, looking down on the company with a definite air of satisfaction. My Uncle Lancaster was standing next to him, with my new aunt seated at the King's other hand. It was a clear display of unity between them.

'It is surely my uncle who has played the main part,' I suggested.

'They've worked together, the pair of them, but even your uncle could not have brought this about without the King's active consent and assistance. They were both well aware of the stir it would cause, and neither of them gives a damn if it displeases others.

It's a demonstration of power, my dear; to be precise a demonstration of who now wields it in this England of ours. Those who dislike it may scratch themselves where it itches, but no more than that.'

'I'd not thought of it like that,' I said.

'Well, of course it's not the main issue. Your uncle had done this for love of Dame Katherine and their children, and I for one think that speaks well of him as a man. It must have cost him a great deal of money, to say nothing of the trouble involved. Everyone calls him proud, and perhaps he is. Yet surely no more than is proper in a son of King Edward. There's another side to him, Constance. I've known him since he was a snot-nosed brat, and I've often marked that in his dealings with his own family, and even with his servants and tenants, he is more often than not the soul of kindness. Even in my own dealings with him, I've always found him fair, even generous. I had your cousin, Catherine, in my charge for some years, and her father saw she lacked for nothing, and never questioned any expense I incurred as her governess. To do him justice, I believe him a better man than most.'

I shook my head. 'His generosity did not extend to my father, that's for sure. Not so much as a clipped groat spared from the huge fortune he brought back from Castile, or from the fat pension granted to him. He's quite forgotten that my mother's claim to that throne was as good as my aunt's, or very close. If we were talking of lands in England, there would have been an equal partition between them. I think he treated my father meanly, if not unjustly, when he could easily have afforded to give him some portion of the money. I doubt Harry shares your high opinion of his father either.'

'He is a dutiful son, nonetheless, and will accept the change, however much he may dislike it. I fear his tragedy is that he was born too late. In King Edward's day, he would have been leading an army in France, and doing well, I think. As it is, he's a man without purpose, or at least without the work that a man of his birth should have. He can only stand around, twiddling his thumbs. The King does not trust him, and gives him no responsibility.'

'Do you wonder that the King does not trust him, my lady?' I stared at her, puzzled by her kindly assessment of my cousin. 'I need not remind you he was one of those who had you banished from court, as though you were a thieving chamberer, dismissed in shame for stealing a trinket. Though, of course, they went on to do much worse. Let us not pretend any of it was done without Harry's assent, at the very least.'

'I believe he tried to save Burley, Constance.'

'Hmm, well he did not try hard enough, evidently. That poor, gentle old man! I saw him die.'

She looked shocked. 'You did?'

'I was in attendance on the Queen that day.'

'I marvel that she allowed it! Whatever was she thinking about? You were a child, my dear, and it was not by any means a fit sight for your eyes. A beheading! Of a man you knew well, and liked! I wish I had been there to prevent it.'

'Well, you were not, because of *them*. Anne was left with very few ladies to wait upon her, and I was by far the highest in rank. Besides, I was not a child any more. I was fully twelve, a woman in the eyes of God, and it was my *duty*. I remember all who were there and how they bore themselves. I dream of it to this day.'

She took my hands, bowed her head over them. 'Poor child! I really had no idea you suffered that. Curse those Appellant dogs for sending me away; I should never have permitted it, and Anne, God pardon her, should not have permitted it either.'

'As I said, it was my duty. I don't regret that I was there, because it made sure that I shall never forget the debt, or think well of the likes of Harry Bolingbroke.'

*

Alianore, Lady March, was also at Nottingham. She was lodged with her parents, just as in the old days, but had not arrived with them, but had made her way from Ludlow with her own considerable train of followers, the men clad brightly in their red and green Mortimer liveries.

'I had expected your brother to be here,' she said irritably. 'Ned promised he would be, in the last letter I had.'

I explained he was in France.

'I'm well aware of that!' It was not quite a snap, but it was slightly too brisk to be polite, even between friends. 'The point is, he said he would be here. I suppose he and Mowbray are finding Paris too agreeable, and so they linger.'

I doubted that. 'You seem to be in an ill mood, like several others here. Your sister of Arundel, for example. Your other sister of York. Is it for the same reason?'

She snorted. 'No, not at all. If your uncle wants to make himself look like an old fool, troubling Pope, King and a parliament about such a matter, that's his business. The lady herself is gracious enough, all things considered. I had to be here, to stand for Roger and show goodwill. I did hope, though, that as my reward I should at least have the pleasure of seeing Ned again. You know how matters stand.'

Strictly, I suppose, I could have said that I did not. No one had ever said, in plain words, exactly what there was between Edward and Alianore — or rather what was not. Even Alianore had never confessed her secrets to me in any detail. Nor had I probed. It was obvious enough though, given that whenever we were at court they were almost always together, often in quiet corners. Not everything has to be made explicit.

I wanted to tell her that if she was wise she would not put too much trust in my brother Rutland, who was too busy making his way in the world, and too callous, to spare much thought to her feelings.

However, I was too much of a coward; besides, I knew she would not heed me.

'He could arrive any day,' I said, to placate her. 'We are to move to York for Easter. If he does not come here, he will certainly be there, because he and Mowbray have to report to the King on their dealings with the French.'

'What with Ned and March, I seem to have been born to suffer fools,' she said impatiently. 'Though that my husband is a fool is no news to you, or to anyone in this entire castle. Do you know what he's done now? He's only broken the peace in Ireland, that's all. He's at war with O'Neill in Ulster, over his lands there. The King is furious with him, or so I gather. He's to be recalled — which is very bad news as far as I am concerned, since I shall be expected to share his bed and board. He'll be sorely scolded, at the least. Told what a fool he is. Perhaps stripped of his office as Lord Lieutenant. In which case, he'll stay here in England and expect to live with me *all the time*! Or part of it, anyway. I know he keeps a whore at Wigmore. With any fortune, he'll prefer her company to mine.'

'Has my Cousin Richard spoken to you of this?'

'No. Not directly. I dare say he's more important business to occupy him than a conversation with me. I had the tale straight from my father, so I doubt I'm being deceived. Only Roger could be so *stupid*!'

We walked along in silence for a minute, passing a small group of minstrels who were toying with their instruments, preparing against their performance later in the day. Their music was solemn, as befitted the season.

'It may be,' I said, 'that you don't have the full tale, or even the half of it. Roger may have his reasons for fighting. What if this O'Neill, or whatever he's called, attacked *him*? Or disobeyed him? Roger would have to maintain his authority, would he not? He could not sit there on his hands if he is facing defiance. Surely the King will see that.'

She sighed. 'It's true that all this arises from O'Neill's complaints to the King.'

'Well, then.'

'But it fits well enough with what I know of Roger, and the solid bone he calls a head. Is it likely that some wild Irishman would dare appeal to the King unless he had a very good case? Such a man would scarcely expect to be believed, not in a dispute involving Richard's own cousin, unless he could at least provide powerful evidence. So I suppose he has.'

'I'm sure it can all be settled easily enough. The King is a reasonable man.'

'Is he? You think so? It's not the first word I'd choose.'

'I doubt he'll ruin Roger over such a matter. It'll be a rebuke at the very worst. What other great lord would be willing to take your husband's place in Ireland or even be envious of it? It's no sinecure, nor even an office of profit, and no one else has even half Roger's lands over there. It would make no sense to remove him.'

'Sense? The rule of England is not based on what makes sense, Constance! I marvel that you think it is. Is it sense to make the second King Edward a saint?'

I shook my head. 'He was God's anointed, deposed by men who had no right or proper authority, and then martyred. He works miracles at Gloucester. Do you not think that sufficient?'

She gave me an uncertain glance. 'I am not a priest to judge, but it seems folly to me, if half what I've heard of King Edward is true. Though I'm not such a fool that I don't see what advantage my uncle the King hopes to gain by pressing the question.'

I sighed. 'Alianore, he was threatened with the same fate. I was there, in the room, when my Uncle Gloucester said it. There's more besides, much worse, that I may not tell you. It's no wonder to me that Richard seeks to secure himself, by whatever means. The sainting of King Edward is but one stone in a wall.'

She shook her head, grunting. 'Joanne is right. When last she deigned to write to me, she said that Richard could do no wrong in your eyes. If you were his leman, you couldn't defend him any more fiercely.'

I would have taken that as an insult from almost anyone else; as it was I laughed it off, and we began to speak of other matters, such as the growth of her children, and the tedium of living on the edge of Wales. Not, in truth, that she cared for any subject other than the continuing absence of my brother. I believe she was quite sick with love for him. It was folly, but not folly such as I could amend.

*

We moved on to York, where the King had decided to celebrate his Easter court. Not all who had been gathered at Nottingham journeyed with us, but then again there were many of the northern lords who came to York, so the total numbers present were scarcely less. The court was lodged in and around St Mary's Abbey, my lord and I having the use of a merchant's large house across the way, which we used chiefly for sleeping and resting, being within the abbey precincts for much of the day.

It was here that my brother Edward and Thomas Mowbray returned to the court, smiling broadly, bearing themselves with a pride that showed in their very way of walking, their sumpter horses laden down with the presents they had received in France. King Richard received them formally of course, with all of us standing around to make a great ceremony of the occasion, in the refectory of the abbey. Mowbray did most of the talking. The treaty was concluded, he told us — though this was no surprise — on the basis of Richard's marriage to Isabella and a twenty-eight year truce. A meeting had been arranged between the two kings to confirm the agreement, but this was but a formality, an occasion for ceremonial. The long war was over.

Most of the faces gathered around the King were composed, if not pleased. Even my Uncle Gloucester, if not content, was no more grave than usual, and did not raise his voice in his objection, as he would have done even a year or two earlier. Only Arundel looked angry, as though someone had just stolen his best horse and left an ass by way of exchange. However, even he kept silent.

Such an occasion would normally have been marked by a great feast; as it was, we were in Holy Week, and so the supper we ate was modest by the standards of the court, although it comprised all manner of fish from salmon and pike to eels, lampreys and cockles. As soon as it was over Richard withdrew into a private apartment, taking Mowbray, Edward and a few others, all members of his Council, with him, no doubt to hear more details of their work in France.

Alianore's face was even more disappointed than that of Lord Arundel listening to news of the treaty. Thomas and I had found a corner in which to seclude ourselves with friends, and we drew her into it, along with John Montagu and his wife. Fortunately, on this occasion Montagu did not wish to preach theology at us. He had a sheaf of poems he had written, and while the rest of us busied ourselves with dice and idle chatter he read some of his work to us. They were on the subject of love, and perhaps not the best choice for the season, but they were entertaining and Alianore was enraptured. It seemed they fitted her mood perfectly, to the point where her complaints were replaced by a pensive smile and a contented silence.

'You write better poems than my brother,' I told Montagu, smiling at him.

Thomas laughed. 'That's scant praise. You might as well tell a man he handles a lance better than a scarecrow.'

'That is unjust!' Alianore cried. 'Ned writes very well; although *his* verses are in plain English.'

'Ah,' said John Montagu, 'my lady of March prefers the

English form? Well, I must own it's becoming ever more fashionable, especially among those who write in expectation of coin from the multitude. French, though, is a more poetic language, and all the greatest poetry is written in that tongue. Our English tongue is certainly plain – and that's its weakness. It lacks all melody. French, I think, is more suited to a noble audience, such as understand its beauty and subtle meaning. As opposed to the yokels and clowns who gather in every alehouse and laugh themselves sick mocking millers, friars and cuckolds. Such rough humour has its place — but that place is not among those of gentle birth, still less those of noble blood.'

'Ned's poems speak of love just as yours do; he doesn't make crude jests. I think, sir, that you should hear his work.'

'Oh, Alianore!' I cried. 'Is not living without meat for forty days mortification enough? I love my brother well enough. There's much to be said in his favour, but he's no more a poet than I am, and I can no more put together a rhyme like those Lord Montagu has read to us than I can fly through the air. If you were to argue that Ned is cleverer than the rest of us, or that he sits a horse very well, you'd be on safer ground.'

Everyone laughed, except Alianore, who looked hurt. I was sorry for that, and sought to make amends by telling the company that I had missed my brother a great deal, and was glad he was home again, and high in favour. So much so that I doubted I should be so fortunate as to gain a word with him, given that he was occupied with great matters of state. This seemed to mollify her a little. She all but smiled.

'I wonder if he has concluded his own marriage?' Thomas asked. 'To the Lady Isabella's sister? I know he was less than anxious to conclude it, and nor can I blame him, given that the girl must barely be weaned.'

'He will do his duty,' I said, 'if it is the King's wish.'

'Perhaps.'

'It will likely come to nothing,' Montagu answered. (He had had his portion in the negotiations with the French, so spoke with some authority.) 'It was never a key part of the peace. More an afterthought. The greater pity is that not all matters between us could be resolved, which is why we have a long truce instead of a final peace. Still, it ends the question for a generation, and after that long a time living in amity, no one in his wits will wish to begin fighting again. My guess is a true peace will emerge from it, and that in fifty years or so, when we are all dust, no one will be able to believe that such a profitless war was ever begun.'

'My father would not have called it profitless,' Thomas said, 'for he made a great fortune from it — as did others. There are many about us, even here, who will sorrow at the end of any prospect of such gains.'

'Gains for some, I grant you,' Montagu said, 'but only at the cost of high taxes for every man to pay. That burden will be taken from the people; that will content them. Unless, of course, we decide upon a great crusade against the infidel instead, which the King favours.'

'I favour it myself. It would be to the benefit of all our souls, and pleasing to God. This peace makes it possible — indeed we would be fighting the infidels as allies of the French. Imagine the combined force of England and France! Who could stand against us?'

Montagu shook his head. 'At my age the prospect is not as shining as it may be at yours. I have begun to prefer my hearth and home.'

'Sakes, man, you are not *that* old! Imagine if we could take Jerusalem. It would eclipse all the deeds of the third Edward. Who then would talk of Crécy or Poitiers? They would seem like petty skirmishes in Ireland by comparison! What good is peace if we do not make good use of the respite?'

'To make war in another place? It's a dream, Thomas. A folly. As bad in its way as the false dream of conquering France. This country has been bled white with taxes for decades. It should be given time to grow and prosper, for our merchants to wax fat on their profits. The French as allies? Who, pray, would command? Would you obey a Frenchman? Would *they* obey an Englishman? Think on it. It would be chaos, and chaos brings about defeat and destruction. Let us stay at home, and breed fat sheep, and take our ease.'

I could see from his face that Thomas was inclined to argue, and I could also sense that it might lead to a quarrel. So I placed my hand on his, and used my eyes to plead for peace. He took a breath, but the moment passed.

This talk of crusades appalled me, but it was nothing new. The King had talked of it, many times, and you will remember that several of his most favoured knights, including Thomas and Edward, had become members of the Order of the Passion of Jesus Christ. I had thought it a dream, a mere game, an idle ceremony, part of the formal dance of diplomacy, not to be taken seriously. Thomas's words suggested otherwise, and I was reminded of his decision to go to Prussia, taken without any discussion with me, simply announced to Elisabeth's guests at Christmas.

I did not quite agree with Montagu, but I agreed this far — that there was plenty of work for us in England, a thousand matters to settle before there was any thought of more vain adventures in foreign lands. As far as I was concerned, my lord had no need to prove himself in martial deeds except, perhaps, those that might be accomplished in a tilt-yard with a rebated spear and a blunt sword. The problem was that he seemed to have other ambitions.

*

At the dawn of Easter Day we went in a great procession through the streets of York to the Minster, where those of us highest in rank filed into the chancel to take our places. The Minster was so full of the aroma of new cloth that it smelled like a draper's shop, even the competing aroma of incense being quite overborne. Not to be outdone by anyone else, I wore my new heraldic mantle for the first time, so that my back was covered by the colours of Despenser and York, not only proclaiming my identity to all present but also serving to keep me warm, for the morning was chill and the bright painted tiles beneath our feet as cold as ice.

After the gloom of Holy Week, the services lit by fewer and fewer candles until we were more or less worshipping in darkness, the great church now blazed with dozens of candles, so that every face, every expression, could be marked. Most were well contented on this joyous day, the greatest of Church celebrations, and we were all impatient for the feast that would follow this service, our reward for weeks of abstinence.

The sacred Host and the Cross were brought out of the Easter Sepulchre and restored to their proper places and the boys of the King's chapel raised their voices in beautiful chant. We went forward, all of us, in due order of precedence, to make our offerings. Archbishop Arundel preached — for this was his own cathedral, not that he saw it very often — a cheerful sermon of the wonder of Christ's Resurrection and of the solemn sacrifice made in redemption of our sin. (He spoiled the effect only a little by speaking briefly of the tares among us, who needed to be rooted out and burnt – he meant, of course the Lollard heretics such as Montagu.)

Then, all at once, it was over, and we were dismissed, like happy children released from the schoolroom, knowing that the great feast lay before us, many happy hours at table filling our stomachs with every delicacy imaginable — *except fish!*

As we made our way to the hall we formed a procession, an informal, happy one, without the marshalling of officious heralds, noisy with chatter as excited voices were raised in anticipation of the meal to come.

I found myself walking next to Harry Bolingbroke. He greeted me courteously, bowing low, and wishing me a joyous Easter.

I could do no less than match his courtesy, of course. I despised him as much as I did any of the Appellants, indeed I thought him in some ways the most unnatural among them. That did not, however, mean that I could behave in an ill-bred manner.

He was still wearing black. It looked sumptuous upon him, it was true, both cloth and embroidery entirely fit for a king, as was his tall, sable fur hat, and I could not help but remark on it.

'I wear it for remembrance of Mary,' he said, solemnly. 'She was a good and dutiful wife to me. Perhaps better than I deserved. It's true I've not had one of my manors demolished by way of a memorial, but that doesn't mean I do not mourn.'

'I believe we may soon be brother and sister, as well as cousins,' I said lightly.

For a moment he looked puzzled. 'Oh, you mean the King's plan to marry me to one of King Charles's daughters, and your brother to another?' He gave an awkward little laugh. 'Yes, I suppose that would make us brother and sister, after a fashion, if it came to pass. However, these negotiations are slow and complex and take time, and much that is proposed never bears fruit. Look at the design to give Guienne to my father. That came to nothing, barely a breath after it was first suggested. Your brother and I are in perfect agreement. We are both of us peculiar enough in our tastes to prefer a grown woman. So we shall introduce every possible delay and objection, until the day comes that everyone forgets that these marriages were ever proposed.'

'You will defy the King?'

He shook his head. 'Certainly not. I'll not make any such error. It's just I believe the question will never arise. Ask your brother. I believe he will tell you the same about his own case. Nine times out of ten, such proposals come to nothing, especially when they are not the main plank of the treaty. I very much doubt I shall ever have the honour of referring to you as my sister.'

'I have scarce had a word with Edward since he came home,' I said. 'He seems ever busy with the King's business. I shall certainly ask him when I have a chance, and also what he knows of this crusade that seems to be in prospect. What do you know of that, Harry? My lord seems to think that he will go, and I'm sure that you'll be even more keen than he is, for all the world knows what a mighty warrior you are.'

I tried to keep the scorn out of my voice, but I fear I did not succeed. However, he merely smiled back at me, as if my compliment was sincere. He always was a most infuriating fellow!

'You flatter me, fair cousin,' he said. 'The truth is, as with my marriage, I doubt that it will come to pass. However, if the King leads such a glorious venture, I shall most certainly follow him. All the way to Jerusalem.'

He smiled again, wryly. I knew his meaning well enough. He did not think Richard man enough ever to embark on such a campaign. He held our cousin in complete disdain.

I did not allow myself to dwell on his contempt for the King. I had a feast before me, and could all but taste the roasted lamb in my mouth. It was strange, but even as I thought of it, I began to feel nausea.

Fortunately, it remained but a feeling, or I should have been shamed before the common people of York who stood watching us as we passed along their streets. As it turned out, I ate very little of that great meal at St Mary's. A little watered wine, and a few wafers, quite sufficed. I could not stomach more.

Hanley Castle

At this great feast of the year, the King wore his crown, as was the ancient custom; and once the dinner was finished sat on a high throne beneath his canopy of estate, looking down on the company, maintaining his silence. All might reverence him — and some were in attendance here for that very purpose — but for the present he would not initiate a conversation, so of course no one could speak to him.

He looked so lonely sitting there, and I am sure he found the custom of the day a tedious duty. Yet he sat there because it was expected of him. In past times he had at least had Anne to keep him company, with whom he might exchange a smile or a quiet word. Now he was alone. Utterly, utterly alone. There were those there, I am sure, who envied his position, who looked on with bitterness in their hearts. I felt only pity, and regret that I could not comfort him with so much as a word. Etiquette, custom, whatever you call it, forbade any such gesture.

Suddenly, Edward was at my side.

'Soon,' he said, glancing towards the King, 'our cousin may have more than England to rule.'

'Do you talk of Jerusalem?' I asked. I couldn't imagine what else he meant, though it made little sense. Even if a crusade was fought, and was more successful than anyone thought possible, any gains would surely have to be shared with the French. Especially as their numbers were certain to be larger than ours, for France can field far more fighting men than England, and always has, time out of mind.

'I speak of the Empire. The German Empire, the Roman Empire, call it what you will, though God knows it has precious little to do with Rome beyond the title. It seems that some of the Electors are unhappy with Wenceslas, and are casting about to replace him.'

Wenceslas of Bohemia was Anne's brother, King of the Romans, so-called, and Emperor in all but name, though never invested by the Pope as was necessary if that title was to be claimed.

I shook my head. 'Is this one of your jokes?'

'No joke at all. Approaches have been made. Though nothing is certain at this time, and cannot be until more of the Electors are won over. Imagine though if it comes to pass! Richard will be a greater lord, by far, than any English king that has lived. How we have come on, my sister, since that day at Sheen when Uncle Gloucester thought to knock you out of his way, when Richard had scarcely any power at all but had to dance to whatever tune the Appellants piped. Look at him now, and imagine him, greater still. We at his side, because we are among the few he can trust. And if he spends half his time in Germany, who do you think will rule here?'

'Others will have the same ambition,' I said.

'Others are not trusted. I am. *We* are. My father might be given the task, while he lives, but he is more interested in his lovely Duchess than in statecraft. So the work will certainly be delegated.'

I sighed. 'I wish you would spend less time dreaming about what may never be, and give more of your company to Alianore. She is only here because of you, and you have scarcely looked at her.'

'Do you forget that I've been occupied with our Cousin Richard's great business?' he asked. 'A man cannot spend all his life running about after ladies like a love-sick puppy. You know that. Thomas, I swear, does not devote his every waking hour to you.'

'He is my husband. It is different.'

'Is it?'

As it chanced, my lord was not so very far away, indeed he was almost within hearing distance, engaged with Thomas Mowbray, John Montagu and some other fellow I could not name, though I had seen his face about the court.

'I wonder what his business is with William Bagot?' Edward asked.

Hanley Castle

'Bagot? Is that who he is? Is he not Warwick's man?' I was puzzled.

My brother snorted. 'At one time. He's been Warwick's man. My Uncle Lancaster's man. Mowbray's man. The King's man. Anyone's man who pays well enough. One of the worst rogues in England.'

'Worse than Arundel?'

Arundel was standing a little way off, with our Uncle Gloucester, their faces serious as they conversed.

'Far worse. At least you know what Arundel stands for, what he believes. You and I may dislike him, but he's honest enough in his way. Bagot would sell his own grandmother for advantage, and truckles to any man if it suits his purpose. If I were you, I'd advise Thomas to be wary of growing too close to such a reprobate.'

'I shall; but he may not heed me.'

He grunted. 'That reminds me. You need to keep him on a shorter leash, and especially if March is brought home. It will profit him nothing to be seen as too close to the Mortimers. I've told you why before this — the matter of their other connections.'

He nodded in the general direction of Arundel, who now had his countess on his arm. I had not noticed Philippa Arundel's arrival — it was as if she had sprung out of the ground — but the sight of her gave me no pleasure. She was whispering in her lord's ear, grinning at him as if they were sharing a joke. They probably were, and I suspected it was the King they were mocking.

'Will March be recalled?' I asked. 'Alianore seemed to think so.'

He shrugged. 'Perhaps. I think Cousin Richard has other matters to occupy him, and his anger has cooled. I will do all I can to keep dear Roger where he is. It's better so. For more reasons than one.'

Alianore was walking towards us, and as soon as he caught sight of her, he abandoned me and stepped forward to bow low before her and kiss her hand.

*

By the time we returned to Nottingham, I was all but sure I was with child again, although I did not boast of it for fear of tempting fate. My women, who were as good at counting the passing weeks as I was myself, undoubtedly drew their own conclusions, and I hinted to Thomas that I had my hopes, which pleased him well. However, the only real certainty is when the child decides to kick against the walls of its lodgings, and it was, as yet, too early for that.

'I want you all to see how I am promoted,' Edward said. He produced a parchment from some crevice of his clothing, the King's seal bright at its foot. 'You need not read all the detail. The opening will suffice. "To Edward, Earl of Rutland and Cork, *the King's brother*." See for yourselves. I do not lie.'

He handed it to Thomas, who read it silently before passing it to me. It was not an exaggeration. The words were there, in black and white.

We were gathered in the rather cramped lodgings allocated to Thomas and me. My lord and I were sitting on the bed, Alianore next to Edward on the window-seat. My brother Dickon was sitting on a cushion, serving as a door stop, but also present to pour our wine and wait on us as required.

'So,' I said, 'you intend to marry the child? When we were at York, our cousin, Harry, told me he was sure that it would come to nothing.'

Edward grinned. 'I know not what is more remarkable. That you should talk to Harry of Lancaster; or that he should confide in you. Perhaps it was some kind of Easter miracle. Was there a great flash of light? Did an angel appear?'

'Ned, you should not mock the holy angels,' I objected. 'Have you been listening to John Montagu?'

He snorted. 'I'm not such a fool. These Lollard babblings are dangerous, and I'll have none of them. Nor, I trust, will any of you.'

He glanced around the company, as if to challenge anyone to dissent. It was almost as if he had suddenly become king, not merely the King's brother, such was the note of command in his voice. It made me bristle in rebellion, but I could not disagree with his words.

'I don't think that my new title has anything to do with any marriage,' he said. He allowed us to dwell on that for a moment, and then was away on a different topic altogether 'This is an ancient place, and could profit from rebuilding,' he said. 'If I were king, I'd have it razed and start again from the ground to make it fit to be lived in. Of course, the rock on which it stands is riddled with secret tunnels and passages. Did you know that? Some fellow could walk in here while you're fast asleep and steal your jewels and coin for all that I know.

'Alianore, it was here at Nottingham, and through just such a passage, that my grandfather, King Edward sneaked in with his friends to seize your husband's ancestor, the first Earl of March, that great traitor who brought down the second Edward. Some say he was dragged out of the bed of my great-grandmother, Isabella of France. *That* I beg leave to doubt. Others were taken at the same time, and I think it unlikely that old Roger and Isabella would have had a crowd about them to witness their embraces. I also suspect Queen Isabella would not have deigned to lie with a mere earl, and a newly minted one at that. Still, the fools out there much prefer a bawdy tale to plain truth.'

'Have we nothing better to talk about than ancient history?' I asked.

He shook his head. 'Not so ancient. Your friend, Lady Mohun, remembers it. I know, because I asked her about it.'

'She can only have been a young girl. Not at court, either, but barely out of leading-strings.'

'It was the talk of England at the time, and she was not *that* young. Almost as old as you were when you first came to court to wait upon Queen Anne. She remembers, and much else besides, such as Mortimer and Queen Isabella causing Thomas's great-grandsire to be hanged. It's strange, Thomas, in the circumstances, that you and March are such fond gossips. You've no cause to love that family, given they were the ruin of yours.'

Thomas grunted over his wine. 'You would have me blame Roger for something that happened many years before he was born? Before his father was born, if it comes to that? Well, I don't. The quarrel is buried, and I intend to keep it buried.'

'Yet it isn't truly buried, is it? Are you not busy seeking to overturn the verdict against Hugh Despenser?'

'I am, for the sake of my family honour. It was unjust dealing, and a false verdict, but it was not Roger's fault, any more than it is mine.'

'It's all of a piece, Thomas. That's the point. There was more than one injustice done back in those days, and especially if we agree that my great-grandfather was a saint. If he was, what does that make his enemies? Think on it. Consider who sits on the lands that should be yours.'

I knew that my brother was trying to stir trouble, but exactly what trouble was less clear.

'All this talk of old disputes bores me,' Alianore said. 'May we not talk of something more interesting? Ned, I have seen so little of you since York, and now you weary me with ancient tales. Let us dance. Or read me one of your poems. Or give us news of Paris, and what manner of gowns the French ladies are wearing. Anything! You know I cannot stay with the court for long; that I must soon go back to Ludlow.'

'Ludlow? No need to hurry away to that backwater. Surely you could travel with us at least as far as Windsor?'

'To stand with the crowds and watch my betters proceed to the Garter feast? I think not, Ned. Besides, I've no wish to neglect my children.'

'Have they not nurses, governesses, and other such menials? They would scarcely miss you if you stayed away another month. Whereas I — all of us—' he gestured to include Thomas and me, 'will miss your company most sorely.'

'I doubt it,' she sniffed. 'I might as well have stayed away from court for what I've seen of you. It's a wonder to me that you're not with the King *now*, with his other cronies.'

He shook his head. 'You know of the business that took me to Paris, and there was much to report to Richard, many questions to be answered. Yes, I am often in his presence. He relies on my counsel, and I count myself his friend. If he requires my company, for whatever reason, I can scarcely deny it. Tonight though, as it happens, he is dicing with those with the deepest purses. Your uncle, Huntingdon. Montagu. Mowbray. They put down stakes I cannot match, and in any event, the game is tedious.'

'So we should count ourselves honoured with an hour of your time? *I* should?'

'Alianore, you're not being reasonable. Every hour I'm at leisure is devoted to you.'

'If you're not hunting, or hawking, or fussing over your dogs, or showing off in the tilt-yard.'

'Please, don't quarrel,' I said. 'Let's do as Alianore asked. We could dance.'

'Dance?' Edward glanced around him, surveying our inadequate chamber. 'Where? Two on the bed, two on the floor? With no one to make music?'

'Dickon can play his pipe,' I suggested.

'I'm glad he's capable of something. Truly though, there isn't space. We'd be falling over one another.' He laughed at the thought. Paused for a moment of silence. 'I've just thought of another old tale,' he went on, 'and this one's amusing. Even Alianore will laugh. It's said by some that Uncle Lancaster is but a changeling, the son of a Flemish butcher. Some will surely say that this marriage of his confirms it, since no true-born prince would dream of making such a connection. What do you say to that? Can there be any truth in it?'

'Of course not!' I snapped. 'Only a fool would believe such idle tattle. You've only to look at our uncle to see that he's one of us.'

He shook his head. 'That doesn't follow at all. Richard has a clerk who is the exact image of him. You must have seen the man about the court — his name is Richard Maudelyn. He could be a cousin of some sort I suppose, but I don't know that anyone has claimed him as a son. If you put the King's clothes on him, and trimmed his beard, it'd be hard to tell one from the other. Of course, he's but a clerk, and dresses accordingly, so the chances are you've never even spared him a glance. He exists though. One day I'll present him to you, and you can judge for yourself. Mere resemblance proves nothing.'

'This is dangerous talk,' Thomas said.

Edward shrugged. 'We're quite private, unless you think

some French intelligencer is listening through the wall. Besides, these tales are no secret. My uncle is very well aware of them. It was talked about long before any of us were born, and the rumour has never died out. I don't say it's true, but how can anyone be sure?'

'You wouldn't dare say it to his face,' Alianore said, 'and it would be better not said at all. I wonder at you, Ned, I really do. At times you have no more wits than March — which is to say a sheep! — and you're more reckless, more cruel with your words.'

'I did but seek to make you all laugh,' he said amiably, as though he wanted to appease her. 'It's an old story, and many old stories are mere folly. It's just that — one day — the tale may find a use. Who can say?'

Later, much later, Thomas and I were alone and in our bed, yet not asleep. My brother had given us too much to think about — I kept wondering about those secret passages, and if they existed, where they might emerge. What if a thief or a spy was in hiding, just inches away behind the rendered walls? Was it possible?

Suddenly, Thomas spoke, his voice loud in the silence. 'Some weeks back I said that you enjoyed setting hares running, and you didn't deny it. Now I see it's a family trait. Rutland put more hares to flight this evening than a dozen leashes of greyhounds could hope to catch. What was his purpose? Is it but idle mischief, or is it more than that?'

I shrugged. 'I don't know; but it's certain Ned has always enjoyed the sound of his own voice. Always he likes to lead, and make it seem he knows more than any of us.'

'Well, perhaps he does. No one is closer to the King, unless it is John Huntingdon; so he will know secrets denied to us. I thought he was hinting at his purpose, and yet I've no idea what that purpose may be.'

I frowned. I had no answer, or at least, no answer that I was prepared to make. What had crossed my mind was too absurd, I thought. I didn't want Thomas to laugh at me, or think me a credulous fool.

Edward gloried in being called 'The King's brother'. That much was clear. He had done all in his power to destroy March. Now he was also telling strange tales of my Uncle Lancaster. What was his purpose? Was it possible he thought the throne was within his reach?

I shook my head. That was too much, even for Edward. He could not possibly aspire so high. Or could he?

Eventually, still dwelling on this, I somehow fell asleep. My lord had been snoring for a good hour before I accomplished this end.

***

Chapter 14

Summer 1396

Philippa Fitzwalter was back with me again, and this time it looked very much as if it would be a permanent arrangement. She denied, with some vehemence, that she had ever been reconciled with her husband. She swore she had never had a happy moment either in his bed or at his board. (This I found almost impossible to believe, but it was what she told me.) She spoke of every kind of cruelty — apart from keeping her short of money, a matter on which she devised long litanies. She had been punched; kicked; thrown downstairs so that she almost broke her neck.

It would have been a vile tale, had it been true. However, much as I disliked Sir John Golafre, an insolent rogue if I've ever met one, I didn't believe the half of it. For one thing, she wrote to him almost every other day — or so she said. She was certainly writing to someone, because hardly anyone was allowed to leave Hanley Castle without bearing a letter from her, even if it was only to be taken to Tewkesbury to be handed to the carrier. She received frequent letters too. About every month or six weeks she had one from her mother, Lady Mohun, and these she allowed me to see. The others she kept to herself.

In any event, she claimed that she never wished to see Golafre again; although, if we were to return to court, she would tolerate a meeting. She certainly had no intention of living with him.

It was summer again, and so hot that it was almost unbearable to move, even indoors, even when wearing a simple linen gown and the most modest linen kerchief over the hair. We had the casements wide open, and every so often a bee or some other flying insect would find its way in and buzz about the room until it fell victim to someone's hand or some dog's mouth. At least the occasional breath of cooler air arrived with them, along with the usual sounds rising from the courtyard, men and boys shouting at one another, the occasional clatter of hooves as someone arrived or left on one errand or another, the regular soundings of the great clock. Now and then a cart rolled in with supplies of ale and cider, for we were building up our stocks for the haymaking and the castle brewery could not meet the necessary demand when it must also serve my household. For the majority of our people were at Hanley — only Thomas and his riding-household were away at court.

I sorely missed my greyhound, Edith. Running about the park in her usual, joyous way, she had collided with a tree. At first I had thought her knocked unconscious, but it soon became clear she was dead. Another link with my days of innocence was gone. A precious gift from my father.

Philippa could not understand why I still mourned her.

'She was only a dog,' she said, 'and you have others. Thomas would buy you ten more tomorrow if you asked. Besides, she was growing old, and was useless for hunting. You've said it yourself, she could not catch anything.'

It was a waste of breath to try to explain. I glared at her in sign of my annoyance, but I might as well have frowned at a carved stone for all the good it did.

We sat in silence for a good hour.

'Are you uncomfortable, cousin?' she asked at last.

She must have been watching me carefully, as I had not uttered any complaint. I imagined myself quite composed, but I suppose I must have gritted my teeth, or flinched, or stirred in my place without realising that I had.

'The child is kicking,' I said, 'and by the feel of it he's already wearing sabatons.'

She offered a little smile. 'You're sure it's a "he"?'

'No girl could be so restless, or so unruly.'

'If you're right, Cousin Tom will be well pleased.'

Tom? I gave her a glance of irritation. No one called Thomas 'Tom', not even his mother, and certainly not me. Philippa had a way of chopping names that verged on the insolent.

'Not only my lord,' I said, stressing the formality by way of rebuke, 'but also my lady his mother and the whole family. They have waited long enough.'

'Perhaps it would ease you to walk in the garden,' she suggested. 'It's stuffy in here, and the exercise might be of profit.'

So it might, I thought. I was proud of our garden and the changes I had wrought on the neglected wilderness I had inherited. We even had a fountain now, though it only worked as long as the reservoir that fed it did not run dry. There had been so little rain of late that I suspected the flow might be feeble.

I was just about to stir myself when there was another clatter of hooves in the courtyard. Something made me look out, and I saw that the new arrival was a young man in our livery, one of those in attendance on Thomas. It could only be a letter, and with that in prospect I settled myself down again, and waited.

There was but little delay before the fellow was kneeling before me, holding out his message.

'My lord is but a few hours behind me,' he explained. 'The letter will tell you more, my lady, but it's certain he'll be here before supper.'

He looked hot, dusty and flustered from his ride, and I gave orders for him to be served food and ale at once, even before I broke the seal. He had earned that reward, at least.

I had not expected Thomas, so this was a pleasant surprise. The letter told me little more, except that he intended to visit his mother on his way to Hanley, and that he expected that other guests would be with us in a few days. There was no detail as to who these guests were to be, or in what numbers they would appear. For a moment, I was irritated. Surely Thomas realised that it was one thing to prepare for the arrival of John Russell and his lady, quite another to receive the entire court? It could be either, to judge from this missive, or anything in between.

There was no time to muse on it. Orders had to be given, not least an instruction to Hugh Bygge that he and his kitchen folk were to feed, that night, far more of us than he had expected. My people knew their business though, and the castle came swiftly to life with men and boys hurrying about their tasks, airing the guest chambers, setting up additional tables in the hall, broaching casks of ale and cider, drawing our best wine and undertaking all the dozens of small chores that needed to be completed. My part in this was to wander about with my women, checking that all was in hand; but this was next to a formality, done more because it was the custom than because it was really necessary.

I saw to it that my daughter was changed and clean, fit to welcome her father, and had myself changed into a more suitable gown and headdress. The heat of the day was beginning to decline, and in any event there was no more rushing about to do. I had but to settle and wait, although my stomach trembled with anticipation, as though I was but a green girl on her way to a tryst with a secret lover. It was absurd, and I silently reproved myself, but so it was.

At last, he came. I hurried down to the courtyard to greet him, with my daughter walking at my side, holding my hand. I'm not quite sure which of us was restraining the other from unseemly haste, but propriety was maintained. Unlike when he had returned from Ireland, the household saw nothing of my legs, or even my ankles.

I glanced around to see what company he had brought. However, there were no guests, and his following was barely sufficient to maintain his dignity as a great lord. Some of his men, it seemed, had been left behind, or perhaps sent to their homes for a time. This was strange enough to make me wonder at it.

Thomas had brought Bess a present of marchpane, wrapped in red cloth tied with ribbon, but before she could start picking at the knot, he lifted her onto his shoulders and called her his 'lamb.' The child squealed with delight as we processed into the hall and from there up to our solar, my hand resting on Thomas's. It was only when we were in relative privacy that the child was lowered to the ground and my lord and I exchanged a kiss. Only a brief kiss of greeting, for my women were watching, and Philippa Fitzwalter was grinning at us as though we existed for her entertainment. We had to contain ourselves for a while but at least, I thought, this night we would lie in one bed.

Over supper, Thomas had much to tell me of the news and gossip of the court, although as he explained, he had not come from there directly. Lord Zouche had died — the husband of his eldest sister, Elizabeth, a good, loyal man — and he had attended the funeral and given what comfort he could to his sister, who was devastated.

'I brought her to Tewkesbury, to be with my mother. I dare say you will visit them?'

'Yes, of course,' I said. It was a duty, and I added it to my mental list of tasks to perform. 'Is she the guest you mentioned in your letter?'

He shook his head. 'No. It's March.'

I was astonished. For one thing, I had imagined Roger Mortimer to be safely bestowed in Ireland.

'He's at Ludlow, for the present,' Thomas explained. 'He has come home to explain certain matters to the King. First, though, he and I have business. So he will come here, and Alianore will be with him. Their children too, I should expect. Then Alianore will remain here with you, while Roger and I go back to court together.'

I was lost for words. 'Will Edmund be with them?' I asked at last. At least Edmund had sense — he might be an ally I could use.

'No, Edmund remains in Ireland. Minding the shop, so to speak. Is that a disappointment?'

'This business you speak of. Is it the marriage for our daughter?'

'In part. I've a claim to Denbigh, which March holds. I have it in mind that part of Bess's dowry shall be a release of that claim. We also need to talk of other matters, such as how to best secure him from his enemies. It's important that he regains the King's trust.'

'I agree,' I said, 'though how he is to do it, I'm not sure. If he can explain himself, that will be a beginning. Go cautiously, Thomas. Test the ground before you mention this betrothal to the King.'

'I've no intention of mentioning it at all. Not yet.'

I could scarcely believe my ears.

'You must,' I said.

'I see no cause.' He concentrated on his food for a moment. 'The true marriage is a long way off, if it comes to pass. As you know, it may not, for one reason or another. Nothing is binding, nor can it be for years.'

'March is Richard's heir!' I believe I raised my voice, which was discourteous. However, I could not believe he could be so obtuse. The King was already suspicious of March — secret dealings behind his back could only serve to make him more so. We could not afford to lose Richard's favour. All the power we had was built upon it.

I became aware that some of our people were staring at us, and I knew it was because I had used such a tone. Some had probably heard my words. It did not serve to argue in public. So I lowered my head, and focused on the pie I was investigating with my knife. It was a succulent offering of venison, good enough to soothe any temper.

I apologised for my sharpness, but Thomas only smiled and closed his hand over mind to show me, and those around us, that he was not angered by it. Then he turned to his other news.

'The King is to go to Calais in August for some weeks, to meet the French King and settle the treaty between them,' he said. 'It's more ceremony than anything, all is agreed, but you can imagine the preparations, and what's being spent on them, for his Grace is determined that we shall match the French in everything, whether it be in our clothes, or pavilions or our attendants. All must be splendid, and your brother and Mowbray are very busy giving orders and making sure nothing is forgotten. I may be asked to go myself — it wasn't decided when I left — but no ladies will be with us, so you'll not be troubled. The wedding is another matter of course, but by that time you'll be in no proper condition to travel.' He paused to place an affectionate hand on my belly. 'The Duchess of York is still spitting blood about having to go, and I need not tell you why. I've an idea she believes you have got yourself with child as a way of avoiding the occasion.'

He laughed, and I could not help but join in. In truth, the

only small regret I had about my condition was that its timing made it quite impossible for me to attend the King's wedding in November. Fate enjoys playing such tricks on us, but how could I complain? A son for us was more important than anything. I should meet the new Queen in due course and my daughter was promised a place about her. Everything was running our way, and I had no right to quibble with Dame Fortune.

*

I had long thought Roger Mortimer a clumsy, overgrown boy, gauche and somewhat foolish, although amiable and good-natured. Now he was much more obviously a man, with a man's self-assurance. He sat his horse extraordinarily well, even for a practised knight, and was splendidly dressed, as befitted a great lord of his wealth, in the blue and yellow colours of his family, in his case well-cut in rich silk and with so much cloth that his houppelande, once he had dismounted, fell all the way to the ground. It was perhaps a little excessive when worn away from court, let alone for a journey, but it was certainly very fine. About his neck was a livery collar of the White Hart that was so studded with diamonds and other rich jewels that it would, of itself, have served as a knight's ransom.

He greeted us with great warmth, paying me quite absurd compliments, which seemed to me but a hand's breath away from mockery. Yet he was sincere.

We had musicians playing a tune as he arrived, and I believe he gave them nothing less than gold. Then his attention was drawn to two labourers standing by in idleness, stocky young fellows with dark hair. They were first arrivals of a flock of Welsh folk that would descend on us to help with the harvest, as they did each year. I gathered that he had heard them speaking in their language and nothing would serve but he must walk across to greet them in the same tongue and hold a brief conversation. It ended with him pressing coins into their hands.

He explained to us that he had discovered that they were from one of his own lordships, Usk. That, it seemed, was reason enough for him to treat them as if they were there to attend on him, and not merely come to Hanley for the work of the season.

By this time Alianore had descended from her carriage with her children and her women, and my attention turned to her. She hugged me, glanced towards Roger — who was now distributing coin to every man and boy standing by — and rolled her eyes.

'For the love of God, water his wine,' she advised, 'or he will give out his last farthing before the day is done.'

It is no fault in a great lord, or any man or woman of birth, to be seen as open-handed; but perhaps Roger stretched his generosity that inch too far, to the point where it seemed excessive. It was his way, in this and in all else.

At table, he had a great deal to say about Ireland, its people, and their strange customs.

'If I were to choose one man to stand by me in a fight, it would be a Welshman,' he said, 'for there are no better soldiers born. Yet the Irish are not so very far behind. Stubborn devils against any odds, and they don't know the meaning of fear.'

He went on to say that he found the country extraordinarily beautiful, and filled with plentiful game. He would often ride about at large, with but a handful of men, and wear Irish dress — such as it was — as a sign of his good will to the people. I was astonished. Had he wandered from his wits to behave in such a fashion? The King was trying to persuade the Irish lords to dress as Englishmen, and here was his Lieutenant, his potential heir, doing the very opposite. I shuddered to think what Richard would say of it. Would Roger tell him of it as plainly as he had us? Almost certainly! He was no man to adjust his conversation to his company.

As for Alianore, she seemed more contented than she had been for some time; which surprised me at first, until she explained.

We were out in the tilt-yard, the morning after their arrival, watching our husbands hacking away at one another at the barriers with pole-axes. They were thoroughly enjoying themselves, despite the fact that the sun was already beating down quite mercilessly. From time to time they mocked one another with cruel words as is the way with men when they are in competition, especially when they are friends. The wooden framework of the barrier and their half-armour ensured that no harm was done, of course, but it was certainly good exercise. Every so often they broke off, walked across to us like dogs expecting to be patted, and took refreshment. We had a table at hand, and servitors, including my brother Dickon, ready to pour wine for them, or cider if that was preferred. (Wine is very well at table, but does little to cut a thirst worked up by hard labour in summer heat.)

Lady March and I were standing far enough away from our women not to be overheard, even though Philippa Fitzwalter was under the mistaken impression that I required her close attendance. I had to disillusion her on that point, as she was not apt to respond to hints, and she was sadly lacking in common sense.

'Your brother will have told you how matters stand between us?' Alianore began.

I shook my head. It was a reasonable assumption for her to make, but the truth was Edward rarely wrote to me now, and such letters as I had received from him had not mentioned her at all. His news had been of the King and the court and the follies of several of our kindred, not least our stepmother.

'It has come to an end,' she went on. 'He is not what I thought him. In all truth, I wonder if he ever cared for me at all, except as a weapon he might use to hurt Roger.'

'I'm sure that's not true,' I said, drawing her a little closer for I was aware of pricking ears nearer to us than was desirable.

'Oh, it's *very* true. He has a look of you, but you are quite different in your dealings. He has no heart and no loyalty, cares only for himself. I was slow to admit to it, for it was painful to own that I'd been so deluded, but so it is. For one thing, he has another woman. I don't mean the whores all men have, to scratch the itch they suffer when they're away from their wives, or when their wives are big with child. I mean a woman who *matters* to him.'

'He's said nothing to me. Nothing at all. Are you *sure*?'

'I happened to chance upon a letter from her. Ned had scarcely bothered to hide it. I thought it was one of his poems at first, so I picked it up. A very warm letter. I knew then that he was false, but I'd long suspected it. He thinks himself subtle but, really, if you know him, he is not.'

I let out a sigh. 'I'm ashamed that he is my brother,' I said. 'I thought he loved you very much. He told me he wished he could marry you. I thought that was the reason he hates Roger.'

'Oh, he hates Roger well enough. He wanted me to help ruin him, but I would not. I believe that's when he began to find me less pleasing, when he realised I would not be false. Well, not false in that way. Love is one thing, treachery another.'

'Who is this woman?'

'I don't believe it's one of us,' Alianore said. (By this she meant it was someone outside the King's family.) 'No, I think it must be someone a step or two down. Perhaps it's not someone he can marry, but someone he loves. All I can tell you is that she signs herself "G".'

I wrinkled my brow. Struggle as I could, I was unable to think of anyone whose name began with "G".

'Whoever she is,' I said, 'she cannot be as beautiful as you are.'

She shrugged. 'I've wept over him, I grant you; but as you can see, I've not thrown myself into a lake or swallowed hemlock. It's not the end of my life. I've decided to make the most of what I have, as other women do. I'll never have any feelings for Roger, as I told you long ago, but he could be worse. Far worse. When he returns to Ireland, I shall go with him.'

This was a concession indeed. I had never thought to see the day.

'I shall write to him,' I promised. 'Such a letter he shall have!'

She laid a hand on my arm. 'Don't quarrel with Ned for my sake. The cause is not worth it, not now. It will gain you nothing.'

Our children were a few yards from us. Tired of watching the combat, they were wrangling and chasing as young children do. My Bess, understandably, was showing no interest in Alianore's boys, but was attached to Anne, her elder daughter, who had taken charge of their group. Anne was the eldest, and was making a very fair job of her task of commanding them. She was not yet eight, but was tall for her age and very sure of herself. It was strange to think that the new Queen was several months Anne's junior. What madness! I thought. What a sacrifice to make for peace!

'What do you say to this marriage between our children?' I asked.

'I can think of nothing that would please me better,' she said, and smiled at me.

'Alianore, if it was just a marriage between our families I would agree with you. Of course I would! But it's not so simple, as you must see. It touches on the succession, and the King is suspicious of Roger. Need I say why? He sees Arundel as first among his enemies and Arundel is married to your sister-in-law. March's uncle, Thomas Mortimer, is Arundel's lackey, and fought on the wrong side at Radcot Bridge.'

'Roger can't stand the sight of his uncle!' she objected.

'That might be so, but it isn't all. Thomas is related to Arundel through his eldest sister. Her first husband was Arundel's nephew. He himself spent time in Arundel's household and was even knighted by the man. This betrothal is being made quietly, without Richard's knowledge. Do you not see how that could all be presented by an enemy?'

'By Edward, you mean.'

'Yes, by Edward.'

She gave me an impatient glance. 'I think you make far too much of it. What is being talked about is just a betrothal of young children. It isn't even binding. How can there be any objection to that? We are all loyal to the King, not traitors. Apart from that, I think it high time someone told your brother that he does not rule in England. That he should keep his nose out of our family business.'

I was old enough now to know when I was trying to knock down a stone wall with my head. It was clear that Alianore did not share my reservations. Then again, I had to concede she had a point. I owed my first loyalty to my husband, not to Edward. If I could not persuade Thomas to see sense, then I would have to allow events to take their course.

*

'It is all agreed,' Thomas told me. 'The marriage — at some time to come — the settlement over Denbigh, and a bond of mutual support against all others save the King, your father, and your uncles. We have drafted a contract and set our seals to it. The whole matter to be kept privy for the time being. My claim to Denbigh only signifies once Parliament grants my petition, so it's premature to speak openly of it.'

That was the least of it, I thought.

We were alone, and in our bed. The silence of night had already fallen upon Hanley and a cooling breeze was making its way through the open casements, strong enough, at times, to stir the bed curtains. I was quiet, not because I was angry with him, but because I was thinking.

'You do not care for this marriage, do you?' he demanded. 'I've an idea you don't like Roger, either.'

I shrugged. 'I like March well enough.'

'Well, then.'

'I also like Alianore better than any other woman. She's been my friend for as long as I can remember. As good as a sister.'

'I know that. It's what I don't understand.'

I sighed. 'You've just mentioned it. Your petition to Parliament. It's important to you, is it not?'

'You know very well that it is.'

'For the sake of your family honour. Tell me, how do you think petitions to Parliament prosper when the King opposes them? If you lose the King's favour, you lose everything you've gained, and everything you hope to gain. Richard is suspicious of March. Whether he has cause to be, or not, is neither here nor there. All I say is, be careful you don't make him suspicious of *you*.'

'You sound very much like your brother,' he said. I could tell from his tone of voice that he was not pleased with me, or convinced by my argument.

'Ned knows the King's mind better than anyone,' I said. 'He doesn't mean you harm, Thomas. That he's March's enemy I don't deny, but he's not alone in that. Even my father doesn't want March as king.'

That was true. My father and his brothers would never kneel to Roger Mortimer. Nor would their sons. What Parliament thought be damned.

Thomas sighed. 'Even March doesn't want March as king. Has Alianore not told you that?'

'Yes,' I admitted. She had, many times, over the years. 'I'm sure neither of them is ambitious, but the trouble is, no one will ever believe them. My Cousin Richard least of all. There lies the danger.'

'You need not fear,' he said. 'I shall be cautious.'

Cautious? Thomas scarcely knew what the word was. I had an idea that he thought me fanciful, thinking that I imagined dangers that did not exist. Was that not what Alianore had said, more or less?

It made me wonder if they were right. Perhaps, I thought, my wits are scattered. Am I not breeding, and do they not say that women in such a condition have strange fancies? Could it be so?

At least I had said my piece. My advice was given. There was nothing more to be done.

*

Next morning, my lord and his friend March were gone, away to court, and Alianore and I were left to entertain one another. The weather held, and she and I found much to occupy ourselves. We rode beyond the park, to the far end of the Chase. We played games with the children, and with our women. We strolled in the gardens, and sat in the cool of the arbours, reading poetry and laughing over the coarse verses, for what we read was full of ribald tales. We feasted and danced with select guests from the two counties, for I was still doing my utmost to build up our following among the local gentry, hard work though it was. (The Berkeley and Warwick interests were all but set in stone, and Thomas and I had to court the waverers as best we could.)

At last, for want of anything better to do, I took Alianore to Tewkesbury to present her to Elisabeth Despenser. We travelled in my carriage, with our children and Philippa Fitzwalter and a couple of others, with our other women riding behind, and with a good-sized escort to maintain our dignity. (It was not needed for protection — no one in that country would have dared stand in our way — but appearances are important and you must make an impression.)

Elisabeth received us most courteously, although I sensed she was more gratified to see her granddaughter — and indeed Lady March — than she was to see me. We had never really progressed beyond polite tolerance, she and I, although the fact I was with child again did raise me in her estimation. As far as she was concerned, it was my prime duty to give her a grandson. Well, in fairness, there was some truth in that. I was conscious of it myself.

Her eldest daughter, Lady Zouche, was there also. I had, I must own, been somewhat tardy in coming to Tewkesbury to pay my respects and offer my condolences. (It was partly because I was never in undue haste to visit her mother.) I tried to make amends by being as amiable as possible and I said many kind words about William Zouche. I could do this without hypocrisy, for he had been a good man, and a loyal supporter of the King. I had known him from my time at court and I had liked him.

Elizabeth Zouche was quite broken. She could barely speak

coherently, but said she would remain a widow until she died, and gave me the impression she meant to live with her mother in future. She had all four of her children with her. None was above twelve, and none was by Zouche either. They belonged to her first, Fitzalan husband. Still, that was not their fault, and together with my daughter, Alianore's youngsters, and Elizabeth Berkeley, they did much to enliven the house, which was no bad thing. Not even Elisabeth, for all her strictness, could keep them quiet, and with the weather holding they were out in Elisabeth's gardens and in her park, running about together and thoroughly enjoying themselves. It was a delight, and I took pleasure in their giddy doings.

I took less pleasure in the presence of the Earl and Countess of Warwick. Oh, they were there, right enough. Why was I not surprised? They had brought their hawk-faced brat with them, though he was just that little year or two too old to appreciate the boisterous play of his younger fellows. Much of the time he stood by his mother's chair, looking serious and playing with the hilt of his knife. When that grew tedious he ran off with my brother, Dickon, and indulged in wrestling, or fighting with wooden swords, or whatever pastimes boys of that age find interesting. Dickon was the younger of the two, but he held his own, which was pleasing.

Warwick and his lady were subdued, to say the least. His face was longer than ever and somewhat ashen, as if he was just out of a sickbed. I gathered from their talk with Elisabeth that their legal case over Gower was not going well. Their lawyers had resorted to mere delaying tactics, since they feared that the verdict would be adverse. They knew there was nothing to be had from the King. Their petitions to him had been rejected. It made me smile quietly to myself — what on earth had they expected? Richard's memory was just as good as mine. Did they really expect favour after what Warwick had imposed on my cousin?

What were they doing there? It did not take long to uncover their business. They were on their way to Berkeley Castle, there to solemnise the marriage between their son and Elizabeth Berkeley, their conspiracy against us that Elisabeth had sponsored. They were swift to invite Alianore and me to join them, and because it seemed to me that they expected me to refuse, I decided to accept. If you are offered an opportunity to visit the enemy's camp, it's folly not to do so. There is great advantage in spying out the ground.

I sent Philippa, and one of Alianore's women back to Hanley to find changes of clothes, more jewels and a new supply of coin, lending them my carriage for the purpose. I had no intention of appearing at the wedding in the same gown and headdress I had worn to travel to Tewkesbury, and certainly not without an adequate supply of funds. Appearances are everything, and I intended to impress.

They were back before supper, bringing our gear on a pack horse led by one of the men of their escort. I must admit, Philippa chose well. It was the kind of task she enjoyed, and she may well have slipped a coin or two into her own purse. I was not so severe that I objected to that, if I was well served in return. Once my boxes were opened, I saw that I had all that I needed, and more. She had thought of everything, even several changes of gown and linen for my daughter.

Next day, early in the morning, we set out in a great and very impressive procession. Elisabeth decided to ride in Lady Warwick's carriage with the bride, but Elizabeth Zouche accompanied me, as did her children, which meant we were all rather cramped, but it was still comfortable enough, at least until the youngsters became restless, as was inevitable. It was a long journey for them, thirty miles if it's an inch, and although the road is a good one, and at that season free from mud, it took us the whole of the day to reach Berkeley.

Of course, we halted, more than once, to refresh ourselves and rest and water the horses. Also, at my insistence, we paused at Gloucester to venerate King Edward. That did not please Warwick much, but as I pointed out to the company, Lady March particularly wanted to see the shrine and make an offering. This was a surprise to Alianore, but I explained to her that it would please the King if he heard of it, and that her husband needed to please Richard by any possible means.

While we were there, I gave the monks money to say masses for Zouche's soul, which gratified his widow and seemed to make her think better of me. She was still quiet, but for the rest of the journey joined in my conversation with Alianore and Philippa, and even smiled from time to time. I could not dislike Elizabeth Zouche – not least because she had a look of Thomas about her, especially around the eyes and mouth. I had only to look at her to think of him. I hated being apart!

At long last, with all the children more or less in tears and Philippa Fitzwalter growing more querulous by the hour, we came to Berkeley Castle. It was larger than Hanley, and looked more defensible — at least as far as I could judge — but, as we discovered when we entered the building, it was far more old-fashioned. Most of the floors were not tiled, but were just plain stone flags, although plenty of fresh rushes had been spread around and strewn with herbs. The scent of meadowsweet, pennyroyal and lavender rose from beneath your feet as you walked. The walls were covered with rich hangings — the King himself had no better than those in the lord's apartments — but it was clear the roof was leaking. You could see where water had marked the plaster, or brought it down. The rooms were darker than at Hanley — most of the windows were small, and many, even in the best rooms, were filled with horn, not glass.

'Good cousin Berkeley' had no lady to manage his household, of course, but if you allowed for that we were well received. Servants in smart liveries who knew their business hurried to attend to our needs. Wine and wafers were presented to refresh us, and Berkeley himself passed around the room, welcoming us all and ensuring we were comfortable. Then we were shown to our bedchambers so that we might rest and prepare ourselves for supper. It was true that Alianore and I were expected to share a bed, but in fairness we had not been expected, and the castle was crowded. It was a splendid room, with plenty of room for our women and an alcove where the children could be accommodated on pallets. I believe it was where Berkeley normally slept himself — the bed curtains were very rich and decorated with the devices of Berkeley and Lisle.

'Is it here that the second Edward was murdered?' Alianore asked.

I nodded. 'In this castle. So it is said — and right cruelly if the tales are true. I dare say Berkeley's ancestor had a part in it.'

'How shall we sleep? What if the King's angry ghost is still about?'

It was not a wise question, with our women's ears pricking and the children not so occupied with one another that they might not hear us.

'I don't think saints *have* angry ghosts,' I said. 'That is the point. They're secure in heaven. No need to fear on that account.'

She did not look convinced. Nor did one or two of the others, and Philippa least of all. However, I slept just as well as I did at home. There were no fiends abroad in Berkeley Castle, unless you counted certain mortals as such.

When the wedding day dawned, I was not surprised to hear rain beating against the windows. We had enjoyed some weeks of favourable weather, but that never lasts in England; it only promises the onset of a storm. So it was that day; you could already hear the distant rolls of thunder, slowly drawing closer and louder. Even with all the shutters thrown open, it was almost too dark to dress. Still, we made our preparations, Alianore and I agreeing that it was well we were safe inside the castle, with no need to travel.

It was an occasion to wear a gown such as was fit for court, and I chose one of the new style, high-waisted — useful in my present condition, for my waist was not as it was, for obvious reasons — in bright red silk, embroidered with gold letters, 'C' and 'T' powdered everywhere. I covered my hair with the finest caul I had, thick with pearls, with my Garter on my arm, as ever, and a jewel of the White Hart about my neck. You see, I was quite prepared for battle, and this was my armour.

Alianore was equally splendid — although she was one of those women who would still turn heads if she was dressed in sacking and smeared in mud. (I longed to see the paragon my brother had chosen above her, the one he *loved*.)

We walked down to the hall, arm in arm, and found the castle crowded. Guests were still arriving, and in some numbers, the knights and squires of southern Gloucestershire with their wives. This was Berkeley's country, where he was at his strongest, and where the Despenser influence was weak. Even so, Lady March and I made our mark. It was amusing to see the dropped jaws, to feel the stares on our backs. I suppose we could have made a greater stir, given a herald's clarion or two, but it was enough to see the company parting before us bowing and making way.

When my father taught me to play chess, when I was but a child, I remember him saying that for every move there is a counter-move. This is true in life as much as it is in chess; the difference is that in life the game never ends, as long as you have children, or grandchildren, or nephews, to carry it on.

I was looking for my counter-move, and the options did not look promising. There were few people here that I knew well. Elisabeth was no help. The little bride had been in her guardianship and the hawk-nosed brat was her godson. I had an idea she had had more than a hand in making this marriage. (What she thought she was doing, I have no idea.)

My eye settled on Sir James, Berkeley's heir male and younger brother. Here at least was a chink in the Berkeley armour, though I did not know him well. I made a point of cultivating him and his wife, and it was not hard to please them. It was not long before I was hinting that a future marriage between our children might be a possibility. They were by no means averse, and I sensed a useful alliance. Their lands were not vast, but they were well-placed, and included the castle at Raglan, between Gloucestershire and Glamorgan. Besides that, of course, James stood to inherit this very castle from his brother, and much of Gloucestershire with it. It was a friendship well worth cultivating, and I did not so much invite them to Hanley, but insist they must visit us, as soon as my lord was home. (It did not harm to mention that he was at court, summoned there to advise the King on certain matters. A little profitable embroidery of the truth is a useful ingredient of any argument.)

Lord Berkeley had spared no expense. He had gathered so many musicians and minstrels to play in the gallery that I doubt there was another one to be hired in the whole county. Right loudly they played - *Merry It Is While Summer Lasts* is the one I recall, because I found myself singing along with it. There was prophecy in the words, had I known.

We crowded into one of the chapels to hear the couple exchange their vows — or at least, those of us who could squeeze in did so. There was nowhere near room for all, and even knights and their ladies found themselves outside, listening but not seeing.

Alianore and I were, of course, at the front, and watched the children as they exchanged their vows. A part of me pitied them, another part, strangely was proud of them. They both behaved perfectly, spoke in clear, firm voices so that all could hear their responses. Little Elizabeth Berkeley was a very amiable child —

perhaps Elisabeth Despenser deserved credit for that at least — but even the hawk-nosed brat carried himself well, and smiled at his bride as if to reassure her. What their real feelings were I cannot say, but they gave the impression that they were content. There was to be no bedding of course; they were far too young for that, especially the girl.

The ceremony concluded, we went in procession back to the hall for the feast, the musicians playing their merry tunes as we walked. The meal put before us was as splendid as you could expect at court, and the music continued while we ate, with a series of jugglers and dancers and tumblers appearing in the space between the tables. I was soon enjoying myself more than I had thought possible, given the company.

Once the meal was done there was no shortage of people wanting to be presented to Alianore and me, and we took over one of the window embrasures in the hall and held court. Sir James and his lady were anxious to be of service and made many introductions. Some of the men sent their wives to approach us, others were bold enough to speak for themselves. Much of what was said was mere commonplace nonsense, amounting to nothing, but occasionally there was some small complaint, some son or daughter who needed to take service, and I took careful note and promised to do what I could, even offering to do so much as write to the King on some fellow's behalf.

It would have been helpful to have a clerk there to take notes, but I had a good memory in those days, and I had been trained to remember faces and put names to them. In any event, it was nine parts a matter of being gracious, only one part of making promises.

The fellow that impressed me most was one of my lord's own retainers. He wore our griffin badge about his neck, but at first I could not place him, which was a fault in me. Thomas did not have so many men at his call that I had an excuse to forget one. He was, I suppose, about forty, not overly tall, with hair the colour of a raven's wing and a merry glint in his brown eyes. He was also most courteous, kneeling to kiss my hand, and his voice was mellow and urbane. Who could it be?

Then I remembered. He was one of those summoned to Hanley Castle to receive the King. Robert Poyntz of Iron Acton, one of very few followers we had from this part of the shire. He had no tedious requests to make, nor did he make complaint. Yet I took a liking to him. And, judging from some of his comments, I gathered he was no fonder of our host than a man living in South Gloucestershire needed to be to survive with his roof unburned.

It crossed my mind he would make a good Sheriff, such as the King required. I was determined not to forget his name again, but to mention it to Thomas.

*

Next day, the thunderstorms had departed and we had clouded sunshine in its place. There was jousting as part of the celebration, with the little bride on a large chair in the centre of the stand to queen over it and award prizes. (She had, of course, a jury of ladies to advise her, and she was a sensible child and took advice good-naturedly.)

Her husband was too young to compete with the older men, but the day began with him and other young fellows riding at the ring, which was a fair test of their skill. He won his competition, received some trinket from his little wife, and then settled down on a chair next to her to watch the sport.

It was all you would expect a joust in the depths of Gloucestershire to be. The best of the knights and squires were competent, and I'm sure that none of them lacked courage. However, in matters of skill they were far behind the likes of Sir John Russell, or Golafre, let alone Huntingdon. Still, it was an entertainment to occupy us, and no one was killed.

It was coming to a conclusion when I saw a whole column of horsemen arriving, making their way around the castle to the jousting field. My first thought was that here were challengers, come to improve the sport. Perhaps Berkeley had arranged it so. (It would not have surprised me if Harry Bolingbroke himself had decided to take part, given that he enjoyed jousting and was happy to gain easy victories in country tournaments.)

Then I noticed the banner. It was Roger Mortimer's, and there he was, at the head of his men. He was not in armour, but in ordinary riding-clothes, much less fine than those he had worn when he arrived at Hanley. He had the look of a man who had ridden hard.

Berkeley, who looked astonished, hurried forward to greet this unexpected guest. They spoke together with Roger gesturing in the direction of our stand. It was clear that he wanted Alianore. That was not strange it itself. What was strange was the manner of his arrival and his evident urgency. It struck me that bad news was on its way. My thoughts flew to Thomas. Had some ill befallen him? My stomach suddenly trembled, as if I'd not eaten for a week. I had no choice but to sit there, doing my best to look composed, while Roger made his way to us. He was moving as quickly as a man could without running, but it seemed to take an age.

He reached us at last, somewhat breathless, and gave a hurried greeting to Alianore and me. We were of course in a stand packed with other people, every eye was on him and every ear turned towards us.

'My lady,' he said to Alianore, 'you must make ready to leave at once. We must return to Ireland as quickly as we may.'

There was such urgency in his words that she rose at once, without a question. In that at least her impulse was correct. This was no place for a debate.

I realised I must go with them if my questions were to be answered, and I had any number. We formed quite a procession, with our women and pages trailing behind us, but it was better than talking before half of Gloucestershire.

'Where is Thomas?' I asked. 'Is he not with you?'

Roger shook his head. 'He's still with the King.'

My worst fears eased.

'Have you ridden far today?' I asked.

'From Worcester. I sought you at Hanley Castle, and was told you were both here. So I followed.'

'Then you've travelled far enough for one day.' I sighed. Did I really have to explain every detail? 'You'll need to go back to Hanley. Alianore's gear is still there, for the most part. You'll kill your horses if you make even half that journey today. They need rest, and fodder. So do you, Roger, by the look of you.' I glanced at the position of the sun. 'Even with fresh horses, you'd not win your way back. It would be full dark before you even reached Gloucester. Let us all go tomorrow, together. The next morning, you can be off as soon as it is light, with no real delay.'

Alianore added her pleas to mine, saying it was far too late to make any distance that day. Besides, what was the cause of this haste? Was there evil news from Ireland?

Roger's face twisted with anxiety. For a moment I thought he might start crying, for he looked very much like a little boy, frustrated at losing some childish game of chance. He shook his head, muttered some words I could not catch, and then yielded.

'Very well,' he said. 'It's true about the horses. I doubt they'd manage more than another five miles, for we've ridden at a good pace. I shall stay here until morning — but then we go. Back to

Hanley, then to Ludlow as quickly as we can travel. Then to Chester, and Ireland. I shall not feel safe until I have a ship beneath my feet, and I'm out at sea.'

'Is the King angry with you?' I demanded. 'Is that what's wrong?'

'No, but he would be, if he knew. I am bound by oath not to speak of it. There can be no harm to him, if I am not in England.'

This babble made no sense at all to me, but he would not explain. Alianore pressed him, but he kept repeating that he was bound to silence by a most solemn oath. He could not, or would not, explain. Something, or someone, had put the fear of God into Roger Mortimer, that at least was plain.

*

That night I had to lodge with Elisabeth, as it was only reasonable that Alianore and Roger should lie together. I hoped, moreover, that in privacy she might manage to extract some sense from him. The confident, expansive Roger who had arrived at Hanley was replaced by a tongue-tied bumbler who scarcely seemed to know what to do with himself. The change was extraordinary.

Elisabeth saw fit to question me.

'What is it that you are about here, daughter?' she demanded.

I gazed at her, not quite taking her meaning. 'Why,' I said, 'I'm here to look after my lord's interests, as is my duty. What else?'

'And you think to do that by *flaunting* yourself before all?'

I shook my head. Indeed, I laughed aloud. '*Flaunting* myself? You make it sound as though I've been parading naked on the high table. I've not even danced; though not for want of being asked. Even "dear cousin Berkeley" was courteous enough to offer, but I thought it wise to decline, for the sake of my child. It seems I can do no right, according to you, madam!'

'You are here to stir trouble. I am not a fool, Constance.'

I shook my head. 'It's not I who maintains criminal gangs in this county. That's Berkeley, and it's the scandal of the shire. Nor have I ever levied war on the King, like Warwick. Nor is it I who have fostered an alliance between them, against my lord's interests. Yet you dare to say that *I* stir trouble?'

'If you had any sense, you would seek peace,' she said. 'An accord is better than a quarrel, and an accord can be achieved. As I intend to tell my son.'

I bit my tongue out of respect for her age; apart from that, I wanted to sleep, for I was very tired.

We set out very early, after breaking our fast in some haste and saying an even hastier farewell to our host, and also to Elisabeth, who had decided to remain for a few days before taking the bride back to Tewkesbury. I did not sorrow at the parting.

It was a long journey back to Hanley, and not a quiet one, because Alianore was anything but content.

'Roger went to see his sister, at Reigate,' she explained. 'He was bidden there for dinner. He'll not tell me much more than that, but from what I can make out, the conversation turned his stomach. Well, you can imagine what *that* was about, with my Uncle Arundel! There were others there too, although he'll not say whom. Well, he let slip that one was *his* uncle, Thomas Mortimer. That's no surprise is it?'

Given that Thomas Mortimer was Arundel's lackey and had been for years, it was not.

'He'll not say what was talked about,' Alianore went on.

'Whatever it was, he was sworn to silence. I think we can guess though, don't you? If we don't, you can be sure that others will. Roger has ruined *everything*. Now he runs away, which makes it ten times worse. If the King was suspicious of him before, he'll be even more so now, won't he? Nor can I wonder at it. Why did he have to go there? He has no sense *at all*.'

It was unfortunate that this was all said before Philippa Fitzwalter, but there was no help for it. Alianore was far too angry to contain herself, and all I could do was tell Philippa that all this must be kept between us.

I could not understand what Roger was about, and when at last we reached Hanley, and I had settled him in my solar to rest before supper, I did my best to make him see sense.

'Roger,' I said, 'whatever oath you may have sworn, it cannot override your oath to the King. It really is that simple. If there is some treasonous plot against him, then, no matter who is involved in it, it's your duty as a loyal subject to report it to Richard. Anything less, and you run the risk of being accused of treason yourself. *And perhaps others with you.*'

I was thinking of Thomas, of course. Out of loyalty to his friend, he had gone far out onto a limb, and that limb was rotten and could snap beneath him.

We were quite alone, the three of us. Roger, Alianore and I. After I had spoken, the silence was intense. Alianore sat stiffly in her chair, deadly quiet. Roger trembled with uncertainty. I paced. Yes, I paced, like one of the lions in the Tower, up and down the room. I could feel the rage swelling inside me, the passionate desire to slap this fool of a man as though he was a witless child. Pacing was the only way to control my temper, to keep me from flying at him. That he had endangered himself was one thing. It was quite another that he had put my husband in peril. Thomas would not be running off to

Ireland. He was in reach of the King's anger because of this dolt.

'It isn't treason,' he protested. 'It's mere words. Folly. Words spoken in drink. It can't come to anything without me, and I will have no part of it, as I told them. That's why I want to be in Ireland. While I'm there, they can't even use my name. Richard is safe. Do you not see it?'

'It will come out, nevertheless!' I all but spat at him. 'Someone will talk. Arundel is *watched*. There will be spies in his household, and your very flight will add credence to whatever tale they tell. Your only hope is to get to Richard first, before someone else tells the story.'

'I've told you — I am sworn to silence.' He shook his head, and for a moment I thought he would start weeping. 'They made me swear, on the sacred Host.'

I had already answered that point. Now I lost my temper.

'I swear, by Our Blessed Lady, that if harm comes to a single hair of my husband's head because of your folly, you will find in me, Roger Mortimer, such an enemy as will make your present enemies seem like beloved friends!' I strode over to him, stared directly into his eyes. *'Do you understand me?'*

He nodded, miserably.

'Constance!' Alianore was staring at me. 'Please. The whole household will hear.'

'I don't give a dog's turd if the Prior of Malvern hears me!' I raged at her. 'This could be the ruin of all of us.'

'I will not allow any harm to come to Thomas,' he promised. 'Not if it costs me my life. There is no danger to the King, or I should not be sitting here. It was just *talk,* as I said. Foolish talk. You know what Arundel is like. I wish I hadn't gone there. I only went to see my sister. Not for any evil purpose. Surely you believe that?'

My rage was beginning to ebb. I lowered myself onto the window seat. It had been a long day, I was feeling uncomfortable, and I was tired. So very tired.

'I know not what to believe,' I said, 'since you will tell but half the tale. Besides, I am not the one who matters in this. It's the King, and what he believes will depend on what he is told, and by whom. This I do know, that flight is often taken as a sign of guilt, and you will not be there to defend yourself.'

He just sat there, looking miserable. Perhaps he saw his error, and also saw it was too late to amend it. Alianore shifted in her place, laid her hand on his as a gesture of comfort. I was beginning to feel ashamed, for my loss of control over my tongue, for my discourtesy to a guest. Yet I was still too angry to apologise. I sat there in silence, worrying about what might happen to Thomas, my fancies running wild.

*

The hay harvest was well under way, and the sheep shearing had begun, before Thomas returned to Hanley.

'I am here but for a little time,' he said. 'The King expects me to go with him to France, and that means I can spare but a few days. I wanted to see you though, *treschere.*'

I had an idea that he had hoped to see Roger Mortimer also, but Roger and Alianore were long gone; if they were not in Ireland by now, they would certainly be on the sea, unless contrary winds had kept them mewed up in Chester.

'What Roger is about I do not know,' he said. 'He gave out some tale of news of trouble in Ireland, but there was more to it than that. He said it was better I did not know, since that way I could swear to be in innocence of it. I know it has something to do with his visit to his sister, and Arundel, but more he would not say.'

There were too many ears pricking for my liking; luckily, the weather was fine, so, as I usually did when secrecy was necessary, I suggested we should walk in our garden.

'As bad as that, is it?' he asked, once we were out there. He understood my intent.

'I can't tell you the full tale,' I said, 'for he was sworn to silence. Alianore and I prised some of it from him, and it was easy enough to guess the rest, or at least to suspect. He could be right though. You might in truth be better not knowing.'

'Tell me,' he said, sighing.

I explained what I knew and also what I had surmised — Arundel, and others, had sought to involve March in some scheme of treason. A proposal so dangerous that Roger had thought it better to flee to Ireland, since he did not choose to betray the proposals to the King.

'Blood of God, this is worse than I feared!' he said, sitting down on one of the turf seats. 'You did well to bring us out here before you spoke of it. Roger gave out he had word of trouble in Ireland, that he had to go back before matters grew worse there. Even that was not well received. If word of this should reach the King —'

'How can it not?' I asked. 'Arundel is much suspected. It's certain there'll be people in his household, reporting on his doings. He isn't a subtle man. More the sort to bawl his intentions to the world at Paul's Cross.'

'That's true, at least,' he sighed. 'He speaks plainly, and cares not who hears. I know that from my time in his service. He would not be having this conversation in his garden, but in his hall, before half the household. Roger would have been wise not to go there.'

'He wished to see his sister. So he said. I doubt he expected to be inducted into a plot. My Cousin Richard, of course, may well not see it that way. I don't know what we can do. We ask for trouble ourselves if we keep silent, and if we tell what we know, what then? We've no proof. Nothing beyond what Roger said to me, and that amounts to a gabbled tale at second hand. It will not serve.'

Thomas shook his head. 'Let us pray to all the saints that it was indeed nothing more than wild talk. The oath though — that's what makes it worse. More suspicious. You don't put a man on oath over a few words spoken in drunken folly.'

'You're right, but I can't see that any harm can come to the King. Whatever Arundel may want to do, he has not the power. Not even *with* March, let alone without him. That means our best course is to keep silent — and hope there are no consequences. Not for March, and not for you.'

He was silent for a time, considering that. 'Speaking of brothers and sisters, have you written to Rutland recently?'

'Not for some weeks.'

'He seems to know a great deal of what passes in our household. I'd not want him to hear of this.'

'Thomas,' I said, a little indignantly, 'there's nothing in any letter I send to my brother, or my father, or anyone else, that you may not see. Shall I let you read them before they are sealed, so you can scratch out anything that displeases you?'

'Of course not!'

'You may, if you wish.' I made a point of sounding hurt. 'Or shall I but put on oath, as March was?'

'Your word suffices with me.'

'I hope so.'

He took my hand. 'I trust you, *treschere*. But if your brother's information does not come from you, we must have a spy in our household.'

My brother had been paying for information for years. Even when we were serving at court together, little more than children, he had been rewarding anyone who brought news to him. He would be doing more than that by now, I was sure.

'It would be a surprise if we did not,' I said.

*

A few days later, John Golafre arrived at Hanley. He was courteous to me — more courteous than he had ever been in all the years I had known him — and civil to his wife, although she made no move to embrace him, and gave only the barest of answers when he spoke to her. It seemed to me that the knight had aged since my last sight of him, and he had a weariness about him, as though his journey from the court at Eltham had quite sapped his strength.

He bore a letter for Thomas from the King, which I presumed was a summons to follow Richard to France. Unfortunately, my lord was not with me. He was out on the Chase, hunting with some of the men of our household and a few guests, including Sir John Russell. We had hopes of having Russell elected to Parliament for Worcestershire. That was a tough nut to crack, such was Warwick's power in the county, but we were making use of all our influence as well as that of the King. It was one reason why Thomas had been working with William Bagot. He might be as great a rogue as my brother had told me at York, but he knew how to put pressure on those who needed to feel it, and had many connections in the shire.

Golafre was most unusually taciturn. He took wine and wafers and then asked for ale, saying he had a thirst that nothing less would resolve. He answered my questions politely. The King was in good spirits and much more like himself. My father was in good health, and at court, while his Duchess was enjoying herself, dancing at every opportunity and admired by all. However, he did not expand on any of this. Nor did he make mocking comments, as the old Golafre would have done.

'When this duty is done, I have leave to go home to Wallingford for a while,' he said. 'I am bone-weary, madam. I need to rest.'

'If you are ill, sir —' I began, thinking to set our household physician on him. He certainly did not look well.

'Not ill, my lady. Merely weary, as I said. These last few years I've barely been out of the saddle, so far have I travelled on the King's business. I grow too old for such service.'

He was scarcely a greybeard, though he was on the wrong side of forty, as I supposed. Yet his eyes were like those of an old dog, one that dreads to stir from the fire, one whose hunting days are done.

I was grateful when Thomas returned, for it was hard work to entertain Golafre in his present mood, and his wife was no assistance. It was obvious from the look on each man's face that they had had an enjoyable hunt; my regret that I had not been able to ride stirrup to stirrup with my lord. I suppose many would say I could have done, but the child I was carrying was precious, by no means to be risked. I was determined to be cautious.

Thomas opened the letter, and then almost at once looked questioningly at Golafre, as he passed the missive to me. It was as short as could be, was merely an order to give credence to the bearer. At once I felt uneasy. Good news is rarely transmitted by such means.

'My lord, what I am commanded to say is for your ear alone,' the knight told him. His tone was so unlike his normal way of speaking it set me wondering. He could not have been more deferential in his tone.

'My lady and I have no secrets,' Thomas said. 'You may speak before her.'

Golafre suppressed a sigh. He glanced not so much at me, but at my women, including his own wife.

'The King's orders,' he said, briefly.

This was strange. In such circumstances, wives, children and attendants are usually regarded much as dogs are, too insignificant to matter.

'Very well,' Thomas answered. His voice was level, but you did not need to know him as well as I did to be aware he was not pleased. With a gesture he invited Golafre to leave the room with him. I believe they went out into the garden, and it was perhaps a quarter of an hour before they returned. It seemed longer.

I could see at once that my lord was not content, that he was, in truth, very close to anger. However, nothing was said. What talk there was between then and supper was of commonplaces, although of course I also had arrangements to make, to ensure that Golafre and his men were lodged in comfort for the night.

What surprised me was that Philippa Fitzwalter declared her intention to ride off with her husband in the morning. She asked leave, of course, but it was a formality. She was not under indenture, and even if she had been I could not have kept her from her knight. I was not so fond of her company as to think her absence a loss.

'Golafre is ill,' she said, 'and it's my duty to nurse him. That apart, I should like to visit my mother, and go on pilgrimage to St.

Thomas at Canterbury.'

That would all take time, I thought. Lady Mohun could be almost anywhere, for one thing. She was not one to sit quietly in one place, and might even be at court. I told her she might be away for as long as she pleased. As she had declared herself, her first duty was to her husband.

It was only when we were in bed, and alone, that Thomas was able to tell me his news. As I had feared, it was not good.

'I am not required to go with the King to France. Instead, I am ordered to remain in my country until I am told otherwise. The King has somehow heard of our plans for Bess's marriage, and has forbidden the match. March, Golafre says, is suspected of treasonous dealings.'

I let out a breath. It was more than tempting to say that I had foreseen all this, to remind him I had warned him not to be in haste and not to keep anything from my Cousin Richard. It was tempting, but I was not such a fool.

'You will obey, of course,' I said.

'I've no choice, when I'm ordered on my allegiance!' His voice was filled with bitterness.

I sighed. That is the most extreme form of command, and not one often issued to loyal men. It is more usually directed to men on the verge of rebellion. It meant that Richard was furious, not merely displeased. It was wholly excessive, in the circumstances, but it also marked the reality of our position. How were we to amend it? In plain terms, we had no option but to draw back, even to grovel if that was necessary. Without the King's favour, all our ambitions were as nothing.

Of course, it was also true that Richard needed us — at least, he needed Thomas. Thomas was not without power, and I did not believe for an instant that he would not be forgiven. It was all a matter of time, of rebuilding.

I tried to explain this, choosing my words carefully. A good man's sense of honour is a delicate plant, not to be trampled upon, and my lord thought himself slighted. At last, I gave up on the task, and went to sleep.

Next morning, and much to my surprise, Thomas was in a much better mood. Since the King did not require his company, he said, he would attend to outstanding business in Glamorgan. Several of the towns there had requested new charters from him to confirm their privileges. They would pay for this concession, of course, so, he said, he might as well oblige them and profit his own coffers. He had in any case neglected his lands in Wales for too long, and it would do him no harm to show himself to his people and cultivate their loyalty. Since I had been content to bear my daughter in Cardiff, he went on, it seemed to him that it was as good a place as any to bring our new child into the world. Did I object to this programme?

I did not. I did, however, point out that we had unfinished business in Gloucestershire. He had, for example, yet to recommend a man to be sheriff of the county.

'Do you suppose the King's offer still stands?' he asked sharply.

'Of course,' I said. 'Richard's anger will not last now you have submitted. He knows you are loyal, and I'm sure he'd prefer your man to Berkeley's man, or some fellow with Warwick behind him.'

I had already mentioned Poyntz as a candidate. The truth was there was not a great deal of choice. Most of our followers in the county were too young, or too insubstantial to hold such an office. It needed someone who could command.

He nodded. 'I'll make the suggestion. I suppose it can do no harm.'

***

Chapter 15

November 1396 — June 1397

I was not long from going into travail when a letter arrived from Philippa Fitzwalter, so curt as to be almost discourteous. It was a bald announcement that John Golafre had died from whatever illness had been troubling him, and that consequently she would be much occupied with settling his affairs.

I doubted that the brevity of her letter was caused by the depth of her sorrow, but I wrote back with usual wishes that are offered in such a case, and also offered Thomas's assistance if she had need of it. (He was, after all, her cousin, and as close to her in blood as any man, unless you counted her stepson, Lord Fitzwalter, a sullen brute of a fellow.) However, I received no answer. I scarcely noticed this omission, as I had other business to occupy me, as you will understand.

At the end of November my son was born. A healthy, lusty child with a loud cry, greedy for the wet-nurse's milk, his hands grasping every finger shown to him as if he never intended to release them. I was delighted with him, for it seemed to me that it was the beginning of a new age. Any child is a precious gift from God, but a healthy son silences many a carping tongue and earns his mother a new degree of respect. I had every hope he would soon have brothers to follow him, and perhaps a sister or two besides. Hope leaps in us at such times — we have our dreams, and forget that all is in God's hands and that nothing — nothing! — is ever certain. As I have learned, Dame Fortune is cruel and fickle and she loves nothing better than to mock us.

We had, of course, decided to name him for the King. Indeed, I had written to my cousin asking if he would serve as godfather, even though it could only be by proxy, my brother Dickon standing in his place. This privilege had been granted without demur, and there were other signs of renewed favour. For one thing, Robert Poyntz was chosen to be the next Sheriff of Gloucestershire, just as we had requested. For another, we received a silver-gilt cup by way of a christening present, and with it a request that we return to court as soon as I had been churched. We were to be presented to the new Queen.

I had, necessarily, missed my cousin's wedding, as had Thomas, and Isabella's coronation was to be held on the very day I was to emerge from seclusion for my churching, so I could not attend that either. There was nothing to be done about it, but I agreed with Thomas we should not delay further, but return to court just as swiftly as decency allowed. If we were restored to favour, our opportunity must be grasped.

There was to be a parliament held at Westminster, which of course my lord husband had to attend, so it was there that we found the King. There were changes about the court, as ever, but one of the most notable was that he had established a personal guard, made up of Cheshire squires and archers, dressed in a livery of green and white with a cloth badge of the White Hart on their chests. There were quite a number of these fellows, although of course not all were on duty at once, just enough to guard the principal doors and keep watch. They were coarse soldiers, but very loyal; they did not trouble me, even those unmannerly enough to leer.

Richard welcomed us so warmly that I wondered whether Thomas had ever really lost his favour. He told us that we had been sorely missed, and asked where our children were. When I answered that they were both at our London house he insisted that they be sent for. The Queen, he said, would certainly want to see them.

Isabella had been installed in what had been Anne's apartments. She was *tiny*. I had known that she was very young, but somehow she seemed even younger than I expected. She sat there, burdened down in her rich, heavy clothes, her fingers covered with rings, her hair hidden by a headdress that looked too large for her, surrounded by adult women, most of whom were French. I doubt there was anyone else in the room younger than seventeen. Her dolls sat at her feet, neglected.

She ran to Richard at once — or at least she stood up and moved towards him as swiftly as her trailing skirts allowed — greeting him with delight, her voice loud despite hushing noises that rose from one of her older ladies, presumably the one acting as governess.

Isabella's eyes seem enormous in her little face, and her smile was by no means forced, but as natural as that of any child welcoming a beloved father. My cousin calmed her with gentle words, and introduced us both. We were received most graciously, although I could not but think Isabella was behaving much as a child imitating her mother's manners — it was all a game to her.

She certainly could not be accused of being sullen or ungracious. When my children were brought in to the room, she delighted in them both. My son occupied her for a time — her eyes seem to grow even larger as she studied him, and she insisted on taking him in her arms and walking about the room with him, making soft, comforting noises as though she had been appointed his nurse. If anything, Bess pleased her even more. Perhaps this was no great surprise, for I have no doubt she was missing her younger sisters. Soon they were squatting on the floor together, and initiating some game with Isabella's dolls, conversing like old friends and quite forgetting the rest of us.

Richard took the opportunity to introduce us to Isabella's ladies — the one I had rightly assumed to be the Queen's governess was named as the Dame de Courcy. She looked at me as though I was a launderer, but I took that for French manners. I was prepared to give due allowance for their foreign ways, for it cannot be easy to find yourself in a strange land, where even nobles speak your language differently and where most people have no knowledge of it at all. I could only imagine what it would be like not to be able to ask some fellow out in the country to open a gate, or to call on a boy to hold one's horse. It was understandable that these people should stick together and be wary of us.

It was soon agreed that Bess should remain with the Queen for the time being; both girls seemed more than happy with this decree, and there were no tears or protests. My daughter would have her own people to support her, of course, and my son, quite forgotten by Isabella, was taken away to resume his place in our house. He had had quite enough disturbance for one day, and by this time he needed to have his swaddling changed and was keen to make us all aware of it. As I said, he had powerful lungs and it seemed he wanted the entire court to know of his arrival.

'My little wife will not stay here long,' Richard told us. 'I have it in mind to send her to Eltham or Windsor. Either is more pleasant for a child than Westminster, and she will have a household of her own.'

That seemed wise to me, and most kindly meant. Of course, I did not say this to my cousin. It would have been presumptuous.

My Uncle Gloucester was not so careful to guard his tongue. In truth, he was back to his old ways.

'Now that there is no war,' he said, to anyone who would listen, 'there can be no justification for taxation. The King should live of his own. He's received a great dowry from the French King for his marriage to the little Queen. He has his estates, and the profits of wardship and marriage, and all the other feudal dues. He has tonnage and poundage, and the revenues from justice and from the issuing of letters patent and the like. Licences for this, licences for that. It should be more than enough, but he squanders money — your taxes and mine, gentles — on dancing and feasting and keeping a sumptuous court.'

He said these very words and more. I know it because he said them in my presence, not of course, that I was his intended audience. I happened to be passing by as he was addressing a little gathering of fellows of middling importance, some of them his own followers, the great majority of them elected members of the new parliament. What my lord father called 'petty knights and squires from the back of beyond who are so bold as to meddle in the King's business.'

Again, I repeat words spoken in my presence, but in this case the Duke of York was talking to his guests at supper, not to a nameless rabble. Thomas and I were present, as were the Earl and Countess of Kent, my brother Edward, and of course, the Duchess. Unlike my uncle, my father was not seeking to provoke trouble, so he did not speak of such matters to men he barely knew, but kept his opinions within the family.

Later, I contrived a private word with my brother. My father's house at this time lay on the banks of the Thames. It was full dark, but it was a fine, clear night and there was a bright moon. We were outside together, away from the company, on a little gravelled path from which you could look across the water. To my surprise I saw there was a small wherry making its way downriver, its oarsmen working by the light of a lantern.

'In all likelihood, someone on his way to Southwark, for the brothels,' Edward said, answering my unspoken question before I had formed it on my lips.

'What of the curfew?' I asked.

He shrugged. 'Who is there to enforce it? Even such watchmen as there are will always take a bribe; besides, if you carry a lantern and are a man of some standing you're never questioned.'

'You speak from experience, no doubt?'

He laughed. 'What do you think?'

I had it in mind to tax him with his treatment of Alianore, but before I could even mention that, he began to speak to me of Uncle Gloucester.

'Our uncle,' he said, 'is stirring trouble again. It's not just this matter of tax — though that's bad enough — he also says that we are fools to keep the peace with France when their king is mad and while they are weak and divided among themselves. Of course, they suffered great losses at Nicopolis.'

'Nicopolis?'

'You must have heard of the battle, surely.'

I laughed. 'You should try being confined for two months with a gaggle of women. There was no lack of talk, but none of it was of battles.'

He laughed. 'I can think of nothing better, as long as the ladies are kind.' He hesitated, savouring his own wit. 'I'm surprised Thomas didn't tell you of it. There was a crusading army sent east – Burgundians mainly. They were badly beaten by the Turks at Nicopolis, which is in Hungary, or some such place at the back of beyond.' He shook his head. 'It doesn't signify where or how. It weakens the French, and Uncle Gloucester seems to believe that even a small army — say 5,000 men — sent now, could inflict such a defeat on them that they would be forced to make great concessions.'

'But that would be dishonourable!' I objected.

He grinned. 'Quite. But remember what you once said about honour, dear sister. Our uncle's sense of it bows to the profit he imagines. I hoped — I *believed* — that he had come to his senses. He was richly bribed to accept the peace. Yet now he harps on the same old string, and, of course, he has Arundel at his side. It could become very dangerous.'

'I doubt it,' I said, 'for as long as our cousin the King has other uncles to rely upon.'

He held up his hand, as if to forestall me from saying more. 'As soon as this Parliament is over, I have to travel to Germany. (It's about the business of having Richard elected King of the Romans.) While I'm away, you and Thomas must look after our family's interests. I want you to work closely with our father, and if necessary support him in arms. I've already said all this to your husband, but I'm not sure he trusts me. Or that he grasps how serious matters are. Or understands that while Mowbray and I are on our embassy the King will be much weakened. It gives our enemies an opportunity to strike, and it may be they'll take it.'

There was a silence between us for a few minutes. We merely stood there, watching the river. Then I said, 'If you believe there is such danger, is it a proper time for you to go to Germany?'

'Some risk for great reward,' he said. 'If Richard is elected, it will be an end to all threats to him, and we shall gain more than you can imagine.'

'And will he be? Elected?'

'If he is not, it will not be for any lack of bribes. We shall carry great presents with us, and promises of more besides. Mowbray and I will do all we can to see our mission is successful. Do you doubt our skills?'

To be truthful, I did doubt them. Both of them were young and lacked experience in such negotiations. My Uncle Lancaster would have been a more impressive envoy, but it was clear why he was not being sent. He was needed at home to keep his brother, Gloucester, at bay.

'When you come back,' I said, shifting my ground, 'shall I be allowed to meet this new love of yours? The one you have chosen above Alianore? I can only presume she is remarkable. Someone at least Alianore's equal in birth and beauty?'

'It is not your concern,' he said sharply.

'Ah, so it's not someone you intend to marry? Some base-born whore I suppose!'

He turned on me. 'As I have said, it is not your concern. As for Alianore, she chose her path. When it came to the test, she chose March above me.'

'That isn't how she tells the tale.'

'And you, of course, take her word?' He laughed. 'A woman, and your friend, cannot possibly lie. Whereas I am but your brother.'

'I know what you men are like. Ruled by that which dangles between your legs.'

He snorted. 'The Church teaches us we are all sinners. I don't presume to be an exception. However, at least we men have our limits. It is *women* whose lusts are insatiable. As any priest will tell you.'

'Do you speak of *Alianore*?' I raised my voice in fury, for I would not have my friend insulted after he had treated her so meanly.

He laughed as if my words were ridiculous. 'No! Of course not. I speak in general, as you well know. And you provoked me to say it. I don't deny I seek my pleasure like any other man, but you go too far if you say I am ruled by lust. Scarcely, my dear. If I were, I'd have a string of bastards like our Uncle Lancaster.'

It was rich for him, of all men, to speak of provocation. I

sighed, weary of his nonsense.

'Will you marry the Queen's sister?'

He shook his head. 'No. And before you ask, I've told Cousin Richard I have a grown woman in mind for wife, and he has no objection.'

'I see I must ask him who it is, since you will not tell me.'

He smiled. 'Ask him what you please. You will know at the proper time, which is not yet.'

I asked him all manner of questions, but he merely grinned at me and answered none of them. He would not even say whether his chosen lady was an Englishwoman.

My brother knew he had me on tenterhooks, and it obviously gave him pleasure to keep me there.

*

At this Parliament an insolent petition was presented that claimed that the King kept too great a court, and that, in particular, he kept too many bishops and ladies about him.

Richard summoned the Speaker of the Commons before him.

It was a most formal audience, with many of us standing about, quiet as mice and wearing solemn faces. It was also as false as a mystery play, where one baker plays Herod and three others play the soldiers he sends to slay the Innocents. For the Speaker was Sir John Bussy, and Bussy was one of Richard's own men, and sat on his Council. Richard feigned to be angrier than he really was, while Bussy grovelled and pretended to be terrified. It was all for the show of it, to put the Commons in fear.

It may be that even this was not necessary. It was not the

Parliament of old times, dominated by traitors. Bussy soon returned, and with many apologies and deep bows, gave up the name of the offender. The world had changed, and for the better.

It was a little cleric of no importance who had caused all this trouble. Thomas Haxey, proctor for the clergy, who hailed from some God-forsaken place to the north of the Trent. The fellow was brought before the King and Lords in the White Chamber, and there tried for high treason. He was sentenced to death; but no one expected his execution, for he was a priest, and Richard never had a priest killed.

Archbishop Arundel claimed Haxey as such. (Thomas Arundel had lately been promoted to Archbishop of Canterbury, meaning that he sat higher in Parliament than any save the King; but on the other hand, he was no longer Chancellor, so it was a fair exchange.) He took the little clerk away, and lodged him in his prison at Lambeth. Or so he promised. I suppose that in truth the fellow was given the run of his house, library and gardens.

That this petition had others behind it was evident. I believe my Uncle Gloucester himself had dictated it, with Haxey no more than a cat's paw. That the little priest was an insolent dog cannot be denied; but I am sure he would not have dared to put forward such a libel without the prompting of powerful men. Of course, nothing could be proved, but everyone *knew*.

*

I had written to Lady Mohun to ask if she had news of her daughter, Philippa Fitzwalter, for it seemed to me that the grieving widow might well be living with her mother. Had she not told me that she intended to make such a visit?

The answer came back at length, all the way from Dunster Castle in Somerset where Joan Mohun was living at that time. Philippa was not there. Indeed, Lady Mohun said, she had not seen Philippa for months, nor heard from her. She had thought her with me.

It was very odd. I could only imagine she was living on her Fitzwalter dower lands, unless she had decided to place herself in a convent for a time, as is a common practice with widows. (I found it hard to imagine it in her case, for she was about as pious as a horse, but it was certainly possible.) Whatever she was doing, I thought her discourteous not to write either to me or to her mother. However, I had other matters to occupy me, and after a time I gave her no further thought. I judged it likely that, like a clipped penny, she would eventually turn up.

The Parliament was ended. My brother Rutland and Thomas Mowbray, Earl of Nottingham, had set off to Germany with a great company of men and several packhorses loaded with gifts — or plain bribes, call them what you will. My cousin the King had great hopes of the election, and once that was achieved he would certainly accept coronation as Emperor at the Pope's hands. The prize was almost within his grasp.

At this time Roger Mortimer, Earl of March, had his office as Lord Lieutenant of Ireland extended by three years. The King made no secret of it, but announced it before the court, saying that he had full confidence in Roger's governance of the island. My lord husband was very pleased, saying his influence with Richard had borne fruit. He had been carefully, patiently, subtly, maintaining his friend's cause all these months.

Roger's folly seemed a trivial matter in retrospect, no more than a misunderstanding, but I still wondered. As I had told Thomas, Ireland was a place of exile, and while he remained there March was quite unable to develop his power in England. However, I kept these thoughts to myself. I did not want my lord to think that I was forever calling up clouds to threaten his hopes and desires.

Just after Easter, the Earl of Kent was called to God. It

happened very suddenly. He was at Arundel Castle with his wife, visiting her brother, Lord Arundel and perhaps trying to talk sense into the fellow. While sitting at table he clutched at his chest and dropped down, dead as a stone.

It was a great blow to the King, who lost his half-brother and a loyal supporter. It was almost as much of a shock to my father, for Kent had been, I think, his closest friend. As for Joanne, she was completely broken by the loss. I spent many hours in her rooms, trying to console her, and not having any great success. Her brothers and sisters (save for Alianore, of course, for she was in Ireland) clustered around her, weeping and telling anecdotes about their father, but that did not seem to help either. Lady Kent, who had more cause to weep than any of them, was the calmest of them all. The more Joanne wept, the more her mother told her that she must accept God's will. (This is always wise counsel, but scant comfort at such times.)

The heir was, of course, Joanne's brother, Thomas Holland, who became Earl of Kent. He was very tall, very lean, and, like all his family, good-looking. He was also a brave knight who excelled in the jousts. However, it seemed to me he had little between his ears, and his conversation was limited to his hawks and horses. Nevertheless, the King valued him and kept him close at hand, and took his counsel, so, in that way, he directly replaced his father. He was, of course, equally loyal to Richard.

The only remaining brother Thomas Holland had now was young Mun, who still served in my father's household, though by this time promoted to squire and attendant more on the Duke than on Joanne. (The brothers between them in age had both passed to God.) I suppose he was fourteen by this time, and uncommonly handsome for a stripling of that age, and quite conscious of it, keeping his fair hair in long, curled locks and trying hard to grow a beard. It was amusing how he grew tongue-tied in my presence and blushed like a young maid if I spoke to him. I had little doubt that he would soon grow out of such folly. Had my brother Rutland been in England I would have asked him to take the lad to a suitable whore to be educated.

Many of us travelled to Bourne after the Garter Feast to attend Kent's funeral, which was very grand and occupied us for three days of ceremony and solemn feasts, with great gifts for the poor of the country all around.

On the way back to court, Thomas and I lodged at Fotheringhay, our bed being of course in the room that had been provided for me long ago. My father and Joanne seemed inclined to go no further, and we were encouraged to linger with them.

Over supper, on our first night there, my father gave certain instructions to Thomas. At least, that was what I judged them to be.

'There are those about the King who are putting unnecessary fears into his head,' he said. 'My brother, Lancaster, and I will never allow any harm to come him, or to the Queen. We have told him as much. I hope that when you are next in his company you will do all you can to reassure him, because I am not sure we have convinced him that he is safe.'

Thomas shook his head. 'My lord Father, I will do as you ask. Yet my assurance is of little value compared to that you have already given him.'

My father snorted. 'You have the advantage of not being an elder, but a friend. Your counsel may indeed be of more weight than mine. Whether it should be is another matter, but that is the truth of it.'

'I know there are those about the King who are afraid,' I said. (At court you had to be deaf not to hear such fears. Even John Montagu has said to me that he was not sure his head was safe on his shoulders while my Uncle Gloucester was seeking to stir the

Commons to rebellion.) 'Perhaps they have cause. Things are being said that are very similar to the preaching of the Appellants.'

'It is folly!' snapped the Duke. 'Do not meddle, daughter. This is not your concern.'

'By your leave, my lord Father, my son's inheritance is very much my concern.' I did not lower my gaze, as I ought to have done, but held my head high. 'I remember what happened to Burley, de Vere, and the rest. All too well I remember! I have the stink of treason in my nostrils again.'

'Have I not just told you?' My father was fast losing his patience and his voice had risen to the point where it could probably be heard down in the hall. 'There is no treason. No risk. No danger. No one has the power to prevail against the King, and if you think you serve him by pretending that matters are otherwise you are much mistaken.'

I did not dispute with him, but I was not convinced. I remembered what my brother had said. That we must be ready to take up arms if necessary.

Joanne leaned towards me. 'Please, Constance. Let us talk of other matters; not of imagined dangers.'

Yes, I thought, let me ask if any new puppies have been born here at Fotheringhay. Or shall we remark on the number of hairs on my son's head? Perhaps debate the best remedy for a cough? God forbid that we should discuss anything of importance.

I said none of this, of course, as I did not wish to seem discourteous. All else apart, I had to remember that my stepmother had just suffered a great loss. I had no wish to provoke her to fresh tears.

*

It did not help that I still had evil dreams; perhaps they made me more fearful than I really needed to be. Still, I was not alone in my concern, and there were many around the King warning him of new dangers. Not the least of them was his half-brother, John Holland, Earl of Huntingdon, who told everyone who would listen, including me, that we should take up arms to defend ourselves. Then there was William Scrope, one of the sons of Lord Scrope of Bolton. He had spent some years in Ireland as Justiciar but was now home and rising in favour. He was a cunning and persuasive speaker, and he too was busy among the men of the court, warning them that their heads might be made to fly at any moment.

Thomas tried to do as my father had asked him, that is he sought to persuade the King that he was secure. At the same time he assured me — in confidence — that he had warned his retainers they must be ready to come to him with their followers on the instant if they were summoned. He added that his chief concern was that he had too few of them. However, his brother-in-law, Robert Ferrers, had promised to add himself to the Despenser retinue. (His remaining brother-in-law, Lord Morley, was Gloucester's toady, so there was no point in asking *him*.) Our castles, he added, had all been put into a state of defence, especially Hanley Castle. They would not be taken by surprise if matters turned against us.

'It's better,' he said, 'to be prepared for a fight that may never occur than be taken unaware. But I believe your lord father to be in the right. The King is now so powerfully protected that only a fool would rise against him. You can say many things about your Uncle Gloucester, or our friend Arundel, but I do not think them fools. Am I mistaken?'

'No,' I said, 'they are not fools. But many see the world as they do. It is well to be prepared, as you say.'

In June the murmurings of trouble turned into an open quarrel between the King and my Uncle Gloucester. It happened thus

— and it was no proper cause for a dispute at all.

We English had for some years — I cannot say how many, and nor do I care — occupied the town of Brest, which belonged to the Duke of Brittany. This had been in security for a loan, now repaid, but the agreement had been that we could keep it until the end of the war. Well, the war *was* ended, and as the place was not ours it was only right and just to return it. The garrison was brought home, and Richard gave a great feast at Westminster to honour them for their service.

The Great Hall of the palace was in the hands of builders at this time, for the King had ordered it to be re-roofed and made more splendid. However, a temporary wooden hall had been constructed out in the yard, to accommodate parliaments and the courts of law, and it was in this structure that we gathered. It was richly painted and gilded inside, and many of the King's wall-hangings had been brought in to decorate it, so it was not obvious that we were eating in what was really no more than a gigantic barn. A watch of the Cheshire Archers were there as a guard of honour for the King, but they did no more than stand at the doors and along the walls, as silent and motionless as statues.

At first, all went well. The random chance of precedence seated me, on this occasion, between John Montagu, who had just succeeded his uncle as Earl of Salisbury, and, above me, my cousin, Harry Bolingbroke. They were better neighbours than you might have thought, each trying to out-do the other in courtesy towards me. Had I been younger, or more naïve, I might have felt flattered. As it was, I knew they would have treated any other woman of good birth with similar elegant ceremony. Even Lady Arundel herself.

Processions of liveried men and boys brought in course after course, each more splendid than the last, with more dishes than you could count. There was such a quantity of food I believe it could have fed all London, and left some to spare. Music played throughout, minstrels working in a little gallery that had been contrived above our heads. As if this was not enough, there were teams of jugglers and tumblers working up and down the massive hall, and even a man who seemed to eat fire – what the trick was, I cannot imagine. Stewards on horseback rode to-and-fro, supervising all.

The meal was concluded and we were down to the wine and comfits at the end when trouble began. All at once, my uncle, who was seated a few feet away from Richard at the top table, began to shout. At least, so it seemed. It may be that he was merely raising his voice so as to be heard, but I'm sure that he wanted more than Cousin Richard to hear what he was saying. His words were meant for all of us, even the lowest varlet seated at the bottom of the hall.

'These men of Brest, who have faithfully served you,' he cried, gesturing towards the lower tables where some of the fellows were placed, 'are now cast aside, and not rewarded, or even given their proper pay. I think it a great shame on the kingdom, and on *you*, sire!'

Richard answered plainly. Not shouting, but his voice pitched so that he carried the hall. The garrison would certainly be paid, every penny due.

My uncle stood in his place. God knows what he thought he was about. 'Sire,' he said, very loudly, 'you ought first to hazard your life in capturing a city from your enemies before you give up lands that your ancestors have conquered.'

It was a ridiculous argument, for the reasons I have given. The city was not ours by right, nor, for that matter, by conquest. Still, there were growls of agreement from some of those present, especially from lower down the hall where many of the lesser knights and squires were sitting, men who hoped to make their fortune by the sword, some of them my uncle's own lickspittles who wore his livery.

'*What* is that you say?' Richard demanded. This time his voice was raised, for he was understandably angry. His cheeks, usually as pale as milk, were quite scarlet above the line of his beard.

Gloucester repeated his words, slightly more quietly, but spacing his words out as if addressing a simpleton. It was as if he was determined to heap insult upon insult. I might have thought him drunk, had he been another man, but my uncle was abstemious. He was always in full command of himself.

The King astonished me with his patience. At one time he would simply have flown into a rage. Instead, quietly, calmly, he explained the causes of his surrender of Brest; he had no right to it, and so no choice but to yield it. The discharged soldiers would be paid, in full, as he had said, and until they were they would live at his expense. My uncle knew all this very well, of course, but he pretended otherwise so he could claim England was dishonoured.

The hall had grown so quiet that you could hear your own breathing. I looked towards my own Thomas, and saw his expression was grim, that he was ready to spring into action in an instant if fighting began. He was not alone in that; half the hall were reaching for the hilts of their swords, baselards or daggers, if only to check they were loose in the scabbard. Uncle Gloucester looked about him, as if for support, and apparently decided there was not enough for his purpose. He settled back in his place, and spoke fair words, and the King spoke fair words back. No one was in the least deceived.

'So,' said John Montagu, 'it all begins again.'

'With one difference,' said Harry. 'This time I stand with the King, and will live and die in his cause.'

And he looked straight into my eyes and smiled, as if defying me to contradict him.

Then he took up his cup of wine, stood, made an elaborate

bow to the King, and drank deeply to pledge his loyalty. As I watched, man after man stood up to copy his example, and a rippling sound emerged from dozens of throats, a deep roar that turned itself into cheers, and the loud shouting of Richard's name. Again and again, like a chant that had no ending. 'God save King Richard! God save King Richard!'

***

Chapter 16

June — August 1397

It was not long after this that the King received an embassy from Germany, headed by the Dean of Cologne. These men were received with full honour, with Richard sitting in state and the rest of us standing about in serried, silent rows to show our respect for the visitors. The heat was stifling, and I could have wished myself to be sitting by an open casement, wearing my thinnest linen gown and, preferably, with nothing on my head and my bare feet in a bowl of cold water. That of course was impossible. There I was, among the company, weighed down by my clothes and jewellery, and consoled only by the thought that everyone else was as uncomfortable as I was myself. At least, unlike Richard, I did not have to bear the weight of a crown on my head.

The Dean spoke for his fellows, in quite good French that was more or less understandable. He gave the King the most elaborate compliments, a litany of them that seemed to last half an hour. Occasionally, he lapsed into Latin, which I could not follow, but of course, he was a churchman so it was only to be expected he would show off his learning on such an occasion.

He told us that Richard was very close to being elected King of the Romans. This was such momentous news that very few of us were so well schooled that we did not let out a gasp of either delight or surprise, according to what bets had been laid.

Unfortunately, there was a 'but' and it followed hard upon, like a fast horse in pursuit of an ancient ambler. There were those electors who had their doubts, because they claimed Richard could not control his English subjects. How then was he to control all Germany as well?

My cousin's face fell; but he did not lose his composure, as he might have done when he was younger. He did not turn bright red or pace about or throw oaths at them. Instead, he spoke mildly, welcomed them to England and invited them to remain as his guests for as long as they pleased. He could not have been more gracious.

Later that evening, my lord husband had a different tale to tell me. Thomas had been one of those Richard had asked to withdraw with him to offer their advice. It was, I suppose, a Council meeting of sorts, but with no clerks present to record what was said, or who agreed with what proposal.

'The King is furious,' he said, very quietly so that no one could hear him but me. 'He has told us all to summon our retainers and put our household-folk into arms. "I will show them whether I am my father's son!" he said. It has come at last, Constance. We are not waiting to be struck, but strike first. Now there are letters to be written. They must be carried off at first light; though I doubt all my people will be here in time. Now he has decided to act, the King will not long delay. He dare not.'

'At last,' I said, 'he takes his revenge.'

'I think so. Though from what he says, I believe he only intends to imprison your uncle, Arundel, and Warwick for a while. To show that he has the power. That reminds me. There's particular news of Warwick. He's lost his case. Lost it badly. Gower goes to Mowbray, but that's just the beginning. He must also pay the back rents. He loses seventeen manors for eleven years by way of compensation. Whatever else happens, his power is broken. He is no longer any threat to us in Worcestershire.'

'It's the least he deserves,' I said.

'He's an old man, losing his strength. I almost feel sorry for him.'

'That is folly!' I cried. 'He would have your head if he could, and he and Berkeley would rejoice in using it as a football. Spare him no sympathy. They are all traitors.'

'How fierce you are!' he said, pausing to kiss me. 'I should not care to be your enemy.'

*

My lord husband's men soon began to arrive in London, although only those from the counties nearby. Those from Wales, in particular, were still far off, and, as it turned out, were not to arrive until it was too late. Some of those who had appeared were ill-provided, and my women and I were busy for a time sewing Despenser griffin badges onto jerkin sleeves, for some of the fellows had no other livery to distinguish them, being but tenants or the servants of tenants and retainers. Our hall was quite crammed with pallets for them to sleep on, until at last some had to be lodged in adjoining houses, all at our cost.

The King had sent messages to the three he had marked down for arrest to come to court, saying that he wished them to attend a banquet.

My Uncle Gloucester had withdrawn to his castle at Pleshey in Essex. His reply to the summons was to claim he was ill. Perhaps he was; but he had played the game of convenient illness in the past, and so was not believed. Lord Arundel shut himself up in Reigate Castle, and also refused the King's command. Again, this was exactly as he had behaved at the time of the Appellants, when Northumberland had been sent with a force to winkle him out of his stronghold, but had failed.

This time the King was more subtle. He sent for Archbishop Arundel, who came across the river from Lambeth in some style, bringing with him a great train of priests, clerks, singing boys, and I know not what, his great processional cross borne before him. We had all to reverence him, for was he not Primate of All England? He spared himself no ceremony.

My mind went back to when he had arrived at Eltham with my Uncle Gloucester, long ago, looking like an attorney's clerk and constantly wringing his hands. That was a habit he had all but forgotten. Now he walked tall and stately, his head high, looking around at us as if to be sure that we were all bending low enough in his august presence.

The King received him with just as much formality as he had done on that distant occasion at Eltham; perhaps even more. It was not so much a public audience given to a subject — it was more akin to the formal reception of a foreign ambassador with whom negotiations were to be held.

Richard was very courteous. He did not command, as he might have done, but made a request that the Archbishop should go to his brother and invite the man to leave his castle and give himself up. If Richard Arundel did that, he said, if he humbly submitted, it would go much in his favour. On the other hand, if he was obstinate, there would be grave consequences.

'What consequences, my lord King?' asked the Archbishop.

'I shall besiege the castle with all my strength, and all my guns and engines of war,' Richard answered. 'It will certainly fall, sooner or later, and when it does every living thing within its walls will be put to the sword. I should much prefer, your Grace, to avoid such a needless effusion of Christian blood, but I shall not hesitate. The choice lies in Lord Arundel's hands, not mine.'

'Your Highness promises my brother's safety, if he yields?'

My cousin's cheeks flushed, ever so slightly. I knew that he was not far from losing his temper. You could see it his eyes, if you dared look at them. 'I have given you my promise as to his fate if he defies me,' he said, his voice rising slightly.

'Your Grace has pardoned him for his faults.'

'More than once! And he might ask himself why he required such pardons. Let him produce them before Parliament, if it comes to that.'

The Archbishop sniffed. It was a very loud sniff, as if he had a very bad cold. I doubt he had. It was more in the way of a comment. Time went by. I suppose it was but a minute or two, but it seemed an age while the man considered his answers.

He bowed. 'I shall do as your Grace commands,' he said.

That was the end of the negotiation. He backed away from the throne and stalked away, his little army of clerks and boys tripping over themselves as they sought to keep up with him. The Archbishop is — for he lives yet as I write this — no great scholar, no master or doctor of the laws; but he knows how to stride. That and how to destroy better men than himself. May God damn him for the vile politician that he is! (Saving always the reverence due to a prelate.)

*

There was a great feast at Coldharbour, John Holland's house by the Thames, which was supposedly to celebrate the return of my brother Rutland and Thomas Mowbray from their mission to Germany. They had failed in their purpose, but my Cousin Richard did not hold that against them, and they had their places at the high table along with the King, Huntingdon and my cousin Beth, Lady Huntingdon.

It was the more surprising that Warwick was placed there, and that the King appeared to be making much of him. The fool had walked into a trap, doubtless hoping, in his deluded way, that Richard would do something to amend the losses he had suffered by losing Gower to Mowbray. (Men of his stamp can never quite bring themselves to believe that they are less than highly valued or that they do not deserve to be rewarded.)

His long face grew very long, and astonished, when the King's knights and Cheshire men arrived with the wine and wafers. They dragged him to a barge that was waiting at the quay to take him down to the Tower.

Thomas and I went home to our house in Friday Street, which some called the *Bell on the Hoop*.

'There is pestilence three streets away,' he told me, 'and I think it may be good for you to take our son to Caversham before it spreads.'

I disliked this suggestion, for I wanted to be in on the kill, so to speak. However, as my lord said, it would make little real difference whether I was in London or Caversham, since he had no thought of taking me into battle. So, after we had talked for a while, I gave in to his wishes and said I would begin my packing. I myself was not afraid of contagion, but it was true that our son was both young and precious and it was important not to put him at risk. In the summer heat, the insufferable stench of London was growing by the day, and it's well known that disease springs from such bad air.

Then, unexpectedly, my brother Edward arrived, bringing with him his usual tail of idle wastrels. It seemed he wanted to tell us about his mission to Germany, and how it came to fail.

'We came close to our quarry,' he said, lazing in a chair by the fireplace in our solar. He had one knee lifted almost to his chin. I do not know how he found such a posture comfortable, but it seemed that he did. He gestured with finger and thumb. 'Very close! These Germans, though, are a curious sort. Close-mouthed and proud. It's hard to be sure what they're thinking, or even to know whether our bribes were pleasing or offensive. I grant you their wine is well enough and they are generous hosts. Now we come home to — *this*! I know not what my cousin the King is thinking about.'

'You don't agree with the arrests?' Thomas asked. I could tell from his voice he was astonished.

'Of course I agree!' my brother all but snapped at him. 'But this talk of locking them up for a few weeks, and then releasing them, is a child's folly. They must *die*! Anything less, and in some little time they will be plotting revenge for the insult. For insult it is, Thomas, and they are not such men as will swallow it meekly. It touches their honour. None of us will be safe while they are above ground.'

'But Gloucester is your uncle. A prince of the King's blood.'

Edward snorted. 'I'm well aware of that. He's also a traitor and, quite apart from that, if it's a choice between his death and mine, I choose his. God's truth, do you deny he deserves his fate?'

Thomas looked at me, questioningly.

'Ned is right,' I said. 'They should have as much mercy as they allowed to Simon Burley.'

I sensed, as much as anything, that Edward and I had shocked him. He looked very solemn.

'So I shall say to Richard,' my brother went on. 'I should tell you he has asked me to act as Lord High Constable in my uncle's room, so I shall have some authority in matters of treason. He has, moreover, granted me the Lordship of Wight.'

'Wight?' I repeated, for I could scarcely believe my ears. 'The island?'

He grinned. 'What else?'

'I wonder how he would have rewarded you for success, if he gives you the Isle of Wight for failure!'

'And Carisbrooke Castle to go with it,' he said, his smile widening. 'As you know, he considers me his brother, and his generosity is in proportion. There is more to come. For Thomas too. You must see how this ends.'

I did. Three men would be forfeited, and we should have a share in the spoils.

'Will my uncle resist?' I asked.

'Not if he is wise. Anyway, there can be no more delaying. We march *tonight, with* every man we can muster.'

'You know that half my men are still on the road?' Thomas asked.

Edward shrugged. 'I've none of mine, except the household I took with me to Germany and those my father will lend me. It matters not. With all our people, and the Londoners, it should be quite an array. We shall be more than enough, and we're taking the guns from the Tower. One way or another, we shall have him out.'

*

My lord father was ill. At least he claimed to be, and sat in a chair in his bed-gown, looking sorry for himself. I think he was merely tired, for the constant heat had been sapping all of us.

We gathered at his house that evening, for Edward was to lead the van of the King's army — if army it could be called. We had not mustered a quarter of our strength, but my Cousin Richard had decided that there could be no further delay, that we must strike at once with such power as we had. Thomas was, of course, to ride with my brother, and so was Thomas Mowbray who had already made his appearance. All three were in full armour, save that for the time being they were bare-headed. A procession of messengers arrived and left, bearing the King's instructions. Richard was to follow on with the main body, while the Londoners would bring up the rear under their Lord Mayor – that Whittington, the Gloucestershire man, from whom we had once borrowed money.

'There is no need for this force,' my father said, his voice querulous. (The very look of him told me he was feeling quite miserable.) 'My brother will never fight. It's all quite excessive.'

'It is but a precaution, your Grace,' Mowbray said, bowing his head. 'We must consider the King's safety, and take no chances.'

Edward seemed to like Mowbray well enough, and Thomas was quite often in his company these days, even bidding him to sup at our table. For my part, I thought him an insinuating jack, any man's for a shilling. Was he not married to Arundel's daughter? Had he not stood with the Appellants? Yet here he was, on our side — this week at least. Who could say where next week's wind would blow him?

'I doubt there'll be any fighting,' my brother said, 'but what fools we should look if we went to Pleshey unprepared and found ourselves facing all my uncle's retainers and tenants. The show of force will deter any resistance. He is not such a fool that he cannot count numbers. We should arrive with the dawn, and with any fortune take him quite by surprise, perhaps while he is still asleep. All will be well, my lord Father.'

The Duke made a grunting sound. 'I pray you are right. All I know is that I am weary, and must seek my bed.'

He rose, very slowly, very stiffly, and moved off, calling for his attendants as he went, while we made our reverences. Joanne was the first to resume her seat, and she rolled her eyes impatiently, but made no comment, only gesturing to indicate that I should sit next to her.

After an hour or so of waiting, the last messenger arrived from the King. It was time for them to leave, and so I said my farewell to Thomas, kissing him and wishing him well, although I was uncertain as to what danger they faced, whether it was great or trifling. He was calm enough, and my brother was bold and talkative, as if he was relishing the task before him. They mounted up in the courtyard, and Joanne and I stood at a window that overlooked the street to watch them go. Edward was at the front of the procession, with Thomas and Mowbray a little behind, their banners carried above them. After them came the men they had assembled, a strange mixture of well-armed knights and esquires and sundry tenants and servants, not all of them well equipped, and their total number surely not above a couple of hundred. Most were mounted, albeit some on sorry nags. I pitied those few who were not, for it is a long walk from London to Pleshey. Darkness was already falling, and some of the men carried torches to light the way. The moon was out, but it was but at the first crescent of its cycle, so offered little assistance.

There was a short time when nothing happened except that street dogs ran about and drunken fellows bellowed on street corners, while Joanne and I looked at each other and talked quietly of trifles. Then we heard clarions, some way off, then the distant jingle of harness and the sound of hooves clattering over the street paving. It was the King with the main host.

Richard was at the head of this company, riding beneath his banner carried by Sir Simon Felbrigg, and with our friend, Sir John Russell, his Master of Horse, close at hand. Then there was Thomas Holland — Joanne waved at her brother, but all in vain, as his eyes were focused forward and I doubt he knew she was there. Then there was William Scrope with John Montagu — Salisbury as I should call him — and the knights, esquires and yeomen of the King's household, the followings of the three nobles and the Cheshire Archers under their captains. It was much darker now, and their leathery, bearded faces were lit only by the torchlight, with some remaining in shadow, all marching in silence save for the rhythmic beating of drums and the occasional loud outburst of cursing from an officer when some fellow fell out of step or stumbled against his neighbour in the dark.

I had no particular wish to see the Londoners go by, but Joanne insisted that we should. She seemed excited, and as I was both her guest and her stepdaughter I could not well demur, but was obliged to follow her lead.

At last they came — the Lord Mayor, his aldermen and chief men as well-equipped as gentlemen, for whom they passed at a glance. Then their followers, again, only the minority on foot, some having more or less the look of soldiers, others making me think they were fellows who had been dragged from their counting-houses and kitchens to have a bow or a glaive thrust into their hands. Some were mere boys. Half-grown, beardless and awkward.

'Thank God they do not face the French,' I thought. It was

only when Joanne stared at me that I realised I had spoken the words aloud.

'Let us pray for their safety,' the Duchess said.

I had not thought her so pious. However, she loved her brother very much and I think she feared for him. So I followed her to the little chapel in another part of the house and we knelt in prayer for some considerable time, until she was content and I was very tired. Only then was I allowed to withdraw to my bed. It was well after midnight.

*

It was early afternoon of the next day before the men began to return. Among the first was my lord husband, sent by the King as a matter of courtesy to report events to my father. He was out of armour, and looked much as if he had just returned from a hunt, a little heated by the sun, perhaps even a little weary; all that mattered to me was that he was quite safe. He had not so much as a scratch upon him.

The Duke was a little better than he had been the previous evening, though he was still pale and had taken nothing for dinner but a little bread and cheese, as if he was but a labourer on the land. He was fully dressed and on his feet, as anxious to hear the news as Joanne and I were.

'There was no fighting,' Thomas said at once, 'none whatever. The Duke of Gloucester is taken. The King has placed him in Mowbray's charge and ordered him removed to Calais, where he is to be lodged.'

That was the bare bones of it, and I believe it was sufficient for Joanne to know there had been no killing. She looked relieved, even pleased, and sank down on her cushions. My father, of course, was not so easily satisfied. He asked one question after another.

'The Duke had sent most of his household away, for whatever reason,' Thomas said in response to the last of them. 'His wife was with him, and some priests and singing-boys — they came out to greet the King — but there were but a handful of servants, and none of them armed. They could not have held the castle for an hour even if they had tried.'

'Ah,' said my father, taking a deep breath. 'Is it not plain enough? My brother never intended to resist. He must have sent his people away as a sign of good faith. No man planning rebellion would do that. He would have surrounded himself with armed retainers. The King must see it, surely.'

I could not restrain a sigh. My father heard, and glared at me.

'Have you something to say, daughter?' he demanded.

'I think you should ask my brother Rutland about that, my lord Father,' I said. My tone did not please him, as I could see from his expression.

'Why?' he snapped, his eyes glancing from me to Thomas and back again. 'What have I not been told?'

'The King, as I understand it, has decided that my uncle must pay for his offences,' I said. I spoke boldly — I could no longer contain myself.

'*As you understand it,*' the Duke repeated testily. 'Thomas, is your wife's understanding at fault, or is there truth in this? My brother's past faults are long pardoned. I've heard no evidence of new offences.'

Thomas looked awkward. His feet shuffled. 'I do not know the King's mind,' he said.

'You were not at the banquet for the garrison of Brest, my lord Father,' I said, my tongue quite running away from me, 'but you must surely have heard that my uncle insulted the King before the whole company — as good as called him "coward" to his face. Richard has had years and years of such slights. I believe that after today there will be no more. There will be a reckoning for all of it.'

My father sank down on his chair. I expected him to rail at

me, but he did not. Instead he called to one of the attendants standing by, demanding a cup of wine. It was brought at once, and he drank deeply. Suddenly, he seemed older than his years, bewildered.

'I think I must speak to the King,' he said at last, in a strange, quiet voice.

Thomas glanced at me, and I bit my lip. It was tempting to tell the Duke that no appeal to Richard would make any difference; that the business was already settled. Yet I was not sure it was so. I knew my elder brother's intentions, and his influence, but in all truth I was not sure that the King had made a final decision.

My lord husband drew me aside, and spoke quietly. 'We are to go into our country,' he said. 'It's the King's order that we make sure that proper men are elected to the parliament he intends to call. That is our next business, and I think we can guess his purpose. Be gentle with your father. He means well. It does not serve to anger him.'

I nodded. He was right, of course. We had quarrels enough, without disputing among ourselves. My father was loyal to the King, and always had been. He would do his bidding.

*

Thomas and I left London next day, though we had first to venture to Westminster to take our leave of the King. It did not cause much delay, for Richard was much occupied with business and could spare us little time. He repeated his orders though, in my presence. We were to make sure that men were returned to the Commons for Gloucestershire who would do his will, no matter what. He also said that he wished Thomas to bring plenty of armed men with him to London at parliament-time, and promised a licence would be issued for that purpose. Nothing, he said, could be left to chance. Not until the traitors — as he called them — were put down for good.

That Edward was close at hand was no surprise. He was in a merry mood, and I had little doubt that his advice had prevailed. There would be no more talk of a few weeks imprisonment and then a pardon. No, matters had gone quite beyond that.

'Arundel is in the Tower,' he confided. 'He gave himself up, thanks to his brother. The Archbishop, of course, is still at large — for the time being. His work at the time of the Appellants is not forgotten. He was Richard's Chancellor, as you will remember, but he was a false servant and betrayed all his counsel to the rebels. I think we may fairly call that treason.'

'The King will not harm a priest,' I said.

'Why not? Why should priests be held blameless in matters of treason?' He let that hang in the air between us, no doubt intending to shock us, as was his wont. Then he grinned at us. 'You are right, of course. Richard won't harm a single hair of his sacred head, whatever his true deserts. But some other measures may be taken. Against him, and against certain others. We have quite a list of them. Half the leading men of certain counties who rose in arms. If some are pardoned, it does not follow that all shall be. In my new office as Lord High Constable it will be my business to consider the matter, and consider it I shall. Those that do not pay with their heads shall certainly pay with coin. It should be a most profitable business.'

It was clear that he was thoroughly enjoying himself.

*

Our journey to the west was not made in haste. We had most of our household with us, save for those sent ahead to prepare for our arrival, and, for the first few days we also had the company of many of those tenants and retainers Thomas had gathered together, all of whom were now returning home. The heat made the going hard, and if only to spare the horses, we had to stop frequently for rest and refreshment. The thick dust rising from the roads did not make matters easier.

On our way we visited Windsor, to pay our respects to the little Queen, who was living there with her household, and more importantly to visit our daughter. Bess was settled and happy, at least as devoted to Isabella as I had once been to Anne. The difference was, of course, that they were two little girls who played together as well as Queen and attendant.

Some of the English ladies at Windsor were less happy. They complained of the Dame de Courcy, saying that she thought herself more important than the Queen and had little time for Isabella's English attendants, favouring the French completely. Such gossip in a household is not unusual; there are always intrigues between factions. I paid little heed at the time, for it was not my business. As long as my daughter was content I was not concerned.

We rested at Caversham for a full week. Then, by steady stages, we made our way across the high country of the Cotswolds and back to Hanley Castle.

There we set about our business. Thomas had already decided on the two of his retainers who should be elected to parliament, and he summoned them for talks, along with our Sheriff of Gloucestershire, Robert Poyntz. The two candidates were very different men; one sharp as a needle, a lawyer, as I would have known at first meeting just from his way of talking. The other fellow, respectful, to be sure, but dull as the mud at the bottom of a ditch. Still, a man needs no great wits to sit in parliament, if he knows enough to cry out 'yea' or 'nay' at the proper time. All we needed were loyal men, sure to do as the King wished, sure to be guided.

There was a great deal of talking to be done, although it seemed to me that all that needed to be said could have been concluded in an hour. Fortunately, I was not involved in most of the discussions, and that was just as well. We had other guests too, of course. Various knights, esquires and gentlemen from all over Gloucestershire were invited to eat at our table and hunt in our park, and out on the Chase. Some brought their wives with them, and so I was kept busy ensuring that everyone was entertained and made to feel important. There were those who sought places for their sons and daughters (and in one case a husband's bastard) in our household, and expected me to either grant their wishes or persuade my lord to accommodate them.

In my time, I have both had to sue to others and receive the suits of those who have sought my favour, and I know not which is the more mortifying experience. It is not pleasant to plead for advantages, even for one's rights; yet it is equally unpleasant to deal with the requests of others, for you can never satisfy everyone, and some you cannot satisfy at all, no matter what you grant them. They remain ungrateful. It did help a little on this occasion that I had some room in which to steer, for I expected my lord to rise in the world within a few months, and we would then require a greater following and a larger household. So I maintained as many as I could in hope, without promising anything I could not afford.

We had some guests from Worcestershire too, for as Warwick's star fell, ours rose, and there were several men who clearly hoped to attach themselves to Thomas. Sir John Russell, our old friend, was now all but certain of election to parliament, and not a little of this change was due to these shifting sands of power.

On the other hand, not all the men of Gloucestershire we had invited to Hanley obeyed the summons. Some made excuses, while others simply gave no answer. Then there were those we had not even bothered to ask, for they were far too committed to 'dear cousin Berkeley' and could not be won over, except perhaps by a miracle. Though we said our prayers, it was far from certain the election would go our way. If it did not, Thomas was certain to lose at least some of the King's confidence, for he was expected to rule the shire, despite the strength of Berkeley's influence.

'You need not worry, my lord,' said Robert Poyntz. 'I shall manage matters. Though it would help if you would send some of your men in livery to Gloucester, to remind the community of the shire of the King's wishes.'

He smiled, for he was a competent man who knew his business; he knew, I think that a show of strength might do much to tip the balance.

*

So it proved. Both our men were elected at the Quarter Sessions held in the great hall of Gloucester Castle. Thomas and I were not present, of course — it was not our place — but enough of my lord's liverymen were deployed about the place to encourage the voters. Poyntz made his appearance at Hanley to bring us the news. There had been no trouble at all, he told us. The acclaim of the county community had been quite clear.

That night we had a great feast of celebration, so great indeed that we had no option but to hold it in the Great Hall, for no other room was sufficiently large. We entertained most of the leading men of two counties and many of their wives; to say nothing of their followers and our own. Hugh Bygge and his fellows in the kitchen did not fail us, and the wine flowed freely, while our musicians played in their gallery and kept our feet tapping. Poyntz and our two successful candidates were there, as was Sir John Russell, who had been safely returned for Worcestershire. The other member for that shire had been Warwick's man, but Thomas, Bagot and Russell between them had persuaded him of the error of his ways. He was ours now; no better conclusion could have been achieved.

Next morning, much of the company dispersed; but in the middle of the afternoon there arrived a most unexpected guest. 'Dear cousin Berkeley' himself.

The fellow brought with him a very substantial escort of armed men, greater than his rank justified. Whether he sought to intimidate us, or was afraid of us I cannot say.

Thomas received him in the Great Chamber, and I sat at his

side. I would not have absented myself from the meeting for fifty marks. I knew it would be interesting.

Berkeley's usual complacent expression was missing; he looked rather red in the face, though it might have been caused by his riding in the sun. How far had he travelled? I wondered. Certainly not from Berkeley Castle, unless he had set off in the middle of the night and ridden harder than was wise in such heat. From Gloucester, perhaps? From Tewkesbury? Had Elisabeth given him dinner? Perhaps allowed him a bed for the night? I smiled at him, spoke some commonplace words of surprised welcome. Would he take wine? Wafers perhaps? Fetch them at once for Lord Berkeley, my good fellows.

He looked at me as if I had spat in his face. Then, courteously, he bowed in my direction. 'I am not here to sample your wine, my lady,' he said.

'Then what is your purpose?' Thomas asked. 'We are not usually honoured by your presence at Hanley, cousin.'

'It is useless to speak to that man of yours, the Sheriff,' Berkeley spat out. 'Therefore I have come to speak to you, face-to-face. This so-called election. It was a disgrace! Do you not know that the whole county is speaking of it?' He shrugged. 'Why would you? You do not even live *within* the shire!'

'Yet I hold substantial lands within it, my lady mother holds more, and this place sits close to the boundary. As well you know. I fail to see your point.'

'The point is that your Sheriff did not permit a proper election. That the loudest shouts in the hall were not for your men, and that some who shouted for them had no business being there, for all that they wore your livery. Why, one of the rogues you have chosen holds not a foot of land in the shire. It is a scandal!'

'Hugh Mortimer?' Thomas asked levelly. 'It's true that he has but little land, and that what he has is in Herefordshire, but he is a clever man, and a lawyer of good repute. He will serve well enough.'

'It is unprecedented! Unparalleled! How can a man with no stake in the county *possibly* represent it in the Commons? It is an abuse! A very gross abuse. One that will never be forgotten.'

Thomas shrugged. 'Supposing all you say is true — and I do not admit it, good cousin — there's nothing I can do about it. The Sheriff will have returned the writ. If you're not content, the only remedy is to appeal to the King. If you wish to do so, I cannot prevent it.'

Berkeley snorted, loud as a horse. 'Do you take me for a fool, Despenser?' he asked. 'What remedy shall a man have from *this* King? Yet you and your lackeys have broken law and custom, and sooner or later there will be a reckoning.'

'You threaten me with law?' For the first time Thomas's voice rose a little. 'I fear it not. Let there be a commission sent down here to investigate *all* breaches of the law. One so powerful it cannot be intimidated by the criminal gangs that thrive in the south of Gloucestershire, maintained by certain great men. Let them come I say, as many lords and judges as may please the King to send, and hear and determine all causes. I shall not go in fear. In fact, I should welcome such a commission, as would Judge Cassy and many of the oppressed commons of these parts. If you petition for it, good cousin, I will gladly join you in the request. Indeed, I may be the one to initiate it.'

That was as good a threat, and better, than any Berkeley had issued. We all three of us knew who was behind the criminal gangs. It was no secret. Berkeley kept a small army in his livery, and it was not for them to stand in idleness.

'My brother, the Earl of Rutland, is now Lord Constable of England,' I said. 'His business is to investigate all treasons, not least that of Lord Warwick. What if he chooses to question Warwick's friends? What crawling things might there be to emerge from under stones?'

Thomas placed his hand on mine. 'My lady, do not pursue that hare. Not yet at least.'

I closed my mouth, but I saw from Berkeley's face that my shaft had gone home. It had gone home and he did not care for it. He could not deny he was Warwick's friend — were not their children united in marriage? He stood on shifting ground. He might well be guiltless of any real treason, but was that defence enough? What might probing into his affairs reveal? You might call the maintenance of murderers, ravishers and thieves a kind of treason, if you stretched a point. For all his smoothness, he was certainly guilty of that, and only his power protected him. What if that power was broken?

'I will leave you to your folly,' Berkeley said, 'for I see my words are wasted, and all good counsel rejected. God speed you both. My lord. My lady.'

He made us each a little bow, more hostile than a slap across the face. Then he turned on his heel and walked out.

Looking back, it seems to me that my lord husband and I were like children, playing with fire without realising how badly we could be burnt. It is easy to say such things in hindsight, but at the time we were very well pleased with ourselves. We had overcome our enemies and it seemed to us that we were secure in the King's favour, and nothing evil could ever touch us again.

***

Chapter 17

August 1397

Nottingham Castle. Once again the court was gathered there, at the centre of the kingdom. The weather had broken at last. Our journey from Hanley had been undertaken in pouring rain from the moment we set out to the moment we arrived, and on the last day of the journey we struggled along roads that had become a sea of mud where they were not lakes of standing water. Nor was it any better at our destination. The rain poured down the windows as if full baths were being emptied over the roofs and candles and torches were needed even during the day.

At last it eased, the winds dropped, and it was merely dull outside.

Edward, my brother, seemed to be everywhere, talking to this fellow and that, standing on the edge of this group, listening, holding court in the middle of another, speaking of hunting, of the deer and hare he had chased, of the proper colour of a greyhound. Suddenly, I found him at my own elbow. He wanted to talk to me, it seemed.

'I have a rare treat for you, fair sister,' he said. 'Come to my rooms in the morning. Say an hour before dinner. Bring something to occupy your hands. Some mending perhaps. All you need do is sit, and watch, and enjoy yourself.'

'What's the mystery?' I asked.

'It would spoil the surprise to tell you, but I promise you, it's something you'll not wish to miss.'

'Shall I bring Thomas?' I asked.

He mused on that for a moment. 'I think he may have other

business. But by all means bring him if he has time. Fetch your women too, of course. The more the merrier.'

I was intrigued, and naturally tried to persuade him to tell me more, but he turned as close-mouthed as an oyster. All he would do was grin inanely. Then he walked off, and before I knew it had his arm around John Holland's shoulders and was laughing with him over some matter or other. I thought it entirely possible that I was the subject of the jest. You could never tell with Edward.

I was tempted to ignore the invitation. There was a chance, I thought, that my brother intended to make a fool of me with some jape or other. When it came to it though, my curiosity overcame my caution. Thomas, as it chanced, was wanted by the King for some purpose or other, so I made the visit alone — or at least with only my women to accompany me.

Edward was sitting in a large chair by the fireplace. He twiddled with an elaborate staff that he held in his hands, richly painted and gilded and tipped with gold. It was the symbol of his office as Lord High Constable, and he was like a child with a new toy, quite unwilling to be parted with it for a moment.

'You come in good time,' he said, gesturing towards the window-seat. 'Make yourself comfortable. We should not have to wait long.'

I settled myself, with my women about me and at my feet, while my brother ordered one of his boys to pour us wine, a task that was soon accomplished and with every courtesy. Edward said very little. It was obvious he did not intend to explain himself, and I was in no mood to press conversation on him, so I turned my fingers to the mending-work my women had brought with us, just as he had suggested, and waited. Not that I had any idea what I was waiting for.

At last, one of my brother's men pushed open the door. 'My

lord, the Earl of Derby is here.'

'Well, fellow, don't keep my cousin waiting! Show him in at once!' Edward gave a good impression of being angered by his attendant, although I doubt he really was. There was a grin hovering around his lips.

This was a surprise, I could not deny it. This could not be a chance visit, so it followed that Harry Bolingbroke had been invited, if not summoned. Since when had he jumped to my brother's orders? The visit should properly have been the other way around.

Harry came in, somewhat briskly, two or three of his men at his heels as was to be expected. He did not look content. His eyes went from Edward to me, and showed more than a little surprise at my presence. He looked at me — or rather he peered — and made a small courteous bow in my direction.

(My cousin, Beth, Lady Huntingdon, had told me that her brother was growing short-sighted. Although Harry loved his jousting and hunting, he also loved his books, and never had his nose out of one, so she claimed. That accounted for this change in him.)

Edward did not rise to greet him, as he ought to have done. He merely pointed to the chair opposite him — a smaller, lower chair I noted — and waited for my cousin to seat himself.

Harry settled himself, looking even less pleased. 'Well?' he demanded, after the silence had drawn his impatience.

'This should not take long,' my brother said unhurriedly. He uncrossed his legs and sat a little straighter. 'It is but a matter of giving you your instructions.'

'Instructions?' my cousin repeated. His face reddened. 'Did you say — *instructions*?'

Edward grinned at him. 'Yes. Given in my office of Lord High

Constable. Proceeding from the commands of our cousin, the King's Grace. As is my duty.'

I saw a look on Harry's face such as I had never seen before. In my presence, at least, he had always seemed calm, courteous, composed. I had heard him give the odd sharp retort to other men, but I had never seen him angry. Now, his face was almost purple with fury. He half-rose in his place, thought the better of it, and settled down again. 'Say on,' he spat out.

'The King remembers your offences, as well as those of Mowbray, at the time of the Appellants. However, bearing in mind your youth at the time, and taking the advice of his Council, he is inclined to mercy. The pardons granted to our Uncle Gloucester, to Arundel and to Warwick, are all to be recalled. To be regarded as utterly null, as prejudicial to the Crown. You and Mowbray, on the other hand, will be pardoned anew. All and every previous offence shall be put into oblivion. Indeed, it is the King's intention to reward you with advancement in title.'

Was in my imagination, or did my cousin let out a sigh of relief? Certainly, his colour was less high. He seemed to sit more easily in his place.

'Where is that boy?' Edward demanded, as if the lad had gone into hiding. He had not, but stood in plain sight. Now he advanced hurriedly in response to the call, going on one knee before my brother. 'Pour my cousin some wine, fool! What are you thinking about? Is he to sit there till supper-time, thirsting?'

The stripling hurried to obey, as if his skin depended on it. He was offering a brimming glass to Bolingbroke within half a dozen heartbeats, bowing low over his task.

'I hope it's to your taste,' Edward said, raising his own glass to his lips and taking a long swallow. 'Rhenish. I brought some back from Germany with me. A little sharp on the tongue to my mind, but pleasant enough.'

He touched it to his lips again, and smiled. 'There is, of course, a condition,' he went on.

'*Condition?* What condition?'

'I was about to explain. Some of us will make the accusations before Parliament. I'm sure you remember the procedure, seeing that you were involved in the process last time. In truth, the precedent will be followed exactly. Thomas Mowbray will be an appellant for the second time in his life, this time against his former friends. Quite appropriate, do you not think? The King thought of asking the same service of you. However, he has decided it is not necessary. All that is required is that you give evidence against my lord of Arundel. Since the man is your lord father's enemy as well as the King's, I presume this will cause no difficulty?'

Harry sighed. It seemed to come from his boots. 'What would you have me say?'

'That is for you to determine, good cousin. Our friend Arundel is notably careless in his words. Blunt to the point of folly. I'm sure that during your time at Haringey together — or was it Huntingdon? I forget. Anyway, when you were preparing to make war on the King...'

'I did no such thing!'

Edward held up a hand. 'No matter. As I told you, all errors are pardoned, or *will* be. At that time, shall we say, I'm sure that Arundel said something that was less than prudent. It would be astonishing if he did *not*, knowing our man as we do. If by some great miracle he was cautious, or if, cousin, you simply forget exactly what was said after all this time, then by all means invent something. It really should not stretch your imagination. Something about seizing the King, perhaps.'

'Damn you! This is not to be borne!' Harry stood up, his wine still clutched in his fingers.

'Oh, I think it is, bearing in mind the alternative.' My brother gave him the sweetest of smiles. 'Even your own father said you deserved to be executed. I distinctly remember it. The King is being most generous, and asks for precious little in return. Do you *really* need time to think about it?'

My cousin slammed his wine glass down on the mantelpiece with a force that could well have shattered it. 'I will not forget this,' he said quietly.

'Nor should you.' Edward was not smiling now, but quite serious. 'Such mercy, such *exceptional* royal mercy, should never be forgotten by the recipient. I very much doubt it will be repeated. You will do as you're asked?'

'Yes,' Harry spat out. 'As you say, the man is my father's enemy. I will do it, if only for that reason.'

'Your reasons are neither here nor there, as long as your actions are pleasing to the King.'

My cousin grunted. Then he stalked out, his men at his heels.

Edward and I looked at each other, and then dissolved into laughter. I still wonder whether Harry heard us. If he did not, it would only be because he walked more swiftly than was usual.

'Your lady and I have need of a private word,' Edward said, addressing my women. 'Leave us.'

They trailed out and my brother's servants, instructed by a mere jerk of his thumb, followed on their heels.

'Did I not promise you that our day would come?' He rose from his seat, took two strides across the room and, in token of his delight, embraced me, planting a brotherly peck on both cheeks. 'All those years we waited, and now we are the masters. Just as I said we would be. Richard will repay every insult, and if we cannot have Cousin Harry's head on a spear, at least we have utterly humiliated him. Did you mark the expression on his face?'

I nodded. 'Yes. Although whether you were wise to treat him so, I know not.'

He laughed. 'Wise? I have waited years to see him crawl. Did you not take pleasure in it?'

I could not deny it.

'There is more,' he said, 'although this is strictly for your ears. Your ears alone. If anything but good comes to Richard, it is his intent that I should succeed him. What do you say to that?'

'That it is madness,' I answered. 'They would never allow it.'

'*Who* would never allow it?'

'Those with a stronger claim, of course. Uncle Lancaster. March. Harry, for sure. They will never permit you to take the crown. Not that we should even talk of it. Is it not treason to imagine the death of the King?'

He laughed again, briefly this time. 'Then half the court are traitors, as you well know. Don't worry. Richard will live for many years yet, and those years will be used to clear the way.'

I took a breath. I had suspected his ambition for many months, but had questioned my own judgement. Now I questioned his.

*

That afternoon, in the great hall of the castle, the new appellants gathered to appeal the three imprisoned lords before the King. My lord husband was one of them, of course, with my brother Rutland. Thomas Holland, Earl of Kent; John Holland, Earl of Huntingdon; John Montagu, Earl of Salisbury; Thomas Mowbray, Earl of Nottingham and William Scrope were the others.

It was a mere formality at this point, hastily arranged and no great spectacle at all. They gave sureties to repeat the appeal before Parliament, and that was all there was to it. The only surprise to me was that William Scrope did most of the talking. Then I remembered that his father had spoken for the Appellants all those years ago in Westminster Hall. Even in the smallest matters, King Richard was deliberately following the precedent set by his enemies.

***

Chapter 18

August – October 1397

Astonishing indeed is the suffering of the King. Of late the sun had been concealed behind a cloud, that is to say the King's majesty beneath an alien power, but now in arms he bounds on the mountains and leaps over the hills, and tossing the clouds on his horns he shows more brightly the light of the sun. Kirkstall Chronicle.

*

Thomas and I withdrew to Caversham. I could not love the place as I did Hanley, but I liked it well enough, and it was much nearer to Westminster and London, where we should soon be needed. Thomas had licence to bring a large escort of armed men to the Parliament, for the King was taking no chances, even now, and wanted to be sure that nothing could interfere with his revenge. This time there was no haste. We could assemble the pick of our men, and know that they had ample time to reach us; there was no need to scratch up badly-equipped hinds from our nearest manors.

The long days of late summer passed slowly. Sometimes we hunted in our park. Sometimes, when I felt idle, I would walk with my women in our gardens, or sit and watch the Thames go by.

We had many guests, among them the Earl and Countess of Salisbury, who came up from Bisham by barge and stayed with us for several weeks. William Scrope also visited for a time, bringing his wife with him, supposedly because they were on pilgrimage to Our Lady's shrine, but in truth, I suspected, because he wanted to talk politics with Thomas. He was a clever fellow, Scrope — almost too clever — but I thought him a cold fish and could not bring myself to like him. Sir John Russell was more welcome — he also lingered for weeks, and said he intended to ride to London with us when the time came. Russell had found a new horse for Thomas — a fine destrier he had brought with him from Worcestershire. The price — for all that Russell claimed he was offering a bargain — was outrageous, but my lord could not resist the purchase. Nor could I object, in truth. We were in greater prosperity than we had ever been, and it was not for me to begrudge my husband a horse, or even ten horses. It would serve to make him more splendid in the jousts and (I hoped) would never need to carry him in war.

When at last the time came to make the journey to Westminster, we travelled in a great company, with numerous carts following us to bear all the arms and armour — not because any fighting was expected, but because the King desired the protection of his loyal lords, just in case anyone was fool enough to raise the standard of revolt. It was precaution taken to an extreme; but of course the intention was to overawe anyone who still opposed the King. I did not need to be told that, it was as plain as a hand raised to your face.

Westminster, and indeed London, was thronged with those attending the Parliament and the various retinues. Moreover, Richard's own Cheshire men were everywhere, some on duty around Westminster, others infesting the taverns and alehouses of London itself — and no doubt Southwark too. Even among our people, gathered in our London house, I heard grumbles about these fellows. It was said they were high-handed, swift to draw steel and apt to take what they wanted without paying. It was unfortunate, to say the least — yet I must say that I have never known any retinue made up of saints, not even those of York or Despenser. Livery gives men licence, and some abuse it. I know not how that can be changed, in a world made up of sinners.

*

One afternoon, while all the bells of London were still trembling after making their clamour for the hour of Nones, I received a most unexpected visitor — my cousin, Philippa Mortimer, Countess of Arundel, Lady Pembroke. I was amazed; more than amazed, I found that I had grown rigid with shock.

She was dressed very simply — so much so that I wondered if she had borrowed an old gown from one of her own waiting women. She was not even wearing one or the other of her coronets. Her eyes were red, and she was the colour of parchment.

I was completely lost for words. What could I say? I believe I mumbled something, but it was but a formal greeting, nothing that I thought about or considered.

To my astonishment, she threw herself on her knees before me. This was intolerable. I could not stomach it. I rose, grasped her wrists, and hauled her to her feet. I scarcely knew what I was doing.

'You shall not kneel to me, cousin,' I said. 'I know not why you are here, but as you are you shall sit.' I placed her on a chair, the one that stood on the opposite side of the hearth to my own. My lord's chair, when he was at home, which he was not. Then I turned to one of my women, scarcely noticing which of them. 'Fetch wine for Lady Arundel!' I ordered. I spoke more sharply than I intended, scarcely knowing what I was about. The wine seemed to take an age to arrive, although I suspect the girl had the task accomplished within a minute. I took the glass from her, and put it into my cousin's hand myself. Then I sat down in my place.

'Say what you have to say,' I said.

She took a draught of the wine. Then was silent for what seemed an hour. Again, I doubt more than a minute passed, perhaps less.

'No one has more influence with the King than you do, cousin,' she said. 'I am here to beg you to plead with him for my husband's life. His life only. Nothing more. If you will do that — I am still rich. I have my Pembroke lands at least. — if you will do that, and save his life, you can have anything of mine that you ask. That and my prayers for the rest of my life.'

I shook my head. 'Cousin, you and I have not been friends — ' I began.

'I know!' she interrupted. 'You need not say it. Nor would I be here if there was any other option open to me. You see, I love him, and I will do anything, *anything*, to save his life. Even if it means crawling to you. If you will not do it for me, do it for my brother. Do it for Edmund! I know you care for him.'

I held up my hand. 'I have my faults, God knows. But no one can say that I have ever taken a bribe. You may keep your treasure, cousin. I will not take it. All else apart, it would not serve. Do you not understand? If I went to the King and knelt before him, and if I took Despenser with me, and my lord father and his wife, and both my brothers, and Edmund too and if we all of us knelt together and pleaded for Lord Arundel's life, it would make no difference. You know why that is, without my telling you.'

'Because of things long forgotten.'

'Because of Queen Anne!' I shook my head. 'You may have forgotten. The King has not. The insult at her funeral was unforgivable; but before that was worse. Do you *really* not know? He and my Uncle Gloucester kept her on her knees for *three hours* pleading for Burley's life, and denied her. I know, because I was there, kneeling with her. God's truth, do you imagine the King holds his honour so cheap that he has forgotten *that*? What man of good birth could either forget or forgive such dealings?'

I had raised my voice, and was all but shouting. Yet the strange truth was that I was not really angry. Not with her, at least. We had been enemies for as long as I could remember. We had fought over our dolls, and once I had laid her out on the floor for insulting my mother. She had rejoiced in every petty triumph over me. Now, though, I pitied her. She was broken, defeated, and had not even her son to comfort her. The poor child had died. So yes, I pitied her.

Yet even had she been my most beloved sister there was nothing I could have done for her. If she imagined I had sufficient influence over the King to save her husband's life, she was out of her wits. There was no one in all England — man or woman — who could have turned Richard from his revenge.

She wept and after a while I wept with her, strange though it is to relate. As I have said before, I have never been one of those creatures who sheds a tear over every dead sparrow. So why did I weep with my confessed enemy, over the fate of a man I despised and who, quite bluntly, deserved worse than the axe he was about to receive? I have no answer, and can only say that it was as it was.

After that day, I never saw her again. She married some other fellow to save herself from widowhood, and was fated to die in childbed. She is long gone. I pray for her sometimes, for although we were enemies, she was Edmund's sister, and I have forgiven her. I wish I could forgive all my other enemies, but I am not saint enough for that. I hope they burn in hell. One above all.

*

Thomas looked splendid in the fine red robes he was to wear for the appeal in Parliament — it was a livery provided by the King for him and his fellows, and no expense had been spared. He also looked uncertain — uncomfortable. Younger than his years. Like a boy envisaging his first day of service in a strange household, uncertain what duties would be imposed on him. I hugged him, told him that I had never been more proud to be his.

'Warwick is to be spared,' he said.

'Is he?' This was a surprise to me.

'The Queen has asked for his life.'

I snorted. 'You mean she has been *told* to ask.'

He shrugged. 'What else? She is a child. She does the King's will. As a good wife should.' He gave me a wry smile, provoking me. 'The man is ill, Constance. He is pitiable, as you'd know if you'd seen him lately.'

'You mean that you have?'

'I was one of those sent to speak to him. In the Tower. To offer him life, in return for a confession. The King much values that. It vindicates him, proves that he does justice. The Warwick lands are forfeit of course. He will spend the rest of his life in prison. But he is spared.'

'The King is generous.'

'Yes. There is other talk. It is said your uncle is already dead, in Calais.'

'Is it true?'

He sighed. 'I've not been told. Not outright. Yet I suspect there is truth in the tale.'

'He was ill. So he claimed.'

'Yes, and he seemed a sick man, at Pleshey. But he's not as old as Warwick. The talk says — well, some say the death was not natural. That he was sent on his way.'

I shook my head. 'It will be a lie.'

'Perhaps,' he shrugged. 'It is, in any event, convenient. It spares your other uncle the task of sentencing his own brother to death, which he would surely have had to do. Or the difficulty of his refusing to do so.'

'My Uncle Lancaster would have done his duty,' I said. 'He

would have done as the King ordered — he is loyal.'

'Yes, but if the rumour is true he is spared the decision. We shall soon see. One thing is sure, and that is if Gloucester has been brought back to England it has been done in great secrecy. There is no sign of him. No sign, and no word.'

'The King is not a murderer,' I said. 'If he has a fault, it is that he has been too merciful to those who deserve it not.'

He took my hand. 'Constance, there are those about him who would murder their own mother to gain his favour. Thomas Mowbray is one of them.'

It was Thomas Mowbray who had held my uncle in custody. Mowbray had ever been a rogue, as I well knew. Still, I did not wish to believe it. At least, not the worst.

*

I could not attend the Parliament, obviously, but sitting at home with my women, my mind half occupied by my needlework, I could well imagine it. The King, on his high throne. My Uncle Lancaster, as High Steward, sitting on another throne below him. The peers, temporal lords to the King's left, spiritual lords to his right. The new appellants, my husband and my brother among them, standing in the body of the gathering to make their accusations. The Commons, headed by their Speaker, Sir John Bussy, gathered below the lowest-ranking of the peers, their numbers causing some to spill outside. Arundel? Where was he? Deprived of hood and belt, kneeling before my uncle, enduring his trial. Harry Bolingbroke, wriggling in his place, waiting to give evidence as directed, knowing that some would think him a Judas and despise him. Oh, I could imagine it all very well.

Restless, I found myself at the end in our little chapel, praying for my cousin the King, that he would find peace now that his honour was avenged; that he would face no more enemies, but live out his time in peace, reigning justly over England. I also prayed that he would live long enough to have sons with Isabella, for that was the best outcome for all of us. Any other ending could only mean division, perhaps even civil war. My brother's ambition was pure folly. He was drunk on the power Richard had given him, but that power would only stretch so far. I could see it, even if he could not.

I was still on my knees when my brother, Dickon, came rushing into the chapel.

'Sister,' he cried, 'they are marching Arundel through the city to his execution. I've been out on the street and everyone is talking about it. They say he's to lose his head on the very spot where Burley lost his, years and years ago. Wherever that is. Somewhere up near the Tower, I suppose. Can you not hear the bells?'

Now that my ear attuned to the noise, I could. The slow, mournful tolling of many bells. Some distant, some close at hand, a whole legion of bells sounding at once. The toll of death.

My brother was smiling, though in truth I think he was more excited than joyful. He was all but dancing, as if he could not persuade his feet to stand still. He was still a boy, of course, only twelve, but at that awkward age when boys start to turn into young men, and fancy themselves older and wiser than they are. His voice had lately broken, and was not the asset to our chapel services that it had been.

'May I go to Tower Hill? To see the beheading?' he asked.

He clearly relished the adventure. It was strange to think that he was more or less the same age I had been at Burley's execution, the difference being that I had attended that out of duty, in the service of Queen Anne. He was merely curious to see a man die, to witness bloodshed.

'If you wish,' I said. He was already half way to the door, all but running. 'Be sure to take some of our people with you,' I called after him. 'See to it that neither you nor they are involved in unseemly brawls, or you will answer for it.'

There was no telling what the mood of the crowd would be. Would they pity Arundel, or jeer him? Would a Despenser livery be a provocation? It was too late to consider these matters — he was already beyond recall, fleet as a hare, though not so graceful in his going.

*

Thomas was home before Dickon reappeared. He looked weary, even troubled, yet had the air of a man who wanted to rest after a long day's work.

'Arundel is to die,' he told me, then shrugged. 'He cursed us all. Your Uncle Lancaster and your cousin most of all. He called Harry Bolingbroke a liar and a false knave.'

'For once, he spoke the truth.'

'To do him justice, he often spoke the truth, as he saw it. By this time his head may already be off. Warwick is spared, as I told you. He fell on his knees before the King, before all of us, and made full confession. As for your uncle —'

He shrugged, settled on his chair. I rose, poured wine for him, and placed it in his hand. Then I stood in silence, waiting for the rest.

'Tomorrow, Parliament will be told he is dead,' he went on, after he had sipped the wine and let out a sigh.

'How dead?'

'Just dead. But before he died, he was visited by a judge. He too made a full confession of his faults, like Warwick.'

'That is — useful.'

'Very. It gives the King a reason to seize his lands. Of course, I need not tell you, there are all manner of rumours afoot. Some say Mowbray had him strangled.'

Before I could answer, Dickon came hurrying in, quite breathless.

'I saw it done!' he cried, quite forgetting his manners.

'Dickon,' my lord said solemnly, 'that is no way to enter a room. Go out at once, and return when you have remembered your lessons in courtesy.'

He did not argue, but left us. A moment later, he was back. He knelt. 'My lord. My lady,' he said.

'That's better. Now, boy, tell us your news.'

'Arundel is dead, brother. Thomas Mowbray and Tom Holland took him to the scaffold. The people didn't like that. One his daughter's husband, the other his nephew. There was sour talk of it.'

'It was their duty,' I said. 'The people do not understand such things. I should have thought though that even they, ignorant though they are, would be glad to see the end of such a traitor.'

Dickon thought about it. 'Some did seem pleased,' he said. 'I heard one fat alderman saying it was what he deserved. But most of them were silent. They just watched. I saw his head fly off. You should have seen the blood! I swear there were gallons of it.'

'We do not speak of such things before ladies,' Thomas said, but the reproof was mild. He was well aware that I was not the sort of creature to faint at the mention of bloodshed.

'I'm sorry, sister.' Dickon made a little bow to me. 'Is it all right for me to say that some of the crowd dipped rags in it? As though they thought him a saint. That was funny! Old Arundel a saint!'

'You may go,' Thomas said. 'You've said enough.'

My brother ran off, no doubt to tell half the household what he had seen. It was certain he would be paying a visit to the kitchen, to see what food and drink he could lay his hands on, even if it was but bread and small ale. His appetite was insatiable.

Thomas sighed. 'We are bidden to sup at your father's house,' he said.

That was no great surprise. Since our arrival in London there had been one feast after another. We had even entertained the King under our roof, much to Hugh Bygge's pride and delight, to say nothing of my own. I had almost lost count of the different tables we had visited.

'Your Uncle Lancaster will be there,' he added.

'Indeed? Then I had better begin to make myself fit to be seen. If I wear all my jewels he may even notice me.'

My husband laughed. 'Constance, every man with blood in him would notice you, even if you wore russet homespun and had straw sticking out of your hair.'

It was flattery, but it still pleased me. How could it not?

By the time we reached my father's house, my uncle and his wife were already there, to my great surprise. So was my cousin, Harry, who, if he did not quite look grim, was certainly not his usual composed and complacent self. Other guests included John Holland and his wife, Harry's sister Beth, whose face lightened when she saw me. It was quite a family gathering, although I thought that sparks might well fly. I knew very well that Harry detested John Holland, whom he blamed for debauching his sister and making their marriage necessary. (It must be said that nothing had been done against Beth's will, as she had told me many times. She found it a subject for boasting rather than complaint.)

Last to arrive was my brother, Edward. He apologised profusely for his lateness, even to the point of mockery. He told us the King had kept him at Westminster, on urgent business that could not be avoided. I caught his smile — it pleased him no end to stress, in such a company as this, how important he had grown, how much Cousin Richard relied on his counsel. I knew him too well, suspected his delay in coming to supper was deliberate.

'Well,' said my Uncle Lancaster, speaking loudly, as if he thought he was still making pronouncements in the parliament hall, 'we have done Richard's will. I only hope he is now content, and will put any other quarrels into oblivion. For all our peace, and for that of England.'

'It seemed harsh to banish the Archbishop,' Harry ventured. 'More so in that he was not allowed to speak in his own defence.'

This was Archbishop Arundel, whom Richard had lately sent into exile.

My brother laughed, unexpectedly. 'You mean he was not allowed to speak in *public*. He spoke to Richard roundly enough — so much so that a lesser man might have lost his head for that alone. I wondered at the King's patience but then, as you all know, he has a great store of that these days. The Archbishop, Harry, can count himself fortunate he is a priest. Richard will never kill any priest, still less a prelate. Yet the man is as much a rogue as his brother was, and twenty times cleverer. You of all people must be well aware that when he was Chancellor he betrayed the King's private policy to the Appellants. Exile is a kindness. He deserved death. If I had been in

Richard's place, the fellow would be on his way to Canterbury, on a bier.'

'I suppose my brother also deserved death,' Uncle Lancaster said. His voice quavered, as I had never known it do before. 'I should at least have liked to hear his defence. Richard knows I would have condemned Gloucester at his bidding; there was no fear of that. I admit, I should then have pleaded for his life. If mercy could be extended to Warwick, could it not also have been granted to one so close to us in blood?'

Edward shrugged. 'His confession will be read to Parliament, honoured Uncle. All men will hear his defence, such as it was. As you know, he was ill when he was arrested. His death was natural.'

Beth, who was next to me, snorted in her wine. 'No man in his wits will ever believe that,' she said quietly, her words intended for my ears alone. 'Not even my John believes it, and he is blockhead enough to believe most things he is told. Mowbray had our uncle choked to death. So is the common talk.'

'Mowbray would not *dare*,' I objected. I spoke loudly enough for Harry to hear — he turned his head in our direction for a moment, then pretended indifference.

Beth shrugged. 'He would not dare without a command from Richard,' she amended. 'What if that command was forthcoming? Why not? The King wanted him dead, as you well know.'

'The King would not do such a thing!' I said.

'Would he not? What if he received counsel to do it? What if someone spoke in his ear? From someone more ruthless?'

She made no direct accusation, but her eyes were on my brother.

'It is a matter I must discuss with Mowbray,' said Harry, into the silence that had fallen. His voice was ice.

'That you will not do!' said his father, very sharply. 'Your Uncle York and I have spent years trying to turn the King's wrath from you, whether you know it or not. Now it is settled. You have regained his trust, and we have peace. If you disturb it, I will not lift a finger to save you, on my honour!'

The silence grew, to the point of awkwardness. Part of me expected Harry to rebel, to answer with equal fierceness. He did not. Instead, he bowed his head. 'As you command, my lord Father,' he said.

Across the room, Edward had taken up a place by the fire, leaning against the mantelpiece so carelessly that I feared his long sleeves were in danger of catching alight. He caught my eye, and smiled as if there was a secret between us.

*

I was Countess of Gloucester now; my lord husband sent me home to Hanley Castle, with the greater part of our household and some of the fellows he had raised from Gloucestershire and Worcestershire as escort. He himself remained with the King.

It was not the only promotion, of course. My brother Edward was now Duke of Aumale. Mowbray was Duke of Norfolk; Thomas Holland, Duke of Surrey; John Holland, Duke of Exeter. That was not the end of it either. My cousin, Harry Bolingbroke, was rewarded for his tale-telling by being made Duke of Hereford. From the sour look on his face I supposed he was not much gratified. Never before had so many new peerages been created in one day.

Some men spoke mockingly of it, calling them the 'little dukes' or *duketti*; but they laughed behind their sleeves, as none dared to question the King openly.

I called at Tewkesbury on my way home, as, of course, I had a great deal of news for Elisabeth. Besides, she was always happy to see her grandson, however little she valued my society.

'My husband hoped to be Earl of Gloucester in his time,' she admitted. 'The family has some claim to it. It belonged to the de Clares.'

Did she think I did not know this? I contained a sigh, somehow.

'Are there lands to support it?' she asked.

'Oh, yes,' I said complacently. 'Several manors, most taken from Warwick and most of them in these parts. Elmley Castle is the best of them. I am to hold them in jointure with my lord, by the King's order. Thomas is also to be Constable of Gloucester Castle and Warden of the Forest of Dean. It makes his power complete, here and in Worcestershire. No one can challenge him now.'

'Hmm,' she said. 'I only wish it had come to him another way. Have you any idea what the great men of this county think of it?'

'I dare say Berkeley is not pleased. He said as much when last he came to Hanley. No doubt because he no longer controls the elections for Parliament.'

'It is not just our cousin, Berkeley. It is most of the better and more discreet men of the shire. They talk at my table, even if they do not dare talk at yours. Thomas has gone too far, too fast, and you, Constance, have encouraged him in his folly. You have destroyed one good man, Warwick, and you have alienated another, Berkeley. Both of them loved and respected by almost everyone here who matters. You have no idea of the damage you've done.'

'Warwick,' I said, meeting her gaze, 'is a traitor. As is any man who sides with him against the King.'

'Warwick is no traitor,' she returned, shaking her head. 'Everyone in this county marvels that he should be thought as such. He was fighting for King Edward in France before you were born, my girl. All he did was seek to rid King Richard of evil councillors.'

'It was not for him to choose the King's advisers,' I said. 'Still less to take up arms against him and cause good men to be murdered by an evil Parliament. He had no right at all. Yet despite all that the King in his great mercy has spared his life. He has no cause for complaint. None whatever. Besides, he has confessed his faults openly, madam. Have you not heard?'

She sighed, settled down onto her chair. 'I know I waste my breath. You see only what you wish to see. Yet I will say this, because I must — you are leading my son, your husband, down a very dangerous path. And for what? Vainglory. That's what it is.'

She really believed that Thomas was my puppet, so little did she know of him! I itched to tell her that I no more commanded him than I did the wind, that his ambition was greater than my own, and scarcely knew limits. I knew it was bootless to try. I might just as well have told her that I intended to crawl to Hanley on my knees; she would as well have believed one statement as the other.

I placed myself on the window-seat, rested there in silence. There was a good hour to supper, perhaps more. Was it better to stay and eat with her, or press on to Hanley? The horses were weary from the miles they had covered that day. They would be better for a night's rest. But here, with Elisabeth glaring at me when she deigned to look at me at all?

I respected Elisabeth and wanted peace with her. I simply could not find the words to sue for it.

'You should be proud of your son, my lady Mother,' I said at last, taking care to speak mildly. 'He is one of the chief men in England now, high in the King's favour, prominent among his advisers. A far greater man than his father was.'

'Yet he is not half as loved!' she cried. She all but choked over her words, and I believe she had tears forming in her eyes.

'He is by me,' I said, no less fiercely. 'He is by me.'

*

Hanley Castle. I was safe at home, and it was as fine and bright a day as you can expect when the leaves begin to fall. There was a wind blowing in from the Malverns, but it was a warm one. Our people were already busy crushing apples for cider, and they were beginning to pluck pears from the trees, ready to make the season's perry. The quinces were ripe in our garden, and everywhere men and boys were occupied in trimming and tidying hedges. I had ridden out over the Chase that morning, not for any purpose, but simply for the pleasure and exercise.

A harbinger had arrived at the castle in my absence. Even as our clock struck twelve, my lord husband rode into the courtyard with his riding-household.

Though we had only been apart a short time I longed to see him and could not restrain myself from hurrying down to meet him. As I did so the beating of the clock bell accompanied my steps, and I was reminded of those bells in London, tolling for Arundel's execution. It was a strange fancy.

As Thomas dismounted, I noted the serious expression on his face. Something was troubling him for sure. He smiled at me, and we exchanged the usual courteous greetings. Yet almost at once the troubled expression returned. I had food and drink set before him, and watched while he picked at it in our solar, but he had very little to say.

'Is something amiss?' I asked him, unable to bear the silence any longer.

He looked at me, and shook his head. 'I have news. I fear you will not like it.'

'You are not angry with me?'

'Of course not, *treschere*! Why should I be angry with you?'

'You seem — I know not what. *Troubled*.'

He smiled at me. An awkward smile. 'I think *burdened* is more the word. This news — I fear it will not please you. I scarcely know how to tell you.'

'My father?' I asked. My first thought was that the Duke must be very ill. Or was it worse even than that?

He shook his head. 'Not your father. Your brother. Aumale as he now is.'

'What of him?'

'He has married.

I felt relief flooding over me. 'Is that all? Who is she? Some great heiress, I suppose?'

'It is my cousin — Philippa.'

I laughed. I couldn't help it. He might as well have named the Queen of Elfland.

'It is true,' he said.

'Don't joke with me! Is it likely my brother would marry *her*? The widow of Golafre, a base-born knight? My brother will be the Duke of York one day. He has higher ambitions still. He would *never* marry someone ten years older than he is, if she is a day, with two husbands dead and no child to show for it. Never!'

'I swear to you on my honour, he has married her. He says he loves her.'

'*Loves* her?' I screamed at him, for my blood was up. 'How can he possibly *love* such a creature? Near old enough to be his mother! If you say she is his whore, that I might believe. I know well enough he is not particular who he puts on her back. Anything in skirts will do. As for love, he knows not what it is.'

There was an enamelled jug, still half full of the wine I had had brought in for Thomas. I could not help myself. I picked it up and threw it, not at him, but at the wall. It hit it hard, bounced off and spilt a good half pint of what was left down the hangings.

'Constance!' he cried. I saw the shock in his eyes. He had never seen me this angry before. Nor, in truth, had anyone else. Well, perhaps Philippa Mortimer, long ago, on that day when I had put her on the floor.

I recalled the letter Alianore had seen, signed by 'G'. *It must have stood for 'Golafre'!*

'That bitch! That whore! My waiting woman!' I hardly knew what I was saying any more, nor did I much care whether it made sense. 'He *can't* have married her! How can such a creature ever be Queen? Or even Duchess of York? Small wonder he knew our business while she was here, it must have been him she was writing to. Taking us for fools, the damnable slut. She must have told him *all* our doings. Even that business of March, which might have cost you your head, or at least Richard's favour. It might have ruined us! She betrayed our trust! She should be whipped through the streets. Made to wear a rayed hood like the common trull she is.'

He stepped forward. 'She is my cousin,' he said. 'Lady Mohun's daughter. A well-born lady, if nothing else. *And now a*

Duchess. Your sister, like it or not. You should not speak of her so.'

'I will speak of her as I please!' I screamed. This time I selected a cushion and hurled it. It missed his head by six inches or so, flew into the fireplace.

What I said after that, I am not sure, but I said a great deal. Another man would have struck me, but Thomas never once laid an angry hand on me in all the years we were together. He was too much a man of honour for that. He used words instead, gentle words that were intended to calm me, but had the opposite effect. I was beyond all reason.

At length he left me. I was so occupied by my fury that I scarcely noticed him go. Yet something drew me to the window, and there he was, mounting his horse. He rode out through the gatehouse alone, with a puzzled selection of his squires and other attendants straggling along behind him, not knowing what he was about.

I began to calm, then. I sank down onto the cushions of the window-seat, vaguely aware that my women were flapping around me like frightened birds, not knowing what to do or say for best. If any one of them had had a grain of sense she would have run off, but none of them had. They were fortunate that my anger was ebbing, that I was merely slumped in my place, gradually recovering my breath.

The clock in the gatehouse sounded the hour, as if it meant to mock me.

END OF PART TWO

HISTORICAL NOTE

Some readers may find it surprising that there was a religious cult around Edward II, but there was, and Richard II did his utmost to have his great-grandfather canonised. He visited the tomb on several occasions, as mentioned in this novel, and had a book of alleged miracles put together. That the project failed was almost certainly down to events in England rather than in Rome.

Only three children of Thomas Despenser and Constance of York are firmly established in history – Elizabeth, Richard and Isabelle. Various people have alleged other children, so I thought the addition of one more was not excessive given the length of their marriage. However, Constance's son, Edward Despenser, is fictional, although such a child *could* have been born. I made Elizabeth rather older than some people guess – but I do stress, one guess is as good as another; no one knows when she was born any more than we know where Constance herself was born.

Anne of Bohemia's cause of death is a mystery, and it is unlikely that anyone understood it at the time. Plague seems unlikely, as only Anne died. One possibility is an ectopic pregnancy, but this can only be a theory. (She really was taking fertility remedies at the time.) The devastation caused to Richard by her death, the demolition of Sheen and the outrageous behaviour of Arundel at her funeral are all factual — even though it is almost impossible to believe the latter.

Thomas Despenser's date of induction into the Garter is unknown. It was sometime between 1389 and 1398. I chose the date I did as it fitted the story, and he had to be given the promotion at *some* point.

My story of the models depicted in the Wilton Diptych is just a whimsy and has no basis in known history. The parallel between the three saints and the three uncles was too tempting.

ABOUT THE AUTHOR

Brian Wainwright has been fascinated by the House of York for all his adult life, and his writing is almost all centred on them. This is his third book about Constance of York, after *Within the Fetterlock* and *Walking Among Lions*. A sequel may well follow. Brian is also the author of *The Adventures of Alianore Audley*, a humorous work set in the times of Edward IV and Richard III with Constance's notional granddaughter as heroine.

Printed in Great Britain
by Amazon

69672d3b-4f5f-4d48-bcd5-28e080ce1e44R01